TERA

From the past comes magic,
from the present, danger, gradually colliding.

Forests cover Terasia's hills and vales, southern border mountains are snow-capped and rivers, cascading from them, eventually make their somnolent, overfed, way into the sea.

Danger lurks in the once homely surrounds of the Margrave's Residence. A simple review turns into a complicated dance. Whom can Prince Arkyn trust? From his first arrival, to his last goodbye, there are challenges and dangers to face. Secrets lurk in hearts which seem open, politics go beyond the Margrave's Court and every revelation leads to more questions. Will he and his developing reputation survive?

Copyright

Book Cover and Illustrations by J.A.Cauldwell

Pennod Press First Edition 2024

ISBN (Paperback): 978-1-917145-07-7
ISBN (ebook): 978-1-917145-06-0

Trigger Warning

This book is fantasy set in a pre-Victorian style civilisation. There are references to unacceptable behaviours including torture, rape, slavery and murder. Other subjects such as suicide, child death and fatal illnesses are touched upon.

TERA

The Erinnan Legacy

Treason and Truth
Book 2 of 12

J.A. Cauldwell

Dedication
For Hugh

Character lists and notes on world building
are at the end of the book

FROM THE PAST COMES MAGIC,
FROM THE PRESENT, DANGER,
GRADUALLY COLLIDING

TREASON
TERA
TRAPPED
TRAGEDY

EVERYBODY HAS A STORY AND SOMEBODY KNOWS IT

Standalone stories that may link to characters from the main series.

TIES

For freebies, The Court Newsletter and to see more details and information on works in progress, please visit https://erinna.co.uk

MAPS

THE OEDRANIAN EMPIRE

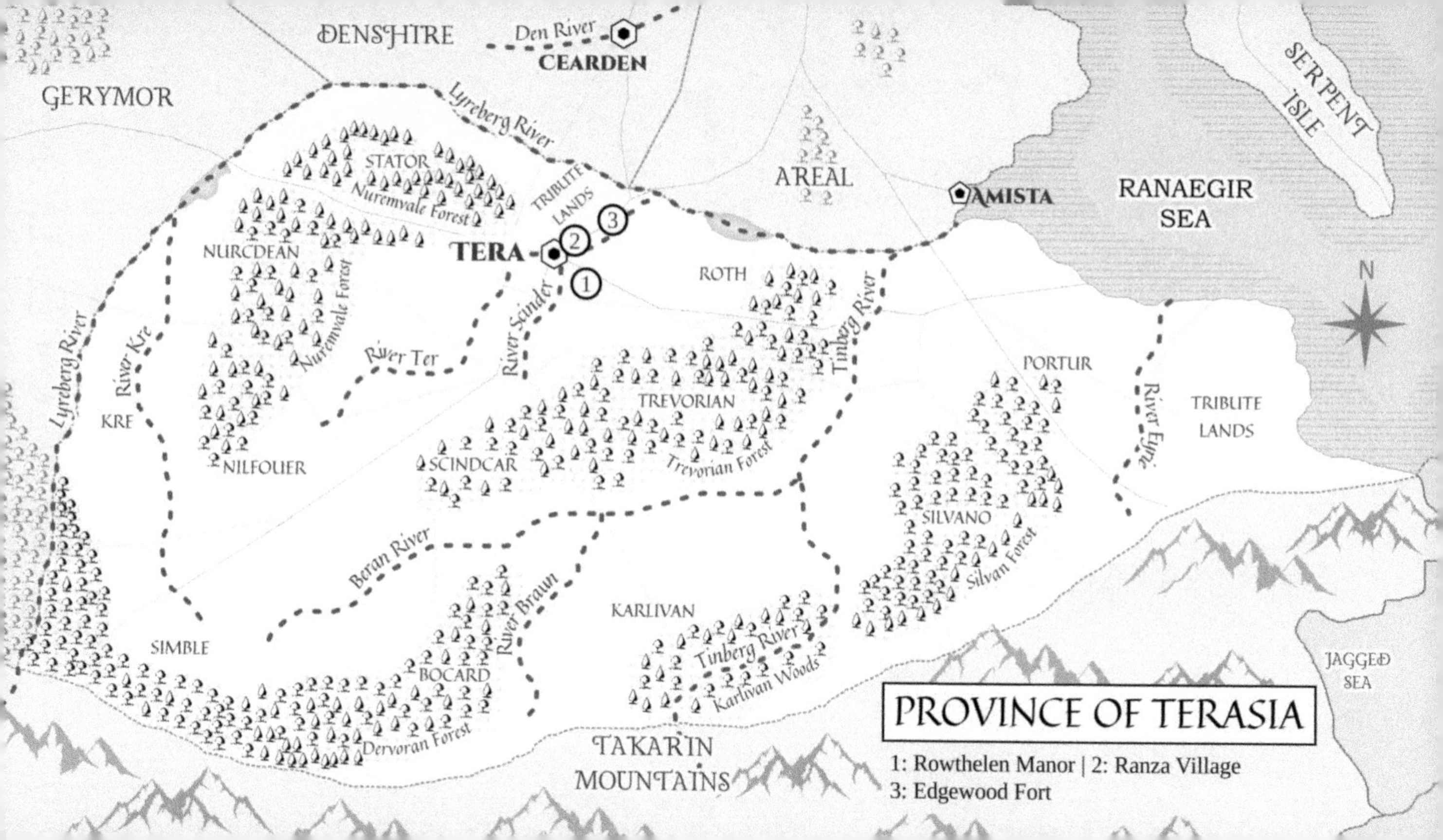

PROVINCE OF TERASIA
1: Rowthelen Manor | 2: Ranza Village
3: Edgewood Fort
DENSHIRE
Den River
CEARDEN
GERYMOR
Lyreberg River
AREAL
AMISTA
RANAEGIR SEA
SERPENT ISLE
N
STATOR
Nuremvale Forest
TRIBUTE LANDS
TERA
NURCDEAN
ROTH
River Scinder
Tinberg River
River Kre
River Ter
KRE
NILFOUER
TREVORIAN
SCINDCAR
Trevorian Forest
PORTUR
River Eyrie
TRIBUTE LANDS
SILVANO
Silvan Forest
Beran River
River Braun
KARLIVAN
Tinberg River
Karlivan Woods
SIMBLE
BOCARD
Dervoran Forest
TAKARIN MOUNTAINS
JAGGED SEA

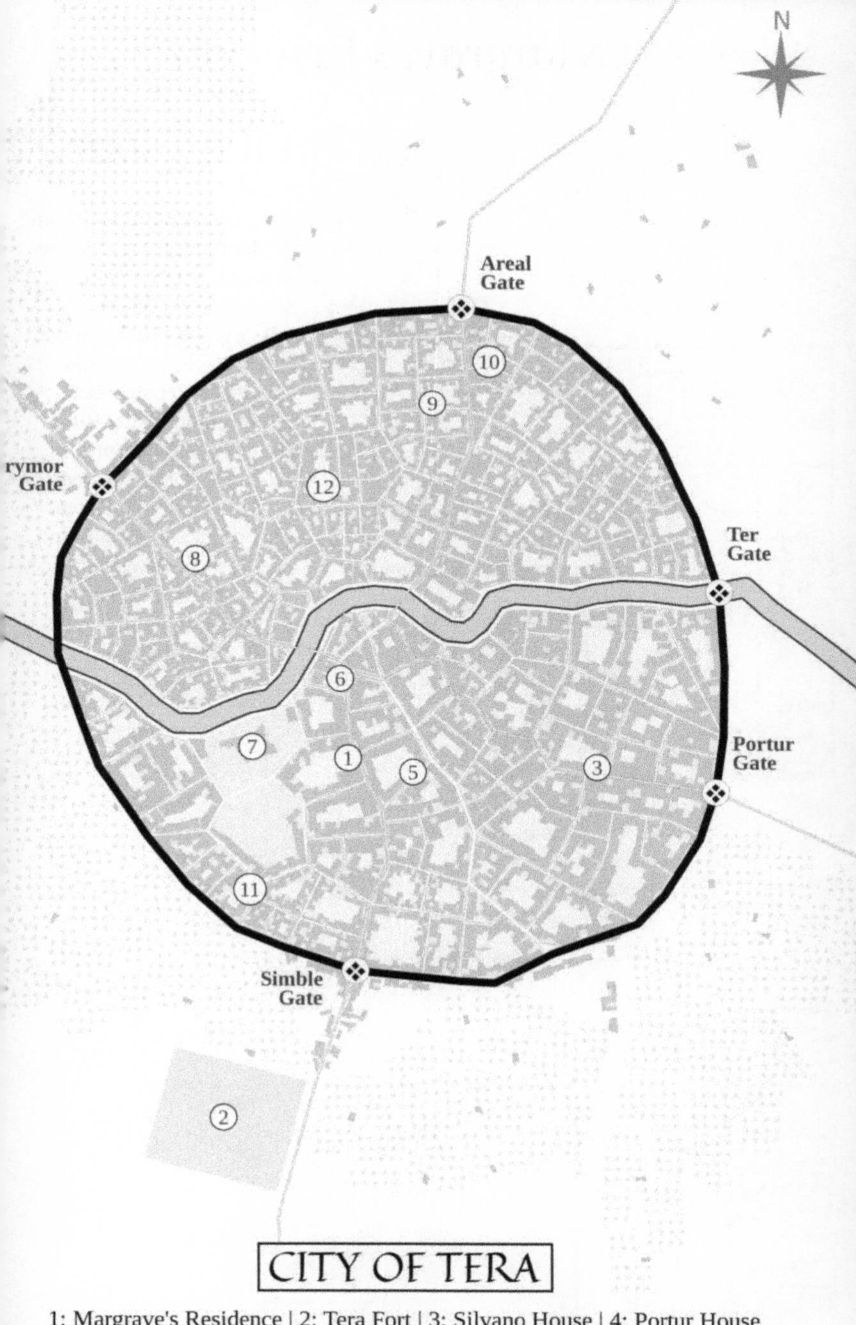

1: Margrave's Residence | 2: Tera Fort | 3: Silvano House | 4: Portur House
5: Library | 6: City Alcium | 7: City Assembly | 8: Wealsman's House
9: Daia's House | 10: Old Ma's | 11: Auldton House | 12: Audit House

Margrave's Residence

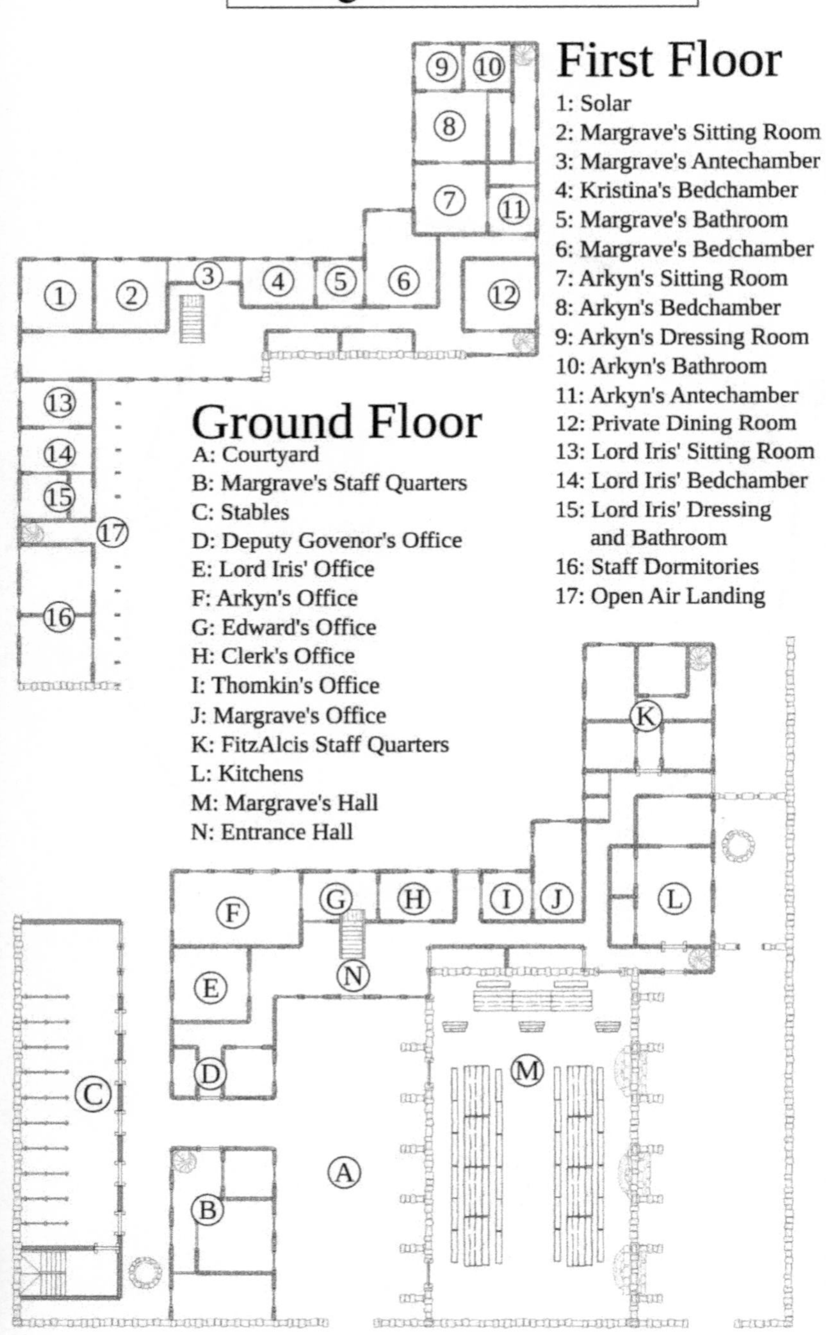

ARCHIVE

FITZALCIS FAMILY TREE

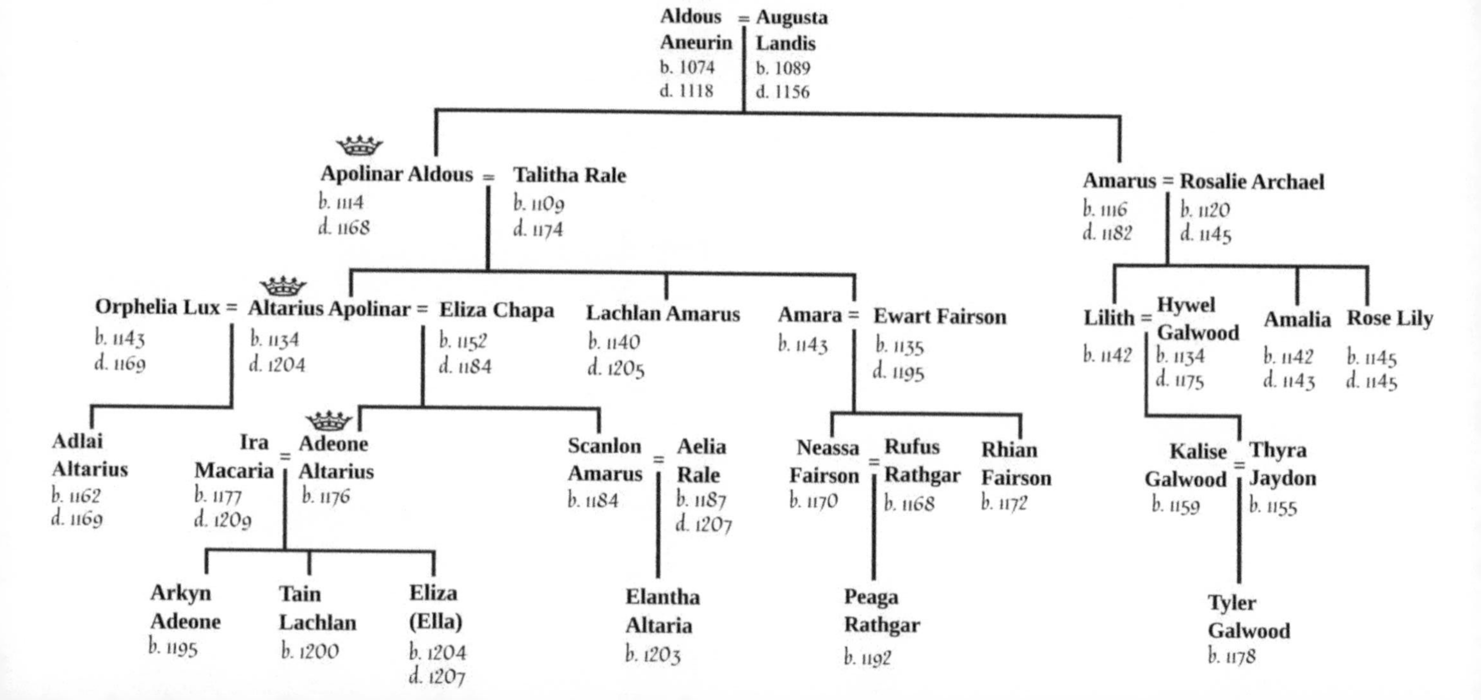

CHRONICLE

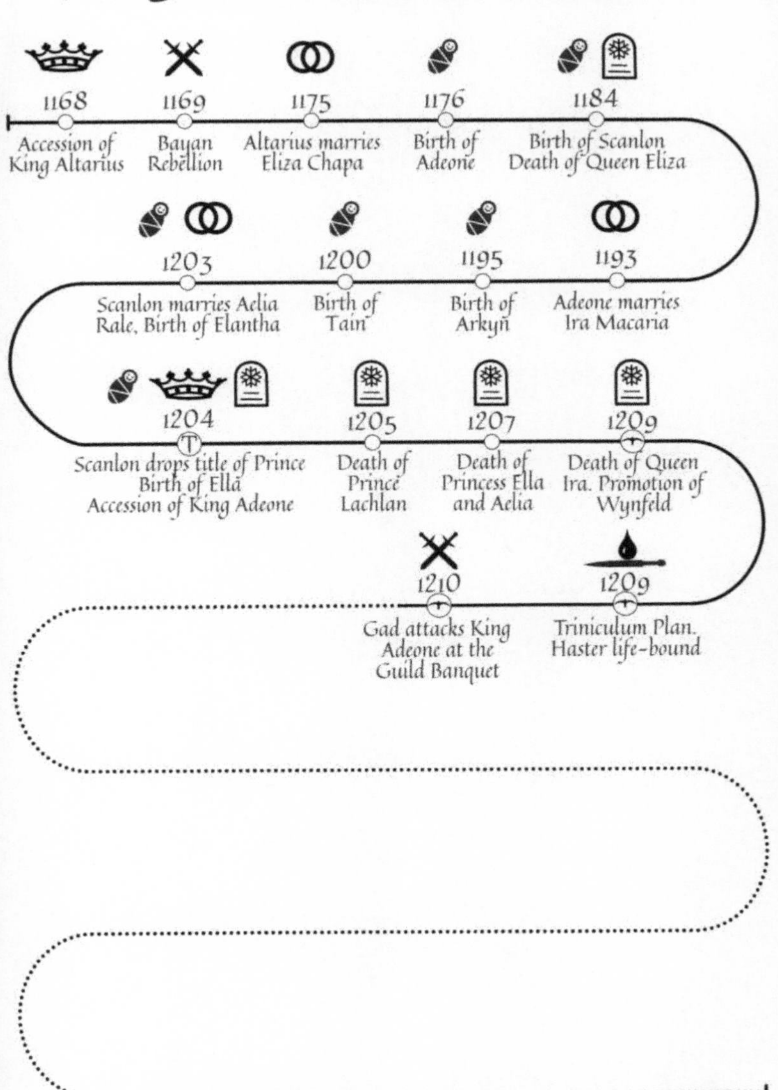

1168
Accession of King Altarius
1169
Bayan Rebellion
1175
Altarius marries Eliza Chapa
1176
Birth of Adeone
1184
Birth of Scanlon
Death of Queen Eliza
1193
Adeone marries Ira Macaria
1195
Birth of Arkyn
1200
Birth of Tain
1203
Scanlon marries Aelia Rale, Birth of Elantha
1204
Scanlon drops title of Prince
Birth of Ella
Accession of King Adeone
1205
Death of Prince Lachlan
1207
Death of Princess Ella and Aelia
1209
Death of Queen Ira. Promotion of Wynfeld
1209
Triniculum Plan. Haster life-bound
1210
Gad attacks King Adeone at the Guild Banquet

TERA

PART 1

Chapter 1
REVELRY AND RIVALRY

Pentadai, Week 45 – 5th Lufial, 19th Geryis 1199

Terasia – Tera – Margrave's Hall

THE MARGRAVE'S HALL in Tera resounded with lively music, awash with colour, an artist's dream or nightmare. How to capture that subtle hue, that brash tone or the complete saturation? How to paint a delicate candle flame guttering in the passage of people? How to paint the merriment and bright eyes of the guests? How to paint the laughing Prince sitting at the dais talking to a friend? How to capture the noise and the atmosphere of the final night of Prince Adeone's visit? Only a good artist would ever try, only an exceptional one would ever admit defeat and only a magical one would ever succeed.

Surveying the hall, Adeone wondered if he'd ever see it again. In twelve years, he'd probably be king and others would undertake the next Terasian Review.

"Her Elegance will be fine, Your Highness," murmured his friend.

"Am I so easy to read?" enquired Adeone.

"No, sir, but your eyes are following a pregnant lady and it is hard to forget the coming events when the empire wishes you both well."

Adeone laughed. "Are they? I never noticed." He changed the subject. Tired of questions on whether he wanted another son or a daughter, haunted by the death of his mother at his brother's birth, he just wanted to know Ira would survive and hoped he'd be home in time for the birth.

Six minutes later, there were new dancers on the floor and Adeone noticed his friend's eyes following a lady. He asked who she was.

The man swallowed. "No-one, sir…" Seeing scepticism, he amended his statement, "Lady Kristina Hale, Your Highness."

"You love her very much, don't you?"

"Yes, but she is to marry our Chief Merchant."

"I could…" Adeone gestured vaguely.

"No, sir, but thank you. I'll find a wife in time."

Adeone grinned. "I'm sure you will. Whether the hypothetical lady knows what's in store for her is another matter… You will write?"

"Of course, sir, if you'll have time to reply."

Adeone shrugged. "I'll make time, my friend. Now, duty calls."

"You could be deaf, sir."

A few minutes later his companion tactfully excused himself and Adeone found the Margrave beside him.

"I must thank Your Excellency for your hospitality and tolerance during my stay."

Portur smiled and seated himself at a nod from Adeone. "The first was a pleasure, the second I don't recall being needed, Your Highness."

Adeone gave him a well-practised sideways look. "An' I thought you an honest man."

"Ah, but time makes a mockery of memory, sir."

Adeone laughed. "I should be thankful for that. Are you pleased with the review?"

"Yes, sir; I think it worked out well for everybody. I hope the next time you visit we'll have the City Assembly rebuilt and the roads in a better state."

Adeone let the comment lie for a couple of moments before saying, "There is one favour I would request of you, unofficially, before I leave... There are two of your lords who, I think, would do well in a high governmental office."

"I tend to agree, sir. Oh, don't worry, I know whom you mean. Give me time and I'm sure they'll obtain posts. You'll miss their company, won't you?"

"Yes, but Festus and Finn are in Oedran, so I'll be causing mayhem there before too long."

"I think, rather, that Your Highness will be working hard." Portur paused before enquiring, "As we're talking of your home, how is Her Elegance?"

"Nearing her time. I hope I make it home before she bears our second child."

"I thought there were nearer two aluna-months before she was due, sir?"

Adeone chuckled. "Doctor Chapa thinks we got the date wrong. I don't argue with him. It looks like there'll be a Munewid prince or princess for the empire."

Portur smiled. "It is said that children born with the year's change bring hope with them, and with the change of century, we would be especially blessed."

Adeone glanced at the Margrave. "Have you never considered marriage, Your Excellency?"

"One day I shall, sir. I need an heir; I am the last of my line and would not face my ancestors thus."

Six minutes later, Adeone was saying, "I must take leave of Lord Roth before I retire."

Moments later, Roth was bowing. Portur was all too aware of the tension between the two men. Sparks had flown between them throughout the review. Often, his deputy had purposefully inflamed the situation;

therefore, he'd been intrigued when Adeone hadn't replaced Roth, seeing beyond the personal affronts to the aptitude of the overlord.

After a couple of minutes of polite but forced conversation, Adeone and Roth took leave of each other.

Once Roth was out of hearing, Portur said, "That man will be the death of me. I must apologise for his intolerable manner, Your Highness. You'll be receiving an apology."

"Your Excellency, don't make an enemy of your deputy on my account. He and I shall soon be out of each other's way; I have little doubt that he will return to his normal endeavours, zealous to prove my decisions wrong."

"He will not find that an easy challenge, sir."

* * *

Three weeks of travelling later, Adeone arrived at Ceardlann. Informed his child was imminent, he hastened to Ira's side and was there as his second son was born on the first day of 1200 – they named him Tain Lachlan and both mother and son survived the birth. With his son is his arms, Adeone remembered what the Margrave had said about Munewid babies bringing hope.

Chapter 2
TERASIA

Alunadai, Week 16 – 22nd Macial, 1st Easis 1211

Terasia – Tribute Lands – Road to Tera

AUTUMN HAD ARRIVED: leaves flamed, nuts ripened and nights brought the first hints of frost. Ominous leaden clouds hid the late afternoon sun and it was *still* raining: a constant, persistent, seemingly never-ending, all-pervading rain. Drizzle became driving rain, turning the road to mud beneath the hooves and wheels of Prince Arkyn's cavalcade. The misty atmosphere hid the hills. Dark conifers loomed on each side, one after another, overbearing, then gone. Out of the blurring mist, their foreboding form came into focus, into sharp relief, before vanishing.

The captain of his guard rode up to Arkyn's shoulder.

"One of the carts seems to be losing a wheel, sir. We should stop."

Arkyn held up his hand and reined in, peering over his shoulder. A group was gathered around one of the furthest carts. "Is there anything of importance in it?"

The Prince's manservant viewed the confusion. "Not of immediate importance, Your Highness. It's to be unloaded on our arrival in Tera.

After the axle broke on the other, we don't have room to redistribute this load either."

"Thank you, Kadeem. We'll just have to see if there is a wheelwright at the village or if they can lend us a cart. Hopefully, they'll have an inn as well."

With mock surprise, the captain said, "After all the careful planning, what would His Majesty say?"

"Mine's a whiskey – as well you know, Fitz. Come on, there's no hope of reaching Tera tonight as planned. I wonder why we're behind schedule."

"I believe the reason is called 'mud', Your Highness – sticky, clinging, pothole hiding, mud."

Turning to his administrator, Arkyn laughed. "You're probably right, Edward. Come on, let's go. The sooner we get to the village, the sooner all of us can be out of this rain. Fitz, detail a group of men to stay with the cart, please."

They reached the village quarter of an hour later, a cluster of a dozen houses spread along the road. They found a hostelry at a minor crossroads. Whilst Fitz dismounted and made enquiries, Arkyn remained in the saddle, surveying the scene. No-one was abroad in the streets, the houses were well built, most had chimneys spewing smoke, but almost all were like the hostelry: low, single storey, with small windows to let in light but not the weather. Many of the windows were glass instead of horn, unsurprising this close to Denshire, but they spoke of an affluence Arkyn hadn't expected. As he squinted through the rain, he thought he spotted a mail-lodge further down the road. That was good: a blacksmith and wheelwright would be nearby.

The hostelry was a pleasant surprise. Inns catered for sleep, but at least with a tavern attached, they had the chance of a hot meal and a comfortable evening, though Arkyn was sure the building wouldn't accommodate everyone. Some would head to the mail-lodge, which kept a few rooms for the mail-riders, and others would find hosts amongst the villagers.

Doors were opening and villagers appeared. He smiled at them, but Fitz returned to say the inn could help. Arkyn dismounted, patting Ponder as his groom came to take his reins and an ostler appeared along with the landlord and landlady. Typically rosy-cheeked, they couldn't do enough to help and before Arkyn quite knew what had happened, he was sitting in front of a blazing fire, tucking into a bowl of steaming vegetable soup. He heard the commotion caused by their arrival, rooms being readied, the jingle-jangle of harnesses as horses were stabled around the village and the sound of Fitz giving orders. It was oddly reassuring. No-one panicking, just general industry.

He finished the soup and realised how damp he was. The rain had worked its way through even his oiled cloak, soaking his tunic and, even now, was still dripping onto the flagstone floor. He chuckled to himself, memories surfacing. There was a polite cough behind him.

"A roaring fire is all very well, Your Highness, but you ought to get out of those damp clothes before you catch cold. You're soaked to the skin."

"I'll dry off soon enough, Kadeem. I was remembering when I fell into the trout stream. I must have been about twelve. I've probably not been so wet since."

Kadeem's lips twitched as he moved over to the table, depositing a pile of clothes. "Did Maria allow you to dry off 'soon enough'?" he asked innocently, holding out the tunic to the fire to warm it.

Arkyn snorted. "No, but we were in private."

"There's a guard on the door, sir."

"Very well. What would I do without you?" he asked rhetorically as he pulled the damp tunic over his head and Kadeem passed him a towel.

Once he was dry and clothed, Arkyn glanced at his sodden manservant. "Now, *you* go and change and eat. Once Edward has done likewise, I'd like to see him. Oh, take the guard off the door – I don't want to deprive our hosts of their livelihood. Instead, Fitz can perch at the end of the bar, as is his wont on his days off. I don't want to intimidate anyone."

Two minutes later, Edward entered, appearing more bedraggled than normal with tousled hair from a quick towelling and a creased tunic. Even then, he could still exude efficiency with disconcerting ease.

Arkyn asked if he'd eaten and warmed up properly.

"Yes, sir. Thank you."

"Good. Have you got the briefing?"

"It's buried deep, sir."

"That won't work, Edward; your papers are never too far away. I can't sit here all evening doing nothing."

Edward's face spoke volumes, including the question, *'Why not?'* He paused before saying, "I'll see if I can retrieve it, sir. I would, however, urge you to rest, Your Highness."

Arkyn smiled. "Advice noted and ignored."

When Edward returned with the briefing, he found Captain Fitz at the end of the bar and a group of weather-beaten elderly men in the far corner watching the scene with interest. As soon as he appeared, they started talking. Fitz seemed happy with the situation, so Edward approached Arkyn and handed him the briefing with a short bow, before standing back a couple of paces.

Arkyn glanced up. "Tonight is hardly normal, Edward. Get yourself a drink and sit down. In fact, get me one whilst you're at it, please. I'm as parched as Denshire."

Six minutes later, Arkyn discovered that sitting in a comfortable chair, drink in hand, was conducive to work. He finished the first part of the briefing and closed the file, placing it on the table.

"Anything to add to that? Other than the weather in Terasia is atrocious."

"No, sir. I'll get Richardson to note it for the next official tour."

Arkyn sat back, laughing. "It might be wise. His Excellency said we should make Tera by mid-morning tomorrow – all being well."

"That's something, sir," replied Edward, collecting the briefing together.

Arkyn, watching him, felt all his reserve leave; he felt really alive and raised an amused eyebrow.

Sensing some change, Edward responded lightly, "I'm a well-known opportunist. I take the chances as they present themselves. I'm sorry, but I'm not giving you the briefing back tonight, sir; His Majesty would have my guts if I did."

"He'd have to find out first," replied Arkyn. "You're probably right. I can't take it in anyway."

One of the old men who'd been watching them hobbled over. "Your 'ighness, work is all very well but you 'ave to relax at some point. Come join us. Bring yon minder as well."

Arkyn smiled at the look on Edward's face. The manner of invitation might have been unusual, but it was full of genuine warmth and concern.

"Ah, but *which* minder is the question. I have quite a collection... Thank you. I'd like to." He pushed himself to his feet.

"That be right, sir. I meant yon minder at t' bar there – not stopped watching you 'e 'asn't – tho' I'm sure this 'ere pen-pusher can find a safe spot for them there papers and join us."

Arkyn turned to Edward. "First, please tell everyone they are more than welcome to come in. The guards obviously can't drink to excess but, with Fitz here, I don't think they'd dare try."

"Very good, sir," replied Edward, stunned.

Fitz, having observed the tableau play itself out, rose and, at a nod from Arkyn, joined the gentleman's table. By the time Arkyn retired for the night, most of the villagers seemed to have forgotten whatever inhibitions they had had. There was talk for years afterwards about how friendly, polite and unassuming he had been. As he got ready for bed, even Kadeem commented on how much good had been achieved. No-one in the village would believe any of the stories Scanlon was sure to put about as Arkyn took on more responsibilities.

Grimacing, Arkyn said, “Yes and I now know more about farming and the taxes of ‘this ‘ere province’ than a hundred briefings could have explained. The odd thing is, I still feel more alive than I have for months.”

“The convivial atmosphere of a tavern, sir. When do you wish to leave in the morning?”

Yawning, Arkyn said eight before wishing Kadeem goodnight and rolling into bed.

Chapter 3
TERA

Cisadai, Week 16 – 23rd Macial, 2nd Easis 1211

Tera

DISTANT MOUNTAINS, wooded hills and surrounding pastures drew the eye from Tera’s stone walls and defensive ditch – once deep and menacing, now shallower through centuries of peace. Within those forbidding walls lay a metropolis of timber and cob. As surely as the River Ter tore the city asunder, bridges stitched the divide – with wharves and docks giving life to the wound. Half-timbered buildings overhung narrow, haphazard, twisting streets whilst movement and bustle hastened through them. It didn’t always dazzle but, to the people of Terasia, it was *their* city and it was home; no place on Erinna could be more beautiful.

Seeing no official welcome as they approached the Areal Gate, Fitz ordered two guards to investigate. They sped off, returning minutes later to say the city guards had had word that the Prince’s arrival had been delayed.

Fitz hesitated. “We were delayed, sir. It’s understandable.”

Arkyn nodded. “We set out early. What do you think?”

Fitz shrugged. “I trust Lord Portur and Wynfeld’s stationed here. I’m sure we’d have heard if owt’s amiss and I know the way to the Residence. We should be fine.”

“If you’re sure, Fitz,” replied Arkyn. “It still feels wrong.”

“Aye, well, Terasians have always had their pride.”

“Yes,” remarked Arkyn dryly. “They killed King Alvern for it.”

“A few centuries ago, sir. I’m pretty sure they haven’t made a habit of it.”

“Well, he could only die once,” muttered the Prince, raising a chuckle from Fitz.

* * *

Riding through the principal streets of Tera without an official escort was complicated. His guards did their best, but keeping his retinue together was fraught with interruptions from everyday city challenges, other carts and crowds. Terasians moved aside where they could, but curious gazes and whispers followed their progress. As they approached the Margrave's Residence, Fitz pointed out the side gateway for the carts to use, whilst he motioned to the gatehouse for Arkyn and his senior staff.

Glad that Fitz was beside him, Arkyn rode into a pleasant courtyard, bounded by the half-timbered house and a stone-built, buttressed hall. The lefthand wing contained an archway – presumably leading to the stabling and gardens – and a flight of steps leading up to a covered balcony.

The atmosphere confused him: somnolent but tense, an animal sensing a predator. Men of the army were strategically dotted around in small groups near doors, silently watching. The insidious atmosphere made him shiver.

An unmistakeably military voice shouted his men to attention. Startled, Arkyn scanned the scene and inclined his head with puzzlement and a brief smile as Commander Wynfeld saluted. What could he be doing at the Margrave's Residence with a plethora of men in attendance?

As Arkyn dismounted in front of the Residence steps, his burgeoning sense of foreboding increased. Handing Ponder's bridle to one of Wynfeld's men, he straightened his tunic before rolling his shoulders slightly, easing the tension.

As he was about to summon Wynfeld, a tall man walked out from the Residence and spoke first.

"I warned the commander you were arriving soon, Your Highness, before he deployed his men."

"Thank you. I know and trust Commander Wynfeld. You are?"

The man's brown eyes flashed. "I am the Deputy Governor, Lord Roth. Lord Portur is prevented from greeting you. Shall we go in, sir?"

In the square-paned windows of the Residence, Arkyn watched a sergeant reporting to Wynfeld. The commander, who had started towards him, turned back, hastily giving orders.

Arkyn's unease intensified as he entered the entrance hall. His attention drawn to the people hurrying to and fro: concern on their faces, whispered conversations carrying the susurration of unease to his ears and, unusually and notably, they were completely oblivious of his presence.

He turned to the Deputy Governor. "What *is* happening?"

"There has been an accident, Your Highness. If you would like to come through, I have had refreshments prepared and will explain whilst you take your ease. Your men are provided for elsewhere."

His anxiety intensified. "My captain, administrator and manservant stay with me."

As Arkyn spoke, Fitz caught his eye. Something wasn't right – Roth's polite demeanour, for a start. Kadeem and Edward exchanged a glance, the sense of disquiet assailing them too. There should have been a proper greeting party of senior officials and lords, and Wynfeld's presence made them all cautious, for he was seldom where he shouldn't be.

They crossed the hallway to an office, where Roth seated Arkyn behind the desk with a stilted deference – as though they were all acting a part. Kadeem stood near the door, Edward waited to the side of the desk as Roth stood centrally in front of it, pushing Fitz slightly to one side. Arkyn couldn't make out what the captain was doing. He seemed to be fiddling with something, but still looking directly ahead. So Arkyn didn't let his gaze drop. Roth didn't notice anything, so intently was he watching Arkyn.

Arkyn said, "I confess, I am inquisitive. There is no official welcome; Your Lordship greets me, not the Margrave; An impromptu military display is apparently occurring here and you coolly inform me that there has been an accident, without *explaining* anything. To whom did the accident befall?"

"It's a long story, sir, better told after you have refresh—"

The door burst inward.

"Arrest him!" snapped Wynfeld, his voice strained and harsh, flying on the wings of panic.

A sneer creasing his face, the Deputy Governor fumbled, trying to draw his sword. Fitz elbowed him sharply in the ribs, causing him to double up as Wynfeld's men surrounded and disarmed him after momentary confusion.

Arkyn rose from his chair, goblet in hand. "Commander, you will please explain this extraordinary behaviour!"

Wynfeld whitened. He croaked, "By Alcis… My prince, you've not *drunk* anything?" the panic almost audible but not yet manifested.

"I have not, though—."

"Well, don't!" snapped Wynfeld, finally revealing how agitated he was. "Kadeem, remove all this; it's poisoned."

Arkyn blanched. Dissociated, he lowered the goblet onto the tray as Kadeem hastily moved everything and urged him to sit down. Instead, Arkyn looked between the captive Roth and Commander Wynfeld.

In a remarkably calm voice, he enquired, "I take it Roth is, to your mind, responsible, Commander?"

"Yes, sir." Wynfeld had seen his Prince become a figure of authority when younger; now he saw, in swift motion, the shadow of a future king.

"Is there *any* doubt, *whatsoever*, as to his guilt?" probed Arkyn, emphasising each syllable. When the Deputy Governor tried to interrupt, he roared, "YOU *WILL* BE SILENT UNTIL I ASK YOU A QUESTION…Commander?"

"No doubt at all, sir. We have sworn testimony."

Arkyn faced the Deputy Governor. "Well? Is it true?"

"Yes, and, by Alcis, I'd try it again," stormed Roth.

"You dare to still stand?"

Forcing Roth to kneel by kicking his feet from under him, the guards jerked his arms up, obliging him to look at the floor. The Deputy Governor struggled, to no avail. The guards strengthened their hold as Arkyn crossed to them.

Drawing his sword swiftly, Arkyn tickled Roth's chin with the tip, before lifting it until the Deputy Governor had to look into his eyes or shut his own and Roth was far too defiant to do that.

"You will explain *why*," ordered Arkyn.

"Ask your father, boy," spat Roth.

Involuntarily, Wynfeld went to intervene, but a slight movement from Arkyn prevented him. He realised his Prince wasn't out of control but, rather, in the tranquil seas of anger.

"Let's see how much of a boy I am, shall we? Commander, I'm guessing the *accident* befell the Margrave, and he has joined his ancestors at Roth's instruction or instigation?"

"Yes, sir, but he meant it for Your Highness," replied Wynfeld, his feet planted foursquare, his hands clasped behind his back, his jaw set.

Arkyn finally looked at him, recognising Wynfeld's restraint, reading it in him as easily as a book. The commander wanted revenge on Roth for the attempt. He shifted his sword. "You will please extract all information required from this person and do your duty. I assume my meaning is understood."

"Men." Wynfeld jerked his head and his men half dragged a struggling Roth out.

As the door clicked shut behind them, the tableau shattered. Arkyn crossed to the window with his back to the room. His household and Wynfeld watched him with consternation. Kadeem murmured something about refreshments and left. Edward followed him to hunt for who was next in Terasian authority. Fitz looked at Wynfeld.

The commander murmured, "I've got men all around the building, but it might be as well to inform yours what's happened. Would you like me to?"

"No, I will. I also need to retrieve my sword chain. Can you stay here?"

Wynfeld nodded. He watched the captain leave, thinking that Fitz had a very simple air for one so devious.

Hearing the door close, Arkyn turned slowly back to the room, shaking.

Wynfeld saw only a traumatised sixteen-year-old boy. He strode over, and with one arm supporting him, carefully took the sword from Arkyn's shaking hand, leaning it up against the wall.

"My prince, please sit down. If you don't, I think you might fall."

"I always can tell when you're worried. How white have I gone?"

"As white as snow, and shaking to boot," murmured Wynfeld.

“I can’t move.”

The commander hooked a chair round behind Arkyn, who collapsed onto it. Their eyes met.

Arkyn whispered, “Was what I did right, Wynfeld?”

“Sir—”

“No, no-one else will tell me; I must know, was I right?”

Wynfeld recognised a genuine need for confirmation. “Yes, I think so. I was impressed; I must admit. I never expected you to hold your own in that manner.”

“Thank you. I must inform my father of events. I can’t imagine what he’ll say.”

“Would you like me to inform His Majesty, Your Highness?”

“No. I had better. That way, at least he’ll see I’m unharmed.”

“I’d hardly go that far, sir; white as mountain snow and shaking, as I said. At least leave it a couple of minutes until you’ve regained colour.”

Arkyn shook his head. “I must do it now. I don’t know what he’ll want done, you see. Will you stay here?”

“Yes, sir.”

* * *

Arkyn called up his messenger, Fafnir – a red dragon small enough to sit on his palm. Requesting a link with the King, an opaque heat haze formed around him. His father appeared opposite, sitting in the King’s chair of the Inner Office.

“What’s happened? Are you at Tera yet?” demanded Adeone, seeing Arkyn’s state.

“Yes, I arrived a short time ago. Sire, Lord Roth has assassinated Lord Portur in mistake for me. He again tried to kill me a few minutes ago. Commander Wynfeld prevented the attempt.”

Silent as he absorbed the information, Adeone recognised that the bland facts hid much uncertainty and emotion. “You are unharmed?”

“Yes, father, just shaken I suppose.”

“What of Roth?” enquired Adeone.

“He is under arrest and interrogation prior to execution, sir.”

“Good.” It reassured and pleased Adeone – even though the idea it should repulsed him. “Is it certain that he was responsible?”

“He admitted it. What do you want doing about the situation, Your Majesty?”

“Arkyn, now is hardly the time for pleasantries. Alcis! Who was responsible for your education? All right, over recent years that was me, but, seriously, what is most important is that you are safe. As to the situation, you’ll have to appoint a new Margrave.”

“Me?” enquired Arkyn, astounded and terrified.

"Yes, *you*. I sent you to Tera confident you could cope with whatever problem came your way. You're my Representative; I trust you. You have the authority to take the oath – so why would I undermine that and you by association?"

"Thank you, father, but I'm not sure—"

"Arkyn, how did you react when confronted with the fact someone had tried to kill you?"

"I, er, I seemed to become someone else. I suppose I was detached, half watching myself, half controlling what was happening." Even saying those words sounds strange to Arkyn.

Yet to Adeone, listening, they were a good sign, and he said so before asking, "What did Wynfeld and Fitz do? Did they interfere with your decisions? What did you do when you heard the Deputy Governor had been arrested?"

"They did nothing to interfere with my decisions, but the commander arrested Roth in front of me when I was about to drink the poison."

Incredulous, Adeone snapped, "You were *what*? Sicla! Wynfeld cut it fine!"

Seeing the fiery annoyance, Arkyn murmured, "I believe he had only just found out."

Realising his son was coming down from the immediate reaction, Adeone said gently, "I hope so. If they didn't advise a different course of action, they thought yours was appropriate. After all, they'll both speak their minds to us. You'll be fine, be yourself. You can do this. I have faith in you and will stand by whatever you decide."

Arkyn whispered, "Thank you, father. I asked Roth 'why'; he said to ask you."

"Roth thinks I overlooked him unfairly at the last review. He's embittered, I assume, but he's a man in your uncle's mould; too hard by far. I never thought he'd go to this extreme and threaten you. I'm sorry. I should have warned you."

"Warning would have made me prejudiced, and the attempt didn't succeed, father."

"You are more forgiving than I am, or maybe life hasn't made you bitter yet," said Adeone sadly. "Promise me never to let it."

"I will try my best." Arkyn hesitated before continuing, "Fitz did something, I don't know what, and Roth couldn't draw his sword. I mean, he also elbowed him in the ribs, but I don't know how he stopped him from drawing his sword."

Adeone frowned, then chuckled. "I bet I do. Terasian swords have a loop on the cross-guard. There's also one on the scabbard or belt. I think they have to be there by law. They were used so people could transport weapons, but not use them during curfews or at alciums. I expect Fitz, being the devious rogue he is, slipped a bar-ended chain between them; it locks the sword into the scabbard. I've seen him do it before."

"Does he always use trickery to protect us?"

"Only when it works." Obviously amused, Adeone continued, "People underestimate him, normally to their detriment. Now, take care of yourself and never forget I'm here if you need me."

"I won't, father. Thank you. What do you want me to do about Roth's estate?"

Adeone considered his son for several moments. "Whatever you think best. I mean that. Set your authority, Arkyn; I will stand by your decision."

* * *

When the connection broke, Arkyn found Kadeem, Edward, Fitz and Wynfeld watching him. Kadeem pushed a goblet into his hand. Arkyn gazed blankly at it.

Wynfeld realised that the second stage of shock was setting in.

Kadeem also noticed. More determined and forthright than normal, he said, "Drink that *without* argument, sir, or I must find a doctor. Quite frankly, I hate to think of the rumours that would cause."

Arkyn drank the warmed wine. Feeling marginally better, he observed wryly, "I should have told His Majesty that I don't have the chance not to look after myself, shouldn't I, Kadeem?"

"Yes, sir. Now you'll please oblige me by eating something. Everything else can *wait*. You can't think about business on an empty stomach after a shock."

"I don't get the chance to try," grumbled Arkyn. "All right. Thank you, Kadeem. Will you permit me to eat as well as conduct business? Today is unusual."

"I suppose it is," replied Kadeem primly.

Arkyn wasn't fooled. "I'll take that as a 'yes'. Commander Wynfeld, please explain the extraordinary events here."

Wynfeld said, "The Margrave was an inveterate eater. When he heard of your delay, he ate the meal intended for you, sir. This morning they found him dead of poison. Roth's deputy sent for me. I'm not exactly sure why me as opposed to the City Guard, but I got here about half an hour before Your Highness. I ordered an interrogation of the kitchen staff. It wasn't hard to locate the boy responsible for adding the 'special seasoning' to the dish. Terrified, he admitted it as soon as he heard what had happened. I got the news as you entered the house. The rest you know, sir."

"Thank you. Who is Roth's deputy?"

Edward replied, "One Percival Wealsman, Your Highness. He's waiting. He was so worried about the situation he returned to see all was well."

"How conscientious of him. Tell me something, Wynfeld, is anything known against him? Has my father a quarrel with him, for example?"

Wynfeld shrugged. "Not that I know of, sir. I think he is trustworthy. He alerted us to the situation, and when I appeared, Roth was badly scared. He'd tried to keep events secret by saying you'd have to take the decisions."

"I suppose, in one sense, he was correct. Edward, please ask Wealsman to join us. What has happened to the boy, Commander?"

"I have him under guard, sir, but we truly believe he didn't know what the seasoning would do."

"Then they'll be no action. See that is known. Nothing is to be said on the matter again. Roth shall take the full consequence of this double treason. I think you may stand your men down as well. As for Roth, do your duty; he is a traitor and murderer."

* * *

Moments later, Arkyn turned to the new entrant: a man in his thirties wearing woollen tunic and hose with mid-brown slightly disordered hair. His hazel eyes were bright and held a sparkle, even with the gravity of the situation. Arkyn nodded to himself. Instinctively, he felt the man would be competent.

Arkyn said, "I take it you are Percival Wealsman?"

Straightening up from his bow, the man agreed he was.

"Why did you alert Commander Wynfeld to the situation?"

"Two reasons, sir. Firstly, I remembered overhearing a comment that Lord Roth made when he heard about your impending visit. It obliquely mentioned revenge on the King. He said that the King would reap the consequences of his decisions. Secondly, I was under instruction from His Majesty to report any strange occurrences – those which might adversely affect Your Highness' stay – to the commander. So, when I reached here this morning and learned what had happened, I alerted him."

"When did His Majesty inform you of your extra duties?"

"I received the letter on the 28th Tradal, sir, shortly before Commander Wynfeld arrived. I assumed my position, being Lord Roth's assistant, made me a useful spy."

Arkyn cringed inwardly. "*Spy* is rather a strong word, Wealsman. I would see the authorisation for that. Also, the former Deputy Governor is awaiting execution for treason; he is not to be referred to as 'Lord'."

Wealsman handed over an official letter addressed to the Assistant Deputy Governor. Arkyn read it – recognising his father's signature but Richardson's handwriting – and placed it beside him.

"Very well. Thank you – for all your prompt action. How much are you now reporting directly to the King?"

"Nothing at all, sir," replied Wealsman. "My remit, as you will have observed, was until Your Highness' arrival."

"Yes. I just wondered if you had accepted it. I have informed His Majesty of events; he has allowed me free rein with the situation. Will you accept that?"

"I should hardly do otherwise, Your Highness."

"That wasn't quite what I asked."

"Yes, sir," said Wealsman, appreciating the Prince's pedantry; it showed someone whom it would be difficult to fool.

Arkyn nodded. "Thank you. Have you seen the review briefing?"

"No, sir. Roth delegated directly to those in charge of the different sections. I oversaw the more day-to-day aspects."

"Very well. Edward will give you one of our copies for now. Maybe you could look over it in the next couple of hours; whilst I attend to the small matter of Lord Portur's death and the attempted assassination of myself."

* * *

A few minutes later, Edward re-entered to find Arkyn once more observing the view and Fitz watching the Prince with concern. Kadeem was obviously trying to decide whether to break the silence. Arkyn turned to Edward.

"Send a runner to the Terazi. If the court is in session, I would ask him to adjourn. I need to convey events here to him as soon as possible, and I require his advice. That's all for now." He watched his administrator leave whilst saying, "Fitz, thank you for your trick with Roth's sword. It could have been much worse if he'd drawn it. You'd better go and keep the guards busy."

Lips twitching, the captain saluted and left. If the Prince kept up this level of autonomy, everyone who expected unease and uncertainty from the young man were going to be shocked, Tera's Chief Judge amongst them.

"I'm afraid this means any itinerary we had has been blasted to the winds by magic," said Arkyn to Kadeem.

"We shall see how they all react in a crisis, Your Highness; I don't envy any of them. Your visit will have caused enough upheaval; this is the beginning of a storm of change for them."

"Yes, with no governor and no deputy governor, it is. My dilemma, though, is I don't really know what I'm doing."

Kadeem smiled. "You're outwardly coping, sir. They will understand. If not, keep them on their toes and, you never know, they might not notice anything wrong."

Arkyn snorted. "You missed your vocation. Do we know what's planned for this afternoon and evening, for example? I suppose the Margrave's Office does. Could you locate the Margrave's secretary? No, hang on, that's Edward's job."

"I'll attend to it, sir. I think you might need Edward. Does Your Highness require anything else?"

"No, thank you." His voice dropped to almost a whisper. "Other than for this nightmare to end."

"Our dreams are what we make them, sir. Nightmares end when we awaken and waking is always sooner than we can anticipate." He bowed and left, fretting about the Prince's state of mind.

Arkyn turned to the window. The rain of the last few days had stopped for now. The clear sky hadn't brought warmth, but it allowed the sunlight to glisten off the sodden garden. He watched a boy and girl on the lawn playing catch. Suddenly, he wanted to see his brother, just for the unending bounce and optimism he held.

Edward returned. "The court is in session, Your Highness. I gave the runner express instructions and a note. We can only hope he follows them."

Arkyn turned from his dreams to his duties. "Then, until we know, where's that briefing?"

"Sir, why don't you rest for a while?"

"Let me think… Because the Margrave is dead, Roth is awaiting execution and Wealsman doesn't know about the review. Lord Iris, as my advisor, is days away because the King wanted to emphasise my arrival; therefore, that briefing and my own judgement are all I can trust. Also, in the absence of anyone else, I'm in charge. Fetch it."

Chapter 4

JUDGEMENTS AND REPERCUSSIONS

Late Morning

Margrave's Residence – Arkyn's Office

THIRTY MINUTES LATER, Edward announced the Terazi – thereby introducing him to the Prince, who saw a well-presented gentleman wearing the green robes of a judge and a discontented expression that furrowed his brow and pursed his lips.

"Your Honour, have you been notified of today's events?"

"I cannot imagine what events you are referring to, but I must inform you I'm displeased with the way I was summoned here, sir."

"Your disquiet is noted; before you continue, however, there is a graver and more immediate concern on which I require your advice."

"Couldn't the Margrave oblige, sir?"

Arkyn explained the events before saying, "Roth is now under arrest and interrogation. He has admitted his guilt, so is also awaiting execution. Terazi, wait a moment. I know what you would say about a trial, but he admitted his guilt in front of me – no trial is therefore necessary. I have consulted His Majesty on this matter."

The Terazi sagged into a chair, his annoyance gone. "By Alcis! Roth a traitor…"

"Yes, his second attack on me sealed the matter."

"I'm not surprised he tried again."

"I do hope that's not a presumption of my character, but rather a summation of Roth's!"

"Of course, sir," replied the Terazi, unabashed. "I've not known you long enough to appraise your character. Though I am confused why you may need my advice?"

"The matter of Roth's estate, Your Honour; I do not know what to do with it or about it. I understand it is forfeit to my father, but the law might allow for clemency."

"In certain situations, yes. That is, at the discretion of the King or His Majesty's Advocates – at least in Terasia – and the agreement of the current Terazi. As both the King's heir and Representative, Your Highness could, therefore, invoke clemency. It allows for retention of half of all property, but it also means Roth's requests and bequests can be upheld, where prudent, and Lady Roth will retain her dower."

"Could you explain what would constitute grounds for clemency and any precedents?"

"Of course, sir. Often, it is to do with the influence the condemned has had over his family and their actions during the period leading to his treachery. There have been cases of clemency in the past, from the first days that Terasia was part of the empire, though there have also been notoriously harsh governors—" The Terazi recollected who he was talking to and changed tack. "Though they're best left to the history books; however, it does mean that there are precedents for almost any action Your Highness might wish to take."

"Do you know much about Roth's situation?"

"Bits, sir. They aren't a united family. Roth's wife is a matriarch and lives apart. His son, Erlan, will have nothing to do with him after Roth objected to his wife joining the family."

To allow himself more time to think, Arkyn asked, "Why did Roth object to his new wed-daughter?"

The Terazi smiled. "It's a strange story, sir. Roth travelled to Denshire as an ambassador for the Margrave. His son, Erlan, went with him. Once in

Cearden, Erlan met and fell in love with the Visir's eldest daughter, Meera. They were both of an age and impulsive. They married in secret and bound themselves so closely afterwards that there was nothing their fathers could do to deny it. Neither Erlan nor Meera have anything to do with their respective families. They're still besotted and untroubled by conscience. It is a love story that may well become legend. Roth let prejudice override his eyes. His son's happy; that is all that should have mattered. The Visir I can't speak for but, as a King's Representative, he probably thought it reflected badly on his authority. Some would, and do, say that if he can't control his family, how can he control a province? It is malicious gossip. He is more than capable. Erlan is likewise a sound man—"

Arkyn's thoughts finished themselves. "In that case, if you will agree, we will invoke the clemency clause."

"Your Highness, I will sign to that. You are certainly merciful."

"Maybe," replied Arkyn dismissively. "The next problem is the governance of Terasia until I appoint the new Margrave. Percival Wealsman, I understand, is next in authority stakes, with yourself as his counterpart in the judicial system. What do you know of Wealsman, Your Honour?"

"He's a minor lord from one of Lord Portur's manors and a good man. Fair, true to himself and his men. He'll defend them with a passion when he feels they are unfairly under attack. Kind, sympathetic but he knows how to speak his mind and does so. He'll tell you his honest views. You can argue with him, whilst sitting on different metaphorical fences, yet somehow end up in a compromise and uncertain as to how you got there. He'll recall incidents and orders easily, but he'll never hold a grudge. He's a good man, sir, cares passionately about Terasia and will be shocked to the core by events here today. I'd trust him with my loved ones' lives, as well as mine."

"Thank you. He didn't mention the connection to Portur."

The judge smiled. "Unless you asked him directly, I doubt he would have done; he prefers to exist in anonymity."

Arkyn raised an eyebrow. "Then he is a rare person. Next, what do you know about Lord Portur's secretary? I haven't yet met the gentleman, but I expect to any moment."

"He's good at his job. Polite, deferential. Truthfully, I've not seen that much of him or his work, but I haven't heard anything bad either."

"That's a good sign. Edward, could you see where the gentleman has got to? Terazi, would you remain here, please? I don't want to disturb your day – I really didn't, I should say – but I would be glad of your advice."

"With pleasure, sir. As to disturbance, the events have been disturbing."

* * *

Edward re-entered alone. "Lady Roth has arrived, Your Highness, in some consternation. She is enquiring after her husband. What would you like done?"

"Show her in, please. I ought to be the one to tell her."

Arkyn pushed himself to his feet as Edward left. He didn't want the interview with its requisite bad news. Realising apprehension suffused his features, he rearranged them until the Terazi saw concern there without there being the hint of indecision or uncertainty.

Announced by Edward, Lady Roth curtsied to Arkyn. "My apologies, sir. I had no wish to disturb Your Highness, but your secretary insisted."

"Thank you, Lady Roth. Please do not concern yourself; Edward was acting on my instructions. I have some grave news. Will you sit?"

"I am perfectly happy standing, sir." Her voice brooked no argument.

"Very well. It is my unfortunate duty to inform you that your husband is under arrest on a double charge of treason."

"You must have made a mistake, sir."

"No mistake. His actions have resulted in the death of His Excellency and nearly myself. I'm sorry."

"*You're sorry!*"

"Yes, I am. He has admitted his guilt in this," responded Arkyn factually.

"He will…there will be a trial?" Her eyes flicked momentarily to the Terazi before returning to meet Arkyn's.

"No. He admitted his guilt in front of me. There is no need for a trial."

"There must be some mistake."

"No mistake, madam."

"Can I see him, Your Highness?"

Arkyn considered her steadily; he turned to Edward. "Get Wynfeld, please."

When Wynfeld had joined the silent room, Arkyn turned from the window. "Her Ladyship would like to see her husband. Is that possible?"

"I have no objection to a visit, sir, but, if possible, not immediately."

"I will see my husband," insisted Lady Roth.

"Madam, you can demand all you want; it will make no difference to my men," stated Arkyn.

"Can you begin to understand—?"

"I don't *have* to! Your husband murdered Lord Portur, attempted to murder me, and all without showing any remorse. He foolishly underestimated me. Do not make the same mistake." (She seemed to sag.) "Get a chair for Her Ladyship, Edward. Commander, at your discretion, send word here when she may see her husband. My lady, I must enquire how much you knew of your husband's activities."

"Nothing, sir, we live apart."

"Then what brought you here in such a hurry?"

"A note."

"Its contents please."

"It said…Goodbye."

"The gist was that, or the whole note?"

"Just that word, Your Highness, just that word. What will happen to him and my family, sir?"

Arkyn considered her; the proud hauteur had been replaced by a defeated air, which ill-matched the starch crispness of her persona. Her strong-boned face had become gaunt, and her eyes haunted. Arkyn crossed to the sideboard, poured a goblet of wine and passed it to her.

The judge smiled at the touch; he began to truly like the Prince.

Arkyn seated himself. "Your husband is divested of his office and title and will be executed. The law states that all his land and property are forfeit to the King; I am, however, going to allow clemency. This means half your husband's property remains with the family. His title passes to his heir and you retain your dower – as I am satisfied you knew nothing of the matter. Your son is, I understand, estranged from your husband, so I have no concerns on his part. Your husband's requests and bequests shall be honoured, as far as is prudent. I have consulted the Terazi, and he has agreed to these proceedings. I hope that relieves your mind."

"Thank you, sir. I don't know what to say."

"Thank you is enough. I also need to inform your son. Can I request anybody to be with you?"

"No, thank you, sir. I ought to present myself to Lady Portur and give her my condolences."

Arkyn blanched. "I wasn't aware that Portur was married. The last information I had was that he was a bachelor."

"He married last week, sir."

"Oh, Sicla! This has been a travesty. Edward, I'll see Lady Portur as soon as possible."

"Your Highness, may I say something?" asked Lady Roth.

Feeling uncomfortable, Arkyn nodded.

"I wouldn't have thought Lady Portur would have been up to receiving anyone officially this morning."

"Thank you, my lady. I hope you are correct. Otherwise, there has been an irretrievable breakdown of manners."

"I think the breakdown is rather in communication, sir. Manners are only applicable if you are aware of the existence of the other participant."

"You are, of course, correct." Arkyn sagged. The report he'd make to his father would be interesting if events continued to occur at the rate they were doing.

Safe in the knowledge that he answered to Lord Scanlon, rather than the Prince or King, the Terazi had watched events with a detached interest. Under the facade that Arkyn now presented, he recognised the worry of an uncertain boy. "Your Highness, you cannot be blamed. I am sure, knowing Her Ladyship, that she would not want you to trouble yourself over the occurrence. If Lady Roth is to present her condolences, maybe I could locate the whereabouts of Lady Portur for her and attend to the matter of finding Lord Erlan Roth."

Arkyn pulled himself together. "Certainly, Your Honour. Lady Roth, please accept my apology for all that has happened today."

"Your Highness, I don't think it is you who should be apologising for almost being murdered."

"Maybe not, my lady, but I offer apologies for the events that have followed."

Lady Roth took her leave, the Terazi following her. Edward stood to one side, uncertainty radiating off him.

Arkyn faced him. "That was an interesting interlude. To whom did you speak earlier?"

"Someone crossing the hallway, sir. I asked who was next to the Deputy Governor in authority – not knowing His Excellency had married. I'm sorry."

"What's done's done. Don't worry. Now, which do I do first? Speak to the secretary, visit Lady Portur or see about Roth's heir and the proclamation of Portur's death? Any ideas?"

"I'm hardly in the right place to advise Your Highness."

"Edward, please."

After a moment's consideration, Edward said, "It may be unwise to visit Her Ladyship without warning. She will be upset and uncertain herself. That leaves the secretary, proclamation and Lord Erlan Roth. I would suggest you speak to the secretary, find out the itinerary for this afternoon and rearrange it if necessary. Then see about the proclamation. By that time, I expect the Terazi will have located Lord Erlan. You can then explain matters to him, send a message to Her Ladyship and either have her attend here or go to her yourself."

"Then see if the Margrave's secretary is here, please."

It took mere moments before Edward announced, "Vincent Thomkins, Your Highness."

"Thomkins? Our diary archivist is a Willim Thomkins," observed Arkyn sitting down and motioning for Edward to stay.

"Yes, Your Highness – my brother."

Stunned, Arkyn enquired, "Master Thomkins, are you aware of the situation?" inwardly pondering what had made one brother travel the length of the empire.

"I found Lord Portur, sir, so am aware he has died; I am unaware of what has become of Lord Roth, understanding, instead, that Lord Wealsman is in charge after Your Highness."

"Yes, he is. Roth is under arrest for treason. Now, Lord Wealsman is unaware of the itinerary for my visit. I'm hoping you know it."

"I have it here, sir."

As he passed it to Arkyn, a knock at the office door preceded the Terazi.

"Your Highness, Erlan Roth was here for a session of introductions this afternoon. I'm intrigued no-one thought that strange. Would you like to see him? I don't believe he has heard about his father, though he may have heard about Lord Portur."

"Please show him in, Your Honour," replied Arkyn, motioning Thomkins to where Edward was sitting taking notes. He watched the auburn-haired man enter and noted the familiar, confused air. He judged Lord Erlan to be in his early to mid-twenties, lean and alert, with eyes that showed the promise of youth still lived.

"Your Highness, I understand you wished to see me."

"I did. It's my duty to inform you that your father is under arrest for two counts of treason."

"There must be some mistake," stated Erlan, thinking precision was rather superfluous – one count of treason was enough to condemn, two was merely perfunctory emphasis.

Arkyn explained the events, wondering how many more times he would have to. He saw the optimism shatter in Erlan's eyes.

"When should I expect Your Highness' commissioners and bailiffs?"

"Are you aware of the clemency provision?"

"Yes, sir, but I can't see the Terazi invoking that."

"He didn't. I did," said Arkyn. "His Honour merely accepted my decision to do so."

Stunned, Erlan blurted out, "Why? I mean… It's not that I'm ungrateful, and I suppose I should be saying thank you, but *why*?"

"You can't help it when your estranged father decides to try to murder me. You couldn't have known about it or, therefore, informed anyone, let alone stopped him."

Erlan swallowed. "Right, sir. Thank you. I, er… I don't know what else to say."

"Thank you is enough."

The Terazi walked up to Arkyn and murmured in his ear.

“Is there another option?” asked Arkyn.

“No, sir. It has to happen for the clemency clause to take effect.”

Arkyn faced Erlan Roth. “You must swear an honour-binding fealty to the King through me and renounce your father in front of witnesses. Are you willing to do that?”

Erlan paused momentarily. “Yes, Your Highness.”

“Then please kneel.”

When the new Lord Roth was back on his feet, he asked Arkyn whether he should attend the afternoon of introductions.

“I’m going to use the opportunity to announce the events of this morning. You may attend or not, as you will. It rather depends on whether you wish to face your peers.”

“I shall attend, if Your Highness has no objection. I will have to present my wife.”

Impressed by the young lord’s resolve to face the unpleasant speculation that would manifest itself, Arkyn said, “I look forward to meeting Her Ladyship, Lord Roth.”

The door had barely closed on the retreating Erlan before Wynfeld was entering to say the former Deputy Governor wasn’t revealing much and it might be a good time for his wife to visit.

“Then find her and say so,” replied Arkyn. “Lord Erlan Roth’s just sworn an honour-binding fealty, but if he wants to be present, I won’t hold him forsworn. His mother may be glad of the support.”

* * *

Half an hour later, Wynfeld returned asking for a private word. Raising an eyebrow, Arkyn dismissed Edward and Thomkins.

“It’s something the new Lord Roth has revealed. He said that the family became estranged after Lord Scanlon visited. That the former Deputy Governor became extremely embittered only after that and that he, Lord Roth, thinks Lord Scanlon had some kind of hold over the former Deputy Governor.”

“I thought it was to do with Erlan Roth’s marriage.”

“I think it might be many things, sir, but I would like permission to search *all* manors of the condemned man.”

“Granted. See that no-one has the chance to interfere. Before you execute him, put the matter of Lord Scanlon to him. I need to know the hold he had. Thank you, Wynfeld. Can you also locate Fitz and send him here, please?”

“Certainly, sir. Might I enquire how you are?”

Arkyn sighed. “I’m trying to deal with things as they arise, but I don’t know if my decisions are right. I’ve told them to tell me if they think I’m wrong, but whether they will…” he tailed off.

"If they thought it would be detrimental, I think they would tell you, Your Highness."

"I hope so. The itinerary is so busy with introductions, banquets and meetings that I wonder how my father manages."

"He's used to it, sir. I'm sure you will become used to it too, but make sure you keep some of every day for yourself. Keep your head high and your heels down and you'll be fine. There are plenty of people willing to give advice if you require it."

"Yes, and it will probably all conflict. I wish Tain were here; he's always so full of bounce; *sometimes* it's uplifting– though never tell him I said that."

"I wouldn't dream of it, sir. I do think, however, it is lucky that His Highness is many miles away in the circumstances."

"You're probably right. Thank you."

Chapter 5
GREETINGS

Afternoon

Margrave's Hall

AN HOUR LATER, Arkyn walked onto the dais in the Margrave's Hall, too nervous to take the hall in properly. Instead of seating himself, he faced the assembled group. In a quiet voice that, nonetheless, held the full attention of the listeners, he began to speak.

"My lords and ladies, it is my sad duty to tell you of the murder of Lord Portur by poison at the hand of the gentleman formally known as Lord Roth, Deputy Governor of Terasia. After a second attempt at killing me, Roth has been executed as a traitor. He admitted his guilt and took the consequence of it."

Many eyes swivelled to where Erlan Roth stood with a lady Arkyn supposed was his wife.

He continued, "My lords and ladies…" (All heads turned back to him) "…Roth's title has passed to his son and half the lands have been retained by the family, on advice received. That is the end of the matter. Having consulted the King, His Majesty has confirmed that I am responsible for appointing the new Margrave. Until then, I will be taking over some of Lord Portur's duties, along with those I already held for the review. Lord Wealsman will be accepting the remainder for the time being. Thank you."

Arkyn seated himself before Wealsman presented and introduced each of the eleven assembled overlords and their wives. When the formalities finished, Arkyn mingled with the crowd, talking to as many of them as possible.

Overhearing a comment, he snapped, “I sent a request to Lady Portur that she was not to trouble herself about attending if she didn’t wish to, Lord Silvano. She has lost her husband; compassion is needed from all of us – especially as the intended victim *wasn’t* Lord Portur!”

Silvano bowed slightly, saying, “My apologies, Your Highness, I didn’t think,” considering Prince Arkyn was showing definite traits of the FitzAlcis: a capacity to deal with the unexpected and flashes of temper. Then there was something new, which he hadn’t witnessed in either the King or Justiciar.

“They are accepted, my lord; I’m afraid I am a bit touchy today.”

Unnerved by the simple honesty, Silvano replied, “That’s understandable, sir. I hope you have not taken a dislike to Terasia through the actions of a… misguided individual.” The pause was so brief that Arkyn almost missed it.

“I would never do so, my lord, and your country is striking…”

They talked pleasantly of the merits of Terasia, but Silvano had reminded Arkyn of his lapse. After a couple of minutes, he extricated himself adroitly and motioned Edward over.

“Present my compliments to Lady Portur and see if she would be up to receiving me. Give her the option of saying no. I don’t want her to feel as though she *must* see me today; if she would prefer it, I can introduce myself tomorrow. Go yourself please.”

As Edward left the Margrave’s Hall, Arkyn found Wealsman beside him.

“Did you mean it, Your Highness, when you said I was taking on some of the responsibilities for running Terasia?”

“Yes, my lord, I did. I can’t manage everything and you are next in authority. Does it pose a problem?”

“Not as such, sir. It just came as a bit of a shock. Rather like finding out you know I’m one of the province’s minor lords. Might I ask who informed you?”

“The Terazi has been very helpful. He has a good opinion of you,” remarked Arkyn with a small smile.

“Better than I deserve, I suspect.”

“We shall see. People tend to hold all sorts of erroneous views; I am not immune from them myself.”

They continued talking until Edward returned; Arkyn excused himself and moved a little way off.

“I do not want to trouble you, Your Highness, but I think that maybe you should visit Lady Portur. She is very distressed. Her maid has told me she's not seen a doctor and won't have one sent for; no-one will go against her."

As Arkyn followed Edward out of the hall, Wealsman found himself temporarily alone. He smiled to himself, thinking of other years when the FitzAlcis had visited until a voice disturbed his vivid memories.

"Well, well, Wealsman, not doing too badly out of this visit already, are you? Rest assured though, at least this time the Margrave *will* change. It is a shame you were born as you were. Governors are overlords... *not minor* lords..."

Wealsman didn't turn around. "Rest assured yourself, my lord, I hold no ambition to be Margrave but, should His Highness ask for my advice, my fealty obliges me to provide an honest and just opinion of all candidates."

"Are you threatening *me*?"

"No, merely commenting with honesty. Although decency would have prevented me from talking about matters such as a new governor whilst Lord Portur lies so recently deceased. Please excuse me, my lord. I must attend to details for this evening's banquet."

Silvano's face would have been amusing to Wealsman had the latter seen it. The overlord didn't know how to respond to either the reply or the rebuke. Wealsman didn't wait for an answer: he simply left the hall.

* * *

Arkyn followed Edward, lost in thought. Nothing had ever prepared him for visiting a widow so soon into her bereavement, and he wondered what he could possibly say to her.

The guard on the doors to Lady Portur's rooms saluted as the Prince passed him and as Arkyn entered the antechamber a maid quickly curtsied, showing them to a small sitting room where Lady Portur was resting.

Shocked by how wan she was, Arkyn drew a sharp breath and knelt beside her.

"My lady, my sincerest condolences. I am sorry I haven't made it here before."

Lethargically, she turned her head to him and tried to rise.

Arkyn placed a hand on her shoulder. "Don't think of trying to get up. I will not stay long to trouble you. I merely wanted to present my condolences and introduce myself. I'd like you to know that your husband's murderer has been dealt with ..." A blank expression suffused her face. Enough was enough. "Have you seen a doctor today?" A slight shake of the head answered him. "Discreetly send for one, please, Edward."

As his administrator left, Lady Portur registered the request. Curling into a ball, she started sobbing. Perplexed, Arkyn kept a reassuring hand on her shoulder until Doctor Artzman appeared.

"Why was Her Ladyship disturbed?" asked the medical man tartly.

Pushing himself to his feet, Arkyn forestalled Edward. Crossing to the doctor, he whispered, "The only way to get *you* here was for me to come. Is there anything you can give her to induce sleep or calm?"

"My apologies, Your Highness. I do have a sedative, if she will take it."

Arkyn said, "Pass me the vial. Is it a complete dose?"

"Yes, sir, just one in a vial; it's safer. What do you plan?"

With a smile playing about his lips, Arkyn murmured, "Merely to pass Her Ladyship a goblet of wine, and then insist that she drinks it. I have a feeling that she will refuse help from you."

"Might I enquire where you learnt that trick, sir?"

"That would ruin an illusion. Please talk to her."

Edward had located the pitcher of wine and goblets. Arkyn poured and mixed the sedative, walked over to Lady Portur and passed her the goblet. She took it and thanked him, sipping it whilst the doctor expostulated with her to take a soporific.

Arkyn said, "I think you are wasting your breath, Doctor. My lady, if you finish the wine, I'll put the goblet somewhere safe." Taking it, he motioned everyone to leave.

Six minutes later, he, Edward and the doctor re-entered. They smiled at each other; Lady Portur was sound asleep.

"Come and check on Her Ladyship in the morning, please, Artzman?" whispered Arkyn. "If she is still in the mood to object, take my name in vain. I am, after all, responsible for more than the subterfuge with the wine, but I wouldn't want anyone to get into that state. Edward, see the maid knows to send for me when Her Ladyship is up to receiving me. Understandably, I don't think she absorbed anything I told her. Let's leave her to sleep."

As he left the chambers with Edward, Arkyn glanced at the tired guard to receive an impeccable salute without any hints of nerves.

"Why are you here, Sergeant…?"

"Dring, sir. Commander Wynfeld's orders – to prevent Lady Portur being disturbed."

"Right. Her Ladyship has retired, so please prevent anyone entering, other than her maids. Give them my apologies, but make them realise those are my orders."

Chapter 6
SHOCK

Late Afternoon
Arkyn's Private Rooms

LEAVING SERGEANT DRING, Arkyn glanced down the main staircase. The entrance hall of the Residence was busy with lords and ladies leaving the introductions. A pang of guilt tugged at him. He should be down there getting to know them but he didn't feel like resuming the mask of a prince and, if everyone was leaving, he didn't feel like extending the event unnecessarily He asked Edward where his rooms were. He'd give everyone several minutes to leave without confusing them.

Edward led the way to the FitzAlcis chambers in the Residence. Specifically set aside for visiting FitzAlcis or their immediate representatives, they consisted of consisted of several rooms: antechamber, sitting room, bedchamber, bathroom, dressing room and servants' quarters. In the Margrave's Residence they were set at the end of one wing, offering a privacy that Arkyn hadn't been expecting.

Acknowledging the guards' salutes, Arkyn entered his antechamber and then his sitting room, caught Kadeem's eye and involuntarily twitched as Edward commented on a mundane issue. He had to be alone. Suddenly, in this safe space, he needed solitude. Too much had happened; he needed time to think.

Having seen the unease, Kadeem said, "It might be best if you saw to His Highness' office, Edward."

Once the door had closed behind his administrator, Arkyn said, "How do you read me so easily?"

"Everyone is a book to be read, Your Highness; with practice, even the long words explain themselves… I'll leave you in peace." Passing Arkyn, he put a drink next to the Prince's hand.

Shaking, Arkyn took a sip. Pacing, he tried to work off his agitation. Swearing, he considered events. He'd ordered a man's death; the man was dead. Him or me, but he had done it; he had been the cause. Portur was dead. No support there. Portur, whom his father said he could trust, who would have acted as an unofficial advisor, who could have helped him. Had he done the right thing with Erlan Roth? Should he have stripped the family of everything? Would his father really agree with the actions he'd taken? Could he explain those actions? Roth was dead. He'd had an overlord executed. His first official decision in Tera: execution. He ended the life of one of the highest lords in the empire. He had killed. Him or me. Him or me…

Sitting down, he rubbed his hands together, then through his hair. He picked up the glass, took another drink, rolling the glass between his hands.

Was it right? What if he'd arrived yesterday? What if he'd pushed on for Tera? What if he'd eaten the meal? What if, what if…? Him or me, him or me…

He got up again. Pacing, clasping the drink in his left hand crushing the fragile glass…

* * *

Someone lifted him off the floor and laid him on the couch. Kadeem was talking to him gently, but he couldn't make sense of the words. He stirred; his hand blazed with pain. Light seared his eyes. The blurry world gradually filled the space. Other figures. Why were they there? All he wanted to do was sleep. He closed his eyes to a slit. That was better. Kadeem's reassuring hand was on his shoulder and he was still talking, but someone else was close by. A reassuring presence. His hand was taken gently yet firmly. He winced. He heard Kadeem's voice.

"You've glass in your hand, sir. Commander Wynfeld's going to remove it."

Arkyn closed his eyes, wanting to snatch his hand away. The tinkle of glass hitting a bowl accompanied stabbing pain as Wynfeld removed fragments. Kadeem wiped his tears away. Embarrassed, he cursed himself for being unable to stop them flowing. The prodding had stopped and his hand was being tightly bandaged. It was somehow reassuring.

Several tones below normal, Wynfeld said, "Well done, my prince, I've known hardened soldiers make more fuss for a smaller wound."

Arkyn stayed silent. Shaking, he curled into a ball. Wynfeld cursed. The clink of a decanter and a beaker was pressed to his lips. Smelling the fruity tones of brandy, he gave into the demand and drank; the warmth seeped through his body along with the overriding desire to sleep.

* * *

Arkyn stirred. How long had he been asleep? He went to move the cover over him and drew in a sharp breath. Of course, he'd hurt his hand. There were soft footsteps he unconsciously recognised as his manservant's. Kadeem pulled back the covers, steadying him, as he swung his legs round and sat up, rubbing his eyes with his good hand.

"What happened?"

"I don't *know*, sir. I surmise that you gripped the glass too hard, and it shattered, embedding shards into your hand. You must have blacked out. All we heard was the crash as you fell. How's your hand?"

"Hurting. Why was Wynfeld here?"

"He wanted to see you but says it can wait, sir."

"What time is it?"

"About half past five, Your Highness."

Arkyn sighed, picking at the bandage. "You'd better let Wynfeld know I'm available if he still needs to see me."

A minute later, Kadeem re-entered to find Arkyn still picking at the bandage. "Is it too tight, sir?"

"It itches."

"It could be a sign that it's healing, sir. Would you like me to re-dress it to see if that helps? The commander was more concerned with stopping the bleeding. It might stand being loosened."

As Kadeem unwound the bandage, Arkyn bit his lip: flesh was parting in several places and the dried blood made it an even less appealing sight.

Kadeem said, "I'm going to get the doctor to check this." Seeing Arkyn wanted to object, the manservant continued, "No, sir. I *am* going to get a doctor. It needs tending. I wouldn't want to face His Majesty if it became infected."

"At least let me wash the blood off."

Whilst they waited for the doctor, Arkyn carefully dabbed at his hand. Warm water first stung, then relieved the pain. Gradually the bowl of water turned red, whilst the slashes on his hand lost colour. There was no way any doctor would leave it unbandaged. The heat of stupidity reached his face. His father, his tutors, had always been clear, appear healthy, appear well, don't show weakness. Bandages on a day where he'd almost been poisoned weren't going to help his authority. Even apart from that, he didn't want the pain, the inconvenience. He wouldn't be able to ride for a while, do everyday things for himself, even eating might be difficult. How had the day turned into such disaster?

He watched Doctor Artzman enter with familiar nerves. Obviously, their earlier meeting with Lady Portur hadn't put this man at his ease. He motioned for Kadeem to explain, looking morosely at his hand as he did so, trying not to pick at the peeling skin.

A few moments later, Artzman gently took his hand, turning it this way and that in the light, before pressing gently around the cuts. "Who tended this?"

Kadeem replied, "Commander Wynfeld. Might I enquire why you wish to know?"

"I was going to congratulate him. There isn't a fragment of glass left. That is impressive. No normal officer I've ever met would make such a clean job of it."

"Commander Wynfeld isn't a normal officer," said Arkyn. "He is an exceptional one; he rose through the ranks."

"That makes sense. I'd like to bathe, then salve and re-bandage this, Your Highness." Artzman got to his feet to cross to the table where he'd placed his bag.

"What are you planning on using, Doctor?" enquired Kadeem. On hearing the reply, he turned to Arkyn, "To my certain knowledge, we don't carry that salve. I'd prefer it to be freshly prepared and by someone who doesn't know for whom it's intended – likewise the painkiller Your Highness is in obvious need of." Seeing the Prince's objection forming, he added, "Sir, you were nearly poisoned earlier, I must take these measures. Your Highness, let me do what His Majesty would expect—"

"Paranoia—"

"Sir, if what your manservant says is true, I think, for all our sakes and peace of mind, his advice is sensible," interjected Artzman. "I will not take offence, nor will my countrymen."

Arkyn sighed. "Thank you. Kadeem, do what you must, though contact the fort first. They might have what you need – that is, if you trust Wynfeld's management."

"I think I do," observed Kadeem wryly. "Doctor, would you mind stepping outside with me for a moment?"

When they re-entered the sitting room two minutes later, the doctor said, "I apologise for interrupting you earlier, Your Highness."

Arkyn glanced at Kadeem's blank face. "Thank you. I will allow it was in a good cause. Kadeem?"

"Wynfeld is having a sergeant deal with the request, sir. He suggested until then that you try some Terasian whiskey."

Arkyn grinned. "He's a dreadful influence."

When Kadeem passed him the whiskey in a tulip beaker, he almost asked why, but the warmth of the ceramic was comforting and felt more secure than cold glass. He took a sip from the overlarge measure and smiled. Wynfeld had been right. The whiskey was worth savouring. He watched Kadeem usher the doctor out and tried to relax. He had a banquet to get through yet. After two shocks, he needed this time to himself.

Chapter 7
RUMOUR

Evening

Entrance Hall

THREE-QUARTERS OF AN HOUR LATER, his left hand bandaged, Arkyn reassured Kadeem he was feeling perfectly well before leaving for his office to see what Wynfeld had wanted.

Edward was waiting for him in the small antechamber to his rooms. As they strolled to the main staircase, the administrator informed him that his office was being relocated and apologised that it wasn't quite ready.

"Should I ask why it's being moved?"

"Fitz's recommendation, sir. It'll now be at the rear of the Residence, further from prying eyes. Lord Wealsman agreed it was sensible. The commander is also waiting for Your Highness and, if I may say so, fretting."

As they reached the entrance hall, Wynfeld saluted, but none of the anxiety left his face. Arkyn motioned for him to lead the way and once in an empty office, asked for an explanation whilst ignoring the solicitous enquiries as to how he was.

Wynfeld said, "It's the information regarding the Justiciar, sir. I don't quite know what to do about it."

"What did the condemned say?"

"I'm not sure I should—"

"Wynfeld, I would remind you I am the King's Representative here, as well as being his son. What did the condemned say about the Justiciar?"

Wynfeld clasped his hands behind his back; there was no way his Prince was going to take it calmly. He decided to let the lesser be the first piece of information he gave. "He advised that the tax records are inspected closely and to avoid talking to anyone higher than the chief scriveners about them."

"Interesting, but that has nothing to do with my uncle. What else?"

Wynfeld swallowed; there was no way around it. "The Deputy Governor mentioned that Lord Scanlon had told him your father wasn't the son of your grandfather. Rather as the condemned wasn't the son of his father. He said Lord Scanlon had shown him proof."

Arkyn stared; half inclined to laugh before reality struck. "Of *which* did he show him proof?" he demanded.

"The condemned *said* the latter, sir."

Arkyn's features darkened as his muscles tightened. "Do you give any credence to the former, Commander?"

"On my oath, no, Your Highness." The more Wynfeld saw of Arkyn, the more intrigued he was. The person who had taught his Prince self-control needed congratulating. After the day's events, Wynfeld thought he'd see more evidence of stress, rather than questions asked with simple, assured authority.

"Did Roth say anything about how far the rumours about my father had gone?"

"He said he never mentioned them to anyone, sir. That he wasn't that foolish because anyone who knew King Altarius and His Majesty must realise they were father and son and, whatever else he thought, he didn't think our King was a bastard in the literal sense of the word."

Arkyn gave a curt nod. "Who was with you in the cell when he made the statement?"

"No-one, sir. He had the sense to request to speak to me alone."

Arkyn cursed to himself, understanding Wynfeld's anxiety. If Scanlon had been spreading that kind of rumour, then it was a dire situation. The more Arkyn considered the consequences, the more worried and preoccupied he became. He called Fafnir and obtained a link with his father.

Adeone was smiling as the link formed. "Causing more trouble?"

"No, sir," replied Arkyn gravely, outlining everything Wynfeld had explained. His angst was clear, but, to his astonishment, his father laughed.

"Not that old chestnut. If as many kings were illegitimate as has been claimed, there would be no bloodline at all. My son, listen to me… I know he's been saying that, but anyone who compares portraits of your grandfather, or knew him, and looks at me has to agree we are related – just as anyone who sees us together says we must be father and son. If Roth didn't spread the rumours, then don't fret. If he did, people may believe what they will. We can't stop them. Do a good job and even if it were true, no-one with any sense will care. Is there anything else bothering you?"

"Erm, I let Roth's family keep half their lands. Was that right?"

"Can you explain your reasons?" asked Adeone.

Arkyn did so succinctly, watching his father's face go from thoughtful to understanding.

"I think that was well reasoned and acceptable given the situation. Erlan Roth will be indebted to you for life, but I can see you didn't do it for that. You've your mother's heart. I'm pleased."

Arkyn blinked hard. "Thank you. I'm sorry to have bothered you."

"Don't be daft. It's better I know. Now, stop worrying about it. What's with the bandages?"

Arkyn told him what had happened, reassuring him that he was perfectly fine.

"I'm glad to hear it," responded his father wryly. "I thought it was only Tain who had inherited my destructive nature."

Arkyn chuckled. "We're both your sons, sir."

"Yes, I know," grumbled Adeone. "Making your beleaguered father worry…" He saw Arkyn's strained face. "Sorry, not the moment to tease you. Don't worry about any of this mess."

"I'll try not to, sir." He composed his features and closed the link. "His Majesty has said to ignore the allegation, Commander, as he knows Lord Scanlon has been trying to spread it for years; however, if I ever find you've mentioned it to anyone else—"

"I'll not be seen for dust, sir?" Wynfeld had to force himself not to smile. It wasn't that he took the threat lightly, he didn't; it was how Arkyn had spoken it, as though he'd been giving such orders for years.

"Something like that, Commander. I do, however, want you to go through Roth's papers with your normal meticulous attention to detail and a scrivener. Check and double-check everything. Speak to his staff. Make it known that if they try to hide anything out of loyalty to his memory, there will be consequences. I might have been compassionate with his estranged family's state, but that does not extend to *his* affairs. Each of the minor lords within his lands must be questioned. Have another discreet go at his son as well. They were on speaking terms before my uncle's visit. If my calculations are right, Erlan Roth's marriage was six years ago, and Lord Scanlon visited this province the year before that. A year is time enough for strains to appear. I don't believe you had the whole of it from the condemned. If Erlan Roth won't talk discreetly, charge him on his fealty but only use that as a last resort. His Majesty does not need lords becoming embittered and I want to leave this province peaceful. Now, I know you've been in this province for some weeks and I can't believe you haven't had your ear to the ground. Anything to report?"

"No, sir. It's very quiet in comparison to Oedran."

"Good. If you haven't already, please change the guard on Lady Portur's rooms. Dring was tired, and that was a few hours ago. Also, thank you for your attentions earlier. The doctor said you did a remarkably good job on cleaning my hand."

"I simply did my best, sir. How long would you like a guard on Her Ladyship's door?"

"At least for the rest of today. I think she needs time undisturbed."

As Arkyn left, Wynfeld saluted, pleased he was posted in Tera. It would be amusing to watch the officials' response to their young Prince, who knew what he wanted doing and whatever he felt about giving the orders would nonetheless give them in such a manner as to make sure no-one would gainsay them.

Chapter 8
PREPARATIONS
Evening
Margrave's Residence

ARKYN FOUND EDWARD waiting patiently outside the room. The Residence seemed to be calming down from a busy day, but there were signs of a hectic evening to come. Those who were milling around were obviously not clerks and officers; they were carrying platters and goblets, or candles and flowers. The steward stood on the doors to the Margrave's Hall, checking everything as it passed him. There were smells of roasting meats wafting through the entrance hall and stealing up the stairs. Arkyn's stomach rumbled, reminding him he needed to eat, but he was more than willing to wait to savour the tastes as well as the aromas.

Arkyn glanced at Edward. "What's next?"

"Kadeem's realised Your Highness should be getting ready for the banquet."

"Then let's put his mind at rest."

* * *

After showing Arkyn to his bathroom and dressing room, Kadeem returned to the sitting room where Edward was waiting. Not to check what the administrator was doing, but for a chat with his counterpart on the Prince's staff. They both had challenging jobs; he in overseeing Arkyn's personal health and wellbeing and Edward in overseeing the Prince's professional reputation and life, and they both held positions that traitors tried to suborn; watching each other, even as friends, was mutual protection.

Grinning at Edward, Kadeem said, "Do you want a drink whilst we've got chance?"

"I wouldn't mind. Who's overseeing this lot this evening?"

"Thomas; he should be more than capable. I wouldn't want him to feel I didn't trust him. Are you organising His Highness' papers, or is Stuart?"

"I am, but as always, it's not that straightforward," said Edward. "It's going to be a long evening."

Kadeem raised an eyebrow. "Don't work all night. He might appreciate it, but he won't condone it. Do you know where you're sleeping?"

"Yes. Thank you for seeing everything unpacked—"

There was a discreet knock and Thomas entered. He looked at Kadeem. "You wished to see me, sir?"

"Whilst His Highness is at the banquet, finish overseeing the unpacking, please. Everything is in the corridor. I have to be with the Prince and I'll want Alan with me – he should be in hall already."

"I'll check. Administrator, what time would you like waking tomorrow?"

"If I've had chance to sleep, seven would be fine, thank you, Thomas. Someone should also be coming to sort out His Highness' private desk."

When Thomas had left, Kadeem said, "Someone?"

"Stuart or one of the clerks. I've got other things to do than supply the impedimenta for this desk." He noticed Kadeem's slightly crooked eyebrow. "Secretary Jacobs recommended Stuart. He should manage arranging ink, parchment, pen nibs and the like. There's no private correspondence yet. Don't you trust Thomas?"

Kadeem chuckled. "More than I admit. The Steward seems to have picked well."

"Let's hope so. Though, as we've said before, we've no chance of replacements this far from Oedran."

"Stop fretting, Edward. What can go wrong? We're only here for a few weeks."

"After earlier, you had to ask that!"

Kadeem chuckled. "I was meaning in the household and staff. The politics of the empire aren't our concern."

Twelve minutes after Thomas left, Arkyn entered the room. "Is there *any* chance they could design some formal tunics with less ostentation, Kadeem? I thought the whole idea of simple tunics was the fact they were *simple.* I understand the merchants wanting to show off their wealth in their clothing, but I thought tradition dictated we were meant to be more restrained."

"I think it's called irony, Your Highness."

"Sure it's not satire? You'd better come and give me a hand with my mantle; it's trickier one handed. Oh, Edward, I've spotted a timepiece. How far back did you get them to set the start of the banquet?"

"An hour, sir."

"No apology for putting everyone out?" asked Arkyn, amused. It was clear Edward was just as determined as Kadeem when necessary.

"No, sir. For that would make me a hypocrite. Lord Wealsman accepted the reasons happily enough and there was no other way to make sure you entered the event refreshed."

"Thank you. Come on, Kadeem. I better finish getting ready."

Kadeem took the simple split rectangle of white silk damask shot with gold thread. He draped it over the Prince's shoulders before arranging the right-hand tail of fabric to drape over Arkyn's left shoulder. He pinned it in place with a jewelled badge of office denoting a King's Representative.

Arkyn raised a sardonic eyebrow at his manservant. "Less is more?"

"More or less, Your Highness," quipped Kadeem, trying to keep a straight face. "This isn't the full scarlet that His Majesty wears."

"No," sighed Arkyn, knowing it would come to him in time. Instead, this mantle was mostly white but had bandings of scarlet and emerald with a gold piping running around the edge. It did match his tunic, he supposed wryly. "I must thank whichever ancestor thought these were a good idea."

"Probably someone who wanted to be warm, sir," remarked Kadeem.

"Or roast. All right, I'll behave. It's just been one of those days."

"It has, sir. I hope this evening is pleasanter than the day has been."

Arkyn swallowed. "Let's hope nothing else happens. The inn last night seems a lifetime away." He re-entered the sitting room, where his administrator was still waiting. "I get the feeling you need to tell me something, Edward, but don't know how to begin. Would I be right?"

"Nearly, sir. I'm unsure if I should tell Your Highness now or tomorrow."

"As we're skirting the issue, now seems best."

"Roth was so certain that he'd succeed in killing Your Highness, that scant work towards the review has been done. We may be in Tera longer than planned."

"I thought we might after the events today. Don't worry about it too much, we'll take things as they come. What has been done?"

"I'm not sure, sir. Thomkins and I have pulled in some City Assembly officials to attempt to work it out this evening. We believe the exchequer has been doing some work and Thomkins assures me the Aedile, who's in charge of public works, should be fine."

Arkyn wasn't certain what he was meant to do in these circumstances, but Edward obviously expected an answer or comment.

"Well, don't work too late. After information received, I'm going to have to examine taxation closely. If the exchequer has begun their summaries, then I will attend to that first. If needs be, I'll work from the ledgers and not worry about seeing a report, though they will need to write one for the records in Oedran. Do we know if any petitions have been filed?"

"I've not yet spoken to Thomkins about that, sir. I'm sorry."

"No need to be. You can't do everything at once. If you're going to be busy this evening, I mustn't keep you. Though, Edward… Get some sleep. In fact, don't work past midnight."

"Thank you, Your Highness."

Once Edward had left, Arkyn caught Kadeem's eye. "When I've returned from the banquet, send Thomas to check that Edward has gone to bed. I don't need my administrator exhausted. Just like you and he don't wish me to become exhausted. Is it tradition, by the way, for you both to conspire in such a way?"

"Yes, sir; although we aren't meant to get caught, I believe."

Arkyn laughed. "It would be the first time you've not got something right. I suppose I ought to face the throng. How long do you think it will go on for tonight?"

"As long as Your Highness wishes."

Chapter 9
BANQUET

Late Evening
Margrave's Hall

ARKYN WALKED into the Margrave's Hall for the second time. Dozens of candles spread their flickering light amongst the guests. Some candles had mirrored wall sconces, reflecting and magnifying the glow they naturally gave. Their light danced off the metallic threads woven into tapestries and wall hangings, hung since he'd left the hall earlier. Table candelabra held sculptured candles which lit gold and silver plate, all engraved with a bear's paw print – the emblem of Terasia – on the symbol of the empire: two moons in eclipse – Cisluna, the smaller, leaving a crescent of Aluna, the greater. Terasia's crescent was black, taken from the legendary star stone gifted to the first Beran by the Majistar Ull. Terasians said that the threads used to outline their flag stood out to better advantage and so they were content with a colour others disparaged.

Overall, the atmosphere the hall exuded was an embrace. After the day's disasters, it went beyond welcoming to comforting. Arkyn felt secure for the first time since he'd arrived at the Residence. He saw Wealsman excusing himself to his companions and crossing to greet him.

"Evening, Lord Wealsman." Arkyn smiled, taking a drink from his server. "This is quite a display…" He indicated the hall with his other hand.

"We do our best. Most of this has been in storage since the coronation, sir… If I might ask, Your Highness, what has happened to your hand?"

"A minor accident, my lord. Nothing serious. My manservant is merely overly cautious; the bandages are for show. If all of this has been in storage for years, it's a shame; it's beautiful."

Recognising a polite warning, Wealsman answered the comment. "It is, sir, but would we notice the beauty if we saw these trappings daily?"

"Maybe not, my lord, but it should be more often than every twelve years. Now, is there anyone seated at the dais whom I wasn't introduced to earlier?"

Wealsman made a round of introductions with such ease that Arkyn relaxed. The demise of both Portur and Roth had meant that the dais seating had been rewritten at short notice. Wealsman had put the Terazi on the Prince's left and himself on Arkyn's right. Tradition dictated that it should have been two overlords instead of the Terazi and Acting Governor; however, Arkyn decided, in the privacy of his head, that the tradition could be dispensed with on such a day and most of the overlords were secretly relieved that he made no comments or tried to rearrange the seating.

Arkyn watched the dancers and tumblers with a smile. He listened to the musicians with a ready ear and was seen laughing at comments from Lord Wealsman. The food he found to his tastes: neither too spiced, nor too bland. The wine he drank watered, but nonetheless he appreciated its body and flavour. He soon appreciated the Terazi's summation of Wealsman; throughout the banquet, Arkyn found himself talking away as to a long-standing friend. He hardly noticed the time passing or the twinges from his hand.

Following the entertainments, he watched as everyone milled around. The musicians continued playing, and some attendees started dancing. Beside him, Wealsman chuckled.

"My lord?"

"It's nothing, Your Highness. Just watching the optimism of youth."

Arkyn gave him a sideways glance.

"Some of the overlords' heirs thinking they can strut and win any of the ladies." He pointed out a couple. "Lord Melek Silvano and Lord Joren Stator."

"I wouldn't have known they were heirs," observed Arkyn.

"There's no reason you should, sir. Lord Joren is Lord Stator's grandson."

"There is no reason I would need to know heirs? Are you sure?" mooted Arkyn wryly. "There is every reason, given our futures. I merely meant that, as they are not wearing formal tunics at a formal Court, it is rather difficult for me to gauge their standing. Their names and families are important, but not as vital as forewarning."

Wealsman glanced at the hall. "They are wearing badges of office, sir."

"Which I can't see as clearly as the stripes of a formal tunic at this distance," said Arkyn with a small smile. "I'll have more forewarning at the next Court, I hope."

"I'll attend to it directly, Your Highness," replied Wealsman carefully.

"Maybe tomorrow would be better. I don't think asking people to change in the middle of the Margrave's Hall is a good idea – however memorable it would make the evening." He dropped his voice. "The ladies they're courting might see more than the gentlemen intended."

A spontaneous burst of laughter escaped Wealsman. Arkyn winked, keeping a straight face.

Half an hour later, Arkyn found himself yawning uncontrollably. He said sheepishly, "I'm not used to this, I'm afraid, Wealsman."

"I don't think anyone – other than, perhaps, His Majesty – is used to the type of day Your Highness has experienced. I hope there are no more such days during your stay in Tera, sir."

"We can hope. Although, neither of us has an easy time coming up…" Arkyn explained what Edward had told him.

Wealsman faced the problem with directness. "I'll get on to the City Assembly tomorrow morning, sir. If he neglected that, there are probably other things that have also been neglected."

"Thank you, though I think at the moment Edward is in a meeting with Secretary Thomkins and several of your officials trying to pull everything together."

"Your Highness is certainly thorough."

"It wasn't my doing. I only found out about the discrepancies shortly before I entered this banquet. Edward is responsible for pulling everyone in."

"Then I must commend your administrator. At twenty-one I thought he was a bit young, but it seems he is, like yourself, easily underestimated."

Arkyn laughed. "I'm not sure if that is a compliment or not, Wealsman. If it is, I thank you for it. If it isn't, I don't think you'd tell me."

Wealsman didn't try to hide his amusement as he asked, "Whatever gave Your Highness that idea?"

"Experience," replied Arkyn dryly.

Chapter 10
MORNING

Tretaldai, Week 16 – 24th Macial, 3rd Easis 1211
Arkyn's Bedchamber

ARKYN AWOKE in the morning and stared at the ceiling, thinking over the disturbing events of the previous day. They had turned into dreams overnight and he needed six minutes to separate the dreams from reality. He decided the dancing bottles in different coloured dresses were a dream, disturbing though they were. He carried on examining the ceiling as Kadeem entered.

Seeing the Prince was already awake, if not sitting up, the manservant gave a short bow. "Good morning, Your Highness. I trust you slept well."

"Yes, so much so I wish I could lie here for another couple of hours."

"I can always inform Edward you're having a late start and leave you to rest. No-one would be surprised."

Arkyn considered the underlying proposition. He mentally shook himself; they might understand, but he still had a job to do, and it was already complicated enough. "Tempting though that is, Kadeem, I'm awake and there's more than enough for me to do. So, you'd better draw the curtains whilst I see if I can gather the momentum to get up."

Kadeem opening the curtains, heard Arkyn take a sharp breath and glanced round. In a couple of steps, he was beside the bed and helping Arkyn to disentangle himself from the bedclothes.

Smiling at his own stupidity, Arkyn said, "Thank you. Next time I get so emotional, remind me not to reach for a stiff drink."

"They say drink is the precursor to pain, sir," observed Kadeem.

"Just go and find me a suitable tunic and leave philosophy for another day – one where I can appreciate the full statement. No need for my sword today, but do attach my poniard. That should be statement enough."

Twenty-four minutes later, Arkyn entered his sitting room. He found Thomas there with a junior member of his household, laying out his breakfast. At a glance from Kadeem, Alan laid down the tray, inclined his head and left. Arkyn nodded at Thomas to continue and asked if Edward had still been working the night before.

"He was settling the last few things, sir."

Arkyn knew what that meant. "Thank you, Thomas, that's all for now."

After Thomas had gone, Kadeem said mildly, "Edward probably never noticed the time, Your Highness."

Arkyn smiled. "I know, Kadeem, I'm not annoyed. How can I be at such dedication? Just make sure that when he's not needed for official work Edward learns how to unwind – likewise yourself. Neither of you has an easy job looking after me; I don't want to make it any harder than necessity requires."

"We're content, sir, but thank you. I shall do my best."

Arkyn tucked into a hearty breakfast of bacon, eggs and Terasian sausages with toast and jam or honey and a variety of fruit should he wish for something sweet. As he was finishing, his administrator entered, looking tired.

"Morning, Edward. I won't be long. How did your meetings go last night?"

"Good morning, Your Highness. They were interesting, sir. Seems our fears were right. Not much has been done; however, I'm reliably informed that everything is in motion for reports to be in by next Alunadai."

"Is this where you tell me I'm not needed yet?"

"I could arrange that, sir, but you did say you wished to start on the initial interviews today—"

"That was foolish of me."

"...And so I've got the Statisman all ready to be interviewed in three-quarters of an hour. This afternoon, Tera's Chief Merchant will be here. Not being part of the City Assembly, he hadn't waited for an official briefing."

"Very sensible of him. Tell me, did you get *any* sleep last night?"

Involuntarily Edward glanced at Kadeem before saying, "Yes, Your Highness. I thought Thomas was reporting that I had retired."

Arkyn raised an amused eyebrow. "Did I tell him to? I must have forgotten to wait for his report. Edward, listen to me carefully: *never*, unless it is a matter of the utmost urgency, work past midnight again – I suppose I should add unless I am also doing so. I am not rebuking your efforts, merely your common sense. I'll admit yesterday was, erm, unique and so that is all I shall say on the matter."

"I shall try to remember, sir," replied Edward with plausible sincerity.

"Good. Kadeem, make sure his timepiece shows the correct time. I'm not going to fall for that trick; Prince Tain has tried it too many times on Maria." As Kadeem chuckled, Arkyn turned back to Edward. "I'll want to see Wealsman when I get to my office in twelve minutes?" He watched his administrator leave. "Before I begin my day officially, is there anything I should know about, Kadeem?"

His manservant replied gravely, "Only one thing, sir. I've taken the precaution of asking Commander Wynfeld to make sure there are always trusted men in the kitchens during the remainder of your stay. He had already placed one of his sergeants there—"

"You're both as bad as each other; however, thank you. Your care and paranoia have been noted, although I think with Roth having been executed, I'm safe enough. How many more discontented souls are likely to try to poison me here?"

"I'd rather not take the chance, Your Highness."

Arkyn sighed. "Probably wise. Could you check these bandages, please? They've loosened overnight."

Arkyn walked through the Residence, again aware of a slight tension and the feeling there was much work being done behind closed doors. Edward met him at the bottom of the stairs and showed him the way to his new office. Overlooking the gardens, with a door to the terrace, it had two levels. The lower half, furthest from the door, appeared warm and welcoming. A roaring fire blazed in the grate, there were fleece rugs, a comfortable armchair and two couches, with a low table and a cupboard built into the alcove by the fireplace. A step up and the rest was clearly an office: his desk and chair, a clerk's desk arrangement, a sideboard with jugs and goblets and several other chairs that could be used as necessary. Arkyn's quick eyes assessed they weren't as comfortable as his. Behind his desk was the door onto the terrace, in front of it was an alert Lord Wealsman who managed a bow worthy of an Oedranian courtier.

"Morning, Wealsman," said Arkyn, hoping the Acting Governor wouldn't be stuffy and obsequious during an official day.

"Good morning, Your Highness. I hope you had an undisturbed night."

Intrigued by the unique way of asking if he had slept well, Arkyn replied in like manner. "I certainly had a comfortable night, my lord. Might I ask why you weren't outside?"

"I was shown in here, sir. I shall wait elsewhere next time."

"Please do. It stops an awful lot of possibly disastrous situations. I don't need you under arrest." Arkyn waved Wealsman and Edward to chairs before continuing, "Given the lack of preparation here, I'm going to be busy and – contrary to what I said yesterday – I am going to be unable to devote much time to the running of Terasia. I have all the initial interviews to conduct before my advisor and clerks arrive from Oedran. Do you think you can cope for a couple of weeks?"

"I'll do my best, Your Highness."

Arkyn nodded. "Thank you. If you need anything signing by a King's Representative, pass it *directly* to Edward. Next, what is happening regarding Lord Portur's funeral?"

"He had no children, sir. I'm going to talk with Lady Portur today; however, I thought Septadai. It's free of other official engagements."

"Do we know how Her Ladyship is this morning?"

"I'm sorry, sir, I don't," replied Wealsman honestly, adding, "I can find out for you, if you wish me to."

Arkyn studied Wealsman and once more liked what he saw. "Thank you, if you could it would be a help. Though, please, for her sake, be tactful. On to other matters, I'll postpone the original interview I was meant to be having with Lord Portur; however, if you've no objection, I have some initial queries I hope you can answer. The other questions, which are still relevant, I'll have sent to you and expect the answers later. Do you have any objection to that?"

"No, sir. I'll do my best to answer whatever I can."

By the time Wealsman left, Arkyn had received a fair summation of what the Acting Governor knew for certain. Unusually, Wealsman admitted if he didn't know something and Arkyn appreciated that far more than he let it show. Overall, it left him thinking the province was in a safe pair of hands for the next fortnight. Especially when Wealsman reported promptly that Lady Portur was feeling better but hadn't yet risen, along with answers to two of the simpler questions.

After Wealsman had left, Edward said, "Forgive me, sir, but something has just struck me as odd. This is the Margrave's *Residence*, and yet the Margrave is using it to help run the province, not just for his own office. The palaces of the empire are used in that way, but generally governors' residences aren't."

"Didn't His Majesty grant some taxes for the rebuilding of the City Assembly, which burnt down in 1198?"

Edward's eyes brightened. "Yes, sir, he *did*. That must be what set off my train of thought. I wonder if that's what the former Deputy Governor meant when he said to examine the province's finances."

Arkyn asked for a sight of the relevant portion of the briefing. His administrator laid his hand on it almost at once.

"How do you manage to keep so organised, Edward? It can be very tiring to watch!"

"If you can't sleep one night, sir, I'll come and show you."

Arkyn shook his head, amused. "That is one soporific I'll happily leave to you. Can you see if the Statisman is here yet, please?"

Whilst Edward was checking, Arkyn saw a note on his desk. He opened it, expecting handwriting he'd recognise. He was disappointed in that and the note wasn't typical for his eyes:

Poison of the mind is like a dagger in the hand of another

Arkyn didn't miss the underlying tones of warning and threat. He screwed it up, and threw it in the fire, wondering how it had come to be on his desk: so few people had access to his office. Although, if finding Wealsman in there had been anything to go by, his junior clerks needed reminding that no-one other than Edward, Stuart, Kadeem and Thomas should enter the office unaccompanied if he wasn't there. Even allowing Thomas unsupervised access was questionable; that morning, however, Arkyn suspected, quite a few people had been in and out of the office. He'd have to remember to ask Edward to have a word with his staff – his office had to be sacrosanct.

Chapter 11
EXCHEQUER AND ENDURANCE

Morning
Arkyn's Office

THE STATISMAN, in a well-tailored linen tunic, bowed clumsily as soon as he was over the threshold. The unpolished gesture, as well as the material, hinted at origins outside the lordships and little preparation.

As he straightened up, Arkyn met his uncertain eyes, then noticed a readjustment, a confidence returning. Was that because of his own youth?

He waved the Statisman to a seat and held the man's gaze as he minced his way over and took it. The confidence began to falter.

Arkyn read the note Edward passed him and handed it back. "Thank you for coming, Rahat. Though the five others you brought with you can return to their normal duties. I'm sure you'll be able to answer my questions.

"As you wish, sir," replied the Statisman airily.

Relaxing back in his chair, Arkyn gave Edward a nod and, ostensibly to pass the time before his administrator's return, asked, "In a province with so many, are you a lord, Statisman?"

"No, Your Highness."

Arkyn waited for Edward to re-enter and take his place before saying, "So, Rahat, tell me about yourself. How did you obtain your position?"

The fussy little man never hesitated. "I worked my way up. Started as an audit runner in the City Assembly when I was seven and then trained as a scrivener or audit clerk. I took the opportunities as they arose and reached Statisman by the time I was thirty-four, six years ago. Someone must have noticed I had a good head for figures."

"Who noticed that aptitude?"

"I don't know, Your Highness."

Smiling, Arkyn said, "Thank you. In summary, you've been doing the job you're in for six years and, having worked your way up, should be cognisant with most procedures used within your oversight. Is that correct?"

Trying to keep the rising panic at bay, Rahat managed to say, "Yes, sir; however. I might not be so knowledgeable about any new practices from the last few years."

Arkyn glanced at Edward. He pointedly waited for his administrator to finish writing before he said, "There should have been no *new* practices introduced without your oversight in the last six years. I know you spoke with Edward last night and I know your department has done some work towards the review. You have my thanks for that. How long have you had?"

Rahat waved dismissively. "About a week to collate everything. I'm sure it'll be satisfactory. My deputies assure me all is well. They have it under control."

"A week to collate statistics and reports for a review is remarkably quick," observed Arkyn.

"You could say we've had twelve years to prepare, sir. Though, when I spoke to the Deputy Governor, he was most aggrieved that the briefing had only arrived a couple of days previously."

Arkyn's brows knitted slightly. "Edward, do you have the records of when the despatches arrived?"

Edward consulted a list. “An aluna-month ago, Your Highness. The former Deputy Governor confirmed with Administrator Richardson they had arrived and been distributed—”

“We got them a week ago,” interjected Rahat.

“I have not said you did not,” rejoined Arkyn. “Edward, continue.”

“Thomkins and I distributed them yesterday evening, sir. Most were still in the despatches box. The Statisman’s briefing wasn’t and a quick look at the former Deputy Governor’s diary does confirm Master Rahat had a meeting with Roth last week.”

Arkyn decided to ignore the bluster that was building behind Rahat’s blush. “Thank you. Statisman, your confidence reassures me that you will have the required reports ready in a week for myself and my advisor to look over. By then, the review clerks will have arrived and can look over your offices to see if improvements are possible.”

“The largest improvement would be to have proper offices for them to look at, sir. Instead of two houses the city apart.”

“Hmm. I take it the City Assembly *hasn’t* been rebuilt then?”

“No, Your Highness, it hasn’t. We never have the money to do it.”

“The King set aside money for the rebuild at the last review. It is your responsibility, as Statisman, to see that the taxes collected are spent as allocated. I hope there are good reasons for the delay.”

The Statisman’s nervous fingers balled into fists. “Sir, I am assured that all is perfectly well. That everything can be explained, that there is no anomaly to worry Oedran. We have dedicated staff—”

“I do not doubt the dedication of your staff, Statisman, but I will need to see where the money has been spent. If that is on areas that require it, then we shall have to rethink the situation. What has happened to the last City Assembly building?”

“It was gutted and is now a shell open to the elements. Unfortunately, the fire which razed it was so fearsome that some of the stone became vitrified.”

“If it was so fierce, why wasn’t half the city burnt with it?”

“Luckily, there are gardens around it that acted as a firebreak. Some buildings were damaged but Lord Portur insisted efforts went to prevent the spread of the fire rather than save the building. It being so close to the river also helped as water was plentiful. That and the storm, of course. It was lightning that started the fire”

Arkyn said, “Right. Returning to more apposite matters, do you feel that you have sufficient staff for your remit?”

“It’s not that I can’t make do, but more staff are always welcome, sir. Running the exchequer would always be easier with more minds.”

"Then I'd like to see a sensible report on your staffing requirements written by someone at chief scrivener level."

"Is there any reason for that specific requirement, Your Highness?"

"Yes, they tend to have more of an idea of what's needed. The further up the management hierarchy one goes the less they know about the work done. Maybe a good example is that you brought others with you this morning. It suggests you may not know all you should."

The Statisman's fists balled again. Had he fallen headlong into a neatly prepared trap? How many more did the Prince have ready?

Arkyn saw the jolt of emotion. Had he been too harsh? Need he have highlighted the double standard? Rahat might be mincing, might be fidgety but he must have worked hard to overcome prejudice to rise to Statisman.

The sun was shining, and it called Arkyn to its embrace after so much rain. He pushed himself to his feet. "Let's take a break. Edward, can you ask them to send in some refreshments please? Rahat, do you fancy a breath of air to clear your head? I'm afraid I've not given you a simple time so far."

Surprised, the Statisman said, "Thank you, sir, it would be appreciated."

Arkyn nodded and together they made their way onto the terrace. They ambled around the lawns talking of nothing apparently substantial, but Arkyn learnt enough to suspect that Rahat's rapid rise to Statisman had made him enemies.

Edward interrupted them, informing Arkyn that Wynfeld wished for a private word.

* * *

When Wynfeld approached, Arkyn acknowledged his salute before motioning that they'd walk and talk. Once assured they couldn't be overheard, Arkyn smiled in invitation.

"When I arrived in Tera, sir, I inherited a scrivener who was, politely, a dimwit. I've a new one going over his records. There's been a consistent shortfall in the taxation funds received by the fort. I assumed you'd wish to know immediately."

"Thank you. Would you like a word with the Statisman after I've finished with him, or would you like to be in the interview and intimidate him that way?"

Wynfeld grinned. "Tempting, but, if Your Highness doesn't wish to raise it straightaway, I'll talk to him later."

"I'll send him along. What did you do with the dimwit?"

"I sent him and a couple more to Oedran and warned the Major why. He'll find them new postings."

Turning back into a carefree youth, Arkyn teased, "Nothing like passing the problem on, is there?"

"Finest military tradition, sir."

"I thought that was drinking too much."

"Second finest military tradition, sir," came Wynfeld's riposte.

Arkyn chuckled. "Ah, but which way do they come round? Is drinking more traditional than passing on problems?"

"I think that depends on which officer you're talking to and how much he's drunk."

They exchanged an amused glance. Suddenly, Arkyn sighed.

"How are things going, sir?" asked Wynfeld, concerned.

Arkyn's eyes traversed the gardens: the mature trees with leaves turning from greens to golds, the pond with its breeze borne ripples, the paths meandering through shrubbery. It dwarfed him, made him feel the impermanence of youth, of his endeavours. Some trees looked old enough to have been mature when Tera fell to Oedran. His inexperience washed over him as though he'd fallen headlong into the pond.

"My age, my lack of knowledge, is showing. I shouldn't be admitting it, should I? I just feel my questions are impertinent, useless, and I can't get at what he's hiding. I'm *sure* there's something."

"Could he be nervous, sir? You have a lot of control over how easy his life will be. I took the liberty of asking Edward how you are coping. He mentioned you'd already made the Statisman reveal more than he wanted to. Maybe your age is your greatest weapon."

"No, my age is— My questions sound daft. They sound like Tain's asking them. Not inconsequential, but just unpolished."

Wynfeld watched the garden. "I doubt Rahat is even considering what they sound like, sir. Speaking from experience, when facing your family, the last thing anyone worries about is whether the questions sound *daft*. You just worry about answering them, about the repercussions if you don't. I've faced His Majesty at difficult times and never once analysed whether questions made sense. I was more worried about how many times I'd broken the rules, how much trouble I was in, how much I'd failed. I never faced His Majesty considering his questions as daft."

"He isn't sixteen!"

"I know, sir, but I saw him when he was and I would have had the same emotions. No-one's criticised your actions yesterday. I expect the Statisman is merely impressed at how composed you are today."

Still uncertain, Arkyn said, "Thank you. I'd better continue with the interview. I wonder if Rahat is ready."

"Whether he is or not, you're in charge, sir. When you feel close to his secrets, don't have a break, no matter how much you want one. He'll crack eventually."

Watching Wynfeld leave, Arkyn stood looking at, but not seeing, the gardens. He heard laughter and two children came running round a bend in the path. They skidded to a halt uncertainly.

Arkyn smiled. "You two have as much energy as my brother. Where do you get it from?"

The girl replied, "I don't know, Your Highness."

"That makes two of us. What are your names?"

"I'm Elsa and this is my twin, Karl."

"I'm pleased to meet you. You were here yesterday, weren't you? Do you live here?"

Karl plucked up the courage to say, "No, sir. Our father is Secretary Thomkins. When he's at work, we're cared for here."

"What about your mother?"

Elsa replied, "She lives in Gerymor, working for Lady Escley. We spend time there and here."

That intrigued Arkyn. "Which province do you consider home?"

Elsa answered Gerymor as Karl said Terasia. All three laughed as Edward appeared.

Sobering up, Arkyn muttered, "I can't hide in the gardens then. It was nice to meet you, twins."

Walking to the house, Arkyn smiled, relaxed. Was it the twins or Wynfeld's doing? It didn't matter. He felt he could face the next interview.

* * *

Once everyone was back in their seats and refreshed, Arkyn said, "After we have finished here, Rahat, I'd like you to visit Commander Wynfeld at the fort. Or rather, I should say, the commander wants to see you. Where were we before the break?"

Too concerned by the fact that Wynfeld wanted to see him, Rahat failed to hear the question.

Realising Rahat wasn't going to answer, Edward said, "You were talking over the reports on staffing, Your Highness."

Arkyn said, "Ah, yes. Now, how are the taxes stored and transported?"

Rahat replied half dismissively, "It's stored in the Treasury House, sir; guarded by the militia and transported in chests – we store coins flat faces together packed in bamboo casings so they don't jingle to let anyone know it is money being transported – each casing burned with a mark."

Arkyn made sure Edward had noted the reply before saying, "My understanding is that bailiffs collect the taxes in rural areas, as they have for centuries, and, in towns, a chief official oversees tax collectors. They then send the tax here. Is any record sent with the carts as to their contents?"

"Sir?"

Arkyn considered the Statisman. "I was thinking that methods unchanged for centuries lay themselves open to abuse. Does a bailiff at one end sign off the carts as containing a certain amount of tax and do scriveners count it again at this end?"

"It isn't deemed necessary, sir. Soldiers accompany the bailiffs and guard the carts. There isn't *chance* for taxes to go missing."

Without looking at Edward's discreetly raised eyebrows, Arkyn said, "Thank you for the clarification, Rahat. Have you ever been directly involved with tax collection?"

"No, sir."

"How is the amount of tax expected deduced? Do you use last year's figures or do you try to predict it more accurately? Say matching up a census with the tax received, then considering factors such as the migration of workers or the economic climate of each lordship."

Rahat took a sip of his drink; the Prince shouldn't *suddenly* be asking that kind of question. "It depends on the year, sir."

Motioning for Edward to note the reply, Arkyn remarked, "You mean it depends on whether you are expecting anyone from Oedran to be examining your books." (Rahat visibly paled.) "Yes, I thought that might be it. Edward, please ask Lord Wealsman to arrange for tax collectors from Tera and an outlying town to be available and at least two bailiffs."

Rahat said, "I can *easily* arrange that, sir; Wealsman will have more than—"

"I am asking *Lord* Wealsman to do it. Have you, in the last twelve years, noticed any sort of decrease in the amount of tax collected?"

Rahat, momentarily unsettled by the Prince's change of direction, gathered his wits to reply. "No, sir."

"Good; however, your report is to include a yearly total for each year since the review before last, as far as possible, and *every* year since the last review. It should also show any increase. You mentioned working from two houses. How do you oversee both?"

"I don't, sir, my subordinates do: one for each house."

Arkyn asked mildly, "Presumably, you work from two different offices, one in each building."

"No, sir, there isn't room. I work from the Auldton House."

"How often do you visit the other?"

"Only as required, sir."

"Required how?"

Rahat realised Arkyn didn't have *any* documents to hand. If he'd been given a list of questions, he'd memorised them. What was more worrying to the Statisman was that he couldn't answer the last question.

Instead, he said, "I tend to wait until my visit would be unexpected."

"Then you don't oversee the other house. Do you trust the head of it?"
"Of course I do, sir."
"Which specific area does he oversee?"
"Tax collection, Your Highness."

An hour later, the Statisman finished answering Arkyn's final question. He couldn't gauge the meeting. Whatever he had expected, it wasn't what had happened. The Prince had stripped the secrets of his office bare without actually removing any of the outer layers.

Arkyn smiled grimly. "Thank you, Rahat. It's been an illuminating meeting. Hopefully, it hasn't been too arduous. Edward, do you have my instructions for the Statisman?"

Edward, making a last note, passed over a shorthand list.

"Thank you. Rahat, please go and see Commander Wynfeld immediately. My clerks will translate that list and have it delivered to your office."

* * *

After the Statisman left. Arkyn let out a deep breath before laughing. There was something infectious about the laugh and Edward joined in. A knock at the door heralded Kadeem, who entered warily, glancing between the Prince and Edward. Arkyn, who'd stopped laughing as the door opened, carried on chuckling as it closed.

Kadeem said, "Your Highness, I came to enquire whether you'd like lunch, but I think I'll just serve it. You seem to be suffering from lack of sustenance. Although it might be supposed that laughter is food enough, sometimes it helps to actually *eat*."

Arkyn chuckled again and then pulled himself together. "I'm not lightheaded in that sense, Kadeem. You should have seen the poor Statisman. He didn't know what to expect when he got here and, by the time he left, he was wondering if it were a dream or a nightmare."

"I wish I'd been here, sir. Would you like lunch?"

Arkyn sighed. "Ever the sensible one, aren't you? Lunch might be wise. I have no idea when I am seeing the next official. Edward?"

"He is due in a couple of hours, sir. Even if he were here, you'd still have time to eat."

Arkyn let Kadeem serve his lunch. Before he ate, he ordered Edward to make sure he had a meal as well. Edward merely bowed and left. Arkyn knew that avoidance.

When he'd finished lunch, he said, "Go and give Edward some food, then stand over him to make sure he eats it, Kadeem. I'm going to sit out in the gardens for a while. Could you ask Wealsman to join me, please?"

Twelve minutes later, on invitation from Arkyn, Wealsman sat down saying, "I hear you've had an interesting morning with the Statisman, Your Highness."

"Who told you that, my lord?"

"Oh, a little whisper is going round at the long sigh that Rahat let out as soon as he was clear of your office, sir," replied Wealsman appreciatively. "Then I received the request to arrange a meeting with certain officials."

"I suppose I did give him a hard time, one way or another."

"Was there any particular reason for it being so hard, sir?"

Arkyn studied Wealsman, liking what he saw. The lord's prompt action had saved his life and as Acting Governor, he had a right to know what was happening.

"Yes, my lord, there was. The former Deputy Governor advised me to examine taxation carefully."

Wealsman nodded. "I'll send for my bailiff, sir."

"It might be an idea to ask him here informally and two others formally. Can you talk to him about whether he sends any information with the tax?"

"I insist a docket recording the amount is included to help the scriveners."

"Good," said Arkyn. "I'm pleased I know at least one person does that. Could you discreetly trace what happens to that docket? Rahat declared they didn't bother with them, that there was no way that tax could go missing."

Wealsman let out a snort of derision. "I think Your Highness is astute enough to see the flaw in that."

"Yes. I nearly laughed. My problem is believing that Rahat is naïve enough to consider it true. Something is happening at the exchequer and I want to know what; moreover, I want to know where the tax is going. Not only has the City Assembly not been built, but there has been a deficit in funds reaching the militia. I now believe I will discover a shortfall in many departments."

Wealsman said, "If every department has had a loss, we're talking thousands of darl a year for *twelve* years. I cannot but hope it isn't as bad as it looks."

"I also, my lord, but, for now, I am assuming that amount."

"What would you like me to do, sir?" asked Wealsman.

"Surely you have enough on running the province, my lord."

"A little bit of work never hurt anyone. I could pull in a couple of people and give them a roasting for you? Tell them I want to see the books as well, that they've let the province down, maybe. I'll be really officious and you can watch the fun unfold."

"You know, Wealsman, I believe you're enjoying yourself," observed Arkyn wryly.

"We all get our entertainment somehow, sir. I could talk to a few of the lower echelons – the people they won't let you get anywhere near – and see if they've noticed anything."

"I've already asked to see a chief scrivener, but feel free. You are right; they will try to stop me talking to anyone who can help. I need another word with Wynfeld. I want to know *who* noticed Rahat had a head for figures and *when*. Then I want to know who recommended him for Statisman at such a young age."

Wealsman smiled. "*Such* a young age, sir?"

Arkyn grinned in appreciation. "I know he was more than double my age now when he became Statisman but, even so, for someone born outside of the lordships, working their way up, thirty-four does seem young…" a movement caught his eye and recognising the lady walking towards them, Arkyn rose. Wealsman followed suit.

On reaching Arkyn, the lady curtsied. "Your Highness, please forgive my lack of welcome yesterday."

"Lady Portur, it's of no concern. Please join us."

Serenely, she smiled her thanks and seated herself. "I hope Percival is behaving himself, sir."

Arkyn's glance was amused as Wealsman enquired,

"When do I ever misbehave, Kristina?"

"All the time from my memory. You took the post out of mischief."

"I can see you know His Lordship extremely well," said Arkyn. "I have already noticed that side of his position appearing. All sobriety at the situation has been lost, I think."

Embarrassed, Wealsman said, "I'm sorry, Your Highness. Lady Portur and I grew up on adjoining manors. We've been told we bickered in our cradles."

"I don't think I heard any bickering, only honesty. Lady Portur, I really do hope you are feeling better than yesterday."

"Thank you, sir. The sleep helped. I believe I have you to thank for that."

Arkyn shrugged. "It was nothing. I hope Your Ladyship will forgive the trickery."

"Certainly. I must admit, Artzman was reluctant to tell me what happened when he called on me this morning. I think you impressed him."

Arkyn ignored Wealsman's curiosity. "The simple addition of a sleeping draught to a goblet of wine seems to be the easiest thing I have done so far—" Arkyn broke off as a clerk appeared and stood patiently several paces away. "I think he's one of yours, Wealsman."

The Acting Governor turned. "My apologies, sir. It can wait."

Lady Portur said, “What?” then seeing Wealsman’s face continued, “Ah.” She turned to Arkyn. “Put him out of his misery, Your Highness. I believe Laus is bringing him news of the annual endurance ride.”

“The what?” asked Arkyn, intrigued.

Wealsman glared at an amused Kristina. “It’s a tradition of Terasia, sir.”

She smiled. “Yes, a lot of grown men, and a few determined women, see how far they can ride within a set time or how long it takes them to do a set distance. He missed this year’s event.”

Arkyn crooked an eyebrow. “Is he any good?”

She pretended to consider. “If winning it every year since 1205 counts as good, I suppose he is, yes. I just don’t say it too loudly.”

Chuckling, Arkyn noticed how Wealsman was trying hard to seem nonchalant. To put him out of his misery, he waved the clerk over.

Seconds later, Wealsman read the name on the note. “Thank you, Laus. Send my congratulations.” Once the clerk had gone, Wealsman added, “Kristina is too kind about my harebrained escapades, sir.”

“If you have won for six years, I rather think congratulations are in order. You’ll have to tell me the history of the sport when Edward isn’t hovering over my shoulder.”

Wealsman crooked an eyebrow. “Do you want to know why he’s waiting, sir?”

“I think I should find out. Yes, Edward?”

Edward crossed over to them and gave a slight bow. “The Chief Merchant is here, Your Highness.”

Arkyn nodded. “Then, my lady, Lord Wealsman, I can’t keep the gentleman waiting. If you’ll excuse me…?”

Wealsman smiled. “You *could*, sir. I think you’ll be amazed at how long people will wait.”

“How long would you wait for then?” quipped Arkyn.

“A minute longer than it takes Your Highness to send for me,” replied Wealsman slickly.

“I’ll test you one day. Maybe I should have said, ‘I *shouldn’t* keep the gentleman waiting’. My lady, I hope to see you later.”

As Arkyn left, he heard Wealsman say lightly, “So then, I always misbehave, do I, *my lady*?”

He heard her tinkly laugh. “If no-one else will tell you, Percival, I thought I should.”

“Maybe they don’t tell me because it isn’t true.”

“Maybe the sun shines at night…”

Their good-natured wrangling faded as the door closed behind Arkyn.

* * *

Chief Merchant Turgar's interview was thorough, direct and informative. He was greying gentleman, who knew his subject, understood opportunity and could speak his mind. By the end, Arkyn felt rather as he had at the inn. He had a wealth of information he never knew he needed and a lot of problems to ponder, not least of which was the fact the road repairs were lackadaisical, the bridge repairs were underwhelming and the Chief Merchant wasn't enamoured with the situation.

Unused to sitting all day, Arkyn got up and stretched when Merchant Turgar left. Edward, pulling his notes together, watched the Prince, half waiting for him to burst out laughing again.

Arkyn met his gaze. "There's more than a simple review to do in this province then. I'm glad Lord Iris will soon be here; his experience may be invaluable. In the meantime, I'm just going to go and see Wealsman."

When Arkyn reached Wealsman's office, he thanked the runner who had shown him the way and nodded to Thomkins to announce him. On entering, he found Wealsman saying rather tartly to a perturbed official,

"…That's your excuse and you're sticking to it! Is that it? Oh, forgive me, Your Highness—"

"Please continue, my lord."

So Wealsman did. "I don't care what your instructions were, Soren! You *do not* move taxes around the province without writing it down in one ledger or another. These ledgers are going to be examined by His Highness and Oedranian scriveners. How long do you think it will be before they notice something amiss?"

Arkyn murmured, "Especially as I'm here now."

Wealsman managed to hide his grin. "Especially as His Highness is here – not that His Highness didn't already suspect something. Great Aluna, I can't believe the whole of the exchequer is malfeasant, or under misfeasance or nonfeasance practice. How did you think you'd succeed?"

Soren opened and closed his mouth, uncertain whether to reply.

Arkyn snapped, "Answer His Lordship."

Half turning towards Arkyn, the official said, "Your Highness, I—"

"Address your answer to His Lordship."

Soren paled. "Lord Wealsman, I was told to refer queries to Rahat."

Catching Arkyn's eye, Wealsman asked Soren, "Did you *ever* question your orders?"

"No, my lord."

"Sicla's Cavern! Did you ever even *suspect* you should?"

"No. It isn't my place to."

Arkyn moved to face the official from behind the desk. Wealsman stepped adroitly aside. Had the Prince had devised the move so he ended up at his right hand?

"If it wasn't your place to question suspect orders, whose was it?" enquired the Prince.

Disconcerted by the change of interviewer, Soren said, "I, erm, I d-don't know, Your Highness."

"No – because it was your place. Answer me truthfully; did you ever privately question the order to move taxes without recording the movement?"

The man looked everywhere but at Arkyn and Wealsman. "No, Your Highness. Tax— It's been done like that since before my promotion six years ago. As it wasn't broken, I didn't try to fix it. Rahat had run a tight ship. It seemed wiser to continue with it than criticise given his post."

Before Arkyn could reply, a knock on the door heralded Wynfeld.

"Might I have a word, sir?"

Arkyn nodded. Two moments later, on his own with the Commander, he muttered, "Depress me further."

Wynfeld smiled. "Surely it's not that bad, sir?" Seeing Arkyn's mood didn't shift, he said, "I've arrested Rahat; I've detained him is slightly more accurate – whilst I find out what is happening."

"I take it he was evasive with you then. Commander, what happened here six years ago?"

"No idea, sir. His Majesty didn't visit. Nor did Lord Scanlon. He'd come the year before – for he had to leave when King Altarius died. He missed the funeral and coronation. I was stationed in Terasia at the time."

"Ah. A year after my uncle visits – and implements some hold over Roth – malpractice enters the exchequer. Does that not strike you as odd?"

"No, sir, simply too coincidental for words – because there *was* a year's wait, it will be difficult to prove anything."

"Especially since I've had Roth executed. Would you suggest I remove from their positions, albeit temporarily, Rahat's two deputies?"

"It might be an idea, sir. They can always join Rahat in a cell and I can put a man on guard outside to catch their conversation."

"So be it. Get Wealsman, please."

Wealsman re-entered the office, bowed with confident ease; he stood, looking efficient, seemingly incurious as to what had been discussed in his absence.

Once the door closed, Arkyn said, "Wynfeld has detained Rahat whilst we determine what has been happening. Do you have any objection to the detention of his deputies? I am guessing Soren is one of them."

"He is, sir, and it might be the wisest thing to do. I'll find someone sensible to head up the office in the meantime. Or no, I'll take over. That might be the safest option."

"Only if you can be on site so they don't destroy anything, Lord Wealsman," interjected Wynfeld.

"Good point," mused Wealsman. "Do you have any ideas?"

"Not really. I don't think it is appropriate to place military personnel in charge of governmental bodies – tends to give the wrong impression. Isn't there a lord who could take charge?"

Wealsman thought for a moment. "Of course there is. I'm a dimwit; Lord Simble should be more than capable."

Arkyn glanced between them. "Any particular reason for the grins, gentlemen?"

"I think the easiest way of describing Lord Simble, Your Highness, is as the male equivalent of Lady Amara," answered Wynfeld.

"So, what you mean is he's cynical, irascible and incorrigible, doesn't believe in tact and, above all, has a sense of humour not helped by being highly intelligent? I do like to be prepared," observed Arkyn.

Wealsman had never met Lady Amara and began to think that might be a good thing. If Simble and she were alike, then one was enough for anyone's acquaintance; however, Simble's very presence would make sure nothing was hidden or destroyed at the exchequer.

Arkyn continued, "My lord, if you would see to informing Lord Simble of his additional duties and Wynfeld will see to detaining the other men, then I have nothing else to add on the matter."

Wealsman and Wynfeld both agreed, and Arkyn left the office. The official inclined his head as Arkyn passed. That, the Prince reflected, was the worst part. To have to pass someone whose liberty you had just removed. He tried to console himself by considering the official's own actions were the cause. He made his way to his rooms and, entering the sitting room, sat staring numbly into the flames of a small fire.

Chapter 12

LADY DAIA

Evening

Arkyn's Sitting Room

TWELVE MINUTES LATER, Thomas entered, confused to find Arkyn there. He apologised nervously for disturbing the Prince.

Arkyn smiled. "Don't worry. I didn't let anyone know I was here; so, please, continue. I'm merely thinking."

After the footman left, Arkyn started counting in his head. He had barely reached eight before Kadeem entered after a knock.

"Can I get Your Highness anything?"

Arkyn laughed. "No, thank you, Kadeem. How long have I got until I must change for tonight's event?"

"An hour or so, sir. Would you like a bath?"

"No, but I might after the banquet if it wouldn't be too much trouble… I've just had to detain two men I've never really met."

"It's said life's challenges come in many forms, sir."

"They do. Well, if I've got an hour, I'll begin to write to Prince Tain."

Arkyn settled himself at the desk as Kadeem left. Tain disliked using messengers and had distrusted them ever since he found out the Herald of Oedran could watch them. The fear was ungrounded; only an order from the King – or Justiciar in some situations – could get them watched. As he wrote, Arkyn realised that was no guarantee they weren't. Maybe his brother wasn't such a fool; however, as others might read letters, Arkyn was careful what he wrote. He could resort to code but codes were breakable. Mostly, he wrote without naming people or places. When Kadeem entered an hour later, Arkyn finished his sentence, locked the desk and handed the key to his manservant to pass to Edward, saying,

"Better than me losing it. You know what I'm like."

Kadeem kept silent. If he agreed it would be a criticism, if he disagreed it would be hypocritical. Arkyn smiled; he liked giving his manservant dilemmas.

* * *

Bustling with people and bedecked with splendour, that evening the Margrave's Hall spoke of welcome and celebration. Minor lords rubbed shoulders with officials of Tera, or snobbishly avoided them, yet there was still a more relaxed atmosphere than the previous evening. Glancing over the gathering, Arkyn cursed. He hadn't had sight of the guest list, but there was more formal wear, which would help. He didn't need to cause unwitting offence.

That evening, storytellers told the myths and legends of Terasia, acted out by troupes of performers and musicians. Arkyn enjoyed the skill of the storytellers. Wealsman dropped in wry observations and quiet comments that made him chuckle. By the time the storytellers finished, Arkyn tried to blink away his tiredness.

Glancing at the Prince, Wealsman saw the slight strain on his face. He poured himself some water and motioned with the jug.

"Thank you, my lord. It might be better than wine," observed Arkyn.

"It is getting quite warm in here, sir. I almost fell asleep, but the musicians obviously noticed and thought we needed thunder."

Arkyn chuckled. "They were skilled. I wouldn't mind reading more about the legends of Terasia."

"I'll find you a text." He noticed Kadeem was standing by with a dish and waved him forward. "I think you might like these. They're a speciality of the area: nuts roasted in honey with sweet spices. We serve them at our banquets for the changing seasons."

Arkyn tried a couple of the sweet hazelnuts. "No-one else wants any of these then?"

"We could never deprive Your Highness," murmured Wealsman easily.

Arkyn snorted and held out the bowl. "Help yourself, my lord."

"Sir?" asked Wealsman, genuinely bemused.

"Well, it's as good a way as any of making sure they're not poisoned," quipped Arkyn.

"Then I am happy to reassure Your Highness," said Wealsman, helping himself, intrigued Arkyn would joke about it then wondering why it should be perplexing; everyone had different ways of coping.

Once the dancing had started, Arkyn asked Wealsman to do a round of introductions. Wealsman rose and, as Arkyn did likewise, pulled the Prince's chair out himself, waving Kadeem off. The manservant watched as Arkyn greeted guests and then noticed a young lady standing alone. The Prince made a comment to Lord Wealsman, who summoned the steward, who replied to a question from Arkyn. Then he watched as the steward took a step back. The FitzAlcis temper had briefly manifested itself. Prince Arkyn dismissed the steward and parted from Wealsman with barely another word.

Arkyn walked over to the lady and inclined his head slightly.

"Lady Daia Sansky, I believe."

"Y-yes, Your Highness," she faltered.

"Would you like a dance?"

If she hadn't been so nervous, Daia might have noticed the terseness of the question. "S-sir?"

Arkyn smiled and it calmed him. "Would you like a dance? After all, your eyes are alight with the music, but no-one seems to have noticed."

"It's b-because I'm a ward of your family, Your Highness."

"Yes, I'd made that connection." Wryly adding, "My nearfather says traditions can be changed, shall we start?"

She grinned but then lowered her gaze, as if remembering a lesson. "I'm not a good dancer, sir."

"Neither am I, but if we don't practice, we'll never improve. So come on, I'm bored of politics."

Wealsman watched as Arkyn and Daia danced. The Prince had told a white lie. He could dance well enough to pretend he couldn't without getting in anyone's way. When the dance ended, Arkyn guided Daia to where Wealsman was anticipating their presence. Arkyn introduced them to each other.

Wealsman said, "I'm pleased to see you again, my lady." He turned to Arkyn. "Are you all right, Your Highness?"

"I'm sure I will be, Wealsman," stated Arkyn. "Will you both excuse me? Thank you."

Once he'd moved off, Wealsman said, "His Highness was distressed, not to mention annoyed, when he realised the lack of proper deference shown to Your Ladyship, your omission from the introductions and your precedence at table being ignored—"

She interrupted softly, "I wouldn't be a bother…"

"You won't be, my lady. You've hardly been to Tera, have you?"

"No, my lord. My governess doesn't think it is appropriate. I am due to return to my lands in the morning. She says a lady shouldn't deal with business and my steward can undertake the interview with His Highness." A new spark lit her eyes.

"Didn't your father let see the workings of the lands? I thought he did. We talked of it on more than one occasion."

"Yes, my lord, but my life changed when he died. No man will wish to marry me if I can run my lands."

Wealsman snorted. "It's not always the case. I suggest that you request to speak to His Highness before you leave."

"I couldn't be an imposition on his more than valuable time."

"I'm sure you could. Everyone else is, after all; it's what makes his time valuable – the complete lack of having any to himself," joked Wealsman with a definite twinkle in his eye.

"Then I wouldn't intrude on those moments—"

They were dancing around each other and the issue. He guided her reluctant steps to where Arkyn was talking to two lords from the tribute lands, whose taxes went straight to Oedran and into the King's private coffers. The lords excused themselves adroitly with an inclination of their heads and smiles.

"Yes, my lord?" asked Arkyn hoarsely.

Wealsman motioned to a server. He passed both the Prince and Daia a drink before taking one himself and dismissing the server by name. Arkyn sipped at the drink then, realising how thirsty he was, he finished the beaker. Wealsman switched it for his own and watched as Arkyn took a further sip.

Sounding better, Arkyn said, "Thank you, Wealsman."

"It's what I'm here for. Might we have a word, sir?"

Arkyn sighed, recognising the tones of an official approach. "Of course, Lord Wealsman."

"I wouldn't be bothering you, sir, but Lady Daia's governess is insisting Her Ladyship returns to her lands tomorrow."

Arkyn caught Kadeem's eye. When his manservant reached them, he snapped, "Inform Lady Daia's household that Her Ladyship is staying in Tera for at least the duration of my stay and for as long as she wishes after that. She is under my family's protection and *no-one* will be forgetting that! Oh, and, Kadeem, she's to be seated at the dais at all functions. Near Lady Portur would be best. That way, when I and others end up talking business, as we certainly shall, they will have congenial company."

Kadeem left thinking the Prince was keeping his temper remarkably well for saying the strain of the last two days.

Seeing Daia's unease, Arkyn glanced in dismissal at Wealsman. The Acting Governor left with thoughts not dissimilar to Kadeem but also wondering if Arkyn ever lost his temper more disastrously. Overlooking a King's ward was not a career-enhancing move. He went to find the steward.

Meanwhile, Arkyn said, "Lady Daia, I'm sorry for that outburst. It was churlish of me. I hope the reason I forget myself is merely the length of the day."

"Your Highness, I can but thank you. I did not want to be either a fuss or a bother, but I did wish to stay in Tera for longer."

"Then you will and you're not a bother. As to the fuss, we'll let those who are paid to deal with such things deal with them – your governess, for a start. What does your steward think he's doing, letting her rule your actions?"

"His own wishes most likely," said Daia. "I'm sorry, sir, I think I must be affected by the length of the day also."

Arkyn chuckled. "Yes, it has been long enough. Shall we watch the melee for a time – instead of being a part of it?"

Daia nodded, and Arkyn guided her to the dais. She was seated with a disconcerting slickness. There'd be speculation on whether the Prince had taken a shine to her for months.

Twelve minutes later, Kadeem made his soft-footed way over to them and stood patiently within a few feet of Arkyn's chair until the Prince raised an eyebrow.

"I've informed Lady Daia's governess, sir. She wasn't happy."

"She has agreed?"

"I'd say rather that she has obeyed, sir. Your Highness…"

"Thank you, Kadeem. Please take your solicitous presence elsewhere."

A couple of hours later, exhausted, Arkyn finally retired from the banquet. He made his rooms before he deigned to show it. He sank onto his bed with a thumping headache to match the rest of his aching body.

Kadeem knelt to take off the Prince's shoes. Thomas had earlier laid out a night-tunic. Helping Arkyn change, Kadeem noticed the prince's under-tunic was soaked with sweat. Understandable after the heat of the hall but worrying if he had become dehydrated. Should he get a lighter weight mantle made or sent from Oedran? No, that was too much fuss. Doors could be opened and fires could burn lower.

"Would you like a bath, sir?"

"I've not got the energy to stay awake long enough. I'll h-have o-one in the m-morning."

Arkyn's eyes were closing on the yawn even as he spoke. Kadeem watched as he collapsed onto the pillows. He rang the bell and when Thomas entered, gently picked the Prince up. Arkyn stirred as Thomas pulled back the covers on the bed.

Kadeem whispered, "Nearly done, sir. Let your dreams take you."

Soothed, Arkyn stilled as Kadeem laid him between the covers. Yet, for all his fatigue, he had a restless night.

Chapter 13
ANOTHER DAY

Imperadai, Week 16 – 25th Macial, 4th Easis 1211

Arkyn's Bedchamber

THE FOLLOWING MORNING, Arkyn awoke and rolled over as Kadeem entered. He coughed to clear his throat and dry mouth.

"The water's fresh, Your Highness," stated Kadeem opening the curtains.

Arkyn pushed himself up with his good hand and reached for the glass. He took a drink before sinking back into his pillows.

"Thank you, Kadeem. What sort of day does it look to be?"

"If I might say so, sir, a typical Terasian one. Heavy drizzle misting the city. It probably covers up much which is better for it."

"Such pessimism is not your normal repartee, Kadeem."

"I'm sorry, sir, maybe I should have said that the mists are like a fog of the mind, revealing hidden beauties as much as they hide that which is disagreeable."

Arkyn laughed. "That's more like it, although flowery for such a dismal morning. I suppose I'd better get up. Is my bath prepared?"

Kadeem smiled. "Yes, sir. Which tunic would you like?"

"I'll let you choose. The same theory, though, as yesterday."

He cleared a tickle in his throat once again and took another drink before leaving for his bathroom. Even after the bath, he still felt stiff and sluggish from the night before. He had to shake himself out of that; there was another full day ahead of him. Once dry, he walked into his dressing room to find Kadeem attaching his poniard to his tooled leather belt. His manservant silently passed him his tunic before finishing attaching the weapon. Arkyn sat to put his shoes on.

Kadeem, noticing he was still favouring his left hand, knelt to help.

Arkyn sighed. "I'm sorry, my agitation the other day has had lasting effects…"

"If you'll forgive me, sir, it probably won't be the only time in your life."

"Hopefully not in such a personal way. Consequences due to official duties I can tolerate, consequences due to being a fool are harder to bear."

"Yet, sir, I feel here in Terasia you will *bear* them well."

"You learnt too much wry humour in Lord Landis' house. Though where you got your philosophy from remains a mystery."

Kadeem chuckled. "It is amazing, or so I have found, the effect His Lordship's manner has on different people, Your Highness."

Arkyn gave a true, whole-hearted laugh. "That is certainly one way of putting it. I have a very unconventional nearfather." After a moment, he sobered up. "I wonder what joys await me today. I'm sure Edward has a long list…"

"More than likely. Your belt, sir."

"Do you ever wonder about the burden you put on me by making me ready for my official duties?" asked Arkyn resignedly.

"All burdens must be borne by someone, Your Highness. The knowledge that I hand you to such duties is mine – your signet ring, sir – however—"

"Thank you. No 'however', I don't think I can stand that this morning. Anything else? Or am I enough of an impeccable Prince for the day?"

Kadeem looked at his master critically. "You are always impeccable, sir, but the bandages enhance the image."

Arkyn snorted. "Thank you. Maybe you could see to them before I breakfast?"

Kadeem did so. Arkyn's hand was healing well, but, for caution's sake, he re-bandaged it. Arkyn considered him wearily; such care could get tiresome.

Sensing the change in mood, Kadeem remained silent and lowered his gaze. He knew when to laugh and joke with the Prince and when to do his job.

Arkyn realised Kadeem was back to being the official servant. If he was to make a light-hearted comment about the bandages, his manservant would be polite but correct in his answer; a servant, nothing more – certainly not someone who would joke and be his confidant when needed.

As Arkyn was finishing breakfast, Edward appeared with a scroll in his hand and a wax tablet at his waist. Pushing himself to his feet, the Prince said,

"What's that scroll I'm trying hard to ignore, Edward?"

"It's Commander Wynfeld's morning report on the situation in Tera, Your Highness. His Majesty finds them useful in Oedran."

"The ever-efficient Wynfeld obviously needs me to find him some more work," grumbled Arkyn. "I'll read it in my office. Can you ask Lord Wealsman to be there?"

A knock at the door heralded Fitz.

Arkyn grinned. "Morning, Captain. All well?"

"Aye, sir. Any plans for today I should be aware of?"

Dryly, Arkyn said, "You'd have to ask Edward. I don't know myself yet. Other than that, carry on as always. I've no complaints."

Fitz winked. "That's good then, sir. Administrator?"

"Nothing that should take His Highness into the city, Captain."

As he left his sitting room, the Prince enquired, "What joys do you have planned for me then, Edward?"

"Two more interviews, sir. One is with the Aedile and one with Master Aldren, the Education Officer, who has oversight of all moral obligations within the city, as well as schooling."

"Sounds like an interesting job." Reaching his office a minute later, he found Wealsman there. He raised an eyebrow at his administrator.

"I anticipated Your Highness might wish to speak to His Lordship," replied Edward, keeping a straight face.

Chapter 14

ERNST

Morning

Arkyn's Office

AN HOUR AFTER Wealsman left, the Aedile entered Arkyn's office. He had been warned that the Prince wasn't quite as innocent as he appeared and had also heard that, after the meetings the previous day, the Prince had ordered three of his colleagues detained and an immediate investigation of their work. He hoped he wouldn't be found wanting in the same manner.

Pleasantries concluded, Arkyn said, "I am assuming, Ernst, that the public works office hasn't received the expected amount of funding for at least the last six years?"

"You're right, sir. We haven't. It's caused a lot o' trouble one way or the other," replied the Aedile with feeling.

Arkyn regarded him with intelligent eyes. "Did you, by any chance, raise it with Rahat?"

"Yes. Didn't make a jot of difference, Highness. He kept prevaricating. Saying they hadn't had the return of tax they expected. I just do the best with what I get."

"I'm sure you do. Can you forward me an honest breakdown of income and expenditure as part of your report, please?"

"Right, sir. I'll see to that. It's lucky you want it honest; *I* don't have the accountants and scriveners to make it anything else."

Arkyn regarded him; the emphasis had been slight, but it had been there. "Are you trying to tell me that someone else does? I would prefer you to state it outright – less cause for embarrassing confusion and recriminations."

Ernst studied Arkyn. The rumours had been true. Not quite so green as he looked this lad. "I think, Highness, you already know that the exchequer has been cooking their books. Their accountants are the best chefs. You get liars, lawyers and accountants and none of 'em are any better than the others."

Arkyn chuckled. It was probably true. "Anyone else's affairs you think I should examine? After all, it would be for the public good."

"I'm guessing you're scrutinising Roth's estate, sir. He gave the orders. Don't let his men fool you. He sent a lot of carts to his manors – *covered* carts."

"Edward, send a courier with the information to Wynfeld, please."

Impressed, the Aedile wondered how swiftly the Statisman had found himself in a cell. They should have heeded the warning when Roth was executed. Whoever said the young were undecided needed to meet their Prince.

"*Apart* from the fact tax has drained from this province as though someone pulled the plug on a bath, is there any particular problem you wish to bring to my attention?" asked Arkyn.

"You mean apart from the fact I'm undermanned and underfunded, under-resourced and think corruption is rife throughout the government of Terasia?"

Arkyn regarded him, lips twitching. "Those will do, with a bit more direction on all of them."

"How long have you got, Highness?"

"As long as it takes. We can always have lunch served whilst we work and this afternoon's officer can have a temporary reprieve."

Arkyn was pleased to see Ernst's bewilderment. Most officials expected others to ignore their concerns. That would never knowingly include him. He jerked his head at Edward, who left to give orders for Master Aldren to be told he might not be needed and for Kadeem to serve lunch at midday, even if Arkyn was still working.

The administrator returned and watched the Aedile for a moment. The man wasn't at all awed by the interview. Edward smiled inwardly; Arkyn had hardly started.

Four and a half hours felt like ten. Wrung out, the Aedile could never accuse the Prince of not being thorough. He couldn't remember what he'd agreed to or everything he'd said. What he now wanted was to go and find a quiet spot, drink a tankard of beer and try to collect his thoughts.

Sitting back after the last answer, Arkyn said, "Thank you, Ernst. That has all been most illuminating. Edward has a list of instructions for you. You've given me much to consider. I hope the report from your department is equally full of detail. We'll certainly need to revisit the costings for the City Assembly. Do you have any final questions for me?"

"No, Highness. Just thanks for listening. It's rare, that is."

"It's why I'm here. Thank you again for your help."

Edward collected his papers together as the Aedile left and Arkyn got up and stretched. "It's half past two, sir. Do you want to see Master Aldren this afternoon, or would you rather wait?"

"Is he here?"

Edward went to leave, but Arkyn rang for Stuart. He put the question to his secretary, who said that the officer wasn't present but could be within half an hour.

"Then please send for him with my apologies for messing around with his day. Tell him to be here in an hour. It should give him time to gather everything together. Did the Aedile say anything as he left?"

"Not within my hearing, Your Highness."

Once the secretary had gone, Arkyn poured himself and Edward a drink. Sipping it, he gazed at the gardens. They were a mass of colour from the whispering autumn leaves. He spotted Karl and Elsa and thought once more of Ceardlann. He'd never finished writing to Tain. Asking Edward for the key to his desk, he left, leaving instructions he was to be fetched *'when the next victim arrives.'*

Chapter 15
LETTERS AND KEYS

Early Afternoon

Margrave's Residence

ARKYN WALKED THROUGH the busy house. Now more used to it, he noticed the lightweight boards covering the walls, painted to give the appearance of carved panels. Were they there to protect whatever was behind them? When the building became offices, Portur must have decided it was better to be safe than sorry. A handful of paintings still adorned the walls above head height. Arkyn smiled. One was of his grandfather as a young man, painted during his visit nearly fifty years before. Above the paintings, a plaster frieze depicted woodland scenes with bears galumphing through foliage. The ceiling had bears' paw prints and crescents in the centre of diamonds. He stopped for a moment on the stairs to look more closely at the frieze, then, realising he was drawing attention, carried on up.

He entered his rooms to find Kadeem and Fitz talking. Both took his appearance with a show of equanimity.

Smiling, he said, "Don't mind me. I'm going to try to complete a letter in the time between interviewing people. Still nothing to report, Fitz?"

"No, sir. Nothing. Seems the assassins have taken heed."

"That spoils your fun."

"I'm sure they're biding their time as always, sir."

"As always, you'll be ready for them."

Arkyn passed into his sitting room and sat at his desk; opening it he took in the sight that met his eyes and paused, glancing around the room. Everything else seemed fine. His gaze slipped back to the desk. There were subtle hints that things had been disturbed, but, half-hidden below some parchment, was the folded corner of a note. He retrieved and read it.

As a caltrop can stop a horse,
so tradition can stop the stampede of change.

Arkyn noted the philosophy behind it, ignored the warning or threat and tossed it into the fire before requesting Fitz and Kadeem to join him.

"Kadeem, has anyone moved this desk since I left it last night?"

"No, Your Highness."

"Thank you. Please get Edward." Once alone with Fitz, Arkyn remarked, "Someone has been in the desk. The letter I was writing is in the wrong place. I always leave the completed part of the scroll furled. It isn't now."

"So much for them heeding the warning," observed Fitz. "I'll get onto the guards."

"Only if Edward didn't enter the desk."

It transpired that Edward hadn't. Fitz left to give the guards a roasting.

"Could anyone have got the key, Edward?" asked Arkyn.

"No, Your Highness. I kept it in my belt pouch or locked in a box in my room whilst I slept. Stuart's there, but I can't believe that he'd have done this."

"No, neither can I, but get him up here for questioning, please."

Six minutes later, Stuart left, exonerated. He hadn't even known Edward had the key. Arkyn realised that, logically, the only people who had known were Kadeem and Edward.

"There must be a second key. I want to know who has it. If the guards are exonerated, I want this room searched for secret doors. There might be an old way into them, like the Servants' Stair into my father's chambers. Fitz will see to it all."

"Very good, sir. Do you mind if, for the meantime, I have a guard stationed here with you?"

"I don't think it warrants that, Edward, but if Fitz thinks differently, I cannot comment."

A couple of moments after Edward left, a guard saluted on entering.

Sighing, Arkyn said, "Find yourself a corner, Halien, and excuse me if I'm not communicative."

Whilst re-reading the letter to Tain, Arkyn considered everything. Both notes had been in places which suggested members of his retinue were responsible, but he wasn't convinced. If any of them held a grudge, something would surely have occurred on the journey. The overtones of the notes were in line with Kadeem's philosophical bent, but Arkyn was sure Kadeem wasn't responsible. He'd worked for him for two years and had been part of his father's and Lord Landis' households before that. Was someone trying to discredit Kadeem? That also suggested someone from Oedran, someone who knew Kadeem's outlook on life. Could it be Edward? Maybe, but Arkyn thought he'd read honesty in the administrator's face. Could the philosophy be a co-incidence? More than likely. Should he tell Fitz about the notes, or even Wynfeld? No. Wynfeld had more than enough to keep himself occupied, and Fitz was already berating the guards. He'd wait. If there were more notes, he might act. For the meantime, he'd continue as normal.

He re-read the letter to Tain; fortunately, there was nothing derogatory or confidential.

Edward entered to say that Fitz would need a plan of the Residence and he didn't want to upset the Margrave's steward or Lady Portur.

"Ask Her Ladyship to join me then and tell Stuart to give my apologies to the Education Officer, if I'm delayed."

Six minutes later, Lady Portur entered.

Arkyn turned to the guard. "Please leave us, Halien."

"I'm afraid the captain was very precise, sir. Until we know what's happened, I'm not to leave."

"Go and tell Fitz that I can appreciate his orders, but I am returning them to him temporarily." Once the door closed behind Halien, Arkyn smiled. "I'm sorry about that, my lady, but there has been an unknown person entering these rooms."

"How did they get in, sir?"

“We don’t know. We need a plan of the Residence, but my guards didn’t want to go heavy-handed to your steward. I hope I can advise him that you have agreed to the request?”

“Of course you can, sir, but this is your family’s Residence, not mine. He is your steward.”

Arkyn regarded her for a few moments. It was true. The official residences of the empire were technically the King’s. Whilst he visited, especially without a governor in place, it was his Residence. He was hosting Lady Portur, not the other way around, unless he wished otherwise.

“Thank you. Did you help with the preparation of these rooms?”

“No, sir. I am, after all, newly arrived in the Residence.”

“Of course, my lady. Did Lord Portur mention anything to you during your engagement?”

“That was quite brief, sir, and the marriage arranged,” revealed Kristina without any hint of subterfuge.

“Then I’m sure the steward can help my men. I’m sorry to have had to ask you all this at such a time.”

“Don’t concern yourself, sir.” She hesitated. “I’ve been wondering if you wish me to leave the Residence.”

“Might I enquire why you’re asking, my lady?”

“As the Margrave’s widow, I have no right to live here. As there’s no heir, the Portur estate reverts to the FitzAlcis and I must return home in accordance with my marriage agreement.” There was something akin to sadness in her voice.

Arkyn watched her carefully. The comment about her marriage agreement spoke volumes. “There’s hardly been chance to investigate the situation yet, my lady, but you are correct, if there was no blood-heir, that is the normal practice; however, do not think that you must return home if you do not wish it. As the widow of an overlord, you have certain rights and we have a duty to defend them.”

She smiled. “I am not complaining about my situation, Your Highness. It is what it is, but after two widowhoods, I suppose I have outgrown my home, and I have found Tera more diverting. It’s been nice to see Percival again as well.”

“I’m sure we can help if diversion is what you require. Although I understand and appreciate your earlier points, I still consider Your Ladyship my hostess, as I would have considered Lord Portur my host. Will you cope with the mayhem?”

Relief suffused her features. “Sir, it will be a pleasure. Thank you.”

“No, thank you. I’ll also examine your situation alongside our wardships, if that helps to ease your mind.”

Lady Portur smiled. “Your Highness has more than enough to do.”

"To mimic Lord Wealsman, a little bit of work never hurt anyone."

"No, sir, but overwork can cause lasting damage, which Percival is apt to forget."

Arkyn sighed. "I'll try to remember that in the coming years."

"I should leave Your Highness to continue. I'll see the steward receives orders to give your men every assistance. Would you like me to slip past the guards unnoticed?"

Arkyn chuckled, suddenly liking her. "I don't think you'd manage it, my lady, but thank you for the offer and for your help."

Twelve minutes later, Edward entered to find Arkyn calmly writing whilst ignoring Halien's presence. He waited until the Prince wiped the pen nib clean before saying that the Education Officer was waiting.

On leaving his room, Arkyn said, "Fitz, any luck?"

"Not yet, sir. We'll get there though. Can I search your rooms?"

"Of course. I'd say excuse the mess, but Prince Tain isn't around to cause it."

Chapter 16
CAPTAIN HASTER

Afternoon

Arkyn's Office

REACHING HIS OUTER OFFICE, Arkyn found Master Aldren waiting along with a second man who saluted as the Prince entered. Arkyn visibly paused.

Edward took in the sight. "Captain Haster?"

"Not captain, Edward," admonished Arkyn. "Stuart?"

The unsettled secretary said, "Erm, Master Haster wondered if Your Highness could spare him a moment. Apparently, it's important."

Arkyn gave Haster an unfathomable expression: important wasn't urgent. "Wait here. Stuart, I'll want to see Wynfeld as soon as I've finished the next interview." He waved the Education Officer into his office.

Two hours later, Aldren left thinking it was he who had been given the education. Arkyn had been pleased to find nothing suspicious in the department other than a distinct and predictable lack of funding. When the officer left, Wynfeld entered and saluted.

Arkyn watched him levelly. "What is Haster doing in the Residence?"

"Helping us catch the man who broke into your rooms, sir."

Arkyn considered that. "All right, I'll see him. You are to stay."

When the former captain entered and saluted, Arkyn snapped, "You are no longer a captain, Haster. A salute is not appropriate."

Haster whitened and bowed. "My apologies, Your Highness. Habit and all that."

"Yes. I would have thought you'd have been more careful about such habits. How did you enter the Residence? And don't say via the front doors."

Haster chuckled. "As it happens, sir, I entered by a little-used rear gate, which I have since told Fitz to watch. I was following a man who should not have been entering."

Still frustrated, Arkyn asked, "What made you suspicious of him?"

"He was in Roth's employ…ment. He… entered the Residence, and I followed, but…" Haster's colour drained further. "He went… went upstairs via the… via the backstairs… Sebas… Sebastian Bondman. He—"

Haster fell.

Horrified, Arkyn watched as Wynfeld checked for signs of life and Edward left to ask Stuart to send for Artzman.

As his administrator re-entered, Arkyn said, "Wynfeld…?" The commander simply shook his head and Arkyn sank onto a chair. "I did it. I was annoyed—"

"Annoyance wouldn't kill him, sir," observed Wynfeld placidly.

"He was life-bound!" Arkyn struggled with himself. "He'd have felt my annoyance."

"But it wouldn't have caused his death, my prince," said Wynfeld carefully, shocked by the revelation. "Life-binds only kill the vassal if they commit treason or treachery." He glanced at Haster. "Admittedly, we don't know if he did and died because of it, but your being annoyed would not have caused this, sir."

Moving around the desk, Arkyn said, "We can find out." He knelt by Haster. Carefully, he placed his hands palm to palm with the former captain's. Nothing happened. Sitting back on his heels, he sighed with relief.

"Sir?" asked Wynfeld, confused.

"The scars from the life-bind would have opened up if he'd died because of treasonous thoughts or actions." He nodded to Edward as a knock on the door heralded the doctor. "I'm not sure you're going to be able to help him, Artzman."

The doctor knelt by Haster's corpse. A few moments later, he agreed. "No, sir, I'm not. I'd seen Master Haster on a couple of occasions recently. His heart was failing."

Wynfeld said, "So this isn't unexpected, doc?"

"No. Not entirely."

"In part?" asked Arkyn.

"Sir…?" remonstrated Wynfeld and was silenced with a glance.

The doctor noticed the look and took in the strangeness of the situation. "Your Highness, I don't know why it would be important, but it wouldn't have taken much overexertion to cause this."

"Thank you. If you could see Master Haster laid out, please."

Six minutes later, alone with the commander and Edward, Arkyn said, "You can tell me I'm not responsible, Wynfeld, but I'll still feel it, so save your breath. I kept him waiting. I was so frustrated he was here when I had other things to attend to."

"As soon as I arrived, sir, he told me what he knew. Time wasn't lost."

"Even so," snapped Arkyn, "he might be alive if I'd been reasonable."

Wynfeld glanced at Edward. The administrator left, almost accidentally taking with him all the papers he could reach easily.

Waiting until the door had closed behind him, Wynfeld said, "The doctor was clear it could have happened at any time, sir, even before he saw you or tomorrow. It was coincidence it happened here." After a moment's silence, he added, "Sitting somewhere else for a time might help."

As Arkyn left for his rooms, Wynfeld caught Edward's eye and waited. It was clear the administrator wanted a word with him.

* * *

The administrator crossed to the Prince's office and waved Wynfeld inside it again.

"Edward, this is irregular."

Ignoring him, Edward closed the door. He took out a small piece of paper from the mass in his arms. "You need to see this, Commander. It was amongst His Highness' documents."

Wynfeld read the note and blanched.

All that can be said to be certain in life is death,
which comes harder when those we love are in great peril.

"I see your point, Administrator. Any ideas?"

"Well, I didn't put it with his documents. It's clearly a threat and I don't know how it came to be in these papers. The writing is standard; it's taught in every school. There's nothing particularly distinguished about it and I expect it was written so that there wasn't."

"Yes. Leave it with me." Wynfeld saw Edward's concerned face. "I won't go blundering around. Check carefully for any others and give them to me if they appear."

* * *

Later, Wynfeld found himself in a link with King Adeone. He watched his King's face apprehensively.

"What happened with Haster?" At the end of Wynfeld's succinct explanation, he asked, "How annoyed was Prince Arkyn?"

Wynfeld snorted. "Certainly not in a murderous rage, sir. I would say highly frustrated rather than angry. Your Majesty, I hadn't realised Haster was life-bound—"

"I didn't announce it. Judge Tancred has confirmed that your Prince's annoyance wouldn't have killed Haster. Are you satisfied his death was natural?"

"Yes, sir. Completely. Doctor Artzman confirmed he was ill. Lord Portur and I had both been using Haster's eyes and ears, so he'd been here a couple of times and the doctor had been called to him before."

"Did Roth know?"

"He may have done, sir, but he wasn't bothered about people like Haster and myself."

Adeone considered. "All right. I'll let it lie. Thank you, Wynfeld."

Chapter 17

SERVING ROTH

Afternoon

Arkyn's Private Rooms

ARKYN HAD REACHED HIS ROOMS without his brain having to consider which turnings to take. Entering the antechamber, he nodded as Fitz saluted. The captain obviously wanted or needed a word with him but, after everything that had happened, Arkyn wanted less responsibility, not more; however, Kadeem wasn't there to take the message and the captain wouldn't report to anyone else. Fitz might give messages to others, but he only accepted Arkyn's authority. Long service and tradition meant that he wasn't part of the army proper anymore and he wasn't part of any 'Guard'. He was Captain Fitz, Officer of the FitzAlcis and Alcis help anyone other than a FitzAlcis who gave him an order he disagreed with.

Arkyn respected the captain for his principles; if he told him to pass the message to Kadeem – when he returned – Fitz would do so, but he, Arkyn, might not receive the whole of it straightaway.

With that in mind, he said, "Come on through."

Once in his sitting room, Arkyn sat down and nodded for Fitz to do likewise.

The captain noted Arkyn's mood. "If it's all the same to you, Your Highness, I'll stand. Once I sit these days, it takes a lot to get me on my feet again."

Arkyn smiled for the first time in what felt like hours. "I wouldn't mind, Fitz… Surely it's a sign you need to retire though."

"Don't you start as well, sir. His Majesty is equally concerned for my welfare. I keep telling him I'd be bored."

"Then there's the question of what we'd do without you, isn't there?" enquired Arkyn wryly. "Now, what did you need to see me about?"

Fitz said, grave as ever, "We've caught the man who broke into your desk, sir."

"Yes, Wynfeld said Haster had passed on the name. I hope we don't need Haster's testimony though."

"Is there a reason we couldn't use it?"

"Yes, he's dead," stated Arkyn. The look on the captain's face made him blush remorsefully. "Sicla, sorry, Fitz, you must have worked with him for years in Oedran. He had a heart attack…" Arkyn explained everything that had occurred with very little emotion to betray his inner angst.

Fitz, listening, heard the angst anyway. "It wasn't anyone's fault, sir. Get that straight in your head. Haster was ill. If you think your temper made it worse, learn the lesson, but don't let it prey on your mind. That way madness lies."

"You've basically just told me off for wallowing."

"Not for the first time, sir. You've all needed the reminder at one time or another."

Arkyn chuckled. "How did we end up with you picking up our pieces?"

"One day I'll tell you the story, sir. When we can find a glass and an evening's peace."

"Fair enough. Has Sebastian Bondman admitted it?"

"In a manner of speaking. I've handed him into Commander Wynfeld's tender care. If he dies on him, I doubt it will be of a heart attack."

Arkyn winced. "I'll not sanction torture. It doesn't warrant that. You said he had admitted to it. Send him for trial. Who is he? I know his name but no more."

"A footman, formally of Roth's employ. He entered the room through a panel by the fireplace from the next room – apparently it used to be a door. I've had a carpenter and joiner working their magic. No-one, and I mean *no-one*, will be entering by that means again. We've searched Bondman, and he had no key on him; however, he had quite a collection of lockpicks; I've apprehended them—"

"Good," interrupted Arkyn. "Did you say he was of Roth's employ?"

"Aye, Your Highness. I think he felt he owed his old master something. He certainly acted like he did."

"Get me Lord Erlan Roth."

Soon afterwards, Kadeem announced Wealsman. Arkyn turned to greet him and recounted what had occurred.

Wealsman said, "I'd heard something of it, sir. I've taken the precaution of stationing a guard next-door. I feel I must apologise also. It's hardly a fitting continuation to your visit and one that no loyal person in Terasia can condone—"

"Yet not of their making, my lord. I shall not exact revenge on those whose actions do not merit it. Nevertheless, my thanks for your apologies, they are accepted. Would you like a drink? Kadeem is hovering, waiting to be useful."

Wealsman smiled. "I could find a home for a whiskey, Your Highness."

Arkyn nodded. "Two whiskeys please, Kadeem, then you can go and see what needs your attention elsewhere."

Drinks in hand, Wealsman and Arkyn sat talking for quarter of an hour about official business, including the exchequer and everything that the Aedile and Education Officer had revealed.

Then Wealsman said, "I hear Lady Daia is enjoying the idea of a prolonged stay. She's a bright lady and shouldn't be confined. Anyway, if I were to be traditional, I'd say she's ready for marriage and she'll never find a husband if she's cooped up in her manor for too long—"

"What a remarkable turn of phrase. Maybe you should meet Lord Landis. I think you might get on well. His maxim is that traditions can be changed. I feel putting the two of you in a room together could be interesting."

Wealsman chuckled to himself. "Then I hope one day to meet him."

"Maybe you shall. You should visit Oedran."

"So I have thought many a time, sir. If I could just click my fingers and get there, I would. Sometimes I wish I was a Shifter."

"Of all the Ullian Spirits that must be one of the most wished for," mused Arkyn. "But wouldn't you say that life could lack something? I mean, if you could disappear here and reappear there, you'd miss so much of the world, wouldn't you? The very vitality of it. The wind, the colours of nature, the smells on the breeze…"

Surprised by Arkyn's poetic stance, Wealsman said, "It would be a quicker journey, sir."

"Yet a less worthwhile one."

"That rather depends on the reasons for your journey and the destination."

"Does it? Isn't all of life one journey? Kadeem always tells me that."

Wealsman snorted. "Your manservant is in the philosophical sense correct, but surely in a practical sense life is full of different journeys, with many destinations."

"Yet that in itself is philosophical, is it not? You cannot deny that life is one long journey because that is a philosophical argument and then say that it is a series of smaller ones, for that is another philosophical argument."

Wealsman frowned. "Yet how else are we to describe life? It surely needs to be compared to something. There has to be a simile for it. As in all things, there must be a description."

"Yes, but it already has one: it is life. A journey through time it may also be, but that is still, in itself, a philosophical description—" He broke off as Kadeem entered and announced Lord Roth.

Erlan entered and bowed. A moment later, he knew it wasn't going to be a polite audience. Arkyn had pushed himself to his feet, his eyes hardening – laughter recently spent was replaced by disapproval. The Acting Governor had positioned himself a step behind the prince, standing foursquare like a guard on parade – emphasis, if it were needed, that it was an official audience even in private rooms.

Arkyn was terse. "My men have, earlier today, arrested one Sebastian Bondman for treason, Roth. He will stand trial. This is by way of a polite warning: no more treachery that traces back to your family or matters appertaining to your authority will be tolerated. Your affairs are under close scrutiny; do not be found wanting again."

Erlan's face set. "Your Highness, I'll discover what's occurred and will endeavour to make sure nothing of this nature happens again. Bondman was meant to be at Rowthelen; with permission, I'll pay a visit—"

Arkyn said, "In which case, I shall not detain you at the current time."

In the privacy of his head, Wealsman winced at the phrase. They were words no loyal lord ever wanted to hear. Erlan was sensible enough not to reply. He bowed smartly and left with determination written over every aspect of his being. Every nuance said that someone was going to pay for endangering the security he had left.

When he'd gone and the door had closed, Wealsman relaxed. "I think that shook him, Your Highness."

"No-one ever told him being the son of a traitor would be easy – even after swearing fealty. I know it's not directly his fault, but he has inherited problems."

"I think he's realising it, sir. We've prevented all movement of his goods and that of the minor lords on his property. As well as on the other half now held by the King. We've summoned each steward and comptroller to Tera to give an account of their manors. There's a detail of soldiers at each manor as well. They are currently searching every building on the properties. So far, nothing has been discovered—"

"I want to know if they find anything."

Kadeem re-entered half an hour later and, standing by the door, hinted to Arkyn that he ought to be getting ready for the banquet.

Arkyn sighed. "Wealsman, would you be kind enough to wait whilst I change?"

A few minutes later, Arkyn re-entered the sitting room, mantle in hand, calling for Kadeem, who had stayed with Wealsman.

"Kadeem, you know I still can't grip things properly with my left hand."

Kadeem went to cross the room, but Wealsman waved him off. The manservant stopped and glanced at Arkyn, who shrugged.

Wealsman said, "Let me, Your Highness." Without appearing self-conscious, he draped the mantle with skilful expertise. "Where is your badge of office, sir?"

Bemused, Arkyn handed it to him and Wealsman pinned it on with the deftness Kadeem normally managed before stepping back.

"There you are, sir."

"Thank you, Wealsman… What are we expecting of tonight's banquet?"

"Nothing too strenuous, sir. It is the merchants and officials of the city. Some of whom you have already met. Kadeem has the guest list for you to look over, as requested."

"Thank you, my lord. I shouldn't keep you from changing for it any longer."

Chapter 18
ARRIVAL AND BRIEFING

Evening

Margrave's Hall

AS HE ENTERED the Margrave's Hall, tiredness crashed over Arkyn; the hall was too garish, the light too bright, the sound too loud. Wealsman was walking to greet him once again, and Arkyn once more asked to be introduced to everyone sitting at the dais. He had read the guest list and Wealsman had annotated it with snippets of information about each guest but, in the heat of the hall, fighting against fatigue, Arkyn couldn't recall any of it.

As he made introductions, Wealsman noticed the Prince's lassitude. It wasn't surprising. He hadn't let up since his arrival. Three banquets on consecutive evenings weren't helping; the kitchens were in uproar. Roth had probably arrogantly assumed they wouldn't happen. The staff would need thanking.

Taking his place at the dais, Arkyn said, "Will you pass on my thanks to the kitchens? They must be feeling the strain."

Wealsman smiled. "Certainly, sir. I was just thinking the same myself."

"Thank you. I notice Lady Daia and Lady Portur are getting on well."

Wealsman glanced at the two ladies, who were talking quietly but constantly. "Yes, I wonder if we'll get a word in tonight."

Midway through the evening, on the edge of hearing, the sound of horses' hooves clattered in the courtyard of the Residence. With so many guests, it wasn't unusual, but the first indication it might have been important was Kadeem walking up to Arkyn's shoulder.

"Lord Iris has arrived, Your Highness."

"What?" exclaimed Arkyn. "Alone?"

"Apparently so, sir."

Arkyn nodded. "I'll be thankful for that. Let him come in."

Wealsman said, "I'll see to His Lordship's rooms, sir."

Ignoring Wealsman, Arkyn rose to greet the travel-stained, white-haired figure of Lord Iris as he approached and bowed – a very exact, courtly bow that spoke of many years' practice.

"Welcome to Tera, Lord Iris. Should I worry there's bad news?"

"No, Your Highness."

Arkyn murmured, "That makes a nice change this week. Let me introduce you first to your hostess: Lady Portur of Terasia, Lord Iris of Oedran."

Iris hid his confusion well as he greeted her.

Arkyn continued, "Might I introduce Lord Percival Wealsman, currently Acting Governor of Terasia, Lord Iris?"

Iris smiled. "You must be having an interesting time of it, my lord."

"In comparison to His Highness, I am having a very easy time, Lord Iris," replied Wealsman placidly. "If you'll excuse me, I'll just go and give orders concerning your rooms. Have you dined?"

Touched by the gesture, Iris said, "Thank you. I haven't. Realising we were so close to Tera, I resolved to reach here this evening."

Wealsman nodded, turning to Arkyn. "Shall I have food sent here for His Lordship, Your Highness?"

"Please, Wealsman."

The Acting Governor left and Arkyn motioned to his vacated place. Servers moved forward to seat them and to pass Iris a goblet of wine. The lord sighed as he sat down.

Arkyn let him take a draught of wine before he enquired, "*Why* are you so early, my lord? Moreover, *why* didn't you tell me that you would be?"

"We were making good time, sir. His Majesty informed me what had occurred on your arrival and suggested that I ride ahead."

Arkyn asked, "What of the other point?"

"A foolish mistake, Your Highness," admitted Iris without hesitation.

"I hope your advice won't be full of the same mistakes. Who else is with you?"

"My man and secretary, sir. I left my grandson overseeing everyone else."

"I wasn't aware Lord Irvin was accompanying you," stated Arkyn, intrigued and pleased.

"He had a hankering to travel, sir, and His Majesty raised no objections."

"Is he going to follow in your footsteps and become an advisor?"

"I can only hope so, sir. After all, an Iris has been an Advisor to the FitzAlcis for many generations."

Wealsman, returning, said mischievously, "I'm not sure His Highness requires one, my lord."

"Lord Wealsman, we all need advisors," observed Arkyn.

Wealsman grinned. "Then you are hiding your requirement extremely well. I'm sure Chief Merchant Turgar will attest that Your Highness hasn't required any help so far."

Iris examined Wealsman with appraising eyes; confused by the lack of formality. Had they been elsewhere, he'd have rebuked the minor lord without hesitation for such familiarity. The Chief Merchant obviously agreed with Wealsman though.

"His Highness has amazed many people over the last few days, Lord Iris; however, you must know him far better than us."

Arkyn blushed. "Lord Iris will be getting a gilded view of my capabilities, if you're not careful."

"I doubt that could ever be so, Your Highness," said Iris courteously.

Arkyn murmured. "Time will tell." His tone changed. "We seem to be talking about duties, hardly a fit topic for such an occasion. Wealsman, find yourself a chair and stop looming. It's depressing. Did you have a pleasant trip, Iris?"

Instead of making the whole of the dais moving one seat to the right to accommodate him, Wealsman ambled to the end where the servers placed a chair and the merchants and officials greeted him with pleasure.

After answering Arkyn's question, Iris commented, "Have I deprived His Lordship of his seat?"

"He won't mind, my lord. He's a minor lord from Portur's lands and extremely good at his job; I don't know what I'd have done without his help, though he'll deny he helped at all."

"That is all the recommendation one should require, but how did Your Highness come to appoint him Acting Governor?" asked Iris, suspicious Arkyn might have been manipulated by a smile and ready manner into making an unwise and ill-advised appointment.

"He was Roth's deputy. Next in the authority stakes. He alerted Wynfeld to the situation and thereby saved my life."

"For which we are all grateful, sir," observed Iris, still far from satisfied; years of experience had taught him that nothing was certain, and rarely as it seemed, in the political manoeuvring of the lords.

At that point, the servers placed a substantial meal in front of him. Whilst he dined, Arkyn talked with Lady Portur.

On turning back to the Lord of Oedran, Arkyn said, "Was that a yawn you just stifled, my lord?"

"I'm afraid so, sir. My age is creeping up on me at last."

Looking over his shoulder, Arkyn caught Kadeem's eye. "Can you see if His Lordship's rooms are ready, please? It seems unfair to keep him here longer than necessary after his ride."

"Word came two minutes ago that they are, sir. If His Lordship wishes to retire, I have a guide waiting to show him the way."

Arkyn crooked an eyebrow at Iris.

"If Your Highness has no need of me, I would gratefully retire," responded Iris.

"Have a restful night, my lord. I'll send for you in the morning, probably about half past nine. Goodnight."

"Goodnight, sir."

Once Lord Iris was out of hearing, Arkyn turned to Kadeem. "Who is waiting to brief His Lordship?"

"Edward, sir."

"Good. See if Wealsman would like to re-join me, please."

Half a minute later, Wealsman sat down. Arkyn apologised for the upset and – at a reminder from Wealsman as to the topic – resumed their interrupted discussion.

* * *

Iris didn't talk to his guide. He was tired and liked everyone to keep to tradition. In that respect, he was about to be disappointed. His elderly manservant met him.

"My lord, Administrator Edward is waiting for you. I tried to discourage him, but he insisted."

Iris sighed. "I'd better see what's so important. I shan't be long, Collins."

The fact that Edward wasn't sitting and hadn't just got up mollified Iris slightly, but not enough for him to hide his irritation.

"Administrator, what is so important that it couldn't wait for the morning?"

"My apologies, my lord. In the morning, His Highness will need me. Therefore, it's better to brief you now, so you can get an undisturbed night's sleep. His Highness likes people to understand the situation fully before he speaks to them, wherever possible."

"Does he know you are here, Administrator?"

"By now he will, sir."

Iris turned a small timepiece his manservant had set on the mantlepiece. "We shall wait for six minutes to see if he sends for you not to disturb me."

As the six minutes passed, Iris studied Edward's face. It gave nothing away. When no message from the Prince arrived, Iris said, "So then, I am not to get the rest I need quite so soon."

"I also would prefer it if this could be postponed, my lord," replied Edward, "but circumstances do not allow it. How much does Your Lordship know of the situation?"

"I know Roth murdered Lord Portur accidentally. Roth meant to assassinate His Highness. He had another attempt at murdering Prince Arkyn before His Highness ordered his arrest and execution. His Majesty has left the decision as to the new Margrave of Terasia to our Prince. That is as much, I believe, as His Majesty knew when he contacted me."

"When did His Majesty contact you, sir?"

"That is immaterial, Administrator. You will please keep to the purpose."

Inwardly cursing the Lord of Oedran's attitude, Edward said, "You will allow, sir, that I am privy to many details that the King and His Highness might wish to keep private. If I don't know when His Majesty spoke to you, I don't know which facts he has omitted under that precaution."

Iris looked as if he had swallowed a lemon. "Yesterday morning, if it is that important."

"Thank you, my lord. How would you like to proceed? I can explain what has happened and you may ask questions as I go or you can ask questions and I can answer them."

Iris snapped, "As I'm unaware of what has occurred, it would be better, would it not, if you did the talking?"

Edward had barely begun the explanation before Iris interrupted.

"To pardon traitors' families is to encourage treachery! Who on Erinna has been advising His Highness?"

Edward stilled. "His Highness made decisions in difficult circumstances. Commander Wynfeld, Captain Fitz and the Terazi were all present at various stages—"

"None of whom is an Advisor to the FitzAlcis! I would have thought Fitz alone would have seen the flaws in the reasoning. The Terazi I can't comment on, but I would have expected more from a commander His Majesty speaks so highly of."

"Commander Wynfeld and his men are the reason the Prince is alive," stated Edward. "He is an exceptional officer and, had he had any, he would have mentioned doubts. My understanding is that His Majesty had no objection and was content with His Highness' reasoning."

"Then I cannot speak to the decision, but might I know the reasons?"

"I would rather you asked His Highness for those, my lord; I am not at liberty to disclose them."

"Then why are you here to brief me?"

"I am here to inform you of what His Highness' decisions have been, not to give you the reasons for those decisions, my lord. Roth's son has assumed the title. His Highness would prefer the events not to be mentioned again, as far as is possible, or at least not to be the subject of gossip and speculation."

"Very well, though I would like to know what steps have been taken on the investigations into Roth's affairs."

"They are in the hands of Commander Wynfeld and Lord Wealsman."

"A minor lord of Terasia has been entrusted with the oversight of dismantling of an overlord's estate?" enquired Iris, perplexed.

"Lord Wealsman is Acting Governor of Terasia and, as such, it comes under his eye as much as the Prince's. He is taking reports when His Highness is unable to. He is *not* making decisions on those reports. Again, if you wish to know the reasons for the decision, then please ask His Highness. I doubt, however, that the Prince will change his mind. Lord Wealsman has been an invaluable assistance and offered much needed support to Prince Arkyn—"

"Doesn't mean I can't question Wealsman's motives. He might be manipulating the situation for his own ends."

Edward began to wish he'd gone to bed. Was Iris always so tetchy? Trying to remain calm, he said, "I don't think he is, sir." Edward continued outlining events. He managed to get to, "Rahat has been arrested, along with his deputies, and his office is undergoing a thorough investigation by Lord Simble, an overlord, and Commander Wynfeld's men. We are still waiting on their initial report," before Iris commented.

"They can hurry it along. Two days should have seen some results."

"We are expecting some sort of report in the morning, my lord."

"Very well. Carry on."

Edward did so, in all – with an initial overview and then a more detailed explanation – the whole briefing took around an hour.

Once Edward left, Lord Iris retired, less than entirely satisfied with what Edward had told him. His young Prince's methods would be a challenge. He couldn't believe the prince had invoked clemency or that the King and Terazi had accepted the decision tamely, but asking the Prince about it was out of the question. It was a past decision, one that required not his advice, merely his knowledge of the verdict. Edward's manner, although exemplary, had made that plain.

* * *

Walking to his room, Edward knew Iris hadn't been happy. Would the Lord of Oedran inform the Prince? If he did, then he, Edward, must accept the consequences. On reaching the room he shared with Stuart, he sank onto the bed.

Bleary-eyed, his deputy asked, "How did the wide take it?"

"Not well. He didn't consider that I'd also had my evening disturbed by his arrival."

"That sounds right. When do they? We're here to be trampled…"

"Some aren't so bad: His Highness isn't."

"Has his moments though."

"We're not paid to comment on those moments, Stuart, as I've told you before."

Stuart's speech was becoming slurred. "Aye, I know. Loyalty is an odd thing, isn't it?"

"You're sleep-talking, I assume. I only wish I were. Night."

"Night, sir. Blow the candle out, for the love of Aluna."

Edward sighed. "When I've got into bed. You'll have to brief His Lordship's secretary in the morning."

"I can't wait. Such an honour, such responsibility."

Six minutes later regular breathing filled the room and the only light discernible was from the moons, but Stuart, for all his body craved sleep, found his mind wouldn't let him rest.

Chapter 19
STRAIN

Pentadai, Week 16 – 26th Macial, 5th Easis 1211
Arkyn's Bedchamber

THE THIRD MORNING after their arrival in Tera, Kadeem entered the Prince's bedchamber. Used to Arkyn having already woken, he was concerned to find him deep in slumber. He drew the curtains. The heavy drapes parted, letting in bright sunlight. Still Arkyn didn't move and Kadeem privately swore. He didn't like waking the Prince. Not because Arkyn objected, but because he was normally an early riser and if he was still asleep, it was because he needed that rest, and Kadeem didn't like upsetting nature's ways.

He walked over to the Prince. "Sir, it's eight o'clock."

Still nothing. Kadeem tried speaking louder, but all he received in response was a sleepful visage. Hesitantly, he shook the Prince's shoulder. Arkyn started awake and, after he'd sat up rubbing at his eyes, cleared his throat. Kadeem passed him a glass of water with a word of apology.

Arkyn looked at his manservant steadily. "Kadeem, stop it. I asked to be woken, and you woke me. I'll get more sleep tonight… hopefully. That is, if no official thinks I need any more honouring or that I need to meet another fifty or so of their ilk. Cheer my morning and tell me I have the evening off."

Kadeem hesitated, taking back the glass. "Erm… You won't be meeting fifty or so people, sir, but I believe you're meant to be dining with the governor…"

"This could be interesting; do the passed-on eat?"

Kadeem smiled. "Theirs is the sustenance of the moons and stars, sir. I meant, of course, Lord Wealsman, as Acting Governor."

Arkyn sighed. "Does Wealsman have to entertain me or I him? In the sense of being hosts."

"I shouldn't have taken the question any other way, sir."

Sotto voce Arkyn said, "*Shouldn't* isn't wouldn't."

"I believe, sir, he entertains Your Highness…"

After having spent three evenings in Wealsman's company, Arkyn started chuckling. The laughter became coughing and then, as he stopped, he sagged into his pillows saying,

"I shall look forward to this evening. My day will be interesting in other ways."

"Interest keeps our minds occupied, sir," observed Kadeem, pulling back the bedclothes.

Arkyn glared at him. Once his manservant had left, Arkyn ran his hand over his head, hoping his headache would disappear. His head felt muzzy as well as painful. Maybe food and more water would help.

Maybe it would have done, but when he looked at his breakfast, his appetite vanished. He toyed with it for some time and managed a few mouthfuls but his head hurt too much and he needed more energy to eat.

Unbeknownst to Arkyn, Kadeem was getting worried. Oversleeping wasn't unexpected. Three very late evenings followed by relatively early mornings made it a certainty, but not eating, *that* was worrying.

When Edward entered and bid the Prince good morning, he got a bland response. Arkyn, glad of the excuse to leave the stuffy sitting room, got up to begin his day. Edward held the door open for him but, as the Prince passed, glanced instead at Kadeem. He read the manservant's concern without a word needing to be said.

For once, Arkyn walked through the Residence in silence. He reached his office beginning to feel slightly better. Whether it was moving around or because he'd eaten something he didn't know, and didn't care. He simply greeted Stuart with a cheerier good morning than he had Edward.

* * *

Sitting at his desk, Arkyn contacted his father before picking up Wynfeld's latest report. Succinctly, it explained that the three exchequer officials were beginning to blame each other, though they might have realised that the guard outside the door, one Corporal Butterworth, could be eavesdropping. Sebastian Bondman had been formally arrested, and the Terazi was preparing to hear the case.

Arkyn asked Edward to file the report and inform Wynfeld that he'd read it. They'd wait to re-interview the exchequer officials until the clerks from Oedran arrived. Time to brood could work wonders. He wrote out a brief statement for the Terazi. As he passed it over to Edward, he said,

"Kadeem says you briefed Lord Iris last night. How did he take it?"

"He was very tired, Your Highness, so I'm not sure it's fair to comment on how he reacted."

"Very well. His Majesty has confirmed he suggested Iris might like to ride ahead, but he didn't expect him to arrive last night. Any word from the Roth estate or Lord Simble?"

"I haven't received anything on the former yet, sir. On the latter, Lord Simble sent his apologies for the delay, yesterday, sir. I expect, from what he said, that he'll bring a report this morning."

Arkyn cleared his throat. "If he does, I'll talk to him about it. I'd better speak to— Come in."

Wealsman entered, accompanied by Sergeant Dring, who saluted smartly and stayed standing by the door.

Arkyn said, "I was about to send for you, my lord."

"I'm pleased to have saved Your Highness the trouble. I've received an interesting report from the closest of Roth's manors. The soldiers have found a vault, about as large as this room, hollowed into a cliff and accessed by an underground passage, its entrance hidden in a stable."

"How was the entrance found?" asked Arkyn.

Wealsman grinned. "After yesterday's events, Lord Roth visited Rowthelen – Bondman used to work between there and Tera. His Lordship put the fear of Alcis into all the staff with the help of the commander's men. After that, one of the younger maids mentioned men had taken chests into the stables. One of the commander's men literally fell into the passage after his colleagues had discovered and removed the cover. They wondered if it was just a pit—"

"Was he harmed?"

"He twisted his ankle, but, other than that, he was fine. There are now several guards on the entrance and the vault is being searched for other exits. Lord Roth asked the maid if she recognised anyone carrying the chests. She gave him their names. One was Bondman, the other has been detained and the rest of the servants are undergoing close questioning. I think the rest of the story is best left to Sergeant Dring."

Arkyn nodded, pleased Wealsman had enquired after the hapless guard. He motioned to the sergeant, who moved forward.

"We followed the passage, sir – must be about a mile. Air holes at certain places would look like rabbit burrows from above. Nothing anyone could get into, anyway. We reached the vault. It must have taken a lot of manpower to make – though the rock is relatively soft as these things go. We reckon there's about fifty chests. All secured and heavy. We took one to the manor and picked the lock. It's full of the bamboo casings holding the darl and talence collected as tax. Lord Roth confirmed that, to his knowledge, his father never kept his personal funds in such a manner."

"Thank you, Sergeant, for a concise report. Is the vault secure?"

"It seems to be, sir."

"Who knows what you've found?" enquired Arkyn.

"Only the men at the manor, Commander Wynfeld, Lord Roth and Lord Wealsman, sir."

"Good, please keep it to that small group. Until I've spoken to several people, the chests will have to stay where they are. Make sure you have enough men to guard the vault day and night. Tell Commander Wynfeld I have ordered it. Other than my congratulations for finding it, that is all for now." As Dring saluted and left, Arkyn said to Wealsman, "We'll have to find somewhere secure in Tera for the money – though I think it is as secure where it is. Is there any indication that they might find similar at other manors?"

"Some are a good day's ride from here, if not more, sir. I'm not sure what we'll find. Commander Wynfeld has a couple of men reading through the late Roth's papers. That might turn up something, though I think he'll have covered his tracks well."

"Yes. Without the hint he gave us though, it might have taken a lot longer to find all this out. I wonder why he hinted at anything."

"Maybe he realised you'd find out anyway and this way he took the blame off other people. He was going to die; might as well help save others, perhaps."

Arkyn shrugged. "Perhaps. Thank you, Wealsman. Can you continue to coordinate things, please?"

Sitting back after Wealsman had left, Arkyn said, "We seem to be getting somewhere with the retrieval of the missing tax. I wonder how much was drained off and *why* he drained it."

"I don't know, Your Highness. Maybe Lord Iris might have some ideas," replied Edward.

"All right, I know he should have been here for that, but I just dislike meetings with my grandfather's former staff. His advisors are still traditionalists. Iris looked like he'd swallowed a lemon at the way Wealsman made a comment to me without first being requested to speak; however, you'd better send for him."

"Very good, sir." Edward left the office thinking that Arkyn had revealed more of his character in that brief statement than in the last year of working with him.

* * *

As Iris entered and bowed, Arkyn said, "Morning, my lord. I hope you slept well. I believe you had a short briefing from Edward last night?"

Iris stood straight as a poker. "Yes, Your Highness, for around an hour."

"Then, in comparison to the officers, you received a short briefing. My administrator is extremely concise. Please take a seat. There have been developments this morning…"

As Arkyn explained, Iris' expression went from blank to blank.

When he finished, Arkyn enquired, "What are your thoughts about the situation?"

"I do not see a flaw in Your Highness' handling of it."

"Are such bland replies your normal style, Iris? No, don't bother answering. I know they are. Can we please just get something clear? When I ask for your *opinion,* I would like to hear it – good or bad. We won't get anywhere if you hide advice behind sycophancy."

Iris appeared disconcerted. "Very well, sir. My answer, however, is the same. I cannot fault Your Highness' handling of the situation. You have identified the one major area of concern and have given orders to find out how, not just why, the tax has disappeared. Addressing the problem of tax collection and transportation to see if the loophole can be closed would be wise – though Your Highness has already begun to consider that, from what your administrator mentioned last night."

Arkyn knew when he was being flattered; Iris wasn't telling the whole truth. He held reservations, but maybe not when it came to the missing tax.

"Yes, I have already put my mind to the question of why the tax is going missing and Commander Wynfeld has men going through Roth's papers," admitted Arkyn. "We shall see what they discover. As to closing the loophole, I have requested tax collectors and bailiffs to be available for interview. I am considering having a system whereby the bailiffs or their lords sign off the carts as containing a certain amount of tax at one end; both on dockets or tally sticks and, possibly, by messenger to the scriveners in Tera." He cleared a tickle in this throat. "Then it is counted again on arrival here and the paperwork is matched up. If there is a discrepancy, the overlord of the area is charged with seeing it right."

Iris nodded. "Sir, that is certainly an excellent starting point and is used in other provinces. Has Your Highness considered only having tax collectors? The local bailiff could accompany them; he should know the financial situation of the people in his area. It might stop blatant corruption."

Arkyn smiled – once Iris stopped giving bland answers, he had good ideas. "I like that plan, my lord. I'm certain there have been bribes before."

Iris, who hadn't expected acceptance without discussion, said, "It might also be worth noting that precipitous change might cause discontent—"

"Not if you make it easy for them to change, my lord," replied Arkyn, coughing slightly. "If you make things easy for people, they will accept it. For example, we'll say the changes will be implemented when they move into a new City Assembly building – it gives a clean break with the past."

"Yes, but will it be too much change at once? People like traditions, sir."

Arkyn finished the beaker of water Edward passed him. "I think if we point out it means their tax won't be going missing and they will get work done, people might put up with a lot – as long as it is easy for them."

"That does have some truth, sir, but it will need to be approached carefully. An incentive to change may be an idea."

Arkyn pushed himself to his feet, pacing, trying to think. With long-held tradition, Iris also stood and was displeased when Edward didn't.

Oblivious to the displeasure, Arkyn walked out onto the terrace and down the steps to the lawn.

Iris would have followed if Edward hadn't intervened.

"Please leave him, my lord. He likes to think undisturbed occasionally."

Iris frowned. "Administrator, it is *not* your place to tell the Lords of Oedran what to do. You should also rise when your Prince does."

Edward was grave as he replied, "I never dreamt it was, sir; however, you will allow, it is my place to see that Prince Arkyn is permitted to work in the way he finds best for himself. He did not ask you to accompany him and, therefore, I am requesting that you do not do so. You may, of course, ignore the request. To address your second concern, I remained seated to continue taking notes."

Iris surveyed him shrewdly, but a knock at the door interrupted them.

Wealsman entered. "Lord Simble has arrived, Edward. Lord Roth says he'll get here this afternoon. I was wondering if I might have a word with His Highness."

Edward smiled. "I will check, my lord."

Once alone with Wealsman, Iris observed, "There is something altogether unruly in that man."

"I obviously haven't met as many secretaries as Your Lordship, but I have only found Edward to be respectful and efficient. He is good at his job and takes a lot of strain off Prince Arkyn. I think he does more than His Highness is privy to."

"That is what I mean. A secretary should only do as he is instructed."

Re-entering, Arkyn overheard the last comment. "However, Iris, an *administrator* should be such that you do not need to instruct him to do anything. I am pleased to say I rarely have cause to ask Edward to do anything other than send for people. He fulfils his duties and more with seamless efficiency. The King chose him for the post; if you have any doubts about his appointment, I would suggest you address them either to His Majesty or myself. Other than that, I would be grateful if you would keep your opinions on my staff to yourself. If I have concerns about Edward's conduct, I will raise it with him. Now, Wealsman, I'm informed Simble is here. Would you have the time to stay and hear what he has to say?"

"Gladly, Your Highness. Shall I show him in?"

"Please, my lord."

Whilst Arkyn had been talking, Edward had retrieved two extra chairs, placing them in front of the desk.

Simble entered and bowed rheumatically, leaning on a silver-topped cane.

Arkyn smiled. "Thank you, my lord. Please come and have a seat. I must thank you for taking over at the exchequer. I hope you've not found it too strenuous."

"Not at all, Your Highness. Just like old times. I used to run the place when I was more chipper."

"That explains why Lord Wealsman suggested you take over. Might I introduce Lord Iris of Oedran? He's the King's Deputy Chief Advisor."

Lord Simble smiled a gappy smile. "We've already met, Your Highness. I hope His Majesty was well when you left Oedran, my lord. I remember him doing the job His Highness is now, but then, so must you."

"I do indeed, Simble."

"Aye, I remember when King Altarius also visited. Must be forty-eight year ago now. As I *recall*, I put your nose out of joint with Lady Amara that time."

Arkyn was grinning to himself, half wondering which lord would remember he was there first. He sat down unobtrusively, raising an ironic eyebrow at Edward, who tried and failed to keep a straight face.

Iris said lightly, "I cannot remember whose nose was put out of joint. I merely remember whose I broke."

"Yes, so do I. Shall we have a replay?"

Arkyn caught Wealsman's eye. Both laughed at the same moment.

Arkyn enquired lightly, "My lords, what *would* Lady Amara say to this display now? Thinking about it, what did she say at the time?"

Simble replied, "Oh, she said she was flattered, but we could go on fighting till the moons had set and it wouldn't make the slightest difference. She had already set her heart on another, but she did have a dance with me. She was beautiful in her youth was Princess Amara."

"She's beautiful now," murmured Iris unthinkingly.

Arkyn nodded; it did sound like his great-aunt: how to end an argument easily and quickly – tell the contenders neither of them had a hope.

He pretended not to have heard Iris. "I half wish I could have seen that, my lord; however, shall we get on with the matter in hand? Wealsman, maybe you would care to sit in the middle."

Simble regarded the Prince with candid green eyes bright with mischief. They soon became solemn as he stated his findings. "Sir, I don't think you're going to like much of this. We've worked out that there has been a drain on the taxes approximately equivalent to five per cent over the entire twelve years since the last review. That, though, is the average or mean. The mode was around fifteen per cent two years ago. Some fleecing is expected, but I am mystified why the scriveners weren't concerned. Actually, I think some were, but no-one listened. Alcis only knows what Rahat thought he was doing. His department is a complete shambles. Even with the deputies missing in action – normally a blessing – it took me a day to find anyone who knew what was happening. Most were trundling along without a thought for the rest of the process. He'd weeded out anyone with a real brain who couldn't hide it. I've got scriveners examining the figures but it can't be denied that there have been thousands of darl a year disappear unheeded. As for the late Roth, I can only say I'm glad he's late – 'cause if he weren't he soon would be. I'm ashamed of my country, Your Highness. The whole fiasco…"

Arkyn let him continue for six more minutes before interrupting. "How long will it take for you to get the paperwork in order?"

"I reckons about an aluna-month, sir," confessed Simble. "Might just do it in a cisluna, but that week might make the difference. Certainly can't do it in less without more scriveners. Doesn't help we're on two sites, the length of the city apart."

"No, I accept that. Wealsman, is it possible to find help from elsewhere?"

"I'll see what can be done, sir; however, I think it would be best for Lord Simble to assume that there won't be any."

Arkyn glanced at Iris. "Anything to say, my lord?"

Still stinging from the dressing down he'd received over Edward and the reminder of an incident almost fifty years old, Iris said, "Only that Your Highness' requests should be met."

Arkyn let Wealsman and Simble see him sigh. "Lord Iris, this province is working without a governor, deputy governor or assistant deputy governor, without a head for the exchequer and without the two deputies as well. It is also an overlord down and Wealsman and Simble are trying to fill all those jobs. I am sure that if it's available, Lord Wealsman will find the help. I prefer the honest answer that there might not be to broken promises. Maybe you and Lord Simble could put incidents of the past aside and work together to get the exchequer up to scratch before the team arrives?"

Surprising himself at the way the diatribe came out, Arkyn inwardly blamed it on the heat of the room and his headache, but knew he'd have to apologise to Iris eventually.

Iris pursed his lips. "Very well, sir. I will try to get the exchequer up to scratch."

Arkyn looked him straight in the eye. "I'm sure Lord Simble will be glad of any *help* you can offer, my lord. For now, thank you. It might be better if you worked out a plan without me interfering."

Iris and Simble left with contrasting thoughts on the Prince's actions.

* * *

Once he had heard their footsteps retreat, Arkyn turned to his administrator saying, "I *don't* have a problem with the way you work, Edward. I couldn't ask for a better administrator. Lord Iris can accept that or return to Oedran."

Disconcerted, Edward said, "Thank you, Your Highness. His Lordship is one of the old school."

"Yes. I think he just proved that." Arkyn jerked his head at Edward and the administrator left. "Wealsman, you would tell me if you thought some of my decisions weren't in the best interests of Terasia, wouldn't you?"

"Of course I would, Your Highness, though hopefully diplomatically. So-called 'yes men' aren't of help to anyone."

"No, I know. Iris might be said to be one. Once you get past it, though, he does give good advice. I just can't handle him well currently."

"The only thing I think you might have done that wasn't the best idea, sir, was pulling him up for perceived faults with others present – although the criticism of Edward *was* unfounded… Sir, are you feeling quite well?" he enquired, noticing strain lines on the Prince's face.

"A trifling headache, my lord. I'm fine."

"Shall I leave you in peace?"

* * *

Once outside, Wealsman ignored the official waiting for an interview and drew Edward to one side. "I think His Highness is ill. Would you suggest I send for Artzman?"

Edward's eyes flicked fleetingly to the office door. "If you really think that, then yes, my lord. How did you notice? His Highness hides things well."

"He's admitted to a *trifling* headache and there is sweat plastered across his brow, but the room is quite cool."

"Get the doctor to his rooms. I'll try to get His Highness there. Stuart…" When the secretary reached them, Edward murmured, "Send to Kadeem. It seems His Highness is unwell, though do it discreetly please."

Stuart wrote out a brief note, biting back the comment that he didn't need to be told to be discreet. Edward and Wealsman parted company, and the administrator entered the office. He found Arkyn with his head on his arms.

Quietly he said, "Sir, I think it would be better if we cancel this morning's interview."

"Edward, I am perfectly all right."

Risking everything, Edward observed, "No, Your Highness, you're not. I've never known you admit to a headache. There's sweat across your forehead and you're shaking. You're finding the light hard going and you've been blunter than I ever remember you being before today. You're not fit enough to be working this morning, sir."

Dumbfounded by Edward's speech, Arkyn took a moment to reply; when he did, it was with the assured authority he had found since arriving in Tera. "Edward, if I say I'm all right, then I am!"

Edward took a breath to reply, but there was a knock at the door and Kadeem, who'd been in the entrance hall, entered. His gaze took in the scene. He jerked his head at Edward. The administrator left and the first thing he did when he got outside was to tell the official that he wouldn't be needed immediately.

Inside the office, Kadeem said, "Sir, you are not well."

Arkyn lost all patience. "Kadeem, I am perfectly fine!"

Kadeem shook his head. "Your Highness, I wouldn't be doing my duty if I accepted that. You've been tiring quickly, you're not eating and are appearing drawn. Please talk to Artzman. Lord Wealsman is concerned and so are Edward and myself. We would just like to make sure."

Arkyn sighed; he didn't have the energy to argue. "Very well, but I don't want to be put in this position again. Is that clear?"

"Crystal, Your Highness. Thank you."

Arkyn merely nodded and Kadeem held the door open. Edward glanced in concern at a grim Kadeem. All three made their way to Arkyn's chambers. They found Wealsman in the antechamber talking to Artzman.

Arkyn greeted them with resignation and continued with Kadeem and the doctor into his sitting room.

"His Highness doesn't look too happy," observed Wealsman to Edward.

"No. I don't know what Kadeem said to him, but I'm sure we're in line for a dressing down soon."

"Me included – when he discovers I sent for Artzman."

"Let myself and Kadeem take the rap for that, my lord."

"No, Edward, that would be highly unfair," chided Wealsman.

They waited in silence for about twelve minutes until Kadeem came to say the prince wanted to speak to them. They entered his bedchamber as Artzman left.

Tucked up in bed, Arkyn glanced over at their entry.

Wealsman pre-empted him. "Your Highness, please don't blame your household for this. I sent for Artzman and alerted them to the fact you weren't well."

Arkyn said tiredly, "I know, my lord, and, through my stubbornness, I wouldn't admit I was ill. There's too much to do, you see."

"I know, sir. I'm sure we can muddle through. Don't worry about the review. Lord Iris will cope."

Arkyn gave the slightest of nods. "Edward, I have flu. Alcis only knows how I picked it up, but you'll have to work with Lord Iris for a bit… I'd like a word with Lord Wealsman alone." (Both members of his household left.) "Thank you, Wealsman. I am feeling quite rough. I just thought I'd overdone it. Hopefully, I won't be laid up for too long, but let Iris know that if he hinders my administrator, I won't be happy. Can you also apologise to His Lordship for my manner this morning? I am feeling bad about it."

"Your Highness, I'm sure His Lordship will understand. Now, get some rest." Without waiting to be dismissed, Wealsman left. He found Kadeem outside. "I'll inform His Majesty."

"Thank you, my lord, but I should do that."

"I know, but I could do with a word with King Adeone anyway regarding the review."

PART 2

Chapter 20
WEALSMAN
Late Morning
Margrave's Office

WEALSMAN RETURNED to his office and called Magucan, his black griffin messenger. He obtained a link with the King.

Adeone said spritely, "Percival! How are you? Is my son behaving himself better than I did?"

Wealsman had used considerable artifice, helped by a magical spirit, to make people forget that he and the King had been companions during the last review. The picture he'd commissioned a true artist to paint, of the last evening of Adeone's visit, had stayed in a private room at his manor, where none realised its importance.

"Other than not admitting he was ill… I'm afraid Prince Arkyn has a touch of flu, Your Majesty."

Adeone sobered, considering his friend. "Is it serious?"

"We don't think so. Doctor Artzman has seen him. It took his household quite a bit of determination to get that far. Edward and Kadeem are both expecting a roasting when His Highness is feeling up to it."

"They'll not get one from me. I appointed them for their sense. Should I come down to Terasia?"

"Much as I think he'd be pleased to see you, sir, I don't think it is that serious. Mind you, it might be fun to see some people's reaction to the idea."

Adeone snorted. "You always did have a twisted sense of humour, my friend."

"I try, Sire, I do try. Oh, your hunch about our tax was correct – up to fifteen per cent embezzled in one year alone. On individual budgets, slick accountancy could have hidden it by rounding figures, then rounding percentages."

"Yes, I have a feeling it isn't only Terasia," stated Adeone. "Portur alerted me last year; I think he began to seriously consider why the City Assembly hadn't been built. He knew I'd want answers."

"Did you tell Prince Arkyn any of the suspicions?" enquired Wealsman with narrowed eyes.

"No, I wanted to see how far he would get on his own. If he hadn't found the trail, I would have pointed him in the right direction eventually. How are you coping with him?"

"Well, but he still doesn't know I know you any better than any other minor lord. His sense of humour is less controversial than yours, but his perspicacity definitely comes from you."

"Flatterer."

"Surely, sir, you like hearing plaudits?" said Wealsman, openly grinning.

Adeone's face matched his. "Only if they're plausible. We do, however, have a problem: with Arkyn ill, the review must wait."

"Actually, I've been thinking; Prince Arkyn was getting close to finishing the initial interviews and Edward has all the notes from those. He knows His Highness well enough to know what was going through his mind. If he briefs Lord Iris fully, then His Lordship could continue with the interviews. By which time the team from Oedran will have arrived. They'll have more time to do a thorough investigation. By the time His Highness is recovering, they should have the majority of reports ready. He can then read them and start to make decisions."

"I don't want him overdoing things when he's recovering, Wealsman!" snapped Adeone.

"I'm sure we can control his workload, Sire. He can't travel easily in winter, especially after an illness, and the review will take the whole of the autumn; the scale of the exchequer problems alone is tantamount to that. He can recover, undertake the review at an easy pace and travel north during the spring."

Adeone considered briefly before saying, "I'll agree to Iris finishing the initial process and overseeing the investigations. Nevertheless, I want my son to make the decisions but, Percival, I am relying on *you* to see he doesn't overdo things – keep an eye on him."

"Don't worry. I will. I promise you that."

"Good. I'll inform Iris he has extra responsibilities."

* * *

Once the link had broken, Wealsman sat thinking. Arkyn's illness was an unfortunate complication during a troublesome visit. He rose and, telling Thomkins if anyone started asking for him, they'd have to wait, walked through the Residence to visit Lady Portur. When she heard that Arkyn was ill, she immediately became concerned, talking over what might be needed.

Laughing, he said, "Kristina, he has plenty of people looking out for him. I doubt he'll want for anything. He'll sleep the next few days away. The doctor is perfectly capable."

She sighed. "I know, Percival, but I can't help myself. What did the King say? And don't prevaricate. *I* know you know him better than you let on."

"He's worried, but hiding it well. I've said we'll take care of the Prince until the spring. He shouldn't ride north in winter after flu."

"No, he shouldn't. Percival, have you ever thought about who will be the next Margrave?"

"Briefly, but I've been too busy to give it serious consideration. I can only think it will be Silvano or Stator; they're the highest in precedence."

"Yes, but… Can you see either of them doing a decent day's work?"

Chuckling, Wealsman said, "Probably not. They'd have to learn though. Lord Portur did work hard. It'll be strange to have a new Margrave after eighteen years."

"Yes. I'll miss him."

"Did you love him?" enquired Wealsman before he could stop himself.

She looked at him, bemused. "No, not love as such. He was company. I don't think there have been many people in my life who I have truly loved."

"I know what you mean. I loved a lady once, but her father refused me permission to marry her. I never stopped loving her."

"I didn't know you'd ever considered marriage. Who is she?"

"I might tell you one day," answered Wealsman sadly.

"No time like the present," she teased.

"Ah, but I don't think this would be a nicely wrapped present. One day I'll tell you." Sensing her interest being roused, he changed the subject – there were too many vivid memories he didn't want to awaken. "So, what are you going to do now you're a widow again?"

She hesitated. "Hopefully *not* return home, but I'm not with child, so the estate reverts to the FitzAlcis. I don't know if I'll be able to stay on it or not. I've got to clarify the situation soon. It's a shame His Highness is unwell. He promised he'd speak to me about it. I'll have to move out of the Residence after he appoints the new Margrave."

"I can always talk to the King," offered Wealsman instinctively.

"No, I couldn't ask you to do that; he has more to worry about."

"Why? One, you didn't ask. Two, it is his business. He wouldn't want you to worry if he can allay your concerns. Three, you really ought not to return home. Your first husband's family are a bunch of harridans and ghouls who never wanted you to marry in, so pushed you out. Lord Portur had no family. In marrying him, you became his next of kin. His estates might be subject to the King's whim, but you will get an annuity. His Majesty isn't such that he would refuse you that, and he will respect your rights."

Standing by the windows, Lady Portur was hugging herself.

Wealsman walked over to her. "Kristina, I'm *not* going to let you worry about all this. There is, after all, a simple way of sorting it: I talk to Adeone."

"Would you really?"

Wealsman chuckled. "Of course. There's nothing I like more than talking to the King. Next time Dragoris appears, I'll speak with Adeone about it. I promise. What's the worst we can do?"

She laughed. A crisp, clear sound that tugged at long-held memories for Wealsman. Absentmindedly, he reached out and put a loose strand of hair behind her ear. She stopped laughing, but her eyes were still alight with fun when she enquired,

"Who is she, Percival?"

He looked at her, bewildered. "You need to ask?" Seeing she still didn't realise he gave up all pretence. "*You* are the only lady I've ever loved." He studied her face. Her eyes registered shock before she whispered,

"Me? Why on Erinna would you love me?"

"Oh, I don't know. Maybe it's the fact you're not only beautiful in face but in mind as well. Maybe it's because you tease me, maybe it's even because I'm a fool. How can I love someone who I've known all my life? Who accepts me for who I am and can see straight into my very soul? Kristina, I've always loved you since I understood what love was. I can't explain it. I might have been able to fourteen years ago when I approached your father, but now all I know is that I love you with every fibre of my being. Maybe it's even the fact that I never want to lie to you."

Before she could stop herself, she said, "You've managed it well enough for the last few years."

"I didn't lie. I couldn't tell you. If you reciprocated my feelings, we were in a hopeless position. We couldn't marry. Your father would never give his permission."

"Who says we'd have asked him? I wish I'd known. I've fooled myself you never cared for me like that for so long and only accepted the other marriages because I thought you saw me as a friend… I'd have…"

She got no further before she found Wealsman had tentatively and instinctively drawn closer to her. What followed set the record straight. When Wealsman reluctantly released her, he said,

"*Now* will you stop worrying about the future?"

"Are you planning to ask anyone's permission *this time*?"

"Yes, one man's and I can't see *him* saying no. With the advantage that no-one will dare argue with him."

"You *can't* ask the King!" she exclaimed, horrified.

"Why not? Technically, you're under his protectorship."

"Yes, but, even so, that *is* a technicality. My marriage agreement—"

A discreet knock on the door preceded Lady Portur's maid entering. "Lord Hale is here, my lady."

"He didn't take long," muttered Wealsman.

He glanced at Kristina and then nodded to the maid, who stood to one side as Lady Portur's father entered.

"Well, Kristina, when are you coming home? I'll have to find another husband for you, I suppose. Will you ever breed?"

Wealsman's hackles rose. "I'd have thought a bit of understanding would be better, Hale! Your daughter has suffered a bereavement."

Lord Hale sneered. "I should have known I'd find you here."

"Yes, in my capacity as Acting Governor of Terasia at His Highness' appointment."

"What does His Highness think about you visiting my daughter in the middle of a busy day?"

"If he hadn't just been taken ill, I would suggest you ask him. I was informing Her Ladyship, as his hostess, what was occurring under her roof. I must also inform Your Lordship that, due to the high number of people staying here because of the review, there is no room for you and your attendants at the Residence."

Sneeringly, Hale said, "I would have thought that was up to the hostess."

Lady Portur tried to diffuse the situation. "I'm afraid, father, the hostess' view is also the same. Lord Iris arrived last night. He has the final guest chambers. Everyone else has been billeted out – including Lord Iris' grandson; however, I will send for refreshments at least."

Wealsman said, "Lord Hale, you were right: it is a busy day. I must leave you to a reunion with your daughter. Lady Portur, I hope I shall see you later." As the door closed behind him, he heard Hale say,

"You won't be able to stay here. That only leaves you the possibility of coming home again. I'm only thinking of your best interests…"

* * *

Walking through the Residence from Lady Portur's rooms to the ground floor office set aside for Lord Iris, Wealsman was suddenly aware of the constant hum of conversation within the Residence. It wasn't loud, but there were waves within the sound that crashed upon his consciousness as he descended the stairs. Sound from the entrance hall carried more than that from elsewhere. He made a mental note to ask staff to keep conversations low during the Prince's incapacitation. Crossing the entrance hall to the office that had originally been set aside for Arkyn, he smiled at Iris' secretary before entering what was now Iris' office.

"Has His Majesty spoken to you yet, my lord?"

"Yes," replied Iris tartly. "His Majesty isn't planning to declare another King's Representative in Terasia currently and is willing to trust Your Lordship with signing important and sensitive documents. I do hope you won't prove his trust misplaced…"

Wealsman was thinking, *'If you only knew; how I hope I can see your face when you find out.'*

"…So it seems you'll be responsible for Terasia as though you were Margrave. Be mindful that you'll be handing over the responsibility. I shall be keeping His Majesty informed of developments here, whatever they may be. This is His Highness' first official posting, but it is not mine. I hope you bear that in mind."

"His Majesty is astute, my lord, and His Highness has inherited those qualities, I'm sure. You may rest assured that I shall care for Terasia as though it were my own country. Maybe we should *both* make sure we have reports to give the King. Much as I enjoy being demeaned by an acquaintance of such short standing, there is work to do."

Iris opened his mouth to say something.

Wealsman pre-empted him. "My lord, you are concerned for His Highness and that may have made you forget yourself; I can appreciate and understand that, but, please remember, Lord Iris, you are a guest in this province."

"Is that a threat, Wealsman?" demanded Iris.

"No. It is a request that you remember a fact. Honestly, I do not threaten you; I have a wish to stop this situation becoming acrimonious for both our sakes. We both serve the FitzAlcis; there is no point in a power struggle between us. I shall attend to Terasia and make sure you receive whatever support you require for the review, in line with His Majesty's instructions. The King has spoken highly of you to me and I hope to see more of the courteous side I witnessed with your arrival."

Iris pursed his lips. "I'm sorry, Lord Wealsman. I am, as you have realised, concerned for His Highness."

"So are we all. Talking of the Prince, I have some messages for you. Firstly, if you hinder Administrator Edward's endeavours, His Highness won't be happy. Secondly, he apologises unreservedly for his manner this morning."

Iris snorted. "I doubt, with regards to his administrator, I'd be successful if I tried. Edward was trained by the King's Administrator. The FitzAlcis obviously approve of the methods; therefore, I cannot comment further."

"Quite, my lord. I should leave you to continue. You have much to catch up on before restarting the interviews."

Iris sighed, all anger gone. "Thank you. I'm sorry for my earlier words; they were unfoundedly sharp."

Wealsman regarded him, seeing in the depths of his eyes a deep-seated anxiety that he was sure wasn't just for the current events. "It is of no matter, Lord Iris. It is a stressful time."

Seeing understanding in Wealsman's eyes and hearing the truth that the words *were* disregarded, Iris felt comfortable confiding, "On top of all this, the nearfather of my children is dying."

"Didn't you request to stay in Oedran?" enquired Wealsman.

"No. His Majesty wished me to be with the Prince. I am an advisor, a Lord of Oedran and an official of the FitzAlcis. My private affairs are for the times they don't need my services."

* * *

Wealsman returned to his office, thinking hard. Everything that had just occurred began to niggle at him. As no-one was waiting to see him, he obtained another link with Adeone.

"Twice in one day, Percival? I am honoured."

"I'm sorry, Sire. I've just spoken with Kristina – Lady Portur—"

"Portur married *Kristina*? He told me it was the widow of a merchant who was rather shy, so I never talked with her."

"Her first husband was Merchant Crabson. She was about to marry him when Your Majesty was here. The 'shy' bit I'll try and reconcile somehow. I'm not sure that's her."

"In *twelve years,* is it unreasonable that I've forgotten whom she was marrying? We don't all have your excellent memory," grouched Adeone.

"Sorry. She's worried about the future and doesn't want to return home, sir. I've told her she won't have to, but Hale has arrived and the first thing he started saying was he'd have to find another husband for her. It made me so *mad*. It didn't help that I'd just told her I loved her and always have done but, even so, she is worried enough about what will happen, without Hale getting in the way."

Adeone had let out a snort of disgust. "Tell your Kristina that she can continue to live as Lady Portur for as long as she wants. I will talk to the Portur steward and let it be known that I consider her as the chatelaine of the lands and he is certainly *not* to accept anyone else as such without my say so. Hale can go and bury his head in the sand of Denshire. I'm not having Her Ladyship distressed." Adeone's eyes twinkled merrily. "Just out of interest, what *was* her reaction to the news you've always loved her?"

"A berating for not telling her sooner."

"But it only took you about *twelve years,*" teased Adeone.

"More like nineteen, sir. It took me five to ask her father permission to marry her, which he then refused."

Adeone regarded him seriously. "Do you still want to marry her?"

"It doesn't matter if I do, sir; it's as hopeless now as ever before—"

Adeone smiled. "Lady Portur is the widow of an overlord and under my protection. If I believe her situation damages that standing then—"

"You're not going to become *traditional*, are you? After all Lord Landis has done."

"In this case, maybe I am – just don't tell him. Percival, her situation means I can override her last marriage agreement. That means that her father has no say and I don't care two hoots of a deaf owl if you marry her – as long as she wants to marry you without coercion, that is. Do you want me to have a word with Lady Portur and Lord Hale?"

Wealsman thought for a moment. "Could you make it seem like we hadn't spoken, sir? Kristina can be rather perceptive when it comes to my machinations."

Adeone nodded. "I'll add it to the list of highly important things to do, shall I? Alongside surviving assassination attempts."

"Hopefully, the example you gave will be higher on your list, sir."

"Maybe. Now, what else are you bothered about? Don't try to deny it. I can read you like a book!" Seeing Wealsman's face, he added, "Don't prevaricate either. I *can* be discreet."

Defeated, Wealsman said, "It's just one thing… Lord Iris seemed, understandably, preoccupied that the nearfather of his children is dying. I got the feeling Iris wishes he was with him."

Adeone swore. "Why didn't he or Rale say anything to me? Alcis, sometimes I wish they'd just bloody well tell me what they're thinking. There's no way I can recall Iris now. He'd be mortified that you've told me and that I even know he wishes he could be elsewhere… Other than the fact this is you, and you worm confidences out of people before they realise anything amiss, how did you come to be talking about it?"

Wealsman hesitated. "Does it matter, sir?"

"He was rude, wasn't he?"

"You know there are times, Your Majesty, when I wish you weren't so perceptive. He has apologised."

"Anything else?" asked Adeone sceptically. "Bearing in mind I know Iris well and, before you think of saying 'no', you made the last statement formal."

"I knew there was a reason not to be friends with a king; he pulls rank at every opportunity."

"Get on with it."

"He seemed troubled that you'd handed me complete responsibility for Terasia. I believe he couldn't understand how you could trust me."

Adeone's lips twitched. "I often wonder myself. Would it make your life easier if I told him?"

"I don't know, sir. I don't know how obstructive he plans to be. Truth be told, I'd rather no whisper escaped here. If Lord Iris changes his manner towards me there'll be only one reason possible in many people's eyes – as technically, other than the Prince, he's the highest person in the province. The joys of self-serving politics – where would the lords be without them?"

"Now, now, Percival, you're sounding cynical." Adeone continued forthrightly, "Very well, but if Iris gets too officious, I'll take steps. There're more people than you reporting to me from Tera. Commander

Wynfeld for a start, and he knows Iris far better than you do. I wouldn't worry too much, though. Iris will be acidic in private until you've proved yourself, but he'll be polite in public, especially as Arkyn appointed you. He *is* a fantastic advisor but he is of my father's generation: never say anything to the FitzAlcis without first knowing if it's what we want to hear. I sent him with Arkyn to teach him, Iris, different methods. My son, for all he's young, says what he thinks and not having worked with his grandfather is less accommodating to the practices my father thought best. When he's feeling better, you'll be in for an interesting time."

"I think I'm already living it, sir. I like the Prince. He's someone who knows what he wants. Rather like his father."

Adeone laughed. "Your compliments are something I anticipate."

"Who said it was a compliment?"

Adeone shook his head. "Tradition? Take care of my son for me."

Being asked the same thing twice in one day showed Wealsman just how worried his friend was. "Adeone, *that* is *never* in question. I know it's foolish to say this but *don't fret*. Arkyn will be fine. From everything you've ever told me, he's a strong lad. He'll shake this off."

"I hope so. When the review is over, come and visit Oedran. Come here for an extended honeymoon. I suppose I'd better get on with reading some thrilling reports. If it wouldn't give too much away, I'd say tell Wynfeld I'm missing his."

* * *

A couple of hours later, Kristina walked into Wealsman's office. Smoothing her skirts out under her, she sat opposite him, folding her hands demurely in her lap. Her pleasant, mellifluous voice put him straight on the spot.

"I thought your words were, '*When* Dragoris next appears'. Obviously, my interpretation was incorrect, or do I have the situation wrong and it's all a coincidence?"

He blushed. "Ah, erm, I've er… All right, I spoke to the King and instigated the discussion—"

"Percival Wealsman, how long has *he* known you love me?"

"Since the last review," confessed Wealsman sheepishly. "He caught me watching you dance. Kristina, *will* you marry me?"

"You certainly know how to pick the surroundings in which to ask the question. Of course I will. After all, better you than someone my father picks."

Wealsman laughed. "And you accept with all the grace you've always managed. Didn't His Majesty tell you that your father no longer had a say?"

"Yes. He also mentioned he thought a spring wedding would be nice because you're a blooming nuisance. I couldn't disagree. He hopes we'll be happy after so long waiting. As soon as the link broke, father had a request and came out of it very disgruntled. He left soon after."

Both relaxed in their chairs, grinning at each other. They had the King's blessing, everything else was mere detail.

Chapter 21
THREATS AGAIN

Afternoon

Palace of Oedran – Inner Office

IN OEDRAN, Adeone broke the link with Lord Hale, part of him wanting to enjoy the thought of Wealsman getting married, but the other, larger, part of him was too worried about Arkyn's welfare. Having been brooding for too long that day, he rang the bell for his administrator.

"Prince Arkyn is ill, Richardson. Some sort of flu. I'll need to talk to Chapa. The Terasian doctor seems competent enough but, given events there, I'd like an opinion from someone I trust. I've given Lord Iris more responsibility for collating information; however, I want no word to reach his ears that I consider Wealsman a friend. Nothing. I want to see what happens in Terasia with the loss of those in power. I've not declared another Representative and I don't mean to. Let's see who is abysmally foolish enough to play politics. Arkyn won't stand much scheming. On that note, should anyone contact you about leaving Tera, the answer is still no. I'll make that clear to Iris and Wealsman as well. I want whatever poison the Justiciar instilled in that province to work its way out..."

Once in the Outer Office, Richardson put down his note tablet, staring into space for a couple of moments; the King's frankness had been unusual and revealing.

The King's secretaries, Kenton and Jacobs, glanced over. It was rare for Richardson not to exit from the Inner Office and immediately start on whatever the King had requested.

"Got nothing to do?" enquired Richardson.

"Enough, sir," answered Kenton. "Is everything all right? The King's reorganised his day and there's an atmosphere forming that seems to suggest it isn't."

Richardson regarded the junior of the secretaries and thought, not for the first time, that Kenton might only be in his thirties, but he had the cheek of a sixty-year-old.

"Get on with your work. I'm sure you'll find out soon enough."

Kenton smirked to himself. He'd been right. Something was happening.

Jacobs bridled. Didn't Kenton understand the proprieties of being a secretary in the Outer Office yet? Why did he get away with such questions? He watched unobtrusively as Richardson rose once more and knocked on the door to the Inner Office.

Seeing Richardson's pensive mood, Adeone crooked an eyebrow.

"A small thing, sir. Kenton just asked what's happening. Do you want me to tell them?"

"Why haven't you already? Are you worried about their discretion?"

"I might be speaking out of turn, sir, but there are a couple of times I've noticed friction. It's not that I distrust either of them but... I'm being cautious and getting Captain Beaver to keep an eye on them. I get the feeling something isn't right. I do trust them to abide by your orders though."

"I must say, this isn't like you."

Richardson hesitated. "Maybe I'm getting overly cautious, Sire."

"Maybe. Or maybe my unease at the situation in Terasia is infectious. Get them in here. I'll tell them and save you a dilemma. Just one thing... Thank you for your caution. It's better than being rash."

When his secretaries were facing him, Adeone said, "I believe you've been asking what is occurring—"

"Kenton has," groused Jacobs before considering his words or manner.

Noting the King's silence and eye-flick, Richardson snapped, "I don't believe His Majesty wanted clarification, Jacobs! Wait outside!"

Once the secretary had left, Adeone looked at his administrator. "Get it sorted."

Richardson bowed and left. The King was a tolerant man but once his tolerance snapped, he wouldn't be forgiving.

Alone in front of Adeone, Kenton bore up well to the King's scrutiny.

"Why were you enquiring?"

"Something seemed to be troubling Administrator Richardson, Your Majesty. He told me I'd find out soon enough and I was content."

"Would you normally ask?"

After a moment's thought, Kenton said, "After a few incidents in a short space of time, sir. There's something in the wind today. I thought it might be something we would need to know about, and Administrator Richardson might not know how to explain. I thought I'd offer an opening."

"I'm sure, deep down, Richardson appreciates your vigilance, Kenton, but he'll tell you if he needs to. There might be many reasons for keeping silent on a matter. Today is one of those days where we must solve problems first. I am trusting your discretion to keep them private if I tell you what is occurring. Do I have your word?"

"Yes, sir, but if you'd rather I didn't know, I shan't complain."

Adeone smiled. "Your word is enough for me. Prince Arkyn has flu and will be incapacitated for some time. I'm sure you can appreciate the complications this creates for the review."

Kenton's honest care seeped into his words. "Yes, Sire. If there's anything I can do— That is, I hope His Highness recovers swiftly."

"You and me both—"

There was a knock and Richardson re-entered, looking grim. Adeone, seeing it, dismissed Kenton. The junior secretary left more diplomatically than Richardson expected.

Adeone regarded his administrator. "I see what you mean. There's friction there, right enough. How long have they been secretaries?"

"Kenton three years, Jacobs eight, sir," replied Richardson. "I've given Jacobs the roasting of the year. If he doesn't mend his tone then, when I've found someone to replace him and with Your Majesty's agreement, he'll find himself on borrowed time."

Adeone absorbed that. "I trust your management of them and, of the two, I'd prefer to keep Kenton on – there's a spark in his eyes which I like – but if Jacobs reverts to his old self, all well and good."

Richardson relaxed, said, "Very good, sir," and opened the door to leave. He sidestepped as Landis entered.

"You get better every day, Richardson. Premonition is a hard skill to master."

"It saves me the trouble of announcing Your Lordship."

The door closed as Adeone was chuckling at the irony. Landis hardly ever waited to be announced.

Landis wasn't fooled by the laughter. "What's happened, Sire? Your Outer Office has an atmosphere I could stab with my dagger."

"Oh, Jacobs and Kenton have found the meaning of the word rivalry," replied Adeone dismissively, "and your elder nearson has an attack of flu."

"When was he taken ill?" asked Landis gravely.

"This morning. I've given Iris more power, but not as a King's Representative. I've also handed Percival more power as well—"

"Forget the politics. Have you spoken with Arkyn?"

"Yes. Come on, let's go for a sit down and I'll explain everything that's happened…"

* * *

That evening Adeone returned to his chambers after visiting Prince Tain at Ceardlann, yawned and put down a few papers relating to the Rex

Dallin on his desk. He should read them immediately, but he tomorrow was soon enough. Exhausted, he fumbled, sending a pile of blank paper slipping, slithering and wafting over the floor. Cursing, he knelt to pick it all up. He reached to retrieve a stray piece of folded paper under his desk and, half recognising what it was likely to be, reluctantly unfolded it:

The sun's absence makes the stars bright.

A fire erupted in his head at the veiled threat aimed at Arkyn and Tain, though, of those two, he knew it threatened Arkyn more. Before he'd left for Ceardlann, he'd instructed Landis to inform the Court of Arkyn's illness. He cursed. It might be harder to find the perpetrator of the notes. What was more, they were phrased as observations on the world, not direct threats. He couldn't arrest anyone for them, not yet.

Frustrated, even through his befuddled mind, he realised he had a larger problem. His office was almost the most private room he had. It was difficult to enter unobserved – impossible even – for anyone not of his official retinue; therefore, to mention the notes to any of them meant possibly mentioning it to the perpetrator. Not a viable option. Momentarily, he wished he hadn't posted Wynfeld so far south. He needed the commander's discretion. Landis would tell him to chuck the notes on the fire and ignore them. Yet, a few months ago, he'd been listening to similar advice when Gad slashed him across the chest. No. This time he'd follow his instinct, which was not to tell anyone *yet*. He could, however, take steps that would mean that Arkyn was safer.

Ignoring the lateness of the hour, he contacted the commander.

Unfazed by the messenger link, Wynfeld said, "Good evening, Sire. I hope you're well."

"Evening, Commander. Well enough. How's your Prince?"

"Apparently sleeping, sir. The fever's taking hold, but the doctor's on permanent call."

"I can imagine he is," remarked Adeone dryly. "Thank you. See he's paid well for his trouble; should mean he's less negligent. I need you to do something for me. There's been an oblique threat made against His Highness' life. I don't want him left alone at all, but I only want a handful of people with him."

Wynfeld stilled. "Very good, sir. Who?"

"You, Fitz, Kadeem, Lord Wealsman, maybe Lord Irvin and Lady Portur. If possible, however, just you, Fitz, Kadeem and Lord Wealsman."

"Understood. Kadeem was planning on being in the room during the night. May I clarify something, sir?"

Adeone nodded, correctly guessing what was coming.

"Thank you. Is Your Majesty sure of Lord Wealsman's loyalty?"

Adeone considered. If anyone in Terasia needed to understand the full situation, it was Wynfeld – especially with the latest events. "Lord Percival Wealsman, Commander, is as good a friend to me as Lord Landis. He is also one of the best spies I have in Tera, so I'd be glad if you didn't reveal our relationship to anyone. If he'd come and live in Oedran, he'd be one of my Defenders."

Instead of panicking, as most men would have done finding out they'd questioned the King's judgement of his friends, Wynfeld said, "Thank you for the confidence, Sire. Is this why His Highness made Lord Wealsman Acting Governor? It raised some eyebrows."

"It *was* a co-incidence, although I'm hardly upset about it. One last thing, I've split responsibility between Iris and Wealsman. Of the two, listen to Wealsman when it comes to Prince Arkyn's safety and liaise with Fitz. The old rogue knows Wealsman and I are friends, but don't talk to him about it in case you're overheard. I want Fitz making sure no-one unauthorised gets to see the Prince. Oh, if Lady Daia is still in Tera, she can see His Highness, though, ideally, only when he is recovering. He'll need some company and, knowing his age, I don't fool myself that he'll only want male company. Now, I'd better let you get back to your evening relaxing, if you've permitted yourself one."

"You know me, sir."

Adeone snorted. "Yes. So, here's a direct order for you: stop working, get yourself a drink and put your feet up. Tomorrow is another day."

Wynfeld laughed. "Thank you, sir. That's the kind of order I like receiving. I shall do my best. I hope, however, Your Majesty plans to follow the same idea."

Adeone sighed. "I'm straight for my bed. I've been at Ceardlann – Prince Tain has more energy than is seemly in an eleven-year-old."

Chapter 22
A DIFFERENT MORNING
Hexadai, Week 16 – 27th Macial, 6th Easis 1211
Margrave's Residence

WYNFELD ROSE EARLY the following day. He'd obeyed his King but, by idling, his mind had puzzled over the threat originating in Oedran. His King wasn't telling him everything; that was his prerogative, but it niggled. Why would anyone threaten Prince Arkyn at such a distance unless it was to unsettle King Adeone? Was there a connection to the note Edward had found? Leaving a senior captain temporarily in charge of the fort and the morning parades, he made his way to the Residence and the servants' area of Prince Arkyn's rooms.

"Thomas, is Master Kadeem available for a quick word?"

A couple of moments later, slightly bleary-eyed, Kadeem entered and smiled at Wynfeld. "Morning, Commander. Thomas, check Stuart and Alan aren't making too much noise in His Highness' sitting room." When they were alone, Kadeem continued, "What can I do for you, Wynfeld?"

"I should have come last night, but no matter. Our King was in contact with me. He doesn't want our Prince left alone and was specific as to who could sit with His Highness…" Wynfeld gave the list and, as he had, Kadeem frowned at the mention of Wealsman.

"I assume His Majesty is satisfied that Lord Wealsman is loyal."

"Presumably. He was definite about it. We know Lord Wealsman's discreet and at least one lord from Terasia has been trusted."

"True and of all of them, I think, His Highness would prefer to wake up and see Lord Wealsman's face than say, Lord Silvano's," admitted Kadeem, yawning.

"Come again, Kadeem?"

"Lord Silvano annoyed His Highness at the introductions. The Prince isn't prone to grudges but first impressions matter. I'd put Stator's chances slightly higher for the governorship after that."

"Good. Lord Silvano and Roth were too close for my liking," observed Wynfeld. "I'll not tell His Highness that unless he asks me what I think of the candidates, but I'd rather see Lord Stator as Margrave than Lord Silvano. I should leave you to carry on. If you want me to sit with our Prince for a time, you know where I am."

A couple of minutes later, Wynfeld found Edward in Arkyn's office, making sense of the organised chaos to locate the papers Lord Iris would need.

"Morning, Commander. You're about early."

"I could say the same, Edward. Any further thoughts on the note you found the other day? Ideas on how it got there, say?"

"Someone put it there. I don't know whom, and I don't know how. Possibly they came through the outer door. The Thomkins twins might be able to help. They're often in the gardens."

Wynfeld smiled. "Aye, they might. What about this door?"

Edward pulled more papers towards him. "Then Stuart should have seen them. No! Oh, Sicla! We were upstairs being questioned over the farce with the Prince's private desk."

"All right. Are you satisfied that His Highness' retinue can be exonerated? Your options haven't included them."

Edward paused. "I don't see how I can be… Commander, I didn't tell His Highness about the note. If you're going to investigate us all, a sensible precaution I'll admit, then be careful. He should know, but being incapacitated…"

"I understand. I might speak to His Majesty."

"Is it wise to put more onto his shoulders? If he knows the Prince is being threatened, Alcis only knows what he'll do – given our arrival."

"You don't think he has a right to know?"

"Yes, Commander, I do. All I'm saying is be careful of being the bearer of bad news. It was one note, and the Prince didn't see it. If His Highness had seen it or if there had been more than one, then I wouldn't hesitate. I'd say His Majesty ought to be told, but we don't get paid to inform the FitzAlcis every time they are threatened. You know that better than anyone," finished Edward, holding Wynfeld's gaze.

"All right, I take the point. I'll do some *discreet* investigations and if anything emerges that I think our King ought to know about I'll tell him then. Will that satisfy you?"

Edward relaxed. "Yes, thank you, Commander. You'll need a list of people working for His Highness, I suspect. I'll mark on it anyone with unfettered access to His Highness' private rooms and office."

"Thank you. I'm about to go and see Lord Wealsman. Anything you need taking to him?"

Edward smiled. "You're hardly a courier, Commander."

"No, but I have my uses, or so I'm told."

* * *

Wynfeld found Wealsman already at his desk and looking like he'd never left it the night before. He regarded Wealsman with fresh eyes. Keeping the secret of a friendship with King Adeone for twelve years wasn't just impressive, it was astounding in an empire that relied heavily on personal connections. The fact Wealsman had managed it said more about him than anything else Wynfeld had heard. His King was shrewd and Wynfeld had never met someone Adeone considered a friend who he, himself, hadn't liked and formed a respect for.

"Morning, my lord. I have these papers for you from Administrator Edward, and I could do with a word in absolute confidence."

Taking the papers, Wealsman added them to a pile saying shrewdly, "Why, Commander?"

"Many reasons, sir," replied Wynfeld evasively.

Wealsman looked at him even more shrewdly. "If it's so important, let's take a walk in the gardens; it's about time I took a break."

In the nip of a cold but mercifully dry morning, Wynfeld said, "I don't know if I should be saying this, but I know of your friendship with our King. His Majesty himself told me last night."

Wealsman glanced sideways at him. Arms behind his back, he observed, "I expect, knowing the King, he had some good reason for telling *you*."

Wynfeld explained the events that had led to the confidence.

"Right. I can do nothing but confirm it, Commander; however, you would never have doubted His Majesty's word. So why are you treading on cracking ice and talking to me about it?"

"Our King mentioned you were one of his best spies in Terasia and I need such people."

Wealsman laughed. "He said you never miss a trick. I report directly to Adeone."

"I understand, my lord, but if there is anything you think you can't report directly to our King, I hope you will find you can tell me."

"I shall consider it, but, trust me, there is very little I find I cannot tell my friend."

Wealsman was disappointed to see no twitch of emotion on the commander's face. Maybe there was more to Wynfeld than met the eye. The commander had reported directly to the Margrave on arriving in Terasia and the meeting had been an unusually long one.

After a moment, Wealsman said, "You will, I assume, not be telling anyone else."

"I value my commission and my life. I shall not be mentioning what I know to *anyone*; however, I have one favour to request of you."

"Oh yes?" enquired Wealsman, half amused at the slight change that had come over Wynfeld. It wasn't blatant but there was just the slightest hint that Wynfeld had softened around him.

"Can I get a frank opinion on the overlords from you, at some point? You know them so much better than I do and I think His Highness will need a report from me on them."

“Oh, I think I can give you a frank opinion, if that’s what you truly want. Just be sure that the fact I gave it you doesn’t reach *their* ears. I don’t think my appointment to Acting Governor was well received.”

Wynfeld smiled. “I’m here to make sure there are no uprisings due to such decisions, sir. You needn’t worry about them.”

Laughing, they made their way into the Residence before parting company.

Chapter 23
SILVANO

Alunadai, Week 17 – 1st Meithal, 8th Easis 1211
Tera – Hale’s House

THE DAY AFTER Portur’s funeral, in the frescoed and gilt surroundings of his study, Silvano regarded his son with despair.

“You’re twenty-five, Melek! I’ve waited long enough for you to find yourself a woman – one whom you can marry, that is—”

“Father—”

“No. You’ll listen to me, and you’ll listen hard. You need someone who will enhance your reputation. You and your peers may find it amusing to organise what can only be politely described as ‘wild parties’ but it will do you no good for your career in this province. One day you might well be Margrave. Do you want your youth remembered how it is currently thought? Even in my wildest moments, I didn’t get three maids pregnant.”

“I’m not here to make up for your mistakes, father.”

Silvano froze. “You will marry whom I tell you to and do this family some good instead of harm. I’m inviting Hale here to make sure Lady Portur is suitable for you.”

“I won’t be coerced into marrying a *minor* lady,” scoffed Malek.

“You’ll do what I say! She’s the only heiress for the Portur lands. Adding those lands to ours would be worth it. She isn’t a virgin – or at least I assume not – but her last husbands and birth mean she’s trained for a lordship. A perfect match. If you marry her during the Prince’s visit, he’ll attend the wedding. That’ll improve your future career.”

Melek smiled to himself. Lady Portur wouldn’t have to be around for long. Just long enough. “All right, but will the marriage be allowed? We’d have two overlordships.”

“I can’t see that being a problem, not yet. You should have sons. You’re fertile enough; the Portur lands can be in trust for your second, as far as the world is concerned. Think of the richness of those lands, Melek. There’s some of the best land in Terasia within their bounds.”

"Yes, but Hale still has to agree."

"He's a social climber. You don't think his daughter wanted to marry Portur, do you? Or, for that matter, that old merchant. No. She'll be told to marry you and that will be that. No-one else can have thought of marrying her yet. No-one will even have considered it with Portur so recently cold."

Melek began to enjoy the idea. He'd be rich before his father died – richer than his father was. He'd father a child and pack the lady off to a manor whilst he spent his life in Tera, living off the income the Portur lands would provide.

* * *

Admiringly, Lord Hale entered Silvano House. Here was an efficient, well-run, rich household. Marble columns sprang from stone-flagged floors, delicate marquetry and gilding adorned cabinets; glass sculptures and vases from Denshire sparkled in the light from large windows; polished woods contrasted with rich velvet drapes. There wasn't a home-woven tapestry in sight, instead painted silks adorned the walls and busts of ancestors inhabited niches. Finished the year before, the house could never be described as Terasian in style, but Hale didn't care. There was no history for it to aspire to. It reflected the current family, with the busts as an obligatory nod to their ancestors.

A footman took his cloak, and *another* footman showed him through to the study, where Lord Silvano and Lord Melek were. The door closed on the servant and Silvano glanced over.

"Your daughter, Hale, is she fertile?"

He didn't rile. Straight talking meant he didn't have to figure out the meaning. "Yes, my lord. She has her bleeds regular enough. Lord Portur was satisfied; however—"

"What's her dowry? Not that that will make much difference. From you, it can't be much, but her current lands, well, their worth is more important."

"There's a small manor I got when I married her mother, but—"

"As I said, immaterial, though my lawyer will talk to you about it. She is, I take it, obedient? Lord Melek has a fancy to marry her. I take it you can raise no objection. No. Good."

Hale swallowed. Why did this have to happen? "My lord, it's not up to me. I'd like it for Lord Melek to marry Kristina, but she… she came under the King's protection with the death of Lord Portur… and… well…"

"Get to the point!"

"She's… well… she's taken it into her head to marry someone else… and… well… the King… the King has agreed. I'm sorry, Lord Melek, I'd have much preferred her to have married Your Lordship, but there's nothing we can do."

"Who's she marrying?" blurted out Melek.

“Lord Wealsman.”

“That crawler. We can buy *him* off, father.”

Silvano and Hale exchanged a knowing glance.

“No, we can’t, Melek. We can’t. Only Wealsman’s death will prevent this marriage now.” remarked Silvano humourlessly.

“Why? He’s a minor lord. A nobody in effect.”

“Be said! We cannot stop this marriage. The King has agreed to it.”

“Wealsman some long-lost brother of his?” enquired Melek, sneering. “Come, father, you’ve more influence than he has. We can show the King the error in his decision; he’s not always right—”

Silvano whipped round to face his son. “Never say such a thing again! You’re a hair’s breadth from treason. If the King’s decreed something, that is the end of the matter, however much we wish the decision was other than it is. We have no right of petition in this. The Lords Berger defied King Atgas – ever heard of them? No. I’m not surprised. Written out of history. Sicla! Wealsman moved quickly.”

Hale fumed, “Well, yes and no, sir. I refused him permission to marry Kristina near fourteen years ago. This time, they didn’t ask my permission. They went straight to the King. I cannot condone that.”

“Why are you still here, Hale? You’ve nothing I want.”

Hale swallowed. Could he salvage something? “My lord, I was thinking, my son is unmarried.”

“You want me to marry one of my daughters to your nothing of a son? No. My daughters will gain me advantage either here or in the empire. I cannot foresee your family helping that. Have him marry another of your kind… Maybe Wealsman has a sister…”

Hale’s eyes narrowed. “Then I shall not impose on Your Lordship’s valuable time any longer.”

“I’ll show you out, Hale,” offered Melek.

* * *

When Melek returned to his father, Silvano stated, “We’ll have to find someone else for you. How about Stator’s girl?”

“She’s young, sir.”

“Aye, but certainly blooming. You’ve been licking your lips looking at her every time we’ve been at the Residence lately. She’s got good clear skin, childbearing hips and her curves please you – what more do you need? Either Stator or I will be Margrave. It might lead to a good position for you. Maybe an ambassador or deputy governor – like your nearfather was. Yes, I’ll start talking to Stator. Then, whilst I’m thinking of marriages, I might consider the eldest of your sisters.”

“That harridan; marry her out of the province. Her conduct at the Residence over the banquet nights has been wantonly. Have you seen the dresses she wears? What you can see of them. If I am disgracing the Silvano name, I hesitate to mention what she's doing to it. Isn't the Visir widowed? Fathered too many children on his last wife, I heard. He'll be hunting for another one – one more trustworthy than to allow his daughters to marry unsuitably and in secret. I'm sure my beguiling sister is enough to please him and to keep her step-family well in order."

Silvano knew Melek was manipulating him. Still, he might have a point. "It would stop people wondering if she's so beautiful why you're not more handsome. Very well, I shall write to the Visir. Maybe by the Munewid I shall have you both married off. That'll only leave five of you. Your brother might prove a problem though."

"Find an heiress for him – say Gerymor, should be far enough."

"Do you love any of your siblings, Melek?"

"No. They are a sinking ship around my neck. You have taught us to be single-minded in what we want. Talking of which, will you excuse me if I leave you now, sir? I need to see to business in town."

Silvano's gaze raked over his son. "I shall not enquire what business, but, yes, you may leave; however, return for dinner. Lord Irvin Iris is staying with us from his arrival this evening. He is a future Lord of Oedran. You will take the opportunity I have been at pains to provide you with and get to know him well."

"I am always eager for such experiences."

As Silvano watched the door close, he was irrationally uneasy about his son's endeavours in the city. Deliberating on everything Melek had said, he decided his son was right. His eldest daughter wasn't quite the model of decorum she should be. With the Prince's illness, it was unlikely that there would be banquets for some weeks. He'd use that as an excuse to take his daughters back to his manor. Whilst there, he'd examine his accounts and calculate what he could offer as a dowry to tempt the Visir. If nothing came of it, he'd examine other provinces and see if there was anyone with a son whose influence would be important. He might even consider the future Lords of Oedran, Lord Irvin even. One of those would give him influence. Would he have to visit Oedran? That might be a problem if he was going to be made Margrave. Should he wait? If he was a King's Representative, his daughters' worth would be higher. Maybe, however, the idea he *might* be the next Margrave would be better. He wouldn't have to provide such a large dowry for a start. He needed to view those account books and determine how much he could afford. If it wasn't enough, his mines would have to extract more gold on the sly. He didn't need to be taxed any more. Yes, he'd return to his lands and take his daughters out of the way of temptation. Memory returning, he swore, there was an embargo on overlords leaving Tera during the Prince's stay. He needed travel leave.

He'd have to get permission from Wealsman, who, if he knew what was good for him, wouldn't ask too many questions.

* * *

An hour later, the door to Wealsman's office crashed open as Silvano strode over the threshold saying, "Thomkins was lying then: you're not that busy. Have you forgotten the courtesy of rising when an overlord enters?"

"Only when they have forgotten the courtesy of knocking. How can I help you, my lord?"

"I need to return to my lands," stated Silvano. "You must give me permission, I expect. Though what a minor lord is doing as Acting Governor I'll never understand."

"I'm doing the hectic job of governor. Why do you need to leave Tera?"

"I don't have to explain myself to you."

"As I *am* Acting Governor, you do, sir. The King's instructions were clear: reside in Tera for the duration of His Highness' visit – at least two aluna-months. So far, that visit hasn't even been a week and you *need* to return to your lands. I require more than that before I can sanction your absence from the city."

"His Highness, as I understand it, isn't in a fit state to know who is in Tera and who is not," retorted Silvano bluntly. "Therefore, you will please not become overly officious and forget your station in life. You *will* give me leave to return to my lands."

"Lord Silvano, I dislike repeating myself but, until you tell me *what* is so urgent, I cannot permit you to leave Tera. I must also abide by the instructions and injunctions of both His Majesty and His Highness. The King has been quite clear in his communications that he wants all overlords in Tera for the duration of His Highness' visit. It is a few days' ride to your lands, in addition to the time you will require there; tell me the reason I should report to His Highness. For he will want answers, my lord."

"I doubt at sixteen he'll care!"

"Oh dear. You don't know our Prince, Lord Silvano. He already receives daily reports from Commander Wynfeld—"

"Another jumped up nobody. What is his lineage but that of servants and the lesser? I have men of more calibre working in my mines."

"I advise you keep such opinions of Wynfeld to yourself. It is thanks to him the Prince is still alive."

Silvano sneered. "And don't let's forget you, Wealsman."

"I did nothing but what I had been instructed to do, Lord Silvano."

"Yes, that's all you ever do. The lapdog of the FitzAlcis. No free-thinking person would ever—"

"Lord Silvano, please moderate your tone. I accept you are of a higher social standing, but civility is universal."

Silvano stared. "*You* upbraid *me*?"

"Not at all. I just require a little more courtesy."

"Explain to me why I should be polite to someone who is preventing my freedoms?"

"I have no greater wish, right now, than seeing you as far from Tera as possible; however, until you give me a reason, in confidence of course, as to why you need to visit your lands, I can do no other but deny your request."

"It is a private matter."

"Would you expect the King or Prince to accept such an answer?" enquired Wealsman, raising his eyebrow.

"Do you, therefore, think you are as high as they?"

"No, my lord, I am saying, and have been doing so for some time, that I have my instructions from them and act on their authority. I can do no other but carry out their wishes. I need the *complete* reason as I must make a report to His Highness, when he is better, of *all* my decisions during his illness."

Silvano snapped, "Oh forget it. I'll go to Iris," and stormed out.

Wealsman quickly contacted Iris by messenger and explained that an irate Silvano was on his way to him. Iris rose in Wealsman's estimation with his response.

"You told him as Acting Governor he couldn't have travel leave?"

"Yes, my lord."

"Then he won't get any further joy out of me. You're Acting Governor at His Highness' decision, which means I cannot and will not interfere in those decisions you make as that official."

Wealsman's face betrayed slight astonishment. "Erm, thank you, sir."

Iris smiled. "We both serve the FitzAlcis. As you are not hindering me, I shall not interfere."

* * *

Silvano entered Iris' office in the same manner he had entered Wealsman's.

Iris didn't even look up. "Get out! Until you can follow conventional methods of entry, I won't speak with you. I have more than enough to do today. Edward, continue."

Silvano stood for a moment, before turning on his heel and storming out. To Edward's surprise, it was another six minutes before Iris' secretary announced him.

The Overlord of Terasia saw a calm, balding, grey-haired man, with well-etched wrinkles, steely grey eyes and the memory of muscles all too used to wielding a sword. There was no age-born weakness about Lord Iris.

"My lord, I need permission to return to my lands. A private matter that I would not trouble you with."

"I would have advised that you visit Lord Wealsman, as I have no authority to permit your absence. I suggest you use your messenger to deal with matters in your lands. Lastly, I would advise you do not play Lord Wealsman and myself off against each other again! His Lordship *is* the Acting Governor of Terasia. Under normal circumstances, travel leave is a matter for the governor of a province; therefore, your request falls within Lord Wealsman's remit, as I'm sure you'll agree when you've calmed down."

Silvano realised what had happened. "So, he told you he'd refused me and you're going to agree with him because he's the *Acting* Governor. How pathetic. You cannot tell me that, as a Lord of Oedran, you *agree* with Wealsman's appointment to such an elevated post—"

Iris rose from his chair. "Silvano, *we* are *not* required to comment on His Highness' decisions! We are required to accept them, unless or until His Highness requests our opinion. Prince Arkyn knows his own mind and abides by his decisions. If you feel so strongly, there will be time enough, when His Highness has recovered, to file official petitions with him, but I advise you don't. Just remember, he will choose the new Margrave during his stay. Reports on the conduct of candidates during his incapacitation may be pivotal in his decision – along with their presence in Tera."

Silvano hadn't listened to half of what Iris had said. "You're telling me not to complain that I'm forced to remain here… How is that justifiable? Does no-one ever question their decisions?"

Iris' face set. "In a different time, not so long ago, that speech would have seen you under arrest and having your affairs examined. If you continue, it still might. Accept the decision gracefully, my lord – for your own sake."

Silvano had blanched at the mention of arrest. "I'll accept the decision, but not gracefully."

Iris reseated himself when the door had closed on Silvano's retreating back. "Edward, ask Commander Wynfeld to see me when he's next here. There was more than anger in Silvano. There was a bubbling animosity. I cannot see that and do nothing."

Chapter 24
LORD IRVIN

Late Afternoon
Margrave's Residence

THE EARLY EVENING ARRIVED with mayhem in its wake. The clip-clopping clattering of hooves clanged through the Residence courtyard. A voice which seemed more used to lower tones called out,

"All right, everyone – cut the noise."

The noise of hooves resounded, but the chatter died. The personable young man who had spoken dismounted lightly. He eyed the Residence curiously and then grinned as he spotted Iris exiting the building with another man.

"Grandfather."

"Irvin. Pleasant journey?"

"Good enough, sir. They've behaved themselves remarkably well for me."

Iris smiled. "I should hope so too…" He introduced Wealsman, who'd been patiently waiting.

Irvin inclined his head. "I'm pleased to meet you, my lord."

"I you, Lord Irvin. I've got the list of where everyone's billeted – and a group of guides waiting."

"I think they'll be glad, my lord."

"If you'd care to go and take your ease, I'll sort everyone out for you."

"I can't ask you to do that," exclaimed Irvin.

Iris chuckled. "Wealsman offered. I think he rather enjoys being busy."

Irvin glanced between his grandfather and Wealsman. "Very well, sir. Then thank you, my lord."

Iris and Irvin made their companionable way to Iris' rooms. Irvin's gaze constantly taking in the unknown building. Polished wood, tiled entranced hall floor, carvings of varying designs, a handrail smooth through use, polished floorboards, guards on doors and servants in muted colours standing aside – probably some were the guides Wealsman had mentioned – and clerks in their dark tunics stepping back as they passed.

Iris led the way up the wide staircase opposite the front doors. His rooms consisted of a narrow antechamber, small sitting room and bedchamber. Irvin glanced around the sitting room, enquiring where Arkyn was.

"His Highness took ill three days ago and is still in a fever."

Accepting a drink from his grandfather's manservant, Irvin said, "I hope he recovers soon. What's happened about the review?"

"I'm doing some of it, then reporting to His Highness when he's recovered. Would you like to observe some of the meetings? It might help you decide your future path. The King won't wait much longer. He'll expect you to be attending one of the schools next year."

Irvin hesitated. "I still don't know what I want to do—"

"The Prince asked if you would become an advisor. It has suited generations of our forebears. You must decide by the time we return to Oedran; or I'll decide for you. I'll not sanction you joining the army; your mother would never forgive me."

Irvin nodded. It was the same discussion they'd had time and again. His father was also pressurising him to become an advisor; Lord Idris Iris hadn't had any choice, as he constantly pointed out. Deep down, Irvin knew neither had he; if he chose law, they'd talk him round – it made him wonder why he wasn't giving them the answer they wanted. Was he hoping for a miracle? All he wanted to do was to read about the history of Erinna.

Watching his grandson, Iris suspected what he was thinking. As a young man he, himself, had questioned his father as much as he dared, but he'd been pleased he'd followed his advice. He didn't now want to see the tradition end.

Changing the subject, Iris informed Irvin he'd be staying with Silvano as there was no room left in the Residence.

"I don't mind, grandfather."

"You might. Silvano reckons he's destined to be the next Margrave. He's always seeking political advantage and will have told his son to become friends with you. Just be warned. There's also the small fact I annoyed him earlier."

Irvin chuckled. "Grandfather, I can take care of myself."

"I hope that's true. How did you find the rest of the journey?"

"Fine, though the roads could do with a bit of work. They're woefully maintained in comparison to those around Oedran."

"Yes," observed Iris. "It's one of the points His Highness noted, though they've improved in the last fifty years. It doesn't seem that long since I was last here."

"Has it changed much, grandfather?"

"Very little. I remember this Residence as just that. Not offices with the living accommodation severely reduced. It was a happy home. I remember King Altarius here, Prince Altarius he was then. Lady Amara was here as well, a beautiful young princess. She kept us on our toes. I remember the banquets; they seemed splendid. King Altarius in the prime of life… A stickler, no doubt about that, but it was a good time. Everyone knew where they stood and stand we did. There was no sitting if the FitzAlcis were in the room. Not unless you were family or an exceptionally close friend. Lord Ewart Fairson was with us. He did sit, but then he married Lady Amara in the end. Older than her, of course, more of an age with King Altarius, but she loved him. That was plain to see. Aye, I even think he loved her. Really loved her…"

Irvin sat listening to his grandfather's reminiscing with a happy heart. Other than the fact he enjoyed hearing about the past, his grandfather wasn't pressurising him into an action he was reluctant to take.

Half an hour later, Wealsman entered. "Forgive me for disturbing you, Lord Iris. I just came to say I've had Lord Irvin's luggage taken to Silvano House and, when he's ready, Lord Melek is downstairs."

Iris smiled. "Thank you, Wealsman. Irvin, you'd better go and be greeted by your hosts. Be polite."

* * *

In the entrance hall of the Residence, Wealsman made the introductions and, realising that Irvin was shy, made his excuses and left.

With his father's instructions in mind, Melek tried to appear friendly. "Welcome to Tera, Lord Irvin. I hope you had a good journey."

Irvin reckoned Melek was a few years older than him: twenty, maybe twenty-one. They were much of a height, so Irvin noted the momentary disparagement in his host's eyes. The slight sneer that he didn't realise he had spoke more loudly than his voice. Irvin's first thought wasn't about wanting to get to know him better. He stuck to the pleasantries.

"Yes, thank you, Lord Melek, but it is pleasant to be at my destination. Three weeks is a long time to be on the road."

"Yes. Shall we complete the journey? You're staying with my family, I understand."

"I'll be glad to meet them."

"They are waiting for your arrival," remarked Melek, wondering how long he could keep up the pretence.

"Maybe you could point out Tera's landmarks to me as we ride, if we pass any of them."

Melek inwardly sneered. "Of course. It would be a pleasure."

Several minutes later, Irvin dismounted in another courtyard. He passed his reins to a groom and smiled in thanks. The gesture seemed to confuse the man. Two moments later, Malek introduced Lord Silvano.

"Lord Irvin, what can I say but it is a pleasure to have you staying with us. You must, of course, treat this house as your home for the duration of your stay. Anything you need, anything at all, do not hesitate to ask."

"Thank you, Lord Silvano," replied Irvin quietly. "It is a pleasure to be here, and I must thank you for hosting me."

"Think nothing of it, Lord Irvin. Your servants have already arrived. They have accommodation alongside my own and, if you don't mind, they'll abide by the same rules."

"I'm sure they won't abuse your hospitality, my lord, but, as is traditional, if you should find fault with their conduct, I would prefer you to raise issues with me directly. I doubt your house rules are very much different from my grandfather's."

"Of course, it is as you wish it. Now, would you like to take your ease before dinner?" After Irvin agreed, Silvano said, "Melek, show our guest to his rooms, please."

Once in those rooms with the door closed on the Silvano family, Irvin let out a relieved breath, hoping the fawning formality stopped soon. He raised his eyebrows eloquently at his manservant, who returned the gesture. Nothing else needed to be said.

Chapter 25
INVESTIGATIONS

Evening

Margrave's Residence

IRIS WAITED LONG ENOUGH for his grandson to be clear of the Residence before returning to his office. He had several small matters he wanted to complete before dinner. He was still trying to puzzle out how so much tax had gone missing without anyone raising the slightest eyebrow. They'd need to know so they could spot if it was happening in any other province. He had the report from the exchequer and was reading it with a sceptical eye. Its corners were so full of annotation that Edward had asked if he wanted another copy taking.

The administrator was in the entrance hall of the Residence talking to Thomkins. It seemed that most of the day's work was over. On seeing Iris approaching, Edward broke off his conversation and walked over to the Lord of Oedran.

"Commander Wynfeld has just delivered his evening report, my lord. He's waiting for you in your office, and there has been a set of dispatches from Oedran. Some I've passed to Lord Wealsman as they are standard provincial updates. The others I've passed to your secretary. Those of a sensitive nature are in a secure chest in your office. Here's the key. There was nothing urgent. I have removed those marked personal for the Prince from His Majesty, Lady Amara and Lord Landis, but that's all."

Iris nodded. "Thank you, Edward. I shall go and speak to the commander. I shouldn't need anything else from you today. Take the evening off."

"Thank you, my lord, but there are several—"

"Edward, this is an order; take the evening off. His Highness won't thank either of us if you are exhausted. I'm certain whatever you were going to do can wait."

"Very good, sir," answered Edward, noncommittally. "I shall make sure everything is secure first."

Iris watched Edward leave disbelievingly. He noticed Richardson's tutelage of the young administrator, but Edward had certainly developed his own, highly efficient, style and worked more hours than Iris expected.

* * *

Wynfeld saluted as Iris entered the room. The Lord of Oedran considered all the reports and rumours he'd heard about this officer. Two and a half years ago, Wynfeld had been unknown; no-one outside his regiment knew anything of him. Then something had happened, something left to rumour and speculation. Wynfeld had become Captain of Intelligence, head of the spies of Oedran. Now everyone in power knew his name. Some even feared it. Iris realised that he didn't know if Wynfeld was still involved in intelligence gathering. The events at the end of 1210 had changed things. The attack on the King should have seen Wynfeld demoted or out of the army altogether, but Wynfeld had continued in post and, far from being demoted, had been promoted only a short time later. Some believed that the promotion was a way of removing him from Oedran without the King losing face; Iris, however, wasn't so sure, especially when he considered Wynfeld's location.

"Thank you for waiting, Commander. I don't know if this would come under your remit or not, but Lord Silvano visited me earlier—"

"I know, my lord – something to do with returning to his lands."

"That is correct. How do you know?"

"He wasn't happy at being refused and was complaining about it for some time," elaborated Wynfeld. "He was foolish enough to do so in the entrance to this Residence. As our Prince is ill upstairs, I've had guards placed at the bottom of those stairs, to prevent unknown people from walking up them unchallenged. They merely overheard his displeasure."

"I wondered why they'd suddenly appeared," remarked Iris. "Silvano's manner concerned me. He made a comment that would have seen him under arrest during King Altarius' reign. It was only because he was distressed, and I do not wish to upset the fragile equilibrium here, that I have not requested his detention."

Wynfeld stilled. "What was the comment, sir?"

"It is now immaterial."

"No, it is not. You would not be talking to me about it if it had been minor. I might find out by other means, but I would prefer not to."

"Are you still, therefore, spying on us all?" enquired Iris.

"Spy, as His Highness has said, is a strong word, my lord. I am still in a position to collect pertinent intelligence. That is all."

Iris regarded Wynfeld for a moment. "Very well. Silvano queried whether anyone ever questions the FitzAlcis – the implication of tyranny was clear."

"He did *what*? Great Alcis! He's a fool, an absolute bloody fool. Does he truly value his skin so little?"

With a flicker of annoyance, Iris stated, "He certainly has little regard for others' feelings. His comment was disturbing, but it wasn't that which made me concerned; there was something underlying it. Something that *I* think was deep-seated animosity."

"Thank you for alerting me, my lord."

"Might I know what you'll do with the information, Commander?"

"I will note it and place Lord Silvano's house under surveillance, my lord. I know, you see, that Roth was Lord Silvano's closest friend. If I gather any other intelligence of note, I shall decide how to act then. It could just be that Lord Silvano feels he can't show his true feelings at the death of a friend, whatever those feelings might be, given the former Deputy Governor's conduct in the last days of his life."

Iris studied Wynfeld's steady face again. "You don't flinch at doing such a thing, do you? At putting an overlord under observation for one comment and a hunch."

"Do you expect me to wait until there is more cause, and, therefore, in the end, to make an arrest with less information – or not act at all until too late? That happened once. I won't let it happen again." His tone changed. "I'm sorry if you find my methods merciless, my lord, but I have a job to do."

"I find your methods neither pleasing nor displeasing," observed Iris. "I was involved in advising King Altarius to gather better intelligence. Your previous regiment was a result of that. I have heard you made many changes; yet you didn't suffer when the King was attacked last year."

"I followed His Majesty's wishes," replied Wynfeld carefully, for he had offered his resignation and it had been refused.

Iris raised an eyebrow. "As do we all, Commander. Don't let me keep you from your work any longer."

* * *

On reaching the fort, Wynfeld sent for one of his sergeants.

"Dring, I've got a job for you watching Lord Silvano. Seems he's a bit irked by events. Lord Iris is worried and thought he'd concern us as well."

"How kind of him, sir. I'll get onto it straightaway. Oh, there's been a despatch box from Oedran." Dring hesitated. "Have you got six minutes to spare, Commander?"

Wynfeld nodded. Silvano and the anonymous letters could wait for a time.

"Thank you, sir. It may be nothing though," hedged Dring. "There's gossip about a corporal who might interest you…"

Wynfeld listened. The sergeant's mess was agog with the information that a soldier, one Corporal Butterworth, had an aptitude to guess what was happening, the answers to riddles, coming weather, men's emotions, down to how many fingers a man was holding up behind his back.

At the end of the explanation, Wynfeld remarked, "Wasn't he in with us at the Residence when our Prince arrived?"

"Aye, sir. He's the one who spotted the kitchen lad."

"Keep a special eye on him. If you see any of his tricks, watch carefully. We need to know if they are just that."

Once the sergeant had gone, Wynfeld yelled for his clerk and asked to see the despatches. He was halfway through reading one from the captain who'd taken his old post when he realised that he needed to speak to him. It could save him many hours of legwork in Tera.

Once the messenger link had formed, he said, "Beaver… How's it going?"

"Fine. Oedran seems quiet. I hear, however, you have all the dilemmas again, sir."

"What you don't know, and what no-one else will know, so keep quiet on this one, is that Administrator Edward found an unpleasant anonymous note intended for His Highness. I only got chance to talk to the administrator about how it could have got into His Highness' papers after our Prince was incapacitated and so this is completely unsanctioned. Administrator Edward has requested I examine the background of His Highness' retinue. I need our notes from when we vetted them. All cross-references, in fact, everything we've got. Any links to Terasia, any links to anything. I'm hoping the note didn't originate in His Highness' retinue, but I must check them as well as the Terasians."

"Right you are, Capt… Commander."

Wynfeld smiled. "Yes, I still can't get used to my rank either. Any rumours I should be aware of?"

"No, sir. As I mentioned, it's deceptively quiet here."

Wynfeld frowned. "Call me a cynic, but get your ear closer to the ground. Oedran is *never* that quiet. Where's Lord Scanlon?"

"Not too far from you, sir. He's in Denshire, for the law review there. Anguis and Rathgar are with him. Enjoying all the comforts the Visir can provide."

"*Lord* Anguis and *Lord* Rathgar, Beaver! Now, you must have the report to sort for the Palace. Send the information to me by courier through the Major – less chance of interception. I'd also like everything on one Corporal Butterworth, currently stationed here."

Chapter 26

FRIENDS?

Cisadai, Week 17 – 2nd Meithal, 9th Easis 1211

Margrave's Hall

LORD IRIS ENTERED the Margrave's Hall the following evening never considering the differences between the King's Court in Terasia, known as the Margrave's Court, and the King's Court of Oedran. Where the Oedranian Court met daily, the Margrave's Court only came together for great feasts, visits or notable events. The old manorial hall had started hosting the Court when the City Assembly burned down. Homely rather than grand, its plain plastered and panelled walls were welcoming, not ornate. Its long tables couldn't hold the hundreds that the King's Hall in Oedran could, but they were still laden with the feast. The dais was raised by two shallow steps, rather than the more elevated height the dais in Oedran had. Even if it were a smaller cousin of Oedran, it nonetheless held its own for welcoming hospitality.

Wealsman opened the feasting with an easy manner, welcoming Iris and Irvin to Terasia and cleverly weaving in that Arkyn would have been sorry to miss the feast, and that they were all thinking of him and wishing him well. The speech had the desired effect and there was a quieter atmosphere than there might have been. No-one, it seemed, wanted to disturb Arkyn.

"Cleverly done, Wealsman," remarked Iris.

Wealsman chuckled. "Thank you, my lord. I've also given them orders to close the door into the Residence once the food's all here. We'll open the far door if it gets too stuffy."

Iris nodded. "The staff are doing a remarkable job coping with so much upheaval."

"Kristina's excellent at organising people, my lord. As I know to my benefit. I can't wait to see what my household makes of her."

Iris crooked an eyebrow. "Is it likely they'll get to know Her Ladyship?"

Wealsman hesitated, feeling Kristina's gaze on him.

"We've known each other for many years, my lord, but not in Tera itself," clarified Wealsman carefully.

Iris wasn't fooled but turned the talk elsewhere for several minutes before saying lightly, "So have you set a date for the wedding yet?"

"Spring, or so I'm told—" He broke off as Kristina exclaimed,

"Percival, you're hopeless!"

"What? Oh. Sorry. Lord Iris caught me unawares," mumbled Wealsman to a chortle from Iris.

The Lord of Oedran glanced between them. "So, are congratulations in order?"

Wealsman reached for his goblet. "They might have been, but I rather think Kristina will have a lot to say to me now."

"I'm sure Her Ladyship will forgive you my trickery."

On Kristina's other side, Daia asked, "Are you getting married?"

Soon the news had spread along the dais, with some suspicious looks and much curiosity in its wake. It took mere minutes for it to travel around the rest of the hall.

More amused than annoyed, Kristina said, "I was trying to keep a sense of propriety for a bit longer, Percival. Apparently, I needn't bother now."

"I'm sure you'll still manage it," observed Wealsman carefully. "You manage everything else, including me, perfectly."

"Flattery gets you nowhere."

Wealsman watched her for a moment before winking and grinning as she blushed. Sitting between them, Iris shook his head and changed the subject. When the speculation had calmed down, he murmured,

"I presume you have the King's permission, Wealsman."

"His Majesty couldn't have been kinder when I broached the subject."

"Then all I can say is congratulations to you both. You said spring for the wedding?"

"Yes. I think it will suit Kristina's temperament."

"What he means is I'm slightly cold with a promise of warmth—" quipped Kristina.

"I mean no such thing—" protested Wealsman.

Her eyes sparked with delight. "What did you mean?"

Wealsman grinned. "Only that you're a blooming—"

"Careful..." Kristina began, amused, thinking of the King's comment on Percival.

"...Beauty. I was going to say beauty."

Iris laughed out loud. "Very quick, Lord Wealsman. I find, though, that women are sceptical when it comes to compliments made in such a way."

"Oh, mistake me not," answered Kristina lightly. "I'm not sceptical at all. I just don't believe a word he says. Especially when I hear him complimenting me. It is such a rare sensation, you see."

Beside Kristina, Daia had overheard the tone of the conversation. She turned to Irvin. "They seem happy enough."

Irvin smiled. "Yes, they do. I hope their marriage is a fulfilling one, my lady."

"It probably will be." After a few moments' pause, Daia enquired, "How are you finding Tera?"

"Pleasant enough. Though a day is hardly time enough to take in the entire city. I was hoping that Lord Melek might be kind enough to show me around, but it seems he is a busy person and I don't like to intrude on his spare time."

"I'd offer to myself but I'm a relative stranger here."

"Would you really?"

"Yes, but eyebrows might be raised."

"Yes, they may well," sighed Irvin dispiritedly.

Overhearing, Kristina asked, "Eyebrows might be raised at what, Daia?"

"If Lord Irvin and I went round Tera together."

"Maybe, but you're a ward of the FitzAlcis and Lord Irvin is a future Lord of Oedran. No-one can suspect anything amiss. Lord Irvin wouldn't risk his family's reputation and you are highly sensible. I can't see there being a problem."

Wealsman remarked, "Problem with what, Kristina? Me again?"

"No, for a change. Daia and Lord Irvin exploring Tera together."

"No problem at all. I doubt Lord Iris will mind and, anyway, take your horses and a groom with you and the problem is solved."

Turning back to the dais after a word with the steward, Iris asked, "Problem?" By the time they'd finished explaining, he said, "Irvin, feel free to explore; just be careful. His Highness won't need your services for some days. Lady Daia, thank you for offering to help."

"We'll be exploring the city together, my lord. I've hardly been in Tera."

"Then make sure you have a guide with you – even if it *is* only a groom."

Daia nodded in thanks. The focus changed again and, two moments later, they were all once more talking in groups. By the end of the banquet, Irvin had lost some of his shyness in talking to Daia. They found that they had a common interest in history. Iris heard his grandson ask,

"Is it true the Memini's Manuscript is here in Tera, my lady?"

"Yes, but it would take a memor to read it and no-one has admitted to being one, here in Terasia, for many years. I don't believe the book has been read since the Fall of the Cearcall in 600. We're not sure how it ended up in Tera. Later texts say it was located in the old palace after the Fall of the Cearcall, but that building is long since lost and with it any other clues."

"Surely, though, the site of the palace must survive and wouldn't logic ictate that it would be within the walls of Tera? The city is clearly of ncient importance both for government and defence. The ditches that urround it, its walls are of stone and yet most of the buildings are of vood, there must be hints somewhere, if only…"

His grandfather made a mental note to point out to Irvin *again* that he ouldn't make a career out of dead men's bones.

Vatching the Court, Kristina smiled to herself. Knowing most of the ttendees, the patterns made sense to her: the friendships, whether political r personal, stood out clearly. So did the fancies of the young lords once he dancing started. The ladies, playing either coy or demure, never stared, ut, nevertheless, managed to size up the young lords easily enough. The oung lords surveyed the ladies likewise. She could tell who the shy ones vere as they stood quietly by. Lord Melek wasn't one of them; he was tanding amongst his boisterous friends, mimicking others. Attention was vhat they sought, and they received it. A party of ladies walked by; Melek eached out to one of them. Kristina didn't hear what they said, could never ave done so, but the lady obviously didn't know how to respond. Eventually, she gave a small smile and a quick nod. A couple of minutes ater, Kristina saw them dancing together. Melek's hand straying too far for Kristina's liking, knowing his reputation.

Wealsman remarked, "What's Lord Melek up to?"

Kristina didn't stop watching the couple. "I don't know. I'm not sure Lord Stator's too happy though."

Wealsman glanced at the overlord and noted a suspicious mood he was half pleased to see. "I see what you mean. Would you like a dance?"

Kristina glanced at him. "If Lord Iris can spare your company."

Hearing his name, Iris said, "Don't let an aged Lord of Oedran come between younger love."

Kristina grinned. "When I see one, I'll let you know, my lord."

He smiled at her and shook his head slightly, amused. "My lady, you flatter me unfoundedly. Go on, enjoy yourself."

Wealsman pulled out Kristina's chair and escorted her to the dance floor, seemingly unaware that whispers were spreading.

They returned to the dais a few minutes later and sat down next to each other so they could talk more easily.

"I didn't know my father and Lord Melek were on speaking terms," remarked Kristina, watching them.

Wealsman snorted softly. "Maybe Melek is asking him why he permitted our engagement."

Kristina chuckled. "You're incorrigible. You really are."

"You laughed though."

"True. You know, Percival, this banquet seems strange without His Highness."

"Yes, I know what you mean. I'll sit with him for a time tomorrow to give Kadeem a chance to rest. The Prince has been awake today, but I think he's still got a temperature. It's been going up and down for a while, apparently. It'll be some days yet before he's awake for long at a time."

Kristina nodded. "Is he eating much?"

"Something I believe. Why?"

"I was just going to check that everything was well in the kitchens in the morning and thank them for their hard work over the last week. I wondered if there was anything he'd fancy."

Wealsman smiled tolerantly. "I'm sure, if there is, he's made his wishes known… Kadeem seems more than capable."

Kristina sighed. "All right, I'll try to stop fretting, but it's difficult."

Iris said, "It's nice to hear, Lady Portur. His Highness would be touched."

"Thank you, my lord. I suppose I'm aware that what one wants when one's ill is one's mother."

Iris nodded. "I suppose for the young that's true enough. It is a tragedy that Her Grace passed on, but it wouldn't be prudent to mention Queen Ira to His Highness."

Wealsman remembered Adeone contacting him briefly to tell him that Ira had died, remembered the haunted look that his friend had worn, remembered the feeling that he would never get over the loss of his wife. The letter he'd received in the days after had been equally poignant. He, himself, for all he'd never formally met her, had been upset by her passing. He'd talked to her over messenger on a couple of occasions, enough to realise he would have liked to have known her better. Adeone's letters had always included news on all his family and so, in some senses, he had. He half listened to Kristina and Iris talking about her and suddenly couldn't listen any longer. Excusing himself, he left the hall for a breath of fresh air. There were a handful of others in the Residence's courtyard. Two were leaving – one looking particularly queasy. Melek and Hale were once again talking. Hale trying to gain influence again, no doubt.

Needing to be alone, Wealsman nodded to the guards on the Residence doors and then to those at the bottom of the staircase in its entrance hall and took the stairs two at a time. He reached the Prince's rooms and again gave the guards a nod. They barred his way. It was late, and they thought Kadeem had retired. Making his way back to the Margrave's Hall, the corridors were dim. Only a handful of candles in un-mirrored sconces gave light, and Wealsman thought he saw someone move at the far end of the corridor but, not being certain, didn't alert the guards. It was probably a servant going to bed. When he reached the entrance hall, he stopped for a word with the guards. He was still talking to them when Wynfeld entered.

"Evening to you, Commander."

"Likewise, Lord Wealsman. I came to check all's well with the guards."

"They've tolerated me with smiles. I'll leave you to your work."

"If you must, sir."

Two minutes later, both the guards and Wynfeld received drinks and a plate of food apiece, with more sent up to the guards on the Prince's rooms. That said everything about Wealsman that Wynfeld needed to know.

Chapter 27
OF CHARITY

Hexadai, Week 18 – 13th Meithal, 20th Easis 1211
Margrave's Residence

LADY PORTUR WALKED through the Residence for the hundredth time and wondered, as on all the others, how Lord Portur had lived somewhere that had become an office. The constant to-ing and fro-ing of clerks and scriveners drove her mad. There was no way of getting away from it. Her rooms were quiet enough, but the knowledge of what the rest of the building was disturbed her more than she had thought it would. Needing to get out, she went to see Percival. Thomkins announced her without question.

"Kristina… Come to see I'm working?" asked Wealsman.

"No. No point. You never do anything else. I'm going to call on Lady Daia and wondered if you wanted me to do anything for you in the city?"

Wealsman smiled. "Actually, yes, can you call by my house and tell them you need somewhere to relax that isn't full of offices and that they're to look after you?"

"Will you stop reading my every nuance!"

"No. It's a language I learned many years ago. The offer stands. Go there, if only for a couple of hours. Raid my library. Check my cook is up to your standards, though I'm not replacing him. He does some fantastic puddings you'll love—"

"So, you want me to make sure I can eat his cooking so you get his puddings?"

"Yes. What's wrong with that? I'll have fed you."

"Percival Wealsman, you are incorrigible. I shall anticipate the puddings with interest."

"I normally do… Just go there if you want to. I know we're not married yet, but what's mine is yours as far as I'm concerned."

Kristina smiled. "At heart, you're an old romantic, aren't you?"

Wealsman held her gaze, lips twitching. "Only for you."

"What makes you so certain I shan't rob you blind?"

"I know where you live and who your guardian is."

"True." A few quiet moments later, Kristina left, feeling better. She took a litter across the city. It was easier in the close-packed streets. Daia's traditional Teran house had three storeys, the upper ones jutting out to give plenty of space. A housemaid greeted Kristina and showed her through to a pleasant room that currently had an atmosphere at odds with its aspect. Lady Portur put her hand on the shoulder of the maid, who was about to announce her, and shook her head. The maid left.

Daia was saying to a straight nosed lady dressed in grey, "You will please unpack everything again. I have told you before that I am residing in Tera for the duration of the Prince's stay. I believe you were informed that it was at His Highness' insistence."

"His Highness hasn't helped your reputation by demanding you stay. Especially as you now *insist* on going round the city with Irvin Iris. I am saying for *your sake* we should return to your lands."

"*Governess!* You *will not* question His Highness' motives again. It is complete codswallop that he has wrecked my reputation. Complete and utter codswallop…"

"My lady should recall that 'codswallop' is a vile, uncouth word beneath her station."

Kristina from the sidelines remarked, "Codswallop, governess."

Involuntarily, Daia laughed. The governess spun round, shocked.

Kristina continued, "If you're talking of remembering one's place, I would remind you that Her Ladyship employs you. If Lady Daia wishes to stay in Tera and is following Prince Arkyn's instructions, you will do as she, in turn, instructs."

"Might I enquire on what authority you are—"

"Daring to speak to you thus? I am also under the King's protection. Now, I believe Her Ladyship gave you an instruction to unpack. I also believe I overheard the word *'again'*. Might I suggest, to save yourself future work, you don't try to coerce Her Ladyship into any action ever again?"

The governess shot Daia a disapproving look before replying. "My lady is a guest in this house—"

"I am not a child who needs reminding of manners," replied Kristina, self-composed as ever.

Irate, Daia exclaimed, "Governess, you will never be so rude to a guest of this house again! Unpack everything and get out of my sight until I send for you."

The governess bristled as she stalked out, nose held high.

Once the door closed, Daia sank onto a chair. "Thank you."

"Not at all. She is an obnoxious woman."

"She didn't use to be so bad before father died. The day I'm of age, she's in for a shock." Daia suddenly smiled ruefully. "Oh, I'm sorry you had to witness all that."

"I came in towards the end. Your housemaid was about to announce me, but I stopped her."

"Good. I shan't forget her face when you said 'codswallop'..."

Kristina chuckled. "I've been round Percival too long."

"Is he so mischievous?"

"Percival? He has his moments."

Half an hour later, refreshed and relaxed, Daia felt ready for the rest of her day. "I've got to go into the city for a time. Would you come with me?"

"Of course."

"Thank you. Tell me something though, this house... does it feel unloved to you?"

"No," observed Kristina thoughtfully, "just as if the love is away for a time. There's still the atmosphere of laughter here."

Daia smiled. "I thought that myself. My governess said it was unloved."

"No, merely the dust of ages has settled. Tell you what, let's call at your cloth merchant's and order some material for cushion covers and the like. See if we can't bring a permanent, lived in atmosphere back – one where the owner isn't away, but just out calling. You'll be here for some weeks, I suspect. You might as well make it home."

"My steward objects when I 'get ideas'."

"You mean when you exercise your right to spend your own money on what you want?"

Daia sighed. "That as well."

Kristina was slightly terse. "Tell him as a mistress of the house you have a duty to make the house a home. Anyway, it's also fun. Come on. I can look for material for a new dress... even my wedding dress."

Daia laughed lightly. "I think I ought to visit my tenants first."

* * *

Several streets away and half an hour later, Daia knocked at a door. When she walked into the small dark living room with its scrubbed table, small fire and plain furniture, it transported her back years.

Without realising she had said it out loud, she murmured, "I've been here before."

A dry laugh came from an old lady wrapped in rugs by the fire. "That you have, Lady Daia. 'E brought you here when you were a youngster.

Brought you to see me, 'e did. That wee lad of my care. Proud as punch 'e was about you."

Daia struggled with the memory. "Who…?"

"Ah, you won't be a remembering of me. Why should ya? I was sorry to hear 'e'd died. Gone to the blessed heavens 'e has. I looks at the stars every night for his sake."

"Me too," whispered Daia.

The old lady nodded. "A right madcap one in his youth 'e was. Never could wield a sword. What was 'e doing trying again?"

"Thinking of teaching me, I believe."

"Sounds about right. Wanted you to look after yourself, 'e did. Are you looking after yourself, little Daia?"

"I'm trying to."

"Good. That's all any of us can ask of life. 'E used to run here, you know. Years ago. Always used to bring us what he could. Cared 'e did. Always came to see us when 'e was in the city."

"How do you mean…?"

The younger woman who had opened the door murmured, "Don't mind Old Ma, milady. She'll talk of your father for hours, for he had a kind heart. She used to work at your house here. Then she married and Pa died in an accident. Your father saw us right. Now we do what we can to help others."

"I can believe it of him," admitted Daia. "What was your mother's job?"

"Nurserymaid, milady. She married a cooper…"

The old lady chortled to herself. "Aye, I did that. Got board and barrel of laughs for free."

Daia giggled.

The daughter said, "Ma, stop it. That joke is worn as thin as your skin."

"Ah, but my skin still covers my old bones."

Daia smiled at her. "Merriment keeps the blood flowing. I dropped by to see if there's anything I can do for you all?"

There was a knock on the door; Daia nodded to the daughter to open it. It didn't bother her if there were callers. A small raggedy lad entered.

"You ain't got a bowl of soups 'ave ya, miss? I tried everywheres else but ma's still ill and I 'ave to find mesen a job but I can't goes on if I ain't et and ma needs our food to keeps strong."

Two moments later, a bowl of soup was being ferociously eaten. In a dark corner, Daia and Kristina kept quiet.

When he'd finished, the lad said, "Thanks, miss. Anythin' I can do?"

The daughter smiled. "Up to chopping a couple of logs for the fire?"

"Yes, miss. I knows where your axe is."

"Who is he?" asked Daia when they were once more alone.

The old lady muttered, "Young Tommy? 'E's one of the lads of the street. His ma's been ill for some time. She's a seamstress, but she's got the shakes. Tommy's only nine. 'E thinks someone will give him a job if 'e keeps trying but for all 'e's 'ardworking 'e can't find a job. They look at 'is height and laugh…"

"Yet he'll wield my axe as though he's six foot tall," chipped in the daughter.

"He seems an eager lad. It's a shame…" sighed Daia to herself.

"Aye, milady, but he ain't the first in the city, nor the last," observed the daughter. "We dole out the odd bowl of soup to them, not as many as we'd like to, but someone like Tommy, he always gets fed. Always does a job or two for us in payment."

"Who's his landlord?"

The daughter smiled. "You are, milady. They've kept up with their rent as well. Cisluna knows how. Your steward ain't the most understanding of souls, but a man in his position has to see that the rent comes in, no matter how much it is."

Daia hesitated. "Maybe. What's Tommy good at?"

"Talking mostly. Teach him something and he'll learn it. I showed him how to split logs and he'd got the hang of it quickly enough. I'm laying bets that he's a dabster and that the ancient magic is giving him a hand. Why, milady?"

"Curiosity. When you said you couldn't give out as many bowls of soup as you'd like to, why was that?"

The daughter flashed her ma a look, which was ignored. "We does what we can, but we've only what I saved and my daughter earns with cleaning the merchant's house. It's our lot in life…"

"Yes, but you obviously want to do something to help your neighbours…" protested Daia.

"Don't you concern yourself, milady," replied the daughter, trying to brush the matter over.

"I help enough of my tenants elsewhere. I don't see why I shouldn't here."

"Because people find it hard to accept charity, Daia." It was the first thing Kristina had allowed herself to say.

"I'm not going to force it on anyone," replied Daia. "Merely suggest that I did here what I try to at home, and that is help where I find someone willing to do likewise. What do you get paid cleaning the merchant's house?" she asked the daughter, who told her, rather uncomfortably. "I've known better. You work your fingers to the bone to support Old Ma and yourself, yet you still give everything else to help others. If you're willing, I'll pay you double to continue to help others. Do a boiling of soup and get some bread from the baker on the corner. Feed those like Tommy who are trying to help themselves and whom the rest of society has laughed at. I'll give you an allowance every week to buy the food with and charge you no rent."

"Milady, you can't be serious," exclaimed the daughter.

From the corner, Old Ma said, "That's your father in you talking, Daia. Fight the injustice of the world 'ead on and stuff what others think?"

Daia grinned. "Yes, Ma, it's just that. What others think doesn't bother me; they can take a jump from the cliffs of Felsmeer but they won't stop me from trying to help others who weren't born as I am. Will you do it?"

The daughter said, "Aye, I suppose so. I'll have to give notice to the merchant."

Kristina asked, "Which merchant?"

"Crabson, madam."

Kristina snorted. "I was once his stepmother. Don't tell me you'll miss his employ."

Old Ma laughed. "I don't think she'll miss 'im one teeny bit, madam."

The daughter glanced at Lady Portur. "He speaks of you sometimes, milady. Even not having met you, I wanted to shove his teeth down his throat. Ma's right, I'll not miss him." Her gaze returned to Daia. "So yes, we'll give it a good go, milady."

Daia nodded. "Good. I think you might need a hand around the place. To chop wood for the fire. Help scrub veg, and the like. Might I suggest Tommy? I'll see if I can't find his mother something to do as well. Was she a good seamstress?"

"Aye, milady. Worked her fingers to the bone she did."

"Then I'm sure we can find her something to do. Look, can either of you write?" (Both shook their heads.) "Then go to a clerk if you need to contact me. Get him to write the letter. I'll see he's paid."

The daughter glanced at her mother. "Thank you, milady. We'll do our best for you."

Old Ma nodded. "Aye, that we will. Now, if you'll excuse me, it's time for my nap."

"Ma!"

Daia smiled. "Don't worry. We ought to be going. I have several more calls to make."

The daughter wiped her hands on her apron, ready to open the door, but Tommy entered, pulling a basket, which seemed to be as large as he was, into the house.

"Where does ya want the logs, miss?"

Daia simply left the house, leaving the daughter picking up the other handle of the basket and Old Ma laughing to herself by the fire.

* * *

They made several calls and, although they didn't receive such a welcome anywhere else, found out several useful pieces of information. On leaving the last of the tenants, Kristina remarked,

"It seems your steward has forgotten himself."

"Yet what can I do? He's officious, obnoxious and overly obstructive, but I can't get rid of him. I'm not alunan-age, Kristina, and, anyway, who would replace him?"

Kristina thought for a moment. "You're going to have to talk to His Highness."

"If he comes out of this fever. He's been in it for a fortnight."

"Kadeem seems certain it will break properly soon. The doctor is satisfied as well. It's a severe case of flu, but he will recover, Daia."

"Yes, but I want this sorted. Something is wrong because if they're paying so much in rent, it doesn't tally with what my steward is telling me."

"Do you mind if I mention it to Percival?" enquired Kristina. "He might have some ideas."

Daia sighed with relief. "Would you? I haven't a clue where to start. I think my steward's been taking the extra."

Kristina nodded. "We'll get it sorted out, Daia, but it can't change overnight. Don't rush in. Keep your ears open and insist on seeing the books *before* His Highness examines your wardship. You've every right to see them. If you want to put the magic amongst the mundane, organise a dinner party and put your household under scrutiny."

"Whom would you suggest I invite?" enquired Daia.

"Percival, Lord Irvin, myself – that makes a four – then as Percival is there, and experienced at running a manor, ask for his help, maybe?"

Daia laughed. "You're a marvel, you really are. I like this idea. Will Lord Wealsman have time to come?"

With a touch of determination, Kristina said, "Yes – by the time I've finished with him."

"Thank you."

"That's all right. What are friends for? Which is probably exactly why your governess doesn't want you in Tera to make them. Now, what colour do you suggest I get married in?"

Daia considered carefully. "I don't know. You need to make it special though. What colour does Lord Wealsman like to see you in?"

Kristina frowned slightly. "I don't know. Should I ask him, do you think?"

"Maybe. Let's see what we can find first..."

Chapter 28
CONSIDERATIONS

Evening

Margrave's Residence

IN THE EARLY EVENING, Kristina entered the Residence with a parcel of fabric swatches dangling from one hand as clerks were finding their cloaks and leaving. Coming down the stairs talking to Wynfeld, Wealsman looked over as one of the senior clerks bid Kristina good evening. He smiled and half ran down the last few steps.

"What have you got there?"

Kristina eyed him admonishingly. "Never you mind. I'm going to tuck it all away safely, then I'll come and find you."

Wealsman watched her go, shaking his head. "Was it just me, or did Her Ladyship seem to have something on her mind, Commander?"

Wynfeld moved forward. "I would say definitely, my lord. I hope it isn't serious."

"Me too. Join us for a drink."

"If I wouldn't be intruding, I should be glad to."

Six minutes later, divested of cloak and with a serene countenance, Kristina walked into Wealsman's Office smiling.

Without preliminaries, Wealsman said, "I'm not fooled, Kristina, and I doubt the commander is. What's the matter?"

Mask shattering, Kristina seated herself, accepting the drink Wealsman passed her. "I don't know if I… that is, if Daia would…"

"I take it you're concerned by my presence, my lady," observed Wynfeld.

"Not in a bad way, Commander, but I hadn't thought you'd be here."

"I think we can be discreet, Kristina," remarked Wealsman. "I'm sure the commander can, which only leaves me to worry about."

Kristina raised an eyebrow. "I never do anything else, Percival. Daia's steward is charging her tenants double what he's telling her. Her governess is trying to force her to return to her lands. She thinks she's powerless being only eighteen."

Wynfeld spoke before Wealsman could. "She's a King's ward, isn't she, my lady?"

"Yes, Commander, but—"

Wealsman was watching Wynfeld's face. "I think the matter is out of our hands, Kristina."

"Actually, Lord Wealsman, I was going to ask you what you thought we should do," admitted Wynfeld. "I know what our King would do, if he were here, and our Prince, if he were undertaking his duties, but I wonder what *we* can do."

Wealsman shrugged. "All I can suggest is that we keep an eye on the gentleman until His Highness is well enough to look into the matter."

Wynfeld nodded. "Then I shall see to doing just that and make a report to His Highness prior to him interviewing the gentleman in question."

"I can see why the King promoted you," observed Wealsman lightly.

"That's more than I can, my lord," answered Wynfeld honestly. "At least I shouldn't be so perplexed again; I won't rise any higher than commander."

Wealsman knew Wynfeld believed that, but he wasn't convinced. Talk turned to other matters and, half an hour later, Wynfeld left.

"Happier?" asked Wealsman of Kristina.

"Yes… no… I don't know. I just hope Wynfeld's discreet. Why did he ask for your opinion?"

"Adeone's told him of our friendship."

"Really?" exclaimed Kristina, amazed.

"Yes." Wealsman laughed. "You should have seen him when he tried to recruit me to his spy network. He accepted it when I said I only report to Adeone."

Kristina nodded. "Good. How's His Highness?"

"His temperature has started dropping consistently, thank the stars. He should be paying proper attention to the world again soon. In the next couple of days anyway. I'm going to sit with him this evening and tomorrow evening, for longer than normal, so Kadeem can get a rest."

"You're tired as well. Do you think it would be frowned upon if I went to sit with His Highness this evening? I dropped by your house, as suggested. They've not seen you for a couple of days. Why?"

"That long?" said Wealsman flippantly. He saw her frown. "Fine. I've slept here. I've been busy and—"

"Then go home for a proper night's rest!" admonished Kristina. "Go on. I'm sure it will all wait for the morning."

"Kristina, I can't."

"Nonsense, of course you can. I'll even ask Wynfeld to detain you under house arrest to make sure of it. He'd do it. Especially if I pointed out that the King wouldn't want you to be exhausted."

Wealsman looked at her, dumbfounded. "You wouldn't!"

"Oh, my dear, just watch me."

Seeing her determination, he said, "All right, all right, you win. Though if this is what you're like before we're married—"

"Percival, after we're married, I'll know when you aren't at home at night, sooner than two days later, and I'd hope you'd enjoy being at home."

He met her gaze. "If you were at home, I wouldn't be here so late."

"Are you saying that you work late because I'm here or because there's no-one at home?" she murmured, tracing the lines of his hand with her fingers.

"Both." He took her hand, kissing her palm, saying, "I must get on."

"No, you don't. You are going home. Get your cloak and I'll have your horse brought round to the front. Before you argue anymore, I've requested dinner and your favourite pudding for you."

"My servants know what they're in for then."

Kristina accepted his hand as she got up. "Yes, and I, in return, have learnt quite a lot about your habits."

"I will have to make sure that doesn't happen again." Drawing her close, he kissed her slowly.

She whispered, "Don't blame them. They knew I was worried too."

Percival slipped his hand around her back. "I won't, as long as you kiss me again."

Kristina smiled. It was another six minutes before she rang the bell and sent the footman to see Wealsman's horse saddled.

After watching Wealsman leave the Residence, she went upstairs to talk with the Prince's manservant.

"I'm sorry, Kadeem. I've sent Lord Wealsman home for the evening."

"Thank you, my lady. He wouldn't listen to me."

Kadeem had to be more drained than he looked to admit that.

She continued, "I can believe it. He was concerned that he should have been sitting with His Highness this evening. I said I'd sit with the Prince, if that is permitted?"

Kadeem smiled. "Of course, my lady, but I wouldn't impose on your kindness."

"Think nothing of it. Go and get some rest."

"Thank you, my lady, I'll be glad to… I mean…"

"I can pretend I didn't hear that if it makes you feel better. Go on."

Kadeem left.

Entering the Prince's sumptuous bedchamber, Kristina settled herself in a chair. Half an hour later, Thomas entered with a knock and passed her some embroidery her maid had sent.

Working on the monotone border of the embroidery by candlelight, Kristina contemplated how tired Kadeem was. He needed to take a break, or he'd end up ill. Knowing the strictures the King had decreed, Kristina tried to devise a plan so Kadeem could recuperate the following day. She resolved to ask Fitz to sit in the room during the morning, and then Daia could be there in the afternoon. She or Wealsman could take the evening. That would give Kadeem most of the day to himself.

When the manservant entered later, Kristina made the suggestion.
"Thank you, my lady. I'm perfectly content."
Not knowing quite what had come over her, Kristina remarked, "Content isn't necessarily refreshed, Kadeem."
He finally admitted defeat. "If you insist, my lady, I am unable to object."
"I insist," replied Kristina kindly.

Once she had gone, Kadeem closed the door and sighed, privately relieved that she'd persisted. The Prince was stirring but only to roll over once more. Kadeem shook his head; he wished the fever would break, truly break. The Prince's temperature had gone down, but he hadn't woken to the world again yet and Kadeem was concerned. After such a long illness, the time needed for recovery would also be lengthy. Only half his work had been done.

Chapter 29
RECOVERY

Septadai, Week 18 – 14th Meithal, 21st Easis 1211
Arkyn's Bedchamber

ARKYN STIRRED, surfacing from feverish sleep – his body making various demands of him. To open his eyes to the light and to drink – to rid his mouth of the dust of sleep. Someone else was in his bedchamber, he could sense their vigil. He couldn't tell what time it was. The grey light of autumn masked everything, but it must be late afternoon by the deepening darkness. As the watcher realised that he had woken, soft footsteps crossed to his side. He expected Kadeem, but the hand that felt his forehead was female. That was strange, and Arkyn remembered being ill as a child and his mother using the same gesture.

A mellow, soft voice suited to the light in the room enquired, "How are you feeling, Your Highness?"

His throat worked, but he couldn't speak; his mouth was too dry. As if realising it, the same hand held a beaker to his lips. He swallowed the water gratefully and rolled onto his back. His eyes met Daia's and his registered disbelief.

Smiling at him, she said, diplomatically, "Kadeem's taking a breath of air, sir. He's hardly been out of these rooms for days. He thought you wouldn't wake yet."

Arkyn slowly croaked, "Good. He can't always be here."

"You'll not tell him that, sir… I mean, he wouldn't listen… No, that's not what I mean either…"

"I know what you mean." He tried to push himself up but found his arms too weak.

"Hang on, sir, I'll give you a hand."

A few seconds later he said, "You're practised at this."

She grinned. "I don't sit at home all day, sir. I'm often out helping sick tenants. My governess disapproves, but why shouldn't we help them? They help us. There's already enough injustice in the world. It isn't their fault they are born as they are."

"Would you change our society then?"

"No. Nevertheless, I'd happily change certain people's attitudes. Some of my peers think their tenants' issues are their tenants' fault. It makes me mad… I'm sorry, sir, hardly fitting talk for the bedside of a feverish prince."

Arkyn chuckled. "I'm sure I can cope. You know your own mind, Lady Daia. I find that refreshing. So many people are afraid to voice what they feel, especially around my family, that to find someone unafraid is gratifying."

"It must be," remarked Daia, perching on the edge of his bed.

"Yes. So, tell me, why does your governess object?"

"She thinks a lady shouldn't be in contact with anyone below her rank unless absolutely necessary. My father let me be involved in the running of the estate, as well as the house. Now she and my steward make it clear I should be only involved in the running of the house. It's maddening…"

Arkyn frowned. "But they are your lands, my lady. You're not a child. You have every right to voice your thoughts and for them to listen."

"For the most part, they *listen*, but they then don't follow my orders."

"Whom did my father appoint as local guardian here in Terasia?"

"Lord Portur, sir, and His Excellency was attentive enough, or as much as he could be, but I didn't wish to trouble him with the petty nature of my problems. I shouldn't be troubling you either. I was told nothing onerous, should you awaken."

"This isn't. This is me talking about life to someone who might be best described as a nearsister – just don't tell Kadeem."

She laughed. "Is he so determined then?"

"I rarely have to upbraid him. He's trying to do his job under difficult circumstances. Normally, he has excellent reasons for his persistence; my father's orders being one of them."

Their eyes met, both amused.

Daia said, "There's no gainsaying those orders, sir."

"No. I wouldn't have my manservant disobey my father. What's your maid like?"

"My governess says I don't need one."

"Hmm. I ought to have a talk with the lady – when I'm slightly more presentable. How are you finding Tera?"

"Interesting and diverting. Lord Irvin and I have been exploring it together."

"How is he? I really must apologise to him for abandoning him. Although, with you as a companion, I can't see he'll be complaining too much."

Daia blushed. "He seems to be enjoying himself, sir."

Arkyn watched the blush bring life to Daia's face, but, before he could tease her about it, the door opened and, having heard their voices, Kadeem entered to see all was well.

Daia hurriedly pushed herself to her feet, her blush deepening.

Kadeem glanced over, bowed, then smiled – noting the wry humour in the Prince's eyes at Lady Daia's reaction to being disturbed.

In a mock-severe voice, Arkyn chided, "You deserted your post."

"I did indeed, sir, and must ask your pardon…" The effect his unctuous voice gave was undone when, obviously relieved to see the Prince looking better, the manservant added, "However, it seems for the best; you've not been this coherent for days."

"It's nice to know you noticed…" He started coughing.

Kadeem crossed to him and mixed a throat soother. He passed it over, murmuring, "Too much talking, sir."

Once the concoction had relieved his dry throat, Arkyn said, "You're enjoying this, aren't you?"

"Not particularly, sir. I prefer to see Your Highness in full health." He caught Arkyn's eye, adding wryly, "However, if it were Prince Tain…"

Arkyn laughed and started coughing again. "That's not fair, Kadeem. Stop making me laugh." An inward pang made him realise how much he missed Tain's company in ways he hadn't expected. His brother's love of life would have been a tonic no doctor could prescribe.

Kadeem smiled. "I'm sorry, sir, but laughter is meant to be the best medicine."

Arkyn shook his head. "Go on with you. Go and get another breath of air. I'll be all right for twelve minutes."

Once the manservant had left, Daia told Arkyn of her visit to Old Ma and the fact that Tommy might be a dabster – a person who could pick up skills without trouble, a hue of the ancient Ullian Spirit of a manipulator. Talk turned from that to the ancient Cearcall, but Daia soon realised Arkyn was tiring. She excused herself adroitly. As she left, Kadeem re-entered.

Arkyn regarded him. "Thank you. I'm sorry for my behaviour that first day – I promise I'll not be so stubborn headed again."

"Your Highness, I should have handled the situation better."

"I tend to differ."

Kadeem smiled. "Then might I say, sir, that you're not just my master but also my prince. There is no circumstance, no conceivable situation – in any book on protocol – where Your Highness should feel obliged to apologise to me."

"I don't feel obliged to! I wish to and if you're quoting protocol at me, I'll point out that the wishes of princes should never be denied."

Both of them were half laughing, but both also knew they had reached an understanding.

Kadeem said, "I shall accept the apology, sir. Would you like a bath?"

"A slick change of subject in line with your normal practical manner. All we need now is a bit of philosophy; however, in answer to your ever sensible question, yes, please. I ache for Anapara."

Kadeem rang the bell. When Thomas entered, Kadeem asked him to see to preparations.

"What is it, Kadeem?" asked Arkyn when they were once more alone.

"Nothing serious, sir. I've been talking to the doctor here. He mentioned aches might plague you for some time. He suggested that a course of massage might help and recommended a practitioner. I have talked with them and had Wynfeld check them out, I've had Wealsman interview them as well in case Wynfeld or I had missed something—"

"So, what's the problem?"

"The issue is that the practitioner is a woman, and it is better that she works directly on your body, flesh to flesh."

Arkyn raised an amused eyebrow. "Have you spoken to the King?"

"Erm, yes, sir. His Majesty said it's your decision, Your Highness. I or another of your household would be there."

"All right, arrange it. I'm willing to give it a try."

A few minutes later, Thomas entered and Arkyn tried to get out of bed and failed; filleted, exhausted, his muscles weren't in his control, his strength sapped.

Kadeem murmured, "Lie still, sir. Now, put your arms around my neck, and I don't mean strangle me as you probably wish to."

Chuckling, Arkyn started coughing. "Don't make me laugh!"

"Sorry, sir. I'm going to lift you up… nice and steady…" He passed Thomas. "See His Highness' bed is changed and that a light meal is ready in his sitting room, please."

Two minutes later, after various matters had been attended to, Arkyn found his aches easing in the warm water. Kadeem gently washed his face and hair before lifting him out and drying him off. Arkyn was silent, ready to sleep once more, but Kadeem had ordered a meal for him and he did feel hungry. His manservant helped him don a clean tunic before enquiring,

"Can you stand, sir, or would you prefer me to carry you again?"
Arkyn hauled himself to his feet, but his legs folded under him.
Kadeem caught him. "Maybe another day, Your Highness. All days bring something new."
"There's the philosophy," whispered Arkyn. "All right, I'll continue submitting myself to your ministrations."
Kadeem dropped his voice. "Thank you, sir. It does help to have a willing victim – sorry, I mean invalid."
Arkyn chuckled and started coughing. "Not fair."

As they entered the sitting room, Fitz was talking with Wealsman. The captain's eyes narrowed slightly as he assessed Arkyn's state, then seeing the Prince had noticed he winked, grinned and left.
In answer to a raised eyebrow, the Acting Governor said, "I came to relieve Kadeem of his vigil, Your Highness. Master Thomas informed me you'd woken, and Secretary Stuart has left some personal correspondence for you to read, should you wish to."
Kadeem placed Arkyn in a chair with arms before balancing a tray on them. Making sure it was resting safely, he excused himself to attend to the Prince's bedchamber.
Nodding for Wealsman to take a seat, Arkyn breathed in the comforting aroma of vegetable soup and new-made bread. He managed only half the bowl of soup before his arms gave out. Without a word, Wealsman helped him finish the rest, before moving the tray to the sideboard. Through his exhaustion, Arkyn reddened. To be fed and bathed as though a toddler was humiliating. His body, however, was rebelling against him. His legs and arms giving up at the slightest sign of exertion, and his mind was still half asleep, a fog of weariness seeping through him. He'd slept for he didn't know how long, but it was surely enough to leave him better than this. How long had it been? How could he not know? It couldn't be more than a few days. A week at the most. He vaguely recalled surfacing several times, sometimes for a couple of hours, sometimes more, sometimes less, but he hadn't marked time, just fallen back into feverish slumber, oblivious of everything outside his darkened room.

Arkyn and Wealsman were talking when Kadeem re-entered. He moved around, finding a footstool for Arkyn, adding logs to the fire and clearing the detritus of the meal. A couple of moments later, he re-entered the sitting room, hesitated, but overcame his reticence.
"Your Highness, forgive me… I've just found this under the plate on the tray. I believe you've already seen it…"
Arkyn read the proffered note.

"No. That's one I haven't seen before," he admitted, his hand resting limply on the chair arm.

Kadeem blanched. "I'm sorry. I'd never have dreamt of showing it to you if I thought you hadn't already seen it, Your Highness."

Wealsman, taking the note, read it. Irate, he faced Kadeem. "What on Erinna were you thinking? Even had His Highness already seen this, you should never have made him re-read it!"

His befuddled mind wanting to ignore them, Arkyn said, "I'll upbraid my manservant if necessary, Acting Governor. Why *did* you show it to me, Kadeem?"

"To ask how many others you've had, Your Highness. I'm sorry. Lord Wealsman is right – maybe I've lost my objectivity."

Arkyn, by sheer willpower, rose. "No. You haven't. You're also right. There have been others since I arrived. I have ignored them for the pathetic scribblings they are. Who else knows about them?"

"Only we here, sir."

"Right. Burn the note."

Arkyn watched as Kadeem reluctantly did so. His willpower seemed to crumble. Kadeem and Wealsman hurried to help him. He ended up holding one of each of their hands as he lowered himself into his chair.

He murmured, "Forget about that note. On your oaths, forget about that note."

The faces of his companions cleared of preoccupation and, thanking Alcis for the obligations of fealty and oaths, Arkyn listened to Kadeem's fussing.

"What were you thinking of, trying to stand, sir? You know you're not quite strong enough."

Wealsman waited until Kadeem had left before saying, "Nice try, Your Highness. It's a shame I let go of your hand before you got to the bit about oaths."

"You'll forget about it, Wealsman! I'm not adding paranoia to everything else."

"Sir, these notes threaten your life and you're already ill. I can't in conscience do as you ask."

"Wealsman, I gave you an order!"

The Acting Governor knelt by the Prince's chair. "You did, but I'm also vassal-bound to your father; His Majesty would never want the existence of these notes ignored—"

"Wealsman, you will, by no action, be informing my father of these notes, by no slip of the tongue, by no accident or intention. Do I have your word?"

"You have my word, sir. Much as I dread the consequences if anything happens."

Arkyn sighed. "You had to put that obligation on me. I shall make one concession then, no two. If my father should ask specifically, you may tell him. The second, I will allow you to investigate if no-one knows what you're investigating."

Wealsman's brows knotted. "Should make it interesting, Your Highness, but I'll do my best."

Kadeem re-entered to say the bedchamber was ready. Arkyn tried to push himself up.

Wealsman said, "No, my prince, I'll bear this burden if you'll permit me."

Arkyn nodded. Wealsman carefully picked him up as Kadeem opened the door. Arkyn relaxed into the bed and within two minutes appeared to be fast asleep.

Wealsman settled himself in a chair and picked up a book. He glanced at the hovering manservant.

"I'm more than capable of watching His Highness snooze."

"Thank you, sir, but if you have matters which need your attention, I would not interrupt them. Fitz and Lady Daia were here earlier—"

Wealsman smiled. "The matters which require my attention are in this room. Go on. You've been here for days. His Highness is asleep; he'll never know."

Having heard his manservant leave, Arkyn whispered, "Well done. The other matter… it wasn't Daia or Fitz. The other notes were in or on my desk, swamped by paperwork. You'll excuse me if I'm not very communicative."

Wealsman jumped. "Of course, Your Highness. Would it make you feel better if I said I'll count it as a blessing?"

Arkyn chuckled. "I'll ignore that. Goodnight, my lord."

"Night, sir."

Chapter 30
NIGHTMARE AND CHESS

Late Evening
Arkyn's Bedchamber

WEALSMAN SAT with a pencil and a piece of parchment, doodling and frustrated by the impossible task ahead. Discover who had left the notes without raising suspicions, ask questions without alerting Wynfeld and without being arrested for being too interested in the Prince's retinue. Running Terasia suddenly felt simple.

Slipping his well-heeled shoes off, Wealsman got up quietly so as not to disturb Arkyn. Crossing to the window, he twitched the curtain aside, looking out at the gardens, but it didn't help; there was no flash of inspiration. Without being able to ask questions, could he ever discover the perpetrator? He glanced towards Arkyn. Regular breaths reassured him that the Prince was sleeping deeply not fitfully. He padded thoughtfully over to the bed.

'Why have you tied my hands?' He took Arkyn's hand carefully to tuck it beneath them. *'I wouldn't break faith with you but…'* Straightening the covers, he checked Arkyn's temperature. *'…how can I face Adeone if I leave you to be threatened?'*

Arkyn started tossing and turning. Wealsman stilled as the Prince became increasingly agitated. Ringing the bell for Kadeem, he tried to wake Arkyn, cursing quietly to himself.

Soft-footed as ever, Kadeem entered and jerked his head. Wealsman moved swiftly aside. Realising gentle tactics weren't working, Kadeem shook Arkyn harder.

Arkyn woke, shaking. He didn't say anything. Instead, his eyes roved around the room, looking at everything but the two other people there.

Checking his temperature, Kadeem enquired, "Was it a nightmare, sir?"

"Yes."

Kadeem knew from his tone that was as much as Arkyn would reveal. "I'll leave you to sleep, sir."

Troubled, Kadeem left. Arkyn finally glanced at Wealsman, who looked steadily back.

"Don't you want to know what the nightmare was about?"

"I didn't think Your Highness wanted to talk about it."

Arkyn sighed. "I don't." His tone changed. "Help me up, please. I wish to sit by the fire for a time."

"Would you prefer it if I called Kadeem again, sir?"

"No, he'll fuss."

"Let me at least find a wrap for your shoulders, otherwise I might find myself being rebuked – politely, I'll allow."

Arkyn watched Wealsman move around the room with a disconcerting competence.

"Now, sir…"

Recognising the tone, Arkyn grimaced. "Kadeem is paid to fuss, Wealsman. You're not required to."

Wealsman's lips twitched. "I take the hint, Your Highness."

"Good, because it was more of a blatancy. Let's see if I can stand."

Half reluctantly, Wealsman stood aside. Arkyn found he was steadier than he had been, but his legs still buckled. Wealsman caught him and offered support as the Prince fought his way over to a chair by the fire, gritting his teeth in determination until he sank onto it.

"Could you do me a favour, Wealsman, and leave me alone for six minutes? I'm perfectly able to scream should an assassin come knocking."

When the Acting Governor had left, Arkyn relaxed. He'd not been alone since soon after he fell ill. He shivered, remembering the nightmare. The void had been the dark of the deepest night. He'd been falling and, looking up, there'd been a bright line, a rope from which he'd fallen. If he could just reach that rope, he'd be fine, but there were other figures, his brother and father, teetering, tottering, almost falling and Scanlon had been jiggling the rope, trying to tip them off. The surrounding void had contained others he recognised, family who had died: King Altarius, Prince Lachlan, his mother and his sister, Ella. They'd reached out to him, but he belonged with the living. He'd been reaching up when he'd heard a soft voice saying, *'How can I face Adeone if I leave you to be threatened?'* He'd struggled even harder, endeavouring to reach the beautiful light. He'd been a finger's width from catching the line when Kadeem woke him.

The door opened. It couldn't be six minutes, but if dreams could take seconds and feel like hours, then minutes could feel like seconds.

Wealsman knew it was longer. Seeing the Prince was as white as when he'd first woken, the Acting Governor walked over to the decanters and poured a good measure of whiskey. Arkyn took it but, instead of drinking it, placed it by his chair.

Wealsman squeezed Arkyn's shoulder. "It was a nightmare, sir, best forgotten."

"It felt so very real."

"Nightmares often do, sir."

Arkyn studied him. "Do you suffer from them, my lord?"

"I did when I was younger and please, call me Percival, if you wish."

Arkyn didn't seem to hear the request. "How did you stop them?"

"I don't know. I know they dwindled after I started talking to someone about them, but if this was an isolated incident, I'm not sure it would help."

Wealsman glanced at a chair and Arkyn nodded. They sat in silence for a couple of minutes until Arkyn started explaining the nightmare, concluding with,

"…I heard a voice asking how anyone could face His Majesty should something happen to me and I knew I had to reach for the rope, but I couldn't catch hold of it. I kept trying; I couldn't let anyone else suffer."

Wealsman started and paled. Arkyn was paraphrasing his words. The Prince didn't notice; he was too busy staring into the flames and absorbing the warmth. Yet he was shaking, cradling his own body, at the memory.

Wealsman saw again the child who had become a man too quickly. He knew what he wanted to do but didn't know how the Prince would take it.

Throwing convention to the winds, he whispered, "Would you like a hug, Arkyn?"

The Prince never heard him, never heard the unstudied informality that suggested the name wasn't unfamiliar to him without the title.

Ignoring his qualms, Wealsman rose and pulled him into that hug, careful not to touch the Prince's skin. Arkyn relaxed but was all too aware Wealsman wasn't a member of his family or nearfamily. He shouldn't be showing weakness, but he couldn't fight off such concern. Wealsman's company didn't feel intrusive or uncomfortable.

Wealsman, on the other hand, was wondering what Adeone would say when he found out. Maybe it didn't matter. He wouldn't be telling anyone, and he doubted that Arkyn would.

Arkyn broke the hug first. "Thank you."

"It's not a problem."

Biting his bottom lip, as though he was Tain, Arkyn sat back down, folding his legs under him. Wealsman registered the action of a person who felt more at ease. He picked up the prince's drink and passed it to him. This time, Arkyn took a sip. They sat talking for some time, Wealsman keeping both the fire and their glasses replenished.

Kadeem disturbed their privacy, slipping into the room to relieve Wealsman of his watch. Noticing Arkyn had more colour, he made himself busy readying the Prince's bed and his own pallet. Even if Arkyn wouldn't recognise it, Kadeem knew the Prince was tiring.

Wealsman took his cue, allowing the conversation to lull. Three minutes later, the Acting Governor excused himself.

Arkyn finished his drink and pushed himself up. A glare kept Kadeem rooted to the spot. Arkyn managed a couple of steps before his legs folded. Kadeem caught him.

"Everything takes its time, sir."

"With the review continuing, I don't have the time for it to take, Kadeem. I must see Lord Iris in the morning."

"You must see the doctor first, Your Highness. When he says you're fit, I shall inform His Majesty and only then shall I send for His Lordship."

"Kadeem… As you've said, I'm perfectly coherent."

Business-like, Kadeem remarked, "Yes, sir, but I don't recall saying 'fit', 'well' or any other word, or phrase, that would indicate you no longer have flu or suffer from the effects of it. Lord Iris has coped perfectly well for the last fortnight. I'm sure he'll cope for a bit longer."

"How long?" exclaimed Arkyn, aghast. "I can't lie around any longer! What must people think? I'm not here to let others do my work for me."

"Your Highness, no-one questions your dedication or ability to do the review; we're solely concerned for your health. I can't hand you back to your duties before the doctor and His Majesty let me. I can't take the chance. You're feeling better today, but tomorrow—"

"Kadeem, remind me who you work for."

"Ultimately, until you're of alunan-age, His Majesty, Your Highness."

Arkyn had the grace to smile at being outwitted. "I hoped you'd forgotten that."

"With His Majesty requesting daily updates, sir, it is a bit hard to."

Arkyn sighed. "All right, Kadeem, I'm sorry for putting you in an invidious position."

Kadeem smiled. "There's no need to apologise, sir."

"Then I'll try to work out what to do about such dedication. I presume you've been told to stay away from discussing my duties."

"I believe our orders do follow that thought, yes, sir."

"Forewarned. How are my household and staff?"

"Sir…"

"Indulge me and I might raise your pay."

"Is this bribery, Your Highness?" enquired Kadeem, amused.

"Yes. Does it work?"

"I was always taught to be above corruption. Apparently, the rewards are better—"

Arkyn chuckled. "They may well be. Humour me and I won't ask about the review, I promise."

Kadeem hesitated. "All right, Your Highness, I'll answer what I can, but we're all well enough and have no complaint."

"Kadeem…" Arkyn's tolerant voice still told his manservant to stop procrastinating.

Kadeem sighed. "Sir. Edward's snowed under and Lord Iris is re-evaluating his opinion of your administrator. He's all right though; Thomas is looking after him."

"Good. I don't want anyone to become exhausted by working for me."

* * *

Over the next few days, Arkyn fretted. The masseuse revealed that until the doctor declared him fit, a course of massage could harm than help because his body would need rest to fight the lingering infection. She talked him through various oils to help, passing some to Kadeem to add to warm baths. Kadeem, still being cautious, took the name of the oils and sent to Wynfeld to obtain them.

The commander continued his investigations into the anonymous notes, unaware that Wealsman was trying to puzzle out the same problem. Ironically, they each had the other down as a potential suspect. Yet where Wealsman was concentrating his thoughts on the Prince's household and staff, Wynfeld wasn't – he was looking at everyone, as he wasn't aware letters had been found in Arkyn's private rooms. Wealsman discounted Kadeem and Edward, both of whom he considered were too content with their life to disturb the situation. Yet, of the middle-ranking servants and clerks, he had few ideas as to the guilty party. The confusion of Arkyn's first few days in the province, and more latterly his illness, meant that many had had to be in places where their normal status would have debarred them. He needed some sort of proof; he needed a note, but there had been no more.

* * *

Five days after Arkyn's fever had broken, he smiled in welcome. "Come in, Lord Wealsman. You'll have to excuse me; I have a slight cough and my legs are still shaky, though I'm regaining an appetite on the cook's meals; so, I'm glad you could join me for dinner. Even more so if there's a chance I can wheedle *some* news out of you. Kadeem is being annoyingly taciturn."

Blandly Wealsman said, "Sorry, sir, my lips are sealed on the fact the exchequer has given Lord Iris a headache."

"Luckily, I went deaf. So, if we're not to discuss my duties, how about you drop the 'sir' and call me Arkyn? I'm sick of hearing nothing but formality and I can bully you."

'Like father, like son', thought Wealsman. "I'll see how far I can manage to remember that."

"Good. So, what news have you got for me?"

"Not much. Lord Portur went to the heavens shortly after you were taken ill and Lady Portur has decided to marry again."

"That was quick," said Arkyn, astonished. "I take it you are going to tell me who."

"She rather foolishly, in my opinion, decided to accept my offer. We're getting married in spring."

Arkyn smiled warmly. "Congratulations! I hope you'll be happy. Percival, do you, by any chance, play chess?"

"I did, Arkyn. I've not played it for some years."

"Would you give me a game?"

"Certainly, though I warn you, I'm not very good."

"Neither am I; father always beats me."

Wealsman smiled reminiscently; Adeone had always beaten him, as well.

Arkyn continued. "Why haven't you played it for so long?"

"My previous opponent moved on, Your Highness," replied Wealsman, purposefully formal.

Arkyn tutted, "That didn't last long, did it, *my lord*?"

Wealsman pretended to be annoyed at himself. Keeping his acquaintance with Adeone private was tricky, but he was certain that Arkyn would never have permitted him to investigate the notes if he knew of the friendship. He'd have, somehow, forced him to forget: used the binding properties of oaths – which most knew nothing of when they took them – to compel him to disregard the notes. Wealsman would have liked to see if such obligations could have any effect on his memory; it would certainly have put the ancient magic to the test; he could remember exactly what he was doing on any given date. At times, he found it most annoying and so proving he could forget something would come as a welcome change – not that he'd be able to remember forgetting something, or would he? If you truly forgot something, did the memory that you once knew it linger or did that go too?

Wealsman considered it unfair to let the Prince win, but it was a close-run game: Arkyn winning on a hair's breadth from stalemate. It was a long match and by the end of it, Arkyn was stifling his yawns.

Wealsman noticed. "I think we ought to leave the rematch for now."

Arkyn pushed himself up from his chair, steadying himself as he did so. "You're probably right. I ought to lie down."

Seeing how shaky Arkyn was, Wealsman walked over to him.

"Put your arm around my shoulders."

* * *

Once Arkyn was settled, Wealsman walked the short distance to Kristina's rooms thoughtfully.

"How is he?" she asked before he'd even greeted her.

"Shaky. It'll take him some time to get over it. Not a complaint though all evening."

"You were there a while."

"Yes, he trounced me at chess. Do we have some time to ourselves?"

"If you can stay awake. I've told the household to go to bed though."

"I'm sure I'll cope," he replied, holding her smiling gaze.

Chapter 31
OEDRANIAN SUPPER
Septadai, Week 19 – 21st Meithal, 7th Meithis 1211
Inner Office

IN OEDRAN, King Adeone was trying not to fret over what was happening in Terasia. Arkyn would rise to any challenge and his son's retinue were competent. For the moment, his son was being cared for with practicality and dedication. Fitz had told him how hard Kadeem was working and Kadeem had told him precisely nothing about that, only how Arkyn was when Arkyn couldn't. It was oddly reassuring how closely Kadeem guarded his son's privacy.

As far as the official side of Arkyn's visit went, he'd not interfered. Wealsman would deal with provincial matters and Iris had carried out three reviews, the most recent in 1209. Adeone was confident that he would have everything ready for Arkyn on his return to his duties. He also suspected Iris would try to steer his son down a route of less drastic change. He amused himself by imagining how Arkyn would face the hurdle that Iris' traditional methods left in people's paths. Iris was an excellent advisor, and Adeone knew mutual respect would form between his son and the Lord of Oedran, it was just what happened in the meantime.

Richardson entered the Inner Office with a letter in his hand. Adeone eyed him; the smile said it wasn't anything to worry about – or at least the administrator didn't think it was, which, Adeone admitted to himself, was a very different matter.

Adeone took the letter and crooked an eyebrow. Wealsman's official seal, as opposed to the one they used privately to confuse clerks and spies. Curious. Marked private – well, that was normal.

"How did this arrive, Richardson?"

"Special rider, Sire. I was rather intrigued."

Adeone nodded in dismissal and broke the seal. He swiftly read the official invitation to Wealsman's wedding. He chuckled. An official invitation, sent by special rider. Well, that wasn't quite what he'd expected. Wealsman playing by the rules was new. He was still contemplating it when Richardson re-entered, carrying another letter.

"My apologies, sir. This came with the dispatches from Terasia. Anderson's just passed it on."

Adeone saw the seal. "Anderson? Seriously? You let that old rogue handle these?"

Richardson's lips twitched. "He knows *when* to keep his mouth shut, sir, and his methods, although unorthodox, are never malicious."

"True." Adeone broke the seal.

You know you'd like to see their faces!

Wealsman's sloping hand. Short, to the point and full of persuasion.

"Richardson, how difficult would it be to, say, reorganise my diary for spring?"

"In what way *reorganise*, sir?" enquired his administrator warily.

"Theoretically, if I wasn't in Oedran, for say, several weeks."

"It would be—" started Richardson in a cautionary voice.

"See it as a challenge and don't tell *anyone*!"

Richardson hesitated. "Theoretically, sir?"

"Theoretically," confirmed Adeone with a glint in his eye. "I'm going to go down to Court soon. Lord and Lady Landis are due to dine with me later. You, Jacobs and Kenton can finish whenever you wish."

* * *

Quarter of an hour later, he walked through the Palace with a small smile still twitching at his lips. Just the idea of people's faces if he visited

Terasia was worth it. He entered the official Court rooms and passed a pleasant couple of hours talking with various lords and his mother's cousin, Merchant Chapa – who, with his normal incisive observation, noted that the King looked like a boy with mischief still to do.

Adeone was leaving Court when he caught the sound of soft footsteps behind him. He wasn't concerned, for the guards, including Sergeant Hillbeck, were smiling slightly. He was passing through the old greeting room, when very faintly, only just loud enough for him to hear, and certainly not for anyone else to, a voice murmured,

"Our nearfather has a glint in his eye. I wonder what he's planning."

Without turning around, Adeone said, "For that, you'll both dine with me. As for the mischief, if you're not careful, you might find out." He turned and eyed his eldest nearchildren, who smiled warily. Adeone was pleased to see they certainly hadn't expected his response. He continued, "Should I mention your parents are also joining me?"

Julia, who'd uttered the mischievous comment, curtsied. "Good evening, Your Majesty."

Julius rose from a bow. "I apologise for my twin, Sire."

Straight-faced, Adeone confided, "Start apologising for your sister now, Lord Julius, and you'll never stop. How are you both? Enjoying Court?"

"Of course, sir. We get to stay out," replied Julia.

Adeone laughed slightly, "Well, for now, you will have to come and have dinner with me – if you can cope with the honour."

Julius said, "I'm sure we can cope, Sire. Thank you, we'd like to."

"Come on then. I must admit I've been an absent nearfather over recent months."

"I'm sure we haven't noticed, sir," remarked Julia.

Adeone grinned. "So, you haven't missed me then? Isn't it traditional you should?"

Julius interrupted before his sister could say traditions could be changed. "It is, Sire, and no matter what my twin says we have missed Your Majesty. How is Prince Arkyn?"

Adeone appreciated the slickness of Julius' change of subject. "Recovering. He's going to come home in spring. The Acting Governor is reluctant for him to travel in winter after a bout of flu. I must admit I agree with Lord Wealsman, it really wouldn't be a good idea."

They made their way through the rest of the Palace quietly. Richardson was still working when they entered the Outer Office.

Adeone shook his head at him gently, "I said that was it for the evening."

"Yes, Sire, I just wanted to get this done. Your Majesty's diary could *theoretically* be reorganised. Lord and Lady Landis have arrived, but could I just have a quick word?"

Adeone glanced at the twins who stepped back into the Audience Chamber. "What is it?"

"Word has just arrived, sir, that the chief groom has died suddenly."

"Jack?" Adeone's face drained of colour. "When?"

"Just after Your Majesty went to Court. I didn't like to bring the news there."

"Thank you. From recollection he had no family. Can you deal with the arrangements? Don't leave it to the Steward. I want to be informed, for Ira's sake."

"Understood, sir. Do you want me to cancel the dinner?"

Adeone shook his head, took a deep breath, rearranged his features and collected his nearchildren before entering the Inner Office. They shouldn't be bothered by his angst.

Landis said, "Good evening, Sire. If I might say so there is a glint in your eye. Dare I ask why?"

Adeone walked over to his desk, retrieved the invitation from Wealsman, passing it to his friend, who read it.

"Interesting, sir. Are you planning to go?"

Adeone shrugged. "Might not be a good idea; however, I'm sure it wouldn't be the first bad idea I've had. Oh, as you can see, your renegade twins are joining us. I hope you don't mind."

Landis eyed his children. "As long as they behave themselves, Sire."

Adeone's eyes twinkled. "They have been the model of propriety so far, Festus. They haven't missed me at all."

Julia shuffled her feet, embarrassed.

Lady Landis pursed her lips. "Julia, what have I always told you?"

Adeone's lips twitched. He was having all on not laughing.

Julia noticed. "I'm not sure, mother; there is so much you tell me."

Landis sighed. "Julia, don't be rude to your mother. You know full well what she is referring to. Your Majesty, I must apologise."

"I can cope, Festus. She's your daughter."

A couple of minutes later, they entered the triniculum and, for the first time in a while, Adeone missed Ira's presence. He had got used to her not being there, but tonight the blade of loss was again piercing his heart. He sighed gently. Festus noticed and put a sympathetic hand on his friend's arm. They'd known each other for so long that sometimes words only got in the way. Almost as soon as the meal was over, Landis tactfully suggested his children return to Court. Cornelia caught the mood and went with them.

When they were alone, Landis said, "I'm sorry about Jack, but is that all that's bothering you?"

Adeone ran a hand over his head. "I'd almost forgotten until Richardson told me about Jack. I found this on my desk this morning." He passed over a note.

Life's end is always sudden, but the journey might be slow.

Landis swore. "I take it you've investigated."

"No point. The last one arrived in the same way."

Landis shot his friend a look. "How many have you had, sir?"

"Enough. It comes with the job, but these are different. Richardson doesn't find them. They're on my desk in the morning."

"I take it you *have* told Richardson."

"Why wouldn't I have told him?" enquired Adeone.

"So he doesn't know. What did the last one say?"

"What they say is immaterial. They get past guards and secretaries, but they're just letters."

Landis cursed under his breath. "So all the attempts on your life in the last couple of years were inconsiderate coincidences then? Jack died suddenly. Is that a coincidence?"

"Why would anyone harm Jack?"

"Hmm. All right. I see the point. I'll investigate the appearance of these letters discreetly. I'll tell your secretaries I'm doing spot checks as part of my office as Defender of the King's Life."

"What if I tell you not to?" enquired Adeone.

"For once, Your Majesty, I'll ignore your order. As a Defender, it is my responsibility." He grinned. "You gave me the post. Has his Highness found the tax that went missing in Terasia yet?"

"I'm not sure. He's not back at his desk, and I'm not hurrying him. He needs to rest still. More time also means more chance for things to be found. I just wish it had been an easier first review for him, what with poisoning, one of Roth's servants breaking into his private desk—"

"When did that happen?"

"The day before Arkyn fell ill. They sorted it." Suddenly very tired, Adeone said, "Will you excuse me if I simply say goodnight?"

"Of course, sir."

Chapter 32
SOLAR AND STORIES

Cisadai, Week 20 – 23rd Meithal, 9th Meithis 1211

Solar

SINCE THE MORNING he'd been taken ill Arkyn's world had shrunk and, for a while, the small space away from hustle and bustle of the Residence was welcome and comforting. Then, for no reason at all, it became frustrating and demoralising. He couldn't yet resume his duties. Artzman didn't want him to head into the cold, but he needed a fresh perspective. He asked Wealsman for ideas.

The Residence's solar was a similar size to his sitting room: spacious but not vast. By the time Arkyn arrived, the oak and fir fire was blazing merrily in the grate and the sun streaked through the square panes, falling onto seating arranged around the deep window, overlooking the gardens – where fell winds had claimed the fiery autumn leaves, and conifers, in their evergreen shrouds, contrasted with the skeletal forms of their deciduous cousins. In the weak sun, fingers of ice withdrew their bitter grip, and puddles were thawing from their frost induced sleep. Late autumn would soon fall into winter, with its sleet and snows, darker days and longer nights.

Arkyn eased himself into a chair, tilting his face towards the sun. Fitz smiled to himself. He'd told the guards to stay away. Sometimes it was better if they were at hand, other times they highlighted a target's location. He and Arkyn would be all right, just the two of them.

Arkyn saw Fitz's gentle smile. "You can be like a mother hen at times."

Fitz snorted. "Now that's something your father and grandfather have never called me."

"You surprise me. It's nice to be out of my rooms. Did anyone else fall ill?"

"Not that I'm aware of," said Fitz. "Sometimes it's like that. There's no rhyme nor reason to why one person is ill and another isn't. Getting soaked to the skin possibly didn't help."

Arkyn snorted. "It didn't dampen my spirits at the time."

"That sense of humour, though, that's definitely your father," said Fitz. "He's been worried."

"I know," murmured Arkyn. "There's not much I can do to stop that."

"No. Not much. We've tried to reassure him. Lord Iris has been enquiring after your health daily as well."

"Probably wants to know how long he's got until I start interfering," commented Arkyn wryly.

Fitz shook his head. "I doubt that, sir. He's used to that sort of interference. He was one of your grandfather's closest friends and cares more than he shows. I don't think he's ever forgotten your Uncle Adlai or the fever that killed him so young."

Arkyn swallowed. "I forget, sometimes, that Adlai was my uncle. Father doesn't talk of him, but then Adlai died long before he was born. Grandfather didn't ever mention him, not to me. You didn't know him either, did you?"

"No. Lord Iris did. Lady Amara too, of course. They'd be happy to—"

"Sometimes it's hard to ask," said Arkyn sorrowfully, staring out over the gardens.

* * *

Half an hour later, the door opened to children laughing. They stopped abruptly. Elsa apologising hesitantly.

Arkyn craned round, glad of the distraction. "Don't worry. Come in. Karl, you're welcome as well, wherever you're hiding."

"Thank you, sir," said Elsa as she and her brother entered.

Arkyn groaned. "Will you do me one favour today?"

Elsa and Karl nodded in unison.

"Good. I'm off duty and my name is Arkyn. Please use it. Let the adults around here deal with the formalities."

Elsa giggled. "We'll try. How are you feeling? The whole Residence has been worried, the whole city rather."

"Better than I did, thank you. What have you two been doing whilst I've been ill?"

"Lessons. Pa insists," muttered Karl.

Arkyn laughed. "Yes, so did mine. It's very unfair of parents. It spoils all our fun. What exactly are you meant to be learning?"

They talked for some time before they heard a voice calling for the twins.

Arkyn asked mildly, "Why the long faces?"

"It's our teacher."

Conspiratorially, Arkyn whispered, "Let's see if I can't return a favour, if she finds us."

The teacher did. She knew where her pupils were likely to hide. She entered without knocking and stopped uncertainly in the doorway.

Arkyn said, "Come in. I believe I've borrowed the company of your charges. Would it put you out too much if they stayed here for a time?"

Karl and Elsa struggled to keep straight faces as their teacher stammered, "Erm, not, not at all, Your Highness, but Secretary—"

"I'll make it right with Thomkins. Go on. Enjoy your extra afternoon off."

Once her footsteps had retreated, Arkyn grinned. "That's dealt with your lessons."

Giggling, Elsa asked, "Did you ever do that to your tutor, Arkyn?"

"No. My long-suffering tutors – well, they were a good bunch. My father used to turn up unexpectedly and give us an afternoon off."

"Do you miss him?" enquired Karl.

"At times. He's my father, I'm bound to. Don't you miss yours when you're in Gerymor?"

Karl nodded. "But it's better than him and mother fighting."

"How did they come to be split so widely?"

"Lady Escley is Lord Simble's granddaughter. She married Lord Escley, and mother had been working for her here in Tera. She simply decided to go with her," explained Elsa.

"So, when are you going west?"

"Not until next year, sir. Pa's too busy to take us and mother can't get away. They insist we're too young to travel on our own."

"How old are you both exactly?" asked Arkyn. "I've guessed that you're about Prince Tain's age."

Elsa nodded. "To the day. We were born on the Munewid, 1200."

"Were you now? Tradition says the Munewid is a lucky day. It's an interesting game finding people born on the same day."

A knock at the door heralded Kadeem bearing a tray. He noted the presence of two extra people. "I'll return with more glasses, momentarily, Your Highness."

"There's more in that cupboard," said Karl, pointing.

Elsa scrambled to her feet and retrieved two extra glasses. Two moments later, they were sipping warm rosehip and honey drinks.

After half an hour or so, Arkyn finally enquired, "What horrors have I saved you from this afternoon?"

Karl grumbled, "History, dull and dismal."

"Really? I've never found history that bad."

"No, sir, but we're learning of the empire from a different point of view."

Arkyn nodded. "True, or maybe you've not got to the interesting bits. Have you heard Ull's Story?"

Elsa's eyes sparkled. "Yes, we enjoyed *that*."

"How about the Cearcall? Do you know anything about them?" (Karl and Elsa shook their heads.) "Do you want to hear about them? I can't promise to be a skilled storyteller or historian, but I know a bit."

They agreed, so Arkyn settled in to tell them a short history of the Cearcall.

* * *

When Ull, tired from his travels, gifted the last Star Stone of Annire to the novice in the Pale Lands, the Ring of Twelve was born. From a world at strife came a peace enduring. The threads of magic that had streaked through the sky with blinding white light connected and bound magic to the stones. Those who had abused it found justice in its withdrawal.

Ull returned to the mainland, leaving the novice to learn her healing skills and truly become the Meithrin. When news of his death reached her, she looked at the stone and resolved to find the others whom he had mentioned. She sailed for Macia and discovered the Sentire. The islands were settling into a peaceful time. His reading of the weather and the land, of the sea and his fellows' feelings, helped bring a prosperity the islands had rarely known. There were fewer wrecks on the jagged rocks of Gryland, fewer failed harvests and larger catches of fish. They talked as best they could through an interpreter before deciding to sail on. The winds of the Ranaegir took them south to Serpent Isle and to the Espier's land. He needed no interpreter for he could understand all languages. They sailed west and landed at Amista. Deciding that the Wright was closest, they travelled across Areal and entered the country we know as Denshire, then called Cearcallead. In Cearden, an old fort had become a peaceful palace. There they found the Wright. In those days, Cearcallead was a rich country, its land productive, as green as Terasia and as beautiful as Anapara. Only in the very centre of the country was there arid land. The desert which stretches over the country today came much later and the Cearcall never then dreamed they would cause it.

As the four talked, more of the Ring of Twelve arrived. From Terasia and Gerymor came the Beran and Rheol. From the west came the Jeci. From the north came the Amser, the Sennachie, the Memini, the Skifta and the Sundrian. The twelve were met and would meet many times more.

Cearcallead became synonymous with their meetings, for though sometimes they would meet in Tradere, and occasionally at Amista, they preferred the temperate climate and relaxed atmosphere that Cearcallead offered. They took their name from the country and became the Cearcall.

As the years passed, their influence grew. Peace flowed throughout the lands that had once been at war. Trade routes flourished, towns developed, news flowed from place to place. Countries that had been mysteries became friends.

Soon word reached the Cearcall that a child of Tradere, the Amser's country, had shown an ability to sense what people were feeling. The Sentire travelled there; it seemed the child might be another sensor. She wasn't but she was the first of the hues – a medium. Magic was moving, fragmenting, finding new people, children who could wield it. With the knowledge came the question – who raised it first we do not know, but the question was simple – when the Cearcall joined their ancestors, what would happen to the magic they had harnessed? Would the peace they had wrought founder? Would the lands descend once more into the morass of battles – known now as the Age of Emergent Kingdoms? Who would hold the stones Ull had gifted them?

Children were being born who could control magic. Could they find successors? Apprentices they could train both in their magic and their diplomacy. The more the children used magic, the easier they were to find. Eventually, each found an heir to their magic, their spirit in its pure form, and so the stones passed to them on the death of their forbear. By this method of searching and training, the stones passed from hand to hand down generations, gifting greater powers and releasing small amounts of magical energy into the lands. The more there was in the air, the more they produced.

Some of those who showed signs of having a lesser form of magic, of having a hue of a spirit, managed to use this magic and not always for the betterment of their countries. Skirmishes broke out, political and military, and the Cearcall realised the magic Ull had brought was becoming dangerous once again.

Storing magic, taking it out of the air safely, became their goal. They could then draw on it at will, but others, with less righteous aims, could not.

The Cearcall began experimenting. The Sentire discovered the affinity magic has for gold. The Wright, successive Wrights, tried various means of trapping magic with gold. Some experiments ended badly, minor explosions were not unknown and the Cearcall nearly gave up. If storing the magic was more dangerous, then it wasn't worth it? The Wright of the day refused to surrender and eventually he invented globes. We don't know how they were made. No-one has ever melted down one of the golden orbs or dared to cut into one. The globes began to store the magical energy and there weren't further accidents. Confident that they were safe, the Cearcall stored them in the Cearcall Tower, an immense structure in Cearcallead. It was said that you could see the Pale Lands from the meeting room at its apex – although no-one other than the Cearcall ever met there. Not even their apprentices were allowed in. History says that during the later years of the Cearcall, the tower hummed and glowed in the light of the moons.

The advancement of society during the, mainly peaceful, Cearcallian Era was different in each country. It wasn't an empire ruled over by the Cearcall. Each country still had its own government. The early monarchs had agreed they would not claim rights over the Cearcall, so they were without a higher authority to answer to. The rulers asked for advice or help and received it, outwitting many uprisings and uncovering traitors; however, as time passed and memories of war faded, the Cearcall's help could be selective and if they didn't like a regime, they would watch it fall. There was, at one point, a prophecy that said their selfishness would be their downfall. With typical deafness, they laughed it off. For many years, they were right to do so. They weren't all selfish and would help people where they saw the help would be for the better.

Over the centuries, they learnt much; they learnt the ideas people formed could take on more-substantial shapes if the Jeci and the

Sennachie worked with the Sentire and the Wright. Between them, they decided to see if they could personify concepts such as truth and justice, peace and strength. They found briefly that they could. It took twenty-five years before they could personify any concept completely and then they could even hold conversations with them. The Cearcall helped to build the current Justice Hall that stands in Oedran, accidentally trapping Truth and Justice in the walls of the building with a star stone as though it were their prison, although the ideals of truth and justice were not trapped. Many would have us believe it was the foreshadowing of everything that went afterwards – the beginning of the end for the Cearcall: haste, arrogance and recklessness had formed the basis of destruction.

There were twelve countries at this point. The twelve we know today: Anapara, Bayan, Macian Isles, Pale Lands, Serpent Isle, Areal, Iridian (now the Low Plains), Lufian, Tradere, Cearcallead (now known as Denshire), Terasia and Gerymor. Then from the western seas came a rare visitation. Beyond the fire seas is a country known as Wandarin. At least there had been rumours of it. Somehow, their ship had sailed to Lufian. Others must have gone to Wandarin by accident or intention, for they had heard of the Cearcall and came seeking advice. The Wandoril visit had rather unfortunate timing.

* * *

Arkyn paused in his telling to answer a knock at the door.

Kadeem entered. "I'm sorry for interrupting, sir…"

Arkyn sighed, recognising Kadeem's tone. "I believe, twins, my manservant is trying to hint he thinks I'm overdoing it, again. Maybe you'd better go."

They rose, Elsa saying, "Of course, we should have thought. Thank you."

Arkyn smiled. "I've enjoyed myself. Go on; enjoy the rest of your day. I doubt your teacher will bother you again this afternoon." Once they'd left, Arkyn put his head back on the chair, closing his eyes, strains clear on his face.

Kadeem hesitated. "Your Highness, come and lie down for a time."

"When I've some energy. Lose yourself for half an hour. You too, Fitz."

The captain and manservant shared a glance.

"All right, just you, Kadeem. I know defeat when I feel it."

Six minutes later, Arkyn was asleep with the weak sun on his face. Fitz looked at his peaceful features and smiled to himself. In the lines of the Prince's face were all the FitzAlcis he'd ever served. He thought back to those other princes and kings. Not all of them were dead, but those who had known what he'd done for them were. Those who'd known he'd protected King Altarius when he needed it most – when a rebellion had been defeated only for Altarius to return to the destruction of his life in Oedran. Those who'd known that he'd risked arrest for treason, keeping everyone out of Altarius' chambers when he needed time to grieve for a lost family.

Fitz never spoke of that night and no-one ever asked him about it twice, but he was always to be found guarding the FitzAlcis. He'd spent years collecting intelligence, but, in times of stress, he'd always been at their side. Adeone had learned by observation that Fitz was to be trusted and the knowledge had been passed on to his sons. There was very little that Fitz didn't know about the FitzAlcis.

* * *

Arkyn awoke with a jolt an hour or so later.

Fitz asked mildly, "Shall we go and put Kadeem's mind at rest, sir?"

"Is that ever possible?" Arkyn sighed. "Help me up then – if only to keep him happy."

"He's only concerned, sir."

"I know. I don't truly mind. I'm just frustrated at myself."

"Illness takes us all like that, lad."

Arkyn frowned. "Stop listening to Kadeem's philosophy, Fitz. It doesn't suit you at all."

"Right, Your Highness, would you prefer me to say 'so you should be'?"

"I deserved that, didn't I? I'm sorry. I don't make a good invalid."

"No, I'm sorry. My remark was out of order, invalid or not."

"Now you're talking nonsense, more nonsense than normal, that is." Arkyn sighed. "Come on, or else Kadeem will come and fetch me."

They left the room to find Kadeem walking down the corridor. Arkyn raised an eloquent eyebrow at Fitz, but didn't say a word. Fitz fought down a laugh and followed the Prince to his rooms.

Part 3

Chapter 33
REPORTS

Alunadai, Week 21 – 1st Seral, 15th Meithis 1211
Arkyn's Office

ALUNADAI DAWNED, or at least Arkyn assumed it had, with lowering clouds hiding the sun, promising rain. Shirking his duties any longer wasn't an option. Four weeks had passed since he'd fallen ill. Two weeks since the fever had broken its hold on him. Aching muscles didn't, wouldn't stop him from completing the review and having something constructive to do might help his muzzy head.

Kadeem had insisted Edward didn't disturb his morning routine, so he walked down the stairs alone, seeing the entrance hall as though for the first time. The hallway spoke of how it had once been a home. He glanced at his grandfather's portrait; would he recognise the Residence now? Grinning, he pictured his great-aunt here, even then putting people in their places. His heart suddenly ached for home and the familiar.

As he entered his outer office, his legs began to give. Steadying himself, he greeted Edward and Stuart before entering his office. He sank into the chair gratefully. Glancing at the desk, he raised a quizzical eyebrow at Edward.

"Lord Iris' reports, Your Highness."

"Nothing from Wealsman?"

"I'm saving those for a treat, sir."

Arkyn chuckled. "I'll probably need one."

Undoing the ribbon on the first scroll, Arkyn tried to concentrate. Eventually, he gave up and, picking up the reports, moved over to sit comfortably on the couch. With his legs and back supported, his mind cleared enough to focus.

By the end of the first report, he was frustrated. It was full of phrases like 'If I might suggest'. Arkyn knew that one of old. It tended to mean that he ought to do this or that.

The second report wasn't any better. Arkyn put it down carefully on the occasional table. Lord Iris had been an Advisor to the FitzAlcis for over forty years; he understood the politics of the empire better than most, had decades of experience that Arkyn didn't. Was he, Arkyn, missing something? Was he meant to take Iris' suggestions as instructions? He wished his head would clear properly. Should he contact his father, ask his advice? No. It wasn't that the King would mind, but he was in Terasia to gain experience, not to have the answer given to him. In a moment of clarity, the fog of indecision lifted. His father wanted him to make decisions. That had been clear after Roth's betrayal. It was up to him, Arkyn, to determine what to do, not Iris or anyone else.

Pushing himself to his feet, he crossed to the sideboard and poured a glass of water. Leaning against the wall, he watched the drenched gardens. The rain was passing. He opened the sash window a crack, fresh air helping him focus. To determine what to do, he needed the details he'd have gained from all the interviews. Iris' reports made it clear there had been malfeasance in the exchequer, but they also generalised the information. That sort of process had obfuscated the issues there originally. After a time, he collected the reports, rang for Edward, and sent for Iris.

The precise nature of Lord Iris' bow always impressed Arkyn. It was a polished gesture from a man whose age meant a slight stiffening of the joints.

On standing straight once more, Iris said, "How nice to see you once more at your desk, Your Highness."

Arkyn's lips twitched, betraying his amusement. "I'm not sure you will continue to think so, my lord, but you have my thanks for your care. I apologise in advance for this, but I would be grateful if you rewrote your reports to give me facts. Not a hundred and one suggestions to wade through to glean only half of what I need to know."

"I am your advisor, Your Highness."

"Yes, you are, and you are a good one. Make your advice into a separate report. I'm not saying don't advise. All I am saying is give me the facts so that I can assess accurately on which and what I require your advice. I shall give you a few days to unpick and reassemble your reports, but those are my requirements. Get the report on the exchequer to me first. I want to know whether I should release Rahat and his deputies or charge them with fraud."

Iris' reaction was milder than expected. "Very well, Your Highness. If you will excuse me, sir, I shall go and begin."

Six minutes later, Edward entered to find the Prince half lying on the couch.

Arkyn asked, "Did he complain?"

"Not to me, sir. He did say you do your family proud. I think he was impressed you hadn't accepted something that you couldn't work with."

Arkyn smiled grimly. "I don't like doing it, but I know if I don't start now I never will. Plus, as Lord Wealsman would say, it's pleasant to watch people's reactions. Talking of whom, can you please send for him?"

Arkyn briefly considered returning to his desk but thought better of it. Very little of the time he'd spent in Wealsman's company had been formal. Also, Kadeem might have had a point in that he still needed to take things easily.

When Edward announced Wealsman a few minutes later, the Acting Governor took in the scene. "Welcome back to your duties, sir."

"Say it with a straight face, Percival."

Wealsman laughed. "Would you, therefore, suggest I recommend it as a form of torture, Your Highness?"

"Maybe not, my lord. A cure for insomnia though… Pour yourself a drink and tell me if anything is happening in Terasia that I need to know about? To save me having to read anything else today."

Wealsman crossed to the jugs, poured himself a glass of water and topped up Arkyn's. The fact the Prince was half lying on the couch said much. Every other time he'd been in the office, Arkyn had been professional. Either the hours spent together were letting him relax or he couldn't hold himself up.

Putting the glasses down on the occasional table, he eased himself into a chair in Arkyn's eyeline.

Arkyn took a sip of water. "Are things so bad? You've not even started to answer my question about Terasia yet."

Wealsman chuckled. "Sorry, sir. I was thinking. There's nothing so urgent that you need to worry. The good news is that the tax recovered from Roth's manors is entering the city. We've recovered more than enough to bribe an army – without any exaggeration."

"Then be thankful it has been recovered. I'm pleased but don't allocate it. *None* of it is to be used until after I've finished the review. Until then, that money is out of bounds, no matter *who* requests it. If you wish to, write a report of where you feel it should be spent. I'll need estimates for the rebuilding of the City Assembly first. Are there plans drawn up?"

"Yes, sir. Would you like sight of them?"

"Might as well – if only to keep me out of other mischief."

Wealsman smiled. "I'm sure Your Highness doesn't know the meaning of the word."

"You can be unaware of the existence of a word but still behave in accordance with its strictures or meaning; however, I thank you for so complimenting my vocabulary. Your skills as a courtier are unprecedented."

Wealsman snorted. "Your Highness rightly rebukes me. It is I who needs a dictionary."

"Do me a favour and don't get one. You already cause enough trouble."

"Then might I borrow one, sir?" He noted Arkyn's expression. "My apologies. As for what's happening…"

As the Acting Governor talked, Arkyn spent a moment wondering what his father would say if he knew how relaxed he allowed himself to be around Wealsman. It surely wasn't how he was meant to be acting in a province so distant from Oedran.

Chapter 34
MUNDIMRI

Alunadai, Week 25 – 1st Ralal, 1st Ralis 1211

Messenger Link

ON THE FIRST DAY OF WINTER, Arkyn accepted a link with his father and took in the grave note in his eye.

"How's the review going?" enquired the King.

"Nearly complete, Sire," replied Arkyn. "I'm having Rahat and his deputies charged with fraud. I'm not sure both of his deputies will be convicted, but he certainly will. We've recovered about three quarters of the estimated missing tax from Roth's manors. I was thinking of sending the report back with Lord Iris, if that's acceptable?"

"More than acceptable. I need you to break some news to His Lordship. Lord Rale has died. Apoplexy, last night. If Iris asks after Finian, he's going to live with your nearcousins."

Arkyn whitened. "I… Of course, sir. I'll see to it directly. How's Aunt Cornelia?"

"Upset. It's stirred a lot of memories and, with Aelia and Finn gone, it's raw for her. I'm letting everyone think that she and your Uncle Festus were named as Finian's guardians. Rale didn't name anyone, so Finian's actually our ward, but there was no way I was going to force the issue."

Arkyn smiled sadly. "Aunt Cornelia will appreciate that, sir."

"Yes. I hope so. She's my second cousin. I find it easy to forget that but, today, it came home, seeing how upset she was. I'll be ordering Court mourning here for an aluna-month. As you and Iris are in Tera, it might be nice to do the same there."

"Of course, sir. I'll see to it. What about Areal? He was responsible for the province in the Etanes."

"I'll talk with ReJean. His wife's carrying, so given that, I won't force mourning."

Arkyn nodded. "I doubt Lady ReJean will mind. She was very caring when I met her."

"She is. She's got a lovely sense of humour as well. Very pragmatic about things. Teases ReJean in a way I've never known anyone else to."

"He does seem staid."

"He has his moments. I should let you inform Lord Iris. I have a bone to pick with Richardson."

Arkyn discovered the worst part of his job wasn't arresting people. That was easy in comparison to having to tell someone far from home that his friend had died. Lord Iris' normally proud face fought for control. Arkyn passed him a drink and left the room. Edward, waiting outside the office, was perplexed.

"Lord Rale has joined his ancestors. I've just told Lord Iris. He might be a while. I'm going to go and have a break."

"Very good, Your Highness. What about Lord Irvin?"

"Good point. Ask him to join me, please."

Arkyn went to tell Wealsman what had occurred. The Acting Governor became sombre.

"I shall warn Lord Simble. There's no malice in the teasing over the last few weeks, but he ought to be warned that Lord Iris won't be in the mood for it."

"Thank you. His Majesty has asked for an aluna-month-long mourning here as well as in Oedran due to my presence and Lord Iris'. There's no way His Lordship will make it to Oedran for the funeral. That is the most unfortunate part of the empire being so large."

"We'll make the alcium here private for a time, sir."

Arkyn nodded. "That would probably be taken most kindly, Percival. Thank you."

* * *

In Oedran, Adeone broke the link and looked directly at Richardson. "Do I need to ask you to explain the other events whilst Landis and I were at Ceardlann last night?"

Richardson explained how Simkins and he had become suspicious of Landis' questions; how they had realised someone was getting past the guards; how they had taken advantage of Adeone's unpublicised absence following the Mundimri feast to station Hillbeck in the King's Bedchamber. How the sergeant had apprehended a would-be assassin. How the attacker had climbed the old Servants' Stair, entered the bedchamber and in the moments before apprehension thrown a dagger at the bolster pretending to be King Adeone.

"Where is the man now?"

"Still in the cells, Your Majesty. Do you want him brought here?"

Adeone considered. He flicked his eyes at Landis, who nodded slightly.

"Yes. He will find it hard now to deny his intention. If Scanlon, as Justiciar, gets hold of him, it would be extremely unfortunate for all of us. Thank you all for your endeavours." (Richardson bowed and left.) Adeone turned to Lord Landis. "I thought you said you'd be discreet, Festus!"

Landis snorted. "Richardson worked alongside King Altarius as well as Your Majesty. I knew I'd have a near-impossible task convincing him. I should have known it was an impossible task instead — though I am pleased he questions my every move as well. He is a line of defence after all. There have been too many kings betrayed by their friends in our past."

Adeone smiled. "I think Richardson trusts you, though, Festus. Are you thinking of taking him under your eye as Defender of the King's Life?"

Lord Landis was serious as he replied, "I wouldn't dare presume to, Sire. Only a king should ever oversee his staff."

Adeone nodded. "Too true and only a king can."

Jokingly, Landis said, "Any judge would tell you the Justiciar could. True, you'd have to be declared insane for him to do it. Mind you, do you think Chapa would certify you insane? After all, we know you're mad."

"With friends like you, Festus, who needs enemies?"

"Nobody needs enemies, sir, they just appear. I'm impressed with how far Simkins and Richardson got. I'm also extremely pleased you went to Ceardlann last night. Though I'm sorry you didn't get the morning off."

"You are not the only one. I think we're going to have to have a close look at where guards are stationed and when they are there. Are you sure Cornelia can spare you today?"

"She's adamant, sir. We've done what we can at Rale House."

"Thank her for me." Adeone rang the bell on his desk and Richardson entered the office. The King said, "Cancel all immediate meetings, with my apologies to the participants, please, and arrange one with the Captain of the Palace Guard and General Paturn. I also want to speak to the Chief Yeoman about guarding in the city. Then organise a separate meeting with the Steward and I'll need Simkins there for that one."

Half listening, Lord Landis puzzled over the problem of the intruder. His investigations hadn't pointed to an outsider entering the Inner Office. Should he tell Adeone? There was no doubt that the King would have to know what he'd discovered, but was there merit in waiting to see what his suspect would do next? If more letters appeared, then it would prove this latest attack was unconnected to those letters; the more Landis thought about it, the more certain he was. Why, if the intention had been assassination, had the letters been left? There hadn't been another letter since he'd started asking questions, which only strengthened his suspicions as to the perpetrator.

Twelve minutes later, guards escorted the prisoner into the Inner Office. The interview was brief. Adeone asked him if he'd meant to assassinate him. Admitting it, the man signed his life away with the statement. Adeone asked him who else had been involved. The man refused any information, knowing he'd die before the sun rose on a new day with a dagger thrown into his neck, mimicking how he'd have killed Adeone. Bluntly, the King told the guards to try more persuasive methods. As far as the law went, the man was already dead. He hated having to order torture and executions, but it was either his life or theirs.

Not long after the guards dragged out the struggling and condemned attacker, the General and Captain Pixney arrived. The meeting was by no means short, although the outcome was satisfactory. There would be guards posted in the corridor where the stair originated and there would also be a guard in the service corridor outside the King's bedchamber and sitting room. Landis agreed to that, if the changing of the guard at midnight didn't disturb the King. Adeone smiled to himself at his friend's concern. It didn't seem to occur to Landis how many days the King was still awake at midnight. There would also be more regular patrols around the Palace perimeter.

"Have you investigated the passageway at the base of the staircase to see how they gained entry, Pixney?" enquired Adeone.

"Yes, Sire. They must have worked for a couple of hours each night for months. They emptied the cupboards and cut a trapdoor in the back panel. Every night they must have removed it and worked at the bricks and mortar blocking the stair. They gradually removed enough until they had a large enough hole to climb through. They could then make their way up the stairs. The trapdoor wasn't bolted or barred. In fact, the stair has been used as a storage area on occasion."

"You keep saying 'they'," observed Adeone.

"There were at least two, sir, possibly three. The marks in the dust prove that. I think two were small, children probably, used to fit through the small gaps to help enlarge them."

"Children..." Adeone hesitated. "Landis, I won't pursue them, but if you do find out who they were, let them know they've been lucky."

When the meeting was concluding, the General mentioned, in passing, that the Major of Oedran had put in his resignation and would the King accept it. Adeone agreed with the usual caveat that the current Major remained in post until his successor reached Oedran.

The General and Captain Pixney had barely left when Richardson announced the Steward and Simkins. Both they and Landis were surprised when Adeone said,

"Are there any reasons other than security why the Servants' Stair can't be brought back into use?"

The Steward shrugged. "Not from my point of view, Your Majesty. The security hurdle is the largest."

Simkins added, "It could make life a lot easier, sir. The old stair has direct access to the kitchen corridor. It was sealed up for security reasons; however, how much more secure is it having to bring food through the Palace? I think, if there are enough guards on the corridor at the bottom of the stair, it could be safer with it open."

Landis agreed. "It would mean that every entrance to Your Majesty's rooms would be guarded – unless there are any secret passageways into these rooms."

"Not that I've ever been aware of."

* * *

When once more alone with Landis, Adeone poured two drinks. He passed one to Landis.

"Just the Chief Yeomen now."

"Why do you want to see him, sir?" asked Landis, intrigued.

"I want a record kept of who is entering the Administrative Quarter at night. There's one gate from the Lower City—"

"It won't work," said Landis without thinking.

Adeone crooked an eyebrow.

"Sorry, Sire. I didn't mean to interrupt, but I can see flaws with the plan."

The crooked eyebrow stayed crooked.

"There's one gate by road, not by river. There's the Paras and Torport Gates out of the city as well. The Administrative Quarter is home to many people and businesses. All you'll do is cause delays and an effective curfew, which won't be well received. Let alone the fact that people won't want their names on an official scroll, and there's no way of checking if they've given you their true name. Can I ask why you're proposing it?"

"I want to make it more difficult for assassins."

"Understandable, but what you may end up doing is making it more difficult for everyone else. I can see there being much unrest if you were to implement such checks."

"Then what do you suggest, my lord?"

"Better training," said Landis, "for the yeomen and Palace Guard. There's not much else you can do. You could ban weapons in the Palace, Administrative Quarter and the Lower City, but all you'd get is complaints about freedoms being curtailed and half my fellow lords would literally be up in arms about it. So, it wouldn't work. Training might."

Adeone stilled. "Why wouldn't banning weapons work? No, hear me out, Festus. Look at Terasia, before Ancestor Alvern took the province, weapons were banned in their cities. People could transport them, but they had to be tied so they couldn't be used quickly or in anger. They had to be out of sight—"

"Oh good, you're encouraging hidden weapons instead, Sire," muttered Landis.

Adeone snorted. "Just *listen*. Who carries weapons normally?"

"Anyone with sense? Sorry, sorry. Lords, merchants who must protect themselves, some officials, the militia. Most people will carry a knife of some description—"

"That isn't technically a weapon," pointed out Adeone. "It's a daily tool, not something made specifically for protection."

Landis hesitated. "I'm listening."

"Good. I don't want to stop people carrying everyday tools. What I am thinking is to make the carrying of *weapons* illegal in the Administrative Quarter, at least openly and easy to use. That means swords, daggers, poniards, bows, etc. I can't stop the militia. Their weapons are part of their uniform. They are their *tools*. They'd be exempt. Lords, most of the weapons are ceremonial – yes, all right, yours and Iris' aren't but for outside eyes they are. They are part of your formal dress, your tools of your position—"

"You're too crafty for your own good, Sire," muttered Landis dryly.

"I'm ignoring that. So, officials, yes, if someone holds an official post where carrying a sword – such as Defender – is traditionally part of their wear, I won't remove the right. I might institute tokens for people I think need to carry weapons for their own protection; however, for everyone else..."

"They generally don't carry *weapons* anyway," said Landis, a grin spreading. "You'd be formalising what is normal practice. Those who don't carry them anyway won't care and you're not stopping those that do." He frowned. "So, what's the point?"

"The point is that the assassins that my brother is sending after us don't usually fit into one of the exempt categories. It makes it harder for them, but easier for my guards and militia. If they are carrying concealed weapons, it gives guards a slight advantage when they try to draw them. It also gives the impression of a peaceful city."

"You'd want this throughout Oedran? I thought you were talking about the Administrative Quarter."

"I am, for now," said Adeone.

"You'll need the Etanes agreement, sir."

"Only for a law, not a decree," replied Adeone pedantically.

"Your Majesty, I'm not sure implementing such restrictions by decree will go well. Not if it's known to be long term."

Adeone sighed. "I know but Para's Ealdorman. I can't see him agreeing, especially given he's so close to Scanlon."

Landis nodded. "All right. Do a decree for the Administrative Quarter only, time limit it though, say four years—"

"Why four?"

"It's long enough for things to become normal. After you do the decree, petition the Etanes for a new law. If Para doesn't do his job this year, and Lux doesn't next, I'm Ealdorman in 1213 for Macaria's Lordship. I'll do what I can at that point, if it's working, to get it signed by the Etanes. We'll know by then. It's a year and a half away."

Adeone relaxed. "Thank you, Festus. I'm sure Aldhouse will complain."

"Let him. If you're implementing it by decree within your own estate, which the Administrative Quarter is, then his complaints carry no weight."

"You see, you can be helpful."

"I'm Your Majesty's to command," said Landis obsequiously.

"You're something," muttered Adeone.

Chapter 35
DISCUSSIONS

Cisadai, Week 26 – 9th Ralal, 9th Ralis 1211

Margrave's Residence

HAVING SIGNED OFF the review report for his clerks to copy, and having heard from a reluctant Edward the events surrounding Silvano's request for travel leave, Arkyn greeted Lord Iris pleasantly, waved to a chair and requested a briefing on how governors of Terasia were chosen.

Still dressed for mourning in a black tunic, Iris considered carefully what to say. Arkyn was diligent. He had seen sparks of traditional behaviour but also moments of less traditional outlook. He wasn't, therefore, certain how the Prince would pick a new Margrave. The appointment would say a lot about Arkyn, probably more about him than the man picked. Iris knew that one reason the King had sent him to Terasia was to give Arkyn the authority his age might have denied him. He didn't consider that would be effective unless the Prince followed a traditional route, as discontent amongst the overlords would undermine rather than strengthen his reputation.

"Governors of provinces are generally taken from the highest lords of that province, Your Highness. The exception, of course, is the Governor of Areal, whose post is hereditary. In Terasia, the Margrave, as the governor is titled, has always been an overlord since before the province joined the empire. The Kings of Terasia died out, and the overlords picked one of their number to lead them as Margrave. King Alvern's conquest of Terasia did much for the country, but it didn't change the fact that the Margrave is an overlord."

Arkyn enquired softly, "Is it written anywhere that the Margrave *must* be an overlord? Is it law, or a part of the settlement that was reached with Terasia after King Arlis' coronation?"

Iris hesitated. "It is not legally defined, sir, but is such an established practice as to be thought of as inviolable. The appointment of an overlord dispels any problem of private rank versus public rank. For example, Silvano claiming that Wealsman couldn't deny him the right to return to his lands because Wealsman was socially of a lower rank."

Arkyn nodded. "I'm wondering whether I should highlight to Silvano that I know of the incident."

"It would depend on how Your Highness feels, of course, but, if you highlight that you have been told, it could cause discomfort to His Lordship."

"That he may deserve."

"He well might, sir," replied Iris, "but Silvano's reaction when he feels himself discomforted is no certain thing. Stator, for example, would accept the rebuke and that would be that, Wealsman also, but Silvano has a temper on him that might prove disastrous to himself. After certain remarks, I talked with Commander Wynfeld. He has His Lordship under observation but they were words spoken in the heat of the moment. I don't think the commander has any concerns."

Arkyn pursed his lips, thinking. "Iris, are you trying to tell me I might end up having to arrest Silvano if I rebuke him over his conduct?"

"Yes, sir."

"That could certainly be detrimental to the province. Very well, unless his manner grates on me too much, I shall say nothing on the matter. What has been the conduct of the other overlords?"

Iris smiled. "Generally, what you might expect, sir. Most have kept their heads down and come neither to my attention nor Commander Wynfeld's. They have been entertaining each other and have taken the opportunity to further their own interests."

Arkyn gave a small chuckle, then coughed slightly. "Then I hope their time has been productive. Stator – what are your thoughts on him?"

"A pleasant gentleman, sir. His father was the same – solid, loyal to the empire. I don't know of a traitor in the family since this province joined the empire. He's not an astute statesman, nor is he, I believe, exceptionally involved in the current governance of the province. I think he likes to keep himself to himself."

Arkyn sighed. "I'd hate to upset that equilibrium. What of Simble?"

"I feel that given our personal history, Your Highness, it might be better if you seek someone else's opinion on His Lordship."

"Come, my lord, surely you can conquer your youthful differences and advise me impartially."

Iris never hesitated. "Then I shall try, sir. Simble is currently an efficient and effective head of the exchequer. I would say he is a capable man in all he does, but he is getting too old, I believe, to run a province."

"Thank you. Those were the main three that I had in mind. Although I shall interview all impartially, I shall have to take a closer look at others also. Confidentially, Iris, from what I've seen and heard of Silvano, I would rather he held no more power than is currently his. Would you support me in that belief?"

Iris never hesitated. "Yes, sir, I would. His manner is not compliant with His Majesty's regime."

"It would have been with another king?"

"I believe, though I may speak out of turn, that King Altarius would have found in Silvano a proper, rather than an improper, pride," observed Iris carefully. "There is one thing though of which I should make Your Highness aware. It is rumoured that Silvano has written to the Visir offering his daughter, Lady Terasina, as a wife for him. I believe they are in negotiations."

Arkyn sat back. "He, or the Visir, has spoken to the King about this?"

"I believe not, sir. Lord Scanlon is currently in Denshire and I believe has been informed and agreed to the proposal."

"I cannot believe His Majesty would refuse permission for the marriage to take place, but the marriage of a King's Representative needs ultimate sanction from the King, not the Justiciar. Maybe you'd be good enough to remind Silvano of that, Lord Iris."

"I shall attend to it this morning, sir."

Arkyn gave a brief nod. "Thank you. How soon do you believe the marriage will take place between the Visir and Lady Terasina?"

"If His Majesty agrees, I expect this year, or even the end of winter, sir."

With an implacable face, Arkyn mused out loud, "Then that leaves me with a problem. The King ordered the overlords to stay in Tera until I leave. Should I permit Silvano to attend his daughter's wedding?"

Iris recognised that Silvano's conduct had made the Prince angry. It was going to be far easier to advise him now. "Your Highness, Silvano has acted rashly, has forgotten protocol and, on numerous occasions, has been less than decorous. He seems to have forgotten you are of the FitzAlcis and, therefore, deserve the same respect he would give the King, if he were here. I would advise Your Highness to keep him in Tera, where he can be reminded that his actions have consequences."

"Then should I allow his son leave?" enquired Arkyn.

"From something Irvin has told me, sir, I believe Lord Melek has no sympathy or liking for any of his siblings and, I suspect, he is the reason his sister is being married out of the province. He has, I believe, persuaded Silvano to marry his brother to a Gerymorian heiress as well."

"Then either the lady goes to her marriage alone or I allow the females of her family leave and not the men."

"I believe a daughter is always grateful for her mother's presence on her wedding day, sir," remarked Iris, watching Arkyn's face.

"Then if, or rather *when*, Silvano decides to ask for travel leave, I shall deny it to him and his sons. I shall also alert His Majesty to my decisions. Thank you. I think that is all I need your immediate advice on, Lord Iris. I'd like you to be there during the interviews with the candidates for the governorship, especially as they will become a King's Representative, but I hope you will understand if I don't decide for some weeks yet."

"I think that is a wise choice, sir."

Arkyn smiled. "Thank you, my lord. I'm sure you have much to be getting on with. Maybe you could send Edward in."

A few moments later, Arkyn said, "Get me the commander, if he's got the time to spare, Edward."

His administrator grinned. "He's waiting, sir. Something about rumours he thinks would interest you."

Arkyn was amused but terse. "If it is Silvano's daughter, he's late."

"That's not like him, sir. Maybe it's something else."

"Maybe, Edward. Then get me Wealsman. I want his opinion on a couple of matters."

When the door had closed on the rest of the Residence, Arkyn said, "You're getting slow, Commander. Iris has already informed me that Silvano is in discussions with the Visir."

"I thought he might have done," replied Wynfeld, sitting down. "Has he also mentioned that I would recommend that neither Lord Silvano nor Lord Melek leaves Tera?"

"He advised it without saying that it was your thoughts on the matter."

"Then our minds think alike, sir, for I hadn't mentioned it to him."

Arkyn relaxed. "Why did you specify Lord Melek?"

"I'd like to keep the gentleman under my eye for a while longer, sir, and it is easier to do so here. With Lord Scanlon's presence in Denshire, I fear for the safety of my men should they enter Cearden."

"Very well. I'm beginning the hunt for the new Margrave and need a permanent captain to act as liaison with the fort for their safety. I believe you currently have two more sergeants than are necessary at the fort… Do you hold any objection to losing one of them?"

Wynfeld paused. "No, sir, but it might be obvious."

The Prince was terse, "Commander, I'm being so closely watched during this review that anything I do is discovered and reported to Lord Scanlon. It is the obvious thing to promote a sergeant without a unit of men. It sometimes pays to be obvious. Which would you suggest?"

"Sir, I'd like to talk to them about it. They might have a preference amongst themselves."

Arkyn got up and moved until he was holding the back of his forsaken chair, his knuckles white with the pressure. "Are they men of the army or not, Commander? They follow orders."

"Yes, sir, but their work is delicate. I would prefer to leave the one whose presence would yield the highest benefit. I might also advise that the new Margrave could want a say."

Sill straight-backed, Arkyn remarked, "I'm being an officious fool, aren't I?"

"No, sir, you're making your wishes known. I could give you an answer, but it might not be the best solution – that is all I am saying."

Arkyn nodded. "Then you'd better think long and hard about what is. Wynfeld… You could have said 'yes', I wouldn't have taken offence."

Wynfeld chuckled. "Sir, if I'd thought it, I would have said it. I promised His Majesty my advice would always be honest."

"Thank you… Are there any rumours about me here?"

Wynfeld saw the concern on Arkyn's face. "I cannot say there are not. What I will say, sir, is that they aren't malicious. There is relief that you have recovered from your illness and speculation about your decisions, but no detrimental rumour has reached my ears."

Arkyn's face cleared. "That's a near miracle. I'm doing something right."

"Your Highness is certainly doing something right. I think that this review and visit will have proved one thing to people…"

"What is that, Commander?"

"That His Majesty's faith in your capabilities was not just the indulgence of a father but a well-grounded assumption," stated Wynfeld honestly.

"Commander, you'll make a courtier yet."

Wynfeld smiled. "I doubt it, sir. I'm too much the soldier at heart."

"Thank Alcis for that. Thank you, Wynfeld, that's all."

The commander saluted and left. Arkyn heard him say something to Edward and his administrator laugh lightly. He half wondered what Wynfeld had said, but if he started wandering down that path, either paranoia or distrust would result. He glanced at his desk and wanted to be elsewhere. Ceardlann would be favourite or walking in the Rex Dallin, without a care in the world. Teasing Tain and Elantha, talking with them and Cal. Anything other than trying to work out who should be the next Margrave whilst drained of all motivation. He pushed himself up and examined the garden view. Karl and Elsa were either teasing each other or disagreeing about something. He watched them for a couple of minutes and, in watching them, his longing for Ceardlann increased. They'd got a ball and one was holding it before dropping it for the other to catch, or that was what it appeared, but the shady light under the trees made it difficult to see. There was a knock at the office door and Edward announced Wealsman.

Arkyn's eyes met Percival's and the Acting Governor noted the Prince's mood. Edward left and closed the door.

"Might I ask a question, sir?"

"Other than that one?" replied Arkyn pedantically before continuing, "You're going to ask me if I've taken a break this morning, aren't you?"

"Yes, sir."

"That's that dealt with then."

"I'm meant to ignore the fact there wasn't an answer, Your Highness?"

Arkyn's lips twitched. "Wasn't there? That was remiss of me. Sit down and give me your frank opinion on the overlords."

"Very well, sir. Lord Silvano is an officious and obnoxious man, Lord Stator is a steady, well-meaning gentleman and Lord Simble is elderly, irascible, incorrigible and irritating. Lord Trevorian is living in the past – that is, he is slightly senile—"

"He is involved in the running of several towns, I believe," said Arkyn.

"Welcome to government, Your Highness. Lord Nilfouer is, well, he's elderly and doesn't get out much. Lord Bocard's traditional but has limited statesmanship. Lord Karlivan is perhaps the best statesman, for all his shyness is perceptible. Lord Nurcdean is childlike, may be a bonus. Lord Scindcar is a good man, Lord Kre is an able man but persuadable and Lord Roth – for all I think, given several years, that he'll be the best of the bunch – his father's actions and his age alone rule him out of this race."

Arkyn's lips twitched. "Was that such a swift summation because that's all the time you have for them, or because you think I need to take a break?"

"Both, sir."

"I wonder how they'd describe you?"

"I think I can tell you in certain cases. Lord Silvano, for example, thinks I'm a jumped-up runt with delusions of grandeur. It is a great shame that I don't care about his opinion."

"What if he were to report that to the King?" asked Arkyn lightly.

Wealsman had to stop himself saying that Adeone wouldn't listen. "I rank so lowly in this province as to not be worthy of His Lordship's notice most of the time. The events of the last couple of months aside, I doubt he has taken the trouble to consider me. As he only worries about those whom he considers a threat to his position, I would be astounded if he were to report anything to His Majesty."

"What about now? As Acting Governor, you could be a threat."

"Then, I would hope that His Majesty didn't simply take His Lordship's word for it."

"Do you ever wonder about other's opinions, Percival?" enquired Arkyn curiously.

"No, sir. I am who I am; I can't change that, especially not now. I try to be an honest man—"

Arkyn smiled. "I'm *not* criticising you. I was merely interested in your response. I've got to come up with some questions for the interviews. If you've any ideas specific to Terasia, please let me have them. I thought of one earlier, but I don't know if it's too vague… To whom or what should the enduring loyalty of the Margrave pertain?"

Wealsman answered without thinking. "Always the province; for although he must accept direction from the King, sir, he should know how his decisions will affect Terasia and advise the King with that in mind. Personally, I don't think that is a bad question. It has a deceptive simplicity."

"It isn't too much of a trick?"

"It rather depends on the answer you require. My answer, as you heard, would be Terasia, another's might be the King, yet another the empire, each is understandable but opinions might differ on which is correct. It is your opinion that matters, and frankly, sir, the King and yourself will have to work with the new Margrave; therefore, it should be a man who thinks as you think. Especially a man who thinks as His Majesty thinks as the post carries the honour of being a King's Representative."

"Yet he should also be able to work with all the men under his influence."

"Then Your Highness must excuse my frankness if I say that Lord Silvano would not be the best choice."

Arkyn raised an eyebrow meaningfully. "Who could you work with and for?"

"Lord Karlivan, or Lord Kre, sir."

"Thank you. That has given me a lot of information to consider."

"Then consider it over lunch, Your Highness, and digest both at the same time."

Arkyn sighed. "If governors were appointed for impudence, you'd have the job – that and a truly awful sense of humour."

"Thank you, sir. Maybe we should both be grateful they are not."

"Would you so disdain the post of Margrave?"

"As the question of my appointment never arises, I don't think it is important, sir."

"No, but I will have an answer. Would you refuse the post?"

Wealsman laughed. "Your Highness, I would be too stunned to speak. I'm a jester in Court dress. I cannot believe that I would ever make Margrave. If it were offered, as Kristina would tell you, I might accept out of mischief but never conviction that I was the right man for the job."

"Mischief?"

"What else would Your Highness call it?"

Arkyn sighed. "Mischief would fit the mood. Yet you cannot be such a hopeless aristocrat. You are, normally, the Assistant Deputy Governor."

"Yes, sir, but as one of Lord Portur's minor lords, he could direct my obligations."

Arkyn raised his eyes to the ceiling. "Enough. You underestimate your abilities, Percival, and that's that. Now, the lunch you mentioned – dine with me in my rooms."

"If you wish it, sir."

"I do and I promise I shall not talk about matters of state. How are the wedding plans?"

Wealsman sighed. "Can't we talk matters of state instead? I find myself nervous whenever I think about the wedding."

"Then talk the nerves out. Where are you planning to honeymoon?"

Several minutes later, Wealsman was pleased to see that Arkyn's appetite had returned; though, when the meal had ended, Wealsman returned to his office and the Prince, yielding to persuasion, did not return to his.

Chapter 36
ONE DOWN

Tretaldai, Week 26 – 10th Ralal, 10th Ralis 1211
Arkyn's Office

HAVING TAKEN BOTH Edward and Lord Iris' advice, Arkyn drew up the interview order for the overlords. Silvano was first and Arkyn heard it had caused speculation. People were asking why he had suddenly decided to follow protocol after other less traditional decisions. Arkyn wasn't bothered by the pointless speculation. It didn't matter when he interviewed the candidates; they'd all be answering the same questions.

"How would you suggest I handle Silvano, Lord Iris? Should I let him know that I know of, shall we say, controversial matters to which he has been a party?"

Iris hesitated. "I would suggest, to leave those matters lying comfortably under the stones, sir. If you wish to emphasise that you might be privy to compromising details of his conduct, then might I suggest you don't permit him to seat himself straight away?"

Arkyn sat back in his chair. "If His Lordship makes known such a move?"

"I doubt Silvano would, Your Highness. It would detract from the politically confidant persona he exudes at every opportunity."

Arkyn nodded. “Then I shall not request he takes a seat as soon as he enters this office. Anything else, before I summon him, my lord?”

“No, sir. I don’t believe so.”

Arkyn regarded the overlord as he entered. There was a swagger as Silvano made a confident obeisance. Arkyn held the overlord’s gaze as he rose from the bow. There was momentary disquiet brought swiftly under control. Was it because they hadn’t spoken since the introductions? Such a politically adept overlord couldn’t be nervous, could he? As Arkyn greeted Silvano pleasantly, he watched those eyes register the lack of a chair for him and the disquiet returned; the Prince ignored it.

“Lord Silvano, you will have noted, and I know others have done so, that you are the first of the overlords to be interviewed. Do you have any idea why?”

“I had not considered the significance, Your Highness,” lied Silvano.

“How about now I have raised it, my lord?” enquired Arkyn, knowing the lie.

“I can only assume that Your Highness is interviewing us by our precedence.”

Arkyn’s features gave nothing away. “Interesting. You therefore consider that you are the highest overlord of the province. Why?”

Silvano’s face was a picture of confusion. “Sir?”

Arkyn met his gaze. “What makes you the highest lord in the province?”

“Tradition, Your Highness,” replied Silvano matter-of-factly.

“What formed that tradition?”

“I suppose riches, sir,” stated Silvano offhandedly. “After the Lord Portur, the Lord Silvano has the richest land in the province.”

“Thank you. It wasn’t, for example, that your ancestors served their province with distinction, that they fought for the empire or that they even provided support to the Cearcall. It is simply due to *riches*. I wonder if all traditions are so disappointingly banal.”

Silvano hesitated. “It is the only reason I can think of.”

“Have you ever thought that admitting ignorance can be a good thing?”

“Sir?”

Arkyn said, “Answer the question, please, my lord. I ask questions, expecting answers without procrastination.”

“To admit ignorance is not in my nature, Your Highness.”

“Do you consider that as a strength or a failing?”

“I wouldn’t call it a failing, sir, because admitting ignorance demeans the post of overlord.”

Arkyn regarded him critically. “Do you, therefore, claim omniscience?”

“I will say I am normally cognisant of that which is required.”

"Again, not an answer to the question I asked, my lord. Are you omniscient?" reiterated Arkyn, not bothering to hide his frustration.

Silvano eyes darted to the window and then back. "Your Highness, I would say I am omniscient of everything within my sphere of influence."

"What is your sphere of influence?"

"That under my control."

"I do not wish for such a pedantic answer, my lord. Exactly *what* is under your control?" demanded Arkyn.

"My lands and my political influence."

Arkyn made himself relax. Getting riled wouldn't help. "About your political influence, maybe you could explain to me *exactly* what that is."

"*Currently,* with Lord Wealsman as Acting Governor, not as broad as I would wish."

"Again, you are answering me obliquely, Silvano. If you mean none, say none. I have heard that you are a straight-talking gentleman. That must be elsewhere. Do you consider that the answers to my questions are such that you cannot voice them to me?"

Silvano, a tight hold on his normally hot temper, said, "No, Your Highness, although I might say that not all questions can be answered as definitively as Your Highness requires."

"That may well be so, my lord, but your manner suggests that you are merely echoing what you have heard for years. You are playing on your pedigree; however, that aside – the Margrave has many responsibilities. Could you explain what you consider to be the most enduring and important loyalty within those responsibilities?"

"The oath to the King, sir."

Arkyn paused after the answer. It was what he'd expected, but not what he wanted to hear. Then, when Silvano seemed to consider his answer and had opened his mouth to elaborate, Arkyn continued as though there had been no pause.

"The responsibilities that appertain to the post are many and varied. You have stated unequivocally that your primary loyalty as Margrave would be to His Majesty, that is an important point, but others need addressing. You'd be entrusted with the guarding of the province. The militia here would partly answer to you and would have to, given appropriate circumstances, answer to you completely. To take a hypothetical example, your lands border the Takarin Mountains and, as we all know, there are the men of the mountains who have chosen to live outside of the empire. What is your policy for dealing with the Takarin?"

"They keep their distance from my lands, sir. Neither I nor my father have had to develop a policy."

"What would happen if they started, in a cold winter, to try for food at your farms?" enquired Arkyn.

"As my tenants would find it hard to feed themselves, they'd be refused succour, sir," replied Silvano dismissively.

"If the Takarin raided your lands, and you *weren't* Margrave, what would you do?"

"I'd get the men of my lands together to defend them, sir."

"If you *were* Margrave, would you handle the situation any differently?"

"Then I'd ask the militia for help, as I wouldn't be able to devote the necessary time to the problem."

Arkyn again let the answer lie for a moment. Edward, taking notes, contemplated the tableau. Lord Silvano was standing with an overbearing arrogance, which he would no doubt call proper pride, but it wouldn't endear him to Prince Arkyn, who was being watched by Lord Iris.

Not for the first time, Iris considered Arkyn had a deceptive simplicity about the way he presented questions. So far Silvano hadn't noticed their dual purpose, nor had the overlord realised he hadn't answered as Arkyn hoped. The interview hadn't yet changed the Prince's mind.

Arkyn wondered whether to end the interview. Silvano was saying what he believed he, Arkyn, wanted to hear, but he didn't want to appoint someone who would be sycophantic. He didn't want to appoint someone who wouldn't know when to agree, either. He needed an honest man but, in politics, they were rare.

He broke the pause. He'd need reasons to give his father if he didn't appoint in line with tradition. "Lord Silvano, the Margrave's deputy can be his choice or the King's. If you were appointed Margrave, and the Deputy Governor was appointed for you, would you accept the decision if you believed that your new deputy wasn't someone you could work with?"

"If the appointment was by the King or yourself, then I could do no other but I'd like Lord Bocard, sir. I feel that we could work well together and, *traditionally,* both the Margrave *and* his deputy are taken from the highest rank of men."

"It is not for you, Silvano, to teach His Highness protocol or traditions," snapped Iris, having seen Arkyn's gaze harden.

Silvano hesitated, seeing Arkyn's implacable face. "My apologies, Your Highness. I didn't mean that to sound how it did."

"Thank you. I am astounded that such a practised politician would make such a potentially devastating mistake."

Half an hour later Silvano began to have more sympathy for the officers he'd previously disparaged, those who Arkyn had interviewed as part of the review. He'd expected to be able to talk around issues, or talk them out, but the Prince wasn't having any of it. Having had little to do with Arkyn, Silvano found him difficult to read, but most of the empire knew Iris was traditional and Iris was advising the Prince; in that, Silvano thought he'd found an ally.

After Arkyn had received an answer to the last of his questions, the Prince said, "The interview is now yours, Lord Iris."

Iris inclined his head slightly. "Thank you, sir. Lord Silvano, we are all aware of the reasons for seeking a new Margrave. The incidents which greeted His Highness were regrettable, to say the least. If the death had been of another King's Representative and you were Margrave, what would your immediate actions have been?"

"I should have closed the Residence and had the staff questioned by the City Guard. I would then have followed through with anything they discovered."

Iris studied Silvano. Had he heard the question fully? Surely, he'd inform the King. "Anything else?"

"No, my lord."

"Very well. Now, taking the events which greeted Prince Arkyn as they occurred, His Highness was faced with an interesting and intricate situation. He made decisions on the spot and in difficult circumstances. What would your advice have been regarding Roth?"

Arkyn studied Silvano's face carefully as the overlord said,

"Execution, sir. He'd committed treason. There is no other course."

"Quite. What about the Roth lands?"

Silvano paused. "That decision would have been for His Highness and His Majesty to take. Any advice that I could offer would be spurious to the purpose."

"What would your advice have been?"

"I thought I had answered that question—"

Arkyn interrupted. "Then you were mistaken. His Lordship asked for a precise answer; therefore, you answer precisely."

"Sir, I would have considered my advice carefully. I'm not certain I'd have advised clemency, but as Your Highness took that route, I'm unable to criticise that action, even indirectly."

Iris glanced at Arkyn, who gave a miniscule shake of his head.

"Yet we are considering the problem without hindsight," said Iris. "I suppose the question, Lord Silvano, is would you have felt competent to advise His Highness had you held the post of Margrave?"

"I would hope I would have felt competent given that situation, Lord Iris," replied Silvano starchly.

Iris looked again at Arkyn, who motioned to him to carry on. Silvano would never comprehend they wanted a definite, not theoretical, answer.

Iris said, "Thank you. The next question I have for Your Lordship is what your first official action would be, should you be appointed Margrave?"

"It would depend on the time of year that His Highness announces the appointment."

"Thank you. Those are the only questions I had for His Lordship, Your Highness."

Making a note, Arkyn nodded. "Thank you, Lord Iris. Lord Silvano, thank you for attending this interview. I have a couple of things to say. First, you are not to talk to *anyone* about this meeting. Secondly, I am enforcing a ban on entertaining between the overlords during the days I'm interviewing for a new Margrave. That means no invitations to attend on each other. I would rather nothing was *accidentally* revealed. Do I have your word to abide by such strictures for the next five days?"

Silvano's face set and Arkyn knew if anyone else had told the overlord, a dozen objections would have emanated from him.

Instead, the overlord replied, "You have my word, sir."

Arkyn smiled. "Thank you, Silvano, you may leave." Once the overlord had gone, Arkyn let out a long breath. "Edward, please ask Kadeem to serve refreshments. Iris, shall we sit more comfortably?"

Iris nodded and rose. Arkyn pushed himself to his feet and then fell back into the chair. He pushed himself up once more and found Iris beside him.

"Take my arm, sir."

Arkyn smiled. "No, thank you. I have just been sitting for too long. My legs forget they should support me."

Seated more comfortably, Arkyn waited until he'd slaked his thirst before asking for Iris' verdict.

"Not a candidate I should appoint, sir."

Arkyn looked at him, half amused. "I can't say *that* was a bland answer. Unequivocal maybe, bland, certainly not. Why?"

"Various mistakes, sir. His loyalty should be to the province and he should never hesitate in giving advice. Personal preoccupations should never enter official life and a governor should never call on the militia unless absolutely necessary, and certainly not for sorting out minor problems within his lands."

"Our minds are as one, then. I must choose between ten overlords."

Iris was grave. "I might suggest there are only nine, sir – unless you are seriously considering Lord Erlan Roth."

"If candidates keep falling at the speed Silvano did, there'll be fewer than that. Of course, I could defy tradition and seek elsewhere for the Margrave."

"It is your prerogative, sir."

Inwardly amused, Arkyn said, "Which means you wouldn't approve?"

"Your Highness, it is not that I wouldn't approve. The situation might become untenable with anyone other than an overlord in office. We have seen the result of one thwarted overlord with ambition. Should Your Highness not appoint traditionally, then there might be more friction."

"Yet we both know that if I don't appoint Silvano, there'll be friction anyway. He'll not happily accept another as Margrave. In some senses, he's more ambitious than Roth was yet he doesn't have the inclination for such hard work."

Iris was solemn as ever. "Quite, sir. Might I ask one thing?" (Arkyn nodded.) "Will you also appoint the Deputy Governor?"

"Do you advise that I should?"

"It has been known," replied Iris. "I would advise Your Highness to consider doing so, especially if you find two men who might work well together. This province must overcome the effects of Roth's treachery. I mean the long-term effects of the drain on taxes and his mismanagement of the exchequer. I think Your Highness would be best hunting for someone who has universal respect from the lords, City Assembly and the merchants. There is much at stake and tradition at such times holds people together."

"I shall consider it, my lord. There is an hour before Stator is due. Maybe you could fashion your immediate thoughts on Silvano's interview into a report and pass it to Edward."

Iris rose. "Of course, Your Highness." He left with a purposeful gait and an exact bow.

Arkyn flicked his eyes in dismissal at Edward. "Do you, by any chance, have a headache remedy to hand, Kadeem?"

The manservant passed him a vial without a word. Arkyn emptied the contents into his goblet and watered it down before drinking the concoction.

Watching the Prince's face, Kadeem recognised determination. "Will you decide on the new Margrave within the next few days, sir?"

"I don't know. It might become clear but I won't announce it for some time. I want to keep them obedient to my wishes."

"A sensible precaution, sir, but if I might make another observation: if you were to announce the new Margrave, then you could relax and after illness should come—"

"Leave philosophy alone for the moment. I know that argument, but I want to be certain my decision is wise for the province."

Kadeem nodded. "Then, as you'll have many days to consider the candidates, sir, might I suggest you come and rest in your private rooms?"

"You can suggest it, but I haven't got the energy to walk up the stairs. I'll stay here. Lose yourself."

Kadeem smiled and bowed out. He prevented Edward from re-entering the office and told him it was likely the Prince would be asleep when Stator arrived.

Edward said quietly, "He wouldn't let me organise all the interviews on separate days."

"Of course he wouldn't. He thinks he should be able to manage, but it might be an idea to see if he can get an evening alone."

"I'll rearrange his engagements. He was meant to be dining with Lord Wealsman."

Kadeem chuckled. "I'd check before rearranging that. His Lordship does our Prince good and I believe it's two-one to Lord Wealsman when it comes to chess matches."

Edward laughed. "They certainly do get on well."

Chapter 37
PERSONAL PREFERENCE

Afternoon

Arkyn's Office

WOKEN BY EDWARD shaking his shoulder, Arkyn found a thick blanket covering him.

"Their Lordships are waiting?" he enquired, yawning.

"Yes, sir."

"You'd better let them in then." He handed the blanket to Edward. "That had better go back where it was found."

He crossed to his desk as Edward folded and stowed the blanket in a cupboard built into the wall. There was new parchment and a drink to hand as he sat down.

"Was this your work, Edward?"

"No, sir, Kadeem's and Stuart's."

Arkyn frowned, baffled. What had Edward's deputy been doing in his office when he was asleep there? He nearly asked, but his administrator's stance showed Edward had realised there was an issue.

Two minutes later, Iris was seated, and Stator was rising from his bow. Arkyn studied him; he liked the look of the overlord – a solid respectable man with few aspirations, fewer than Arkyn would have liked, it seemed.

"Please sit down, Lord Stator."

"I'd prefer to stand, sir, especially as I believe I am about to let Your Highness down," replied Stator. "I must inform you that I don't want to be Margrave. I have no love of power, find overwork a terminal illness and there are more skilled men for the job."

Iris watched Arkyn carefully as he met the challenge head on.

"What would happen if I thought you were the right person, that a love of power isn't obligatory and that your Deputy Governor would see you don't get overworked?"

"I'd thank Your Highness and then still refuse," replied Stator candidly. "I can think of others better suited to the position."

"Would you mind telling me who?"

Stator did so.

"Thank you. Now, take a seat and explain your reasoning." As Stator did, Arkyn stopped Iris from interrupting. When the overlord had finished, he enquired, "Would you not see his appointment as controversial?"

"A little bit of controversy is how the world gets from yesterday to tomorrow, sir."

Arkyn nodded. "An interesting view, my lord. As you are so determined, there is little point in my asking you a lot of needless questions. Instead, have you anything you'd like to raise with me? It would be better that no-one realises you've refused the post. If you leave now, rumours will start."

Stator chuckled to himself. "I'm sure I could cope, Your Highness, but, as you ask, there is one thing I should like advice on. My eldest daughter is old enough to marry. Silvano has suggested a match with his eldest son, Melek, but I feel that the marriage would be unhappy for my daughter. I know it is traditional that such feelings shouldn't interfere in political decisions, but I'm afraid I have never been a political person. I wish to refuse the marriage, but am aware of Silvano's influence within this province."

"Unofficially, maybe it is time someone questioned that influence, my lord," remarked Arkyn with careful consideration. "Again, unofficially, I might point out that His Lordship hasn't been involved in the running of the province during my visit. The review would never have involved His Lordship, but the oversight of Terasia might have done. As Lord Landis of Oedran says, 'Traditions can be changed'."

Stator's mouth dropped slightly. "Sir, His Lordship is—"

Iris interrupted softly, "Lord Stator, you know I am a traditionalist at heart, but I have not witnessed the political influence Lord Silvano believes he holds. Things might have been different when Roth and Lord Portur were governing the province, but, in politics, a mere day can have a devastating effect on an individual's influence; it has been weeks since Lord Portur was murdered."

Arkyn said, "Lord Stator, if you are trying to determine if I'd raise any objection if you refused Silvano's proposal, then all I can say is I will not. It is essentially a private matter for your families. I can emphasise your decision, should Silvano prove persistent, but I cannot interfere in any other way."

Stator nodded. "I realise that, Your Highness. Thank you. I shall refuse the advances and hunt elsewhere for a husband for my daughter."

"If you have such doubts, it is a wise course of action," remarked Arkyn. "After all, Terasia is not quite as barren of eligible lords as one might suppose, or you could look beyond the province. Denshire or Gerymor are close."

"I think I would miss her too much, sir," murmured Stator, "although Gerymor might well be an idea."

"Yes, your lands border the province, I believe."

"That and Denshire, but if she were to marry beyond Terasia, I would be happier with her marrying into a province with a culture similar to our own. One of courtesans and concubines alongside marriage is strange to my perception, and I can't quite see the point."

"Denshire has kept its customs to suit its situation," observed Arkyn. "They differ from the rest of the empire but that, I suppose, is a result of their negotiating skills; a legacy, no doubt, of the Cearcall."

Stator smiled. "It's probably that all right and the fact they didn't fight the empire but joined willingly."

"Yes, but Terasia didn't fight battles, as such. You simply saw the advantages of stable rule for trade."

Stator forbore from saying that Oedran had closed Terasia's borders and laid siege to major towns and cities instead of fighting battles, razing them to the ground as often as not. "There are advantages in most things, sir. It is a pity that some cannot see it. So many people are trapped by what others think is right."

Arkyn didn't look at Iris. "It is nice to be reminded that not everyone is against change."

"Traditions tend to exist for a reason," cautioned Iris carefully.

Arkyn got up quickly. He crossed to the windows and then turned back to the room, where he found both Iris and Stator on their feet.

"Yes, Iris, they do, but it doesn't mean they are now fitting. Appropriate traditions will not be changed for the sake of change, but where I can improve things for everyone's benefit, I shall. That is the end of the matter."

Stator tried to ameliorate the situation. "My apologies, sir—"

"Stator, I do not need your apology; your comments were valid, appropriate, and I had asked for them. The matter of the new Margrave is of importance for all of Terasia. I believe in giving the ruling lords of a province a say in the matter. To my mind, your thoughts are as valid as tradition."

Realising the atmosphere had become tense, he reseated himself and motioned to his companions to do likewise. Iris continued to stand.

Arkyn glanced at him sharply. "Iris, your feet will wear out. Sit down." As Iris seated himself, his face a careful, neutral blank, Arkyn said, "Lord Stator, who would you suggest for the post of Deputy Governor? Or if you feel unqualified to make that suggestion, maybe you could advise me on the type of person you'd like to see in that post."

Stator considered. He'd been pleasantly surprised by the Prince's readiness to listen and simply accept his wishes. "Your Highness, I feel unqualified to recommend any particular person in this case," commented Stator. "All I would say is that this province may well benefit from younger men being in charge, those who still have life to live and who can bring new focus. This is, you realise, a personal opinion."

"I do realise that, my lord. Thank you for your help. I see I have some thinking to do. The decision won't be made for some time, but I shall give fair consideration to all possibilities."

Recognising the end of the interview from the Prince's tone, Stator rose. "*That* no-one now doubts, Your Highness."

When he'd gone, Arkyn turned to Iris. "Your thoughts, my lord."

"Your Highness seemed to approve."

With restraint, Arkyn said, "Now I'm asking for your thoughts, Iris, without prejudice to my own."

Inwardly frustrated, Lord Iris replied, "Your Highness, I'd say, in a different time, Lord Stator might well have led a revolution. Traditions cannot simply be ridden over roughshod. They have a purpose. His initial suggestion is unthinkable and probably untenable as well. Meritocracy has its place, but I would advise, after the events that greeted your arrival, such a soft-handed approach is unproductive. His Majesty will need a firm hand here. One wielded by a man he can work with and who will work for him without question, without ambition, but above all will accept orders, realising that the King is in charge."

"Then who would you see as Margrave?"

"Sir, I am not here to—"

Arkyn snapped, "I do not wish this situation to get any more protracted. Who would you see as Margrave?"

"Currently I don't know, sir. I know Lord Teran wanted to see Roth in that position. That is impossible now and with regard to his son, my former comments apply. I feel that the King wouldn't want Lord Silvano in the post and I don't know enough of the other candidates. Might I defer my opinion until we've heard them all?"

"Very well. That's all until Simble arrives." He watched Iris' retreating back. How could the lord be so blind?

Lord Simble stated other reasons to Stator, but the outcome was the same: he wouldn't be accepting the post. Therefore, instead of the intended interview, Arkyn spent the time talking about the exchequer problems and changes. Lord Simble had spent the weeks he'd been in charge hunting for someone to oversee the office after he had straightened it out. He had settled on a minor lord whom Arkyn hadn't had dealings with, but, on hearing the suggestion, Wealsman said it was a wise one and so the Prince was content to let the gentleman take over without delay.

The following day, Arkyn noted that his long-suffering administrator appeared more than usually harassed. Knowing Edward's temperament, he decided it wouldn't be prudent to ask him what the matter was. Edward was always competent and efficient. Since they'd been in Tera and especially since Arkyn's illness, he had also become reserved. He was trying to take pressure off Arkyn, and the Prince knew that. To ask him, therefore, to explain why he was stressed might appear an affront to that efficiency. Edward didn't realise that Arkyn had noticed anything amiss. By the early afternoon, after having interviewed Lord Bocard, Arkyn realised that it wasn't temporary stress and so enquired mildly what the issue was. Reluctantly Edward revealed Stuart, Thomas and two clerks had been taken ill.

Edward finished with, "I've borrowed a couple of clerks for the more routine tasks but—"

"Not for the confidential ones. Can't you use one of my clerks?"

Thinking about the anonymous letters, Edward said, "I'd rather not, Your Highness, for various reasons, but I… It's complicated. Please don't ask me to explain." Edward winced; he'd voiced the request unthinkingly.

Arkyn eyed his worried administrator. "If you can assure me that whatever doubts you have are being dealt with in a fair manner, I shan't require an explanation; however, you will request Lord Wealsman joins me and we will sort out the current problem."

"I'm dealing with the issues in a fair manner, sir."

Six minutes later, Arkyn explained the issue to Wealsman before adding. "Edward's borrowed the services of at least one of your clerks for the routine work but for the confidential matters he needs a trustworthy secretary who is experienced."

Wealsman considered for a few moments. "All I can suggest is that my personal secretary lends his services, sir. He's discreet and getting too long a break from work currently. Edward can borrow him for a couple of days to see if they can work together."

Arkyn glanced at his administrator. "Will that suffice?"

Edward hesitated. "Yes, sir, but I'd be happier if he swore some kind of oath."

"Percival?" enquired Arkyn, aware that the oath would transfer loyalty.

Wealsman shrugged. "I think it's highly reasonable."

"Good, then get the gentleman here. What's his name?"

"Laus, sir. Laus by name and louse by nature, according to many…"

On meeting Laus, Arkyn liked what he saw and quite understood how he had ended up working for Percival; it didn't take long for the Prince to discover that Wealsman and Laus had the same sense of humour and approach to formality. Laus was extremely relaxed by anyone's standards. Arkyn had a bet with himself that Iris would disapprove, but, much to his amazement, other than a sharp look, Iris didn't say a word.

* * *

On the last day of the interviews, Erlan Roth entered with a sure but not overconfident step. He bowed, an exact but not sycophantic bow, and then regarded Arkyn with a steady clear gaze. Iris was again reminded that there wasn't even a decade in age difference between the two men.

Arkyn waved to a chair. "What are your thoughts on why this interview is happening, my lord?"

Lord Roth smiled, seating himself. "I think Your Highness is trying to reinforce your earlier actions and, if so, I must thank Your Highness again."

"Your thanks, although appreciated, are not needed, my lord, for I do intend asking you the same questions as your peers. Do you hold any objection?"

"No, sir. If for no other reason than I am a curious soul."

Arkyn proceeded with the interview. He reached the end and Iris – to emphasise tradition, Arkyn was sure – posed no questions. Once it was clear Iris wasn't going to continue the interview, Arkyn said to Erlan,

"My lord, your answers were interesting and in places atypical. Does that bother you at all?"

"No, sir. You might say that my whole life has been that so far."

Arkyn nodded. "You might indeed. The final thing I need to speak to you about is the tax that was found on your lands. Are you satisfied that none of your father's personal funds were with it?"

"Yes, Your Highness. Even if they were half were forfeit to the FitzAlcis. From my father's personal accounts, all his 'official' money was found in the strong rooms of our manors. Anything else is, to my mind, missing tax."

"That does make life easier. I must thank you for your help with the retrieval. It can't have been easy having the militia at your manors. Do you have any issues you would raise with me, Lord Roth? Anything at all."

Erlan smiled. "Nothing, sir. I did what I like to believe any man in my position would have done. Commander Wynfeld and his men were more than considerate. In fact, they shocked and pleased my staff by being so."

"It's nice to know that not all surprises are unwelcome, my lord. Now…"

Once Roth had gone, Arkyn turned to Iris. "Your verdict, my lord?"

"A pleasant fellow, sir, though unsuitable for Margrave."

Arkyn raised an eyebrow. "He was closer on many matters to the answer I wanted than all the rest put together."

"Yes, Your Highness, I realised that, but again I cannot advise you to appoint him –not this close to his father's treason. Given another twenty years, and I'd say he would make an excellent governor or deputy governor, even an ambassador should the need arise for one, but right now I'd say let him simply exist as an overlord, certainly for a few years until he has made his mark and is not living off his father's legacy."

Arkyn found it reassuring that even through his reservations, Iris thought Erlan Roth would one day be suitable for high office. "Very well, then who of the other candidates do you think would make the best Margrave?"

Iris thought for a moment. "Kre, sir. I have not witnessed the side of him that is easily persuaded, which Wealsman said he had, but he is certainly a competent gentleman. His experience of helping to run a couple of free towns shows a dedicated mindset. He wouldn't question the King's authority."

Arkyn hesitated. "So I thought, my lord, but one or two of his answers concerned me, those which I sprung on him, rather than the easily deduced ones. He'd obviously been briefed by an advisor as to what I was likely to ask. I do not object to that, but it does make me wary."

"Would you like a new set of questions drawn up and a second set of interviews arranged, Your Highness?" asked Iris.

"To tell you the truth, I don't think that will help. I think I need time to consider everything I've heard. You have written up your thoughts on the interviews?"

"Yes, sir. I'll give a copy to Edward."

Arkyn nodded, rubbing his hand through his hair. "Thank you, my lord. They'll probably be invaluable. Now, I realise you wish to return to Oedran as soon as possible. I do not wish to inconvenience you, but I am still under doctor's orders and shall not be returning to Oedran until the spring. I have to examine the wardships that my family hold in Terasia. Lady Portur's situation is a formality only, and His Majesty has already intimated to me that he is overseeing it directly from Oedran. That means I only have to examine Lady Daia's affairs, or, rather, her steward's handling of them. Will you stay for a few days so that you can be there? I'm afraid I'm waiting for

Wealsman and Commander Wynfeld to investigate a matter for me, but the interview is set for Tretaldai."

"I wasn't planning to leave until I was certain you had no further need for me, sir, so I can wait for three more days. I'm sure it will take me a week, anyway, to organise my journey."

Arkyn smiled. "It well might. I'm aware that instead of travelling in autumn it is now winter, and I apologise for that. Your help, though, has been invaluable. It can't be easy to work with someone whose ideas don't conform to your expectations; you have been remarkably forbearing."

"Sir, I'm an Advisor to the FitzAlcis. It is my duty to assist."

"Even so, my lord, I thank you for your help. Now, unless you have anything further to add on the matter of the late Margrave's successor, I think, for the moment, that is all I need."

Iris got to his feet. "I shall go and see that all my reports are in order, sir." Once outside the office, he said to Edward, "Will His Highness require mine or Lord Irvin's company this evening?"

Edward glanced at a diary involuntarily. "I don't believe so, sir."

Iris also glanced down at the diary. It clearly had 'no disturbances' marked. He caught the administrator's eye and murmured, "Stick to that, Edward. His Highness needs it."

"Thank you, my lord. I intend to."

The administrator watched Lord Iris cross the entrance hall and smiled to himself. Iris gave off the impression of a restrained and insensitive gentleman, but Edward recognised he had a very caring edge to him.

Chapter 38
RELAXATION

Septadai, Week 26 – 14th Ralal, 14th Ralis 1211
Arkyn's Office

ONCE IRIS HAD LEFT the office, Arkyn relaxed. He had begun to appreciate the Lord of Oedran and to like him, but he still didn't feel entirely at ease around him. Maybe it was the age difference. Arkyn knew such a thing shouldn't matter, but it seemed to. Iris had known four generations of the FitzAlcis, Arkyn included. The Prince, therefore, felt that his actions were being closely watched to compare them to his forbears, even when that wasn't the case. He knew that it was paranoid of him to think they were, but when faced with a lord in his sixties, there wasn't much else that he could think. He also knew that it was a feeling he'd never escape for the next couple of years at least, so he accepted it and only examined his feelings on the matter occasionally.

It was a couple of minutes before Edward entered. The administrator saw Arkyn's drawn face and knew why Lord Iris had been concerned.

Arkyn caught the tone of Edward's mood. "Leave Kadeem to fuss over my health, Edward."

"Sorry, sir. It's a force of habit after His Majesty's instructions."

Arkyn stilled. "And don't rebuke my conscience! Lord Iris should be handing you his reports on the interviews. Just file them away; I'll read them eventually, but I want to make my mind up first before I'm persuaded it's wrong. Is there anything I need to attend to this afternoon?"

Thinking of the report about Lady Daia's staff and also thinking of the way the Prince looked, Edward shrugged. "Nothing that won't wait for the morning, sir."

Arkyn knew that reply. "What will wait for the morning then?"

"A report from the commander and Acting Governor, sir. It isn't marked urgent, therefore I thought—"

"You thought I need the rest more than I need to read it. All right, I promised both you and Kadeem I wouldn't be too stubborn headed, so I shall let it lie. Laus doing all right?"

"I've no complaint, sir, but it's odd. It's like I'm simply showing him things he's forgotten, not having to learn anew."

Arkyn smiled. "Richardson said the same of you, you know, and that you took to your new job with an alacrity he hadn't witnessed before."

"I expect he was being diplomatic, Your Highness."

Arkyn raised an eyebrow. "Tell me, when have you known Richardson to be *that* diplomatic about an underling?"

"Traditions can be changed, sir," quipped Edward sonorously.

Arkyn glared at him, but amusement tinted his voice. "Someone's had a bad influence on you. It can't possibly have been me." He pushed himself to his feet. "How's Stuart?"

"Still ill, sir."

"Make sure the doctor sees him, Thomas and the clerks until they're all well again. That's all for today. I'll put myself in Kadeem's jurisdiction."

Arkyn entered his private rooms and nodded to a junior member of his household, whose greeting was cautious.

Arkyn took pity on him. "Finish what you're meant to be doing, Alan." As the man swept the granite hearth, he asked, "How are you?"

"Perfectly well, thank you, Your Highness."

"Kadeem doesn't work you too hard?"

"Not at all, sir. We're content."

"That's something then. You're not missing Oedran?"

"I think we all do at times, Your Highness," replied Alan. "However, the sensation doesn't last long."

"I'm glad. When you've finished, if you could ask Kadeem to join me, I'd be grateful, but there's no need to hurry. Just tell me if I'm in your way."

"Never that, sir. I'm nearly done. Would you like the fire made up?"

Arkyn looked at the glowing embers. "Why not? It's not the warmest. Have you managed to see much of Tera?"

Alan replied that he'd been out and about on a few errands, that he had enjoyed exploring the markets on his days off and, knowing Arkyn hadn't had the opportunity to tour Tera, described what he could of the city. From narrow twisting alleys, full of half-timbered shops with overhanging storeys and even narrower passages crisscrossing the city, to the river swollen with autumn and winter rains flooding the low-lying banks.

Listening, Arkyn formed a picture of Tera that he could never acquire by visiting it himself. He could never experience the narrow twisting passages as Alan had. The guards around him would detract from the ambience and many of the streets didn't sound fit for coaches. The overhanging buildings probably meant riding was difficult as well; therefore, he'd have to walk and Fitz and Wynfeld wouldn't be happy if he tried to explore a crowded city on foot, especially in a province where treachery had recently been rife. It saddened him because the city sounded fascinating. He realised that he'd not been beyond the Residence since he'd arrived. He'd spent weeks in the same house. Granted, some of the time he'd been feverish or recovering, but how had he not noticed? Is that what official life was? An ornate and elegant prison?

A few moments after Alan left, Kadeem entered. "Your Highness?"

"I've finished working for the day, at Edward's polite, but nonetheless obvious, insistence."

"He has a way with words, sir."

"You can say that again – only please don't."

Kadeem noticed a set of the head and jaws: the Prince was still tense, as well as tired. "Your Highness, might I suggest I call your masseuse?"

"Do I look that bad?"

"Only to those who know you very well, sir. I've spoken to Edward and you're not due to be dining with anyone this evening. Might I suggest that you have a good meal, a hot bath and a massage? The three things normally help."

"I really will have to do something about these good ideas you keep coming up with."

Kadeem smiled. "Praise is a tool of princes—"

"I could try displeasure instead."

"…Hypocrisy of politicians and aristocracy."

"Very quick." Arkyn sighed. "You'd better decide which I need first out of the three on your list and then proceed to order everything."

"Sir. Oh, forgive me, Your Highness, but Alan—"

"Was not expecting me to walk into the room. I'm hardly going to object to him doing his job. I told him to carry on."

"It's not that, sir. Alan has been working very hard since Thomas was taken ill. I thought you'd like to know."

"Then give him my thanks, Kadeem. It is nice to hear praise and not censure. We'll need to go through my household accounts later this next week. Can you see Edward adds it to the list?"

"Of course, sir. Oh, I nearly forgot, there was private correspondence in the despatches: letters from His Majesty, Prince Tain, Lady Elantha, Lord Landis and Master Calumiel. I've put them in your desk."

"I'll read them now. I wonder why Cal wrote."

Kadeem chuckled as he retrieved the letters. "I expect to stop him getting all the blame, sir."

Arkyn laughed. "More than likely. Poor old Cal, he does think of some schemes, but Tain is, I believe, responsible for most. I almost miss them."

When Kadeem left, Arkyn closed his eyes. He was close to finishing all his official work in Terasia; after interviewing Daia's staff, he had nothing to worry about but signing the odd document for Wealsman. That would hardly tax him after the last few weeks' work.

For the first time since he'd set out for Tera, his time was his own. He'd have to find something to do. He wanted company of his own age. He'd talk with Irvin and Daia. The history of Erinna would probably be a part of his and Irvin's talk. He didn't mind that; he could, he was sure, give Irvin a couple of good debates. With Daia would be the chance to laugh and tease and talk about life in general. He smiled to himself, already looking forward to it.

He slipped into dreams. His brother's face, Ceardlann in the summer, Oedran bustling with people. His uncle's face sneered at him from the edge of a pit and he was watching him whilst he fell, still trying to catch the bright line above him. It changed again, and a horse was stumbling, a caltrop in its hoof, and then again it changed into a garden full of lavender at night, and once again into Roth's face the day he arrived. He struggled against bonds holding him back. He wanted to—

He awoke abruptly. Kadeem had shaken him by the shoulder. Ignoring his protestations, his manservant made him take a drink.

Arkyn passed the glass back. "How long…?"

"I wasn't even gone for six minutes. Forgive me, Your Highness, but you ought to see someone; that's the third nightmare since we arrived, that I know of, and—"

"They're a nuisance, Kadeem, and appear when I'm drained. There's nothing else to them." (Kadeem kept silent but still managed to exude scepticism.) "Don't be like that. They will sort themselves. If they've not disappeared by the time I get to Oedran, I'll talk to Doctor Chapa; I'm not going to lay my soul open to Artzman."

"Very well, sir, I realise I'm overstepping certain bounds."

"Stop being obsequious and tell me why you were disturbing my slumber."

"Simply to say I decided the best order would be a meal, bath and then a massage, if that suits Your Highness?"

Arkyn nodded. "It sounds admirable to me. I ought to see what my brother wanted to tell me, or what he'll admit to."

Arkyn read the letters with a ready eye. He'd write to the Comptroller to get an unbiased view of what was occurring at Ceardlann and also to check that the gentleman hadn't torn *all* his hair out.

He'd read all the letters, and shaken his head over his brother's antics, when Kadeem set the table for his dinner. Once the meal had been cleared, Kadeem let him sit for half an hour before telling him that his bath was ready if he wanted it.

"I'm not sure I can move, Kadeem."

"Movement is—"

"Spare me any philosophy. I can't cope with it after today." He pushed himself to his feet. "It should be easy, shouldn't it, picking a new Margrave? There are so few candidates, after all."

"Forgive me, but does the new Margrave have to be an overlord?"

Arkyn sighed. "It's traditional, and I wouldn't like to see Lord Iris suffer apoplexy if I were to pick anyone else."

"Will you announce the new Margrave whilst he's here then, sir?" asked Kadeem, holding the door to the bedchamber open.

"No, I don't think so. He wants to return to Oedran. I still don't know whom I'll pick and I can't, in all conscience, keep him here until I do – especially after Lord Rale's death. I ought to give myself a deadline for the appointment to end this indecision."

Kadeem smiled. "Why don't you make it the Munlumen, sir?"

Arkyn considered. "Hmm. Good idea. Wealsman could then get married in peace too."

A couple of moments later, they entered the bathroom and Arkyn took a deep breath. The room smelt of fir trees. He felt himself unwind and suddenly didn't want to discuss anything vaguely resembling official work. He sat to take his shoes off but found Kadeem had knelt to help, sensing his mood change. Two minutes later Kadeem left and Arkyn relaxed back in the bath not wanting to move. The water was warm and the scent calming.

Drifting off, he awoke with a start. Yawning, he pulled himself out of the cooling water, reaching for a towel. Drying himself off, he entered his dressing room. Kadeem handed him a simple dressing gown. Arkyn yawned again. Kadeem simply smiled at him.

Arkyn shook his head, amused. "Talking won't wake me up."

Kadeem whispered, "No, but it might disturb your contentment, sir. Do you still want a massage?"

Arkyn rolled his neck from side to side. "Yes. I may fall to sleep though."

"I'm expecting it, sir."

"Such faith in me."

Kadeem held the door open for Arkyn. The masseuse was waiting with Alan. Arkyn nodded in dismissal at his footman before greeting the masseuse with a couple of words as she dropped into a well-practised curtsy. When she rose, she averted her gaze from the Prince as he undid his dressing gown and lay on his front. Kadeem drew a sheet over his lower body before standing aside. Arkyn, his head on his hands, closed his eyes as the masseuse began. The warming tones of the oils calmed him, teasing sleep, but he didn't want the massage to stop. He turned his head away from Kadeem.

He awoke in the small hours with covers over him and a pillow below his head. He must have been heavily asleep for Kadeem to have managed that one. Contentment still warmed him. He rolled onto his back, gazing at the ceiling over his bed. His mind became more active as he focused on the world around him. He'd spent too many days in this room since he'd come to Tera and, whatever he told Kadeem, he was still feeling the after-effects of being ill. He was tired and drained most days. He ought to be able to cope, but he couldn't. Maybe he should just accept that. He glanced at the embers of the fire, remembering watching them after the nightmare and, by association, thought about the notes. There hadn't been any for some time. Why? Once Iris was on his way to Oedran, he'd ask Percival what he'd managed to discover. Hopefully, whoever held the grudge had tired of the whole thing.

Chapter 39
WARDSHIPS

Alundai, Week 27 – 15th Ralal, 15th Ralis 1211

Arkyn's Office

THE FOLLOWING MORNING, Arkyn entered his outer office to find Laus waiting. He raised an eyebrow. "Don't tell me Edward's overslept?"

Laus grinned. "Unfortunately not, Your Highness. He's in your office."

"So much for wanting to catch him out. Has he got a pile of documents?"

"He certainly has a couple, sir. He needs a reason for existing."

Arkyn laughed. "Careful, Laus, that's my administrator."

Laus inclined his head. "I'm sorry, sir, I let my natural scepticism overrule my judgement."

"Best way, isn't it?" He was in his office before he realised that he'd never joked with Stuart.

He took in the sight of a well-ordered desk and his administrator checking it. "Morning, Edward. I thought you'd overslept."

"I'm sorry to disappoint you, sir, but Alan has been remarkably efficient at making sure I am awake and breakfasted in time." He hesitated. "Your Highness, Laus, like Alan, has been working exceptionally hard. It seems a shame to lose his help when Stuart returns."

Arkyn said, "I can't in all conscience pinch him from Wealsman, Edward. If he is being that helpful, I'll see if Wealsman will lend him to us until I leave. That way, you can all get a bit extra time off. Stuart especially, when he's recovering, will need it. Will that suffice?"

"Admirably, thank you, sir."

Arkyn seated himself. "So, what *is* this hefty report?"

"The one Your Highness requested on the dealings of Lady Daia's staff. There are also additional notes on the situation from Lord Wealsman, Lady Portur and the commander, all of whom are worried. I've placed with them the standard instructions from His Majesty concerning his wardships; they arrived in yesterday's despatches."

"Thank you, Edward. Did Wynfeld send any verbal message?"

"No, sir."

Arkyn paused. "Must be bad. He normally jokes about something. Is there anything else I need to do before I give these reports my full attention?"

"No, Your Highness."

It took Arkyn most of the morning to read the reports. When he finished, he was fuming. He put down Kristina's report and sent for Wealsman at the end of which he was reassured and had solutions to the issues at hand.

* * *

Two days later, Arkyn was once more watching the garden when Edward announced Daia and her steward. The Prince looked at the steward with interest – an unremarkable gentleman in appearance and manner, neither nervous nor self-assured, a careful, studied, incurious soul. Daia, however, had grown in confidence, and Arkyn was pleased to see it.

A minute later they were all arranged: Edward ready to take notes, Arkyn, Daia and Iris seated and the steward standing in front of the desk feeling increasingly uneasy. Confusing Lord Iris would be much harder than deceiving the Prince.

Arkyn said, "Steward, I have read your report of your stewardship. You have control, currently, of all Lady Daia's assets. Please outline to me your duties and whom you answer to on each one, any instructions you have ever received from His Majesty or Lord Portur concerning those duties."

"Your Highness realises we will be here sometime?"

Arkyn raised a finger to stop Iris from interrupting. "Yes. So, the sooner you start, the sooner you will finish."

The steward audibly sighed. "Very good, sir."

A frown creased Iris' features. The steward shouldn't have questioned the Prince. Arkyn gave him a significant glance. A warning? He didn't fool himself any longer; the Prince's seeming innocence obviously hid greater knowledge. Iris started analysing the steward's account. Something didn't add up. It took him moments to realise that Lady Daia's voice was nowhere to be heard. It was all what the steward thought best.

After the steward finished, Arkyn said, mildly, "Thank you. That was most illuminating. Now, tell me something: do you accept orders from Lady Daia and carry those orders out as you would have done her father's?"

The steward paused. "Excusing Her Ladyship's presence, there are some I haven't."

"Why not? She is still your lady," exclaimed Iris.

"Because, my lord, Her Ladyship is still underage and—"

"*And* nothing, steward! Forgive me, Your Highness, but I cannot believe His Majesty's instructions are so restrictive."

"You are right, Lord Iris, they are not," confirmed Arkyn. "I have had sent to me the standard instructions for every wardship of His Majesty's. These state that once a ward is of cisan-age they can, if they wish, have a majority say in the running of their estates." He turned to the steward. "You should in that instance confine yourself to advice… Is this not so?"

The steward squirmed. "Your Highness, I have given advice—"

"Yet not done what Lady Daia requests."

"Only when it wouldn't be of benefit, sir!"

"Whose benefit?" responded Arkyn deftly.

The steward tried the confusion card. "Sir?"

"When the instructions wouldn't be of benefit to whom?"

"Her Ladyship, sir – who else?"

Iris could restrain himself no longer. "You *do not* question His Highness!"

Arkyn replied to the question. "Maybe yourself or even Her Ladyship's governess? I've had other reports compiled. None of your staff were questioned openly, Lady Daia, but it is astounding what my men discovered anyway. For example, three years ago, when Lord Sansky died, the rent for one of your properties in Tera was half the current rate. Not only that," he faced the steward, "but *you* still record the original amount in the ledger. Before you argue, I have signed statements and have had Her Ladyship's bailiffs watched as they collect the rent… I see you cannot find any words to express yourself, which is perhaps fortunate because there are none to excuse such malfeasance. Your personal affairs are under examination due to your fraudulent dealings. Lady Daia will need to decide how to proceed, but I am relieving you of your post of steward of the Sansky lands with immediate effect."

The steward went an interesting shade, like strawberries in the first days of ripening – mostly white but with hints of red.

Iris was impressed at the speed at which Arkyn had made the justified decision, but the Prince avoided his gaze and Iris had the strange sensation that he was uncomfortable about it.

"Your Highness, you cannot—" started the steward.

"I can, and I'm doing so!" snapped Arkyn. "His Majesty has agreed with the action."

"So I was never going to leave this office with my post?"

"Correct. If you want to know the reasons, think long and hard about whom a steward should answer to and the amount of trust the post entails. *You* abused that trust since shortly after the death of Lord Sansky. *You* acted fraudulently and embezzled funds – as far as possible, those will be recovered. *You* have kept Lady Daia in a state unbefitting to her rank, controlling her movements and purse beyond reason. Furthermore, you have tried to coerce her into actions and have conspired against her, and have taken instruction from none. Lastly, you have compounded these errors by lying to me. Do you think the King doesn't record his decisions?"

"Your Highness is young—"

Iris was on his feet. "To lie about the King's instructions means you are close to treason. You will not insult His Highness again."

His face now the colour of ripe strawberries, the steward glared at Iris before storming from the room.

Arkyn calmly rang the bell on his desk and Laus entered. "Laus, see the steward is lodged in a cell until his temper has cooled."

Laus bowed and left, startled. The door closed on him, leaving the room still and silent for a few moments. It wasn't shock; it wasn't disbelief; it was simply an acceptance that the meeting had ended abruptly. In that pause, Edward rose and poured some drinks. He offered one to the Prince who shook his head.

Instead, Arkyn excused himself and walked onto the garden terrace. He stood feeling the sting of a wintry day on his cheeks, gazing out at the trees, their twigs stark against the blue of a cloudless day. A scuffle drew his attention. The guard by the door was struggling with the former steward. Another, summoned by Edward, joined the tussle and soon the man was led away. Arkyn stood watching the event with a rare disassociation. Guilt burned in him at the same time as a blank emptiness stole his reactions.

Six minutes later, the weight of a cloak being draped around his shoulders brought Arkyn out of the stupor. He glanced round to thank Kadeem, but met Wynfeld's concerned gaze. His mask shattered. Wynfeld guided him onto the lawns and then to a log bench overlooking the rippling pond.

Once sitting, Arkyn half-whispered, "It's not that he got angry, or insulted me – I've had worse from Tain. It's knowing that I had no option."

Wynfeld watched the gardens. "Decisions that take a man's living away from them are often harder than ordering a man's execution. The knowledge that they must live on is more haunting than the knowledge that worldly preoccupations will trouble them no more."

Arkyn swallowed. "I think I'm realising that. I couldn't though, in all conscience, have done anything else – could I?"

"No, you couldn't. If I'd known your wishes, I would have taken the task on myself."

"I hope I never resort to such methods. If it is my decision, then in cases such as that, they have the right to hear it from my lips."

"I never expected anything less of you, my prince, but it doesn't stop many of us wishing we could take the responsibility from your shoulders, even once in a way." Wynfeld let the silence mature before continuing quietly, "It was not solely your decision, my prince. Your hands were as tied as the steward's future is bleak. His actions, his decisions, caused his ruin. Anyone finding out someone they employed had acted so foolishly would have done as you did. Some would have gone further."

Arkyn absorbed that. "Thank you and thank you for listening. Who or what alerted you?"

Wynfeld glanced sideways at him. "Laus isn't such a clown as he appears. I was in the Residence talking to Lord Wealsman. We heard the commotion."

"Then I'm surprised Wealsman didn't appear with you," stated Arkyn.

"I asked him to see about the former Sansky steward."

"Thank you, Wynfeld. You always appear at the right time."

"Pure chance, Your Highness."

Arkyn pushed himself to his feet. "I wonder. Now, I must go and tell the governess that she's dismissed."

"I'll be talking to Lord Wealsman, if you need me, sir."

Arkyn returned the commander's cloak to him. "I'm sure you will, Wynfeld. Thank you." With that, the Prince strode off.

Watching him go, Wynfeld glanced up at the sky, thinking of Queen Ira's dying request to look after her family. He hoped she thought he was doing a good job.

Entering his office, Arkyn enquired if Wynfeld had stopped watching him.

"Only just, Your Highness," replied Iris gravely.

"I *must* have worried him. Have you still got that drink to hand, Edward? Lady Daia, I'm of a mind to dismiss your governess as well. Do you hold any objection?"

Daia looked thoughtful. "No, Your Highness, but I'd like to talk to you privately after the meeting."

"Of course. Edward, show the lady in. I don't think this will take long."

The governess entered. Dressed soberly as tradition dictated for her post, she managed to exude an air of insipidity. Her hair tied loosely would have better suited her personality scraped back tightly; her nose was straight and her lips thin. She curtsied. The shallow and unpractised gesture astonished Arkyn – a lady employed as she was should be able to curtsy, as teaching it to her charges was important.

Arkyn motioned her to a seat and saw Daia watching her governess with an odd expression, as though, like him, she was seeing her for the first time.

The Prince said, "Governess, I assume you know why I've asked to speak to you—"

"Not really."

"That is odd. I had my clerks send you a letter outlining the reasons. Edward, can you please check that it was done?"

"I undertook the task myself, Your Highness," answered Edward. "I sent a letter to the steward at the same time. As he received his, I cannot understand how the governess failed to receive hers. Especially as—"

"I never received it," interrupted the governess primly.

Arkyn enquired mildly, "Are you accusing my administrator of lying to me, governess?"

"I am saying I never received it; I accuse nobody."

"No matter. I'm sure it is easy to remedy." He waited for the governess' face to relax before turning to Daia. "My lady, would you object if I sent a couple of clerks to your house to check? I am rather perplexed as your governess somehow found out the time of her interview without the letter."

Daia murmured, "Please do, Your Highness. I've always heard Edward is precise in all matters."

Iris sat there sober faced but inwardly applauding. The emotion shocked him. Before arriving in Tera, he'd have baulked at the Prince's manipulations. Was he beginning to appreciate the way Arkyn allowed people every opportunity of telling the truth before springing on them the fact he knew the lie? Did it matter? He, at last, understood what the King had meant by saying he wished he could be in Tera to see the fun.

Once Laus had been summoned and told of the errand, Arkyn turned back to the governess. "Now, as you seem unaware of the reasons, let me outline them to you. I have called this meeting to talk about Lady Daia's formal education and the continued need for it…"

The governess couldn't help shooting her charge a supercilious glance.

After a slight pause, Arkyn continued, "…My apologies, that is, *if* there is a continued need for it. Lady Daia will soon be nineteen. In just over a year, she'll be alunan-age and in her majority. Do you believe her education needs to continue for this coming year?"

"Yes."

"Why?"

"She's still young, wayward, headstrong—"

"*Your Highness,* forgive me for interrupting," said Iris. "Governess, do you always speak so of your charge in her hearing?"

The governess bridled. "It is the truth."

"I am not a child," responded Daia.

"No more you are, my lady," observed Arkyn. "Governess, maybe you would care to give an example of Her Ladyship's headstrong and wayward manner?"

"I know not what the expectations of a lady are in Oedran," elaborated the governess superciliously, "but in Terasia they don't visit their sick tenants, they don't disregard advice, and they listen to the other females of their circle—"

Arkyn's lips twitched. "Codswallop. Your passion does you credit, your logic a disservice. A lady of feeling is perfectly at liberty to care about her tenants; in fact, the rewards in loyalty are far superior to those of negligence. Advice may be taken or ignored; it is, by its very nature, transitory. I expect what you mean is Lady Daia does not allow herself to be coerced into, for example, leaving Tera because I haven't helped her reputation—"

The governess whipped round to Daia. "Why you little—"

Arkyn snapped, "Lady Daia didn't, until that moment, know I knew of those comments! They reached my ears by a different source."

"Lady Portur the—"

"*The* nothing! By Alcis, you are trying my patience. There are many other incidents but, for the moment, other matters require attention. Her Ladyship is without a maid. Why?"

"She is not of age."

Arkyn tapped his fingers on the desk. "Immaterial. As Her Ladyship has said, she is not a child. In Oedran a lady has a maid before her fifteenth birthday, sometimes before her brothers' would a manservant. I can think of no reason, other than a desire to restrict her liberties, why you would have ceased her father's hunt for a maid. Maybe you would care to enlighten me."

The governess' jaw hardened; it was an unbecoming gesture. "Such matters are not for discussion with men present."

Arkyn observed far too mildly, "Do not try to embarrass me. Would you have refused to explain to the King?"

"Yes, but not to the late Queen."

Arkyn's features set. The mention of his mother always upset him. "I can't accept that as a reason—"

The governess interrupted him. "I won't explain. The facts might not embarrass you. I'm sure you're worldly enough, but I would still feel uncomfortable."

The insinuation was there; how would a prince know of feminine matters other than by intimate association with a lady?

Arkyn stilled. "Governess, do *not* insult me further. In categorically refusing to answer my questions, you leave me no choice but to dismiss you from your post. Your belongings will be sent to any address you wish. You will not return to Lady Daia's house and will never enter the Sansky lands again. No objection or appeal will help your case. Your actions were unjustifiable and foolish. I'm left questioning how much you have ever taught Lady Daia – for not once have you addressed anyone in this room correctly. You can go."

The governess sat there for a few moments before rising, ignoring everyone in the room and leaving – her back as stiff as a poker, her face expressionless.

Once the door closed, Arkyn sighed with relief. "Lord Iris, regarding any comments you have, I would prefer them now."

"The only comment I have, sir, is that I agree with your actions."

Arkyn nodded. "Thank you. Then that's all. Edward, if you could see there's a brief report on events, I'd be grateful."

Once Daia and Arkyn were alone, she said, "Thank you, sir."

Arkyn smiled. "That's all right. You wanted to talk to me?"

"Mainly to thank you, but also to ask what am I meant to do now?"

"I'm sure you know your staff well enough, but Wealsman has mentioned your deputy steward is worth promoting and we think we've located a suitable maid, but you'll have the last say on her employment."

Daia looked oddly reassured. "Right, Your Highness. What about my 'continued education'? After all, I'm just a 'wayward child'."

Arkyn laughed. "Yes, she had a way with words. I suggest you stay in Tera for the year. Lady Portur says she's happy enough to give you any guidance you may want, need or require. The King and I thought, and with your agreement, we'll make her your local guardian here… Though formally it will be Lord Wealsman and only after I've left. We hope your new arrangements will suit you."

Daia's lips twitched. "They might well. You've been to a lot of trouble, sir; I wouldn't have wanted that. Just— Did you really say *Codswallop*?"

Arkyn laughed. "Yes. Did I get the context right? Lady Portur told me the story over dinner one evening."

Daia chuckled. "Completely right, sir. I can't believe—"

"I like the word. It has a certain presence to it that I think will be amusing. I can just imagine some of the lords' faces if I start using it. Come on, we'd better show our faces before I start *wrecking your reputation*."

They left the room laughing. Arkyn bid Daia goodbye before saying to Edward, "Should anything appear, which can't wait for tomorrow, I'll be in my private rooms. Laus, thank you for earlier. Maybe one of you could send Wealsman a dinner invitation. I'm sure he's working far too hard to welcome my disturbing him now. Also, if Lord Irvin is free, I'd be glad of his company over lunch."

Edward nodded. "We'll see to it, sir." He watched the Prince leave.

Laus behind him asked, "What did he mean? I did my job."

Edward laughed. "That's the Prince for you, always says thank you. Surely Lord Wealsman does?"

"Oh, certainly. I just didn't think it was normal for the FitzAlcis."

"Laus, tell me when you've met any of the FitzAlcis other than His Highness."

Laus took a breath. "Well…" He let it out. "Lord Scanlon in 1204. Very briefly and in passing—"

"Without wishing to criticise, you've just made the point. Will you draft that invitation for Lord Wealsman?"

"Why don't I go and tell him?"

"Because that would disturb him and the Prince didn't want to do that. Alcis, do you ever listen, or do you simply hunt for ways to be informal?"

Laus said, "Would saying 'both' count? All right, Administrator, don't tear your hair out. You'll need it to keep your head warm."

Laus chuckled, writing out an official invitation. Edward watching him shook his head as he contacted Lord Irvin. Lord Iris would say it was the impudence of youth, but Edward suspected that it would still be the same when Laus was sixty. He also suspected Laus wasn't telling him everything about his past, but he was a good worker and he *could* restrain himself.

Chapter 40
ADVISORS AND AN ACCOUNTING

Early Afternoon
Arkyn's Chambers

IRVIN WAS ANNOUNCED so soon after Arkyn reached his chambers that the Prince wondered if he'd been in the Residence anyway. Kadeem served lunch before leaving them to talk for the afternoon.

The friends' talk wandered around many subjects before Irvin confided to Arkyn that he didn't know what he wanted to do with his life. As the talk meandered onto the choices of life, Arkyn mused aloud that they both had it easy in comparison to Tain, who would take up official duties at fifteen. Recognising a mellow mood, Irvin asked about the Princes' education. Arkyn explained that he'd been taught by an advisor and Tain would be taught by a judge and that days away from lessons were rare. Irvin was intrigued that the future justiciar wasn't taught by the current incumbent but Arkyn's tone in replying stopped him from questioning why.

To deflect the interest, Arkyn enquired, "What would you *like* to do, if you had complete control of your life?"

"I don't know, sir, that's the problem. Part of me would like to study law, but then I'd also like to study the history of the empire and the lands before they were united. I'd even like to see if I could find evidence that the Majistar Ull existed. Also, what was here before he arrived? The legends tell us of battles and emergent kingdoms, but what were the boundaries? How did they interact? I don't know. There are a hundred and one questions we don't know the answer to. I'd like to find some of them."

Arkyn smiled. "Why don't you? You enjoy travelling. Why don't you travel around the empire trying to find out? You hold a privileged position as a future Lord of Oedran. You could gain access to most of the libraries in any city."

"Yes, but my father and grandfather want me to train as an advisor. Also, forgive me, but I suppose I want to find out what isn't known. That would mean examining ancient papers, if they exist. I'd dearly like to find a memor and read the Memini's Manuscript with them, the stories it must contain. Yet, who would allow me to even look at more mundane documents?"

Arkyn put his drink down. "You're not without standing, Irvin. It opens a lot of doors. As for the Memini's Manuscript, I think that is far out of our reach. Its history alone means it is a sensitive artefact; I've not even asked to see it, though I'd like to. You could, however, listen to the old stories and record them. I'm sure there is a way around your family's wishes. There normally is."

Animated by the discussion, Irvin exclaimed, “If you have any ideas, sir, I’d welcome them.”

Arkyn thought. Future Lords of Oedran had to be educated in advice, the law, or they had to join the army. The King could determine a different path, but that hadn’t happened in generations.

After a time, he said, “Talk to your father; agree to give the Advisors’ School a chance; it *could* work in your favour. Spend your spare time reading the history you’re interested in. Qualifying as an advisor will open a lot of doors. Just because you are an heir to the Iris lordship doesn’t mean that after your education you must reside in Oedran, or even be an advisor in Oedran. It is only *when* you are Lord Iris you have to live in Oedran. What’s more, if you give the school a chance, you have done what your family wants. You can then pursue your own interests. Your family aren’t to know what you get up to in different provinces. If you tell His Majesty what you’re interested in, he’ll likely leave you alone or ask you about precedents. There you go. Tell Lord Iris and Lord Idris that you want to specialise in the precedents of the early empire. You’d still be an advisor.”

Irvin ruminated for several moments. “I like that plan, sir. It’s quite devious though.”

“You have to be in life. Have you visited the library here? There are some interesting texts on the early emergent Terasia, I believe. The Beran or ‘magic bearer’ had his home here. According to Laioril, it’s only by chance, apparently, that the Memini’s Manuscript is here. You want to talk to him. If you want to know the legends, he is the best. He has enough stories to keep you busy for years.”

“I’ve never actually met him, although I have heard of him, of course. Is it true he camps in the Rex Dallin every year?”

“Yes. I think my grandfather gave his tribe permission. I’d like to know how Laioril persuaded him.”

Irvin nodded. “Is there a library at Ceardlann?”

“Of sorts, though our private diaries are in the Diary Archive in the Palace. The state papers are archived in the Palace as well. They go back for centuries. You want to take a look if you are interested in the history of the empire. I can authorise you to examine the old papers and most up to those of fifty years ago. For more recent ones, you would need the King’s permission.”

Pleased by the gesture, Irvin said, “Thank you, sir, but it is the early years of the empire I am interested in: from the Fall of the Cearcall to the Age of Tyranny.”

Arkyn grinned. “You can certainly read those. I’ll write a note to our archivist. I’ll also introduce you to Laioril when he’s near Oedran. He’s kept myself and Prince Tain entertained for hours. He tells his stories as though he lived through the events. You'd certainly appreciate them."

Irvin smiled. "Thank you, sir. Have you heard from His Highness recently?"

Arkyn laughed. "I received a *small* letter. It took me about half an hour to read. He's having fun learning to plough. Farmer Silversley noticed him watching and offered to teach him. Tain will agree to any mad scheme like that."

"Doesn't the King object, Your Highness?"

"He says no skills learned are worthless," replied Arkyn, thinking he'd better not explain the King had helped. He idly amused himself, imagining what the lords would say if they discovered the King could plough a straight furrow.

* * *

After Irvin left, Arkyn called for Kadeem and told him to bring the household ledgers. His manservant did so, but Arkyn fancied there was something concerning Kadeem when it came to them. Half an hour later, the Prince realised what it was, and it didn't make him happy.

"What's this payment in?"

The manservant paused for a couple of seconds too long.

"Kadeem!"

"Sir, we've been here longer than planned. When Your Highness was ill, Lord Wealsman pointed out that your household funds wouldn't stretch to your extended stay, and it was ridiculous to have to transport more from Oedran. His Lordship insisted Terasia supported your extended stay, Your Highness… Sir… Let me finish…"

It was too late. Arkyn stormed through the Residence and entered Wealsman's office without herald. The Acting Governor, in the middle of a meeting, stood. Arkyn barely glanced at the attendees.

"A word, Wealsman. In my office!"

The door closed on the Prince and left astonishment in its wake. No-one had seen Arkyn so irate. Wealsman quickly excused himself. Halfway across the entrance hall, he spotted Kadeem motioning to him.

"What's happened, Kadeem?"

"He was examining his accounts."

"Ah. How far did you get?"

"Your Lordship insisting Terasia supported His Highness' stay."

Wealsman nodded. "I'll deal with it."

He entered the Prince's office.

Arkyn snarled, "Don't sit down, Wealsman. My funds are a matter for me and my household not, and I repeat, *not* a matter for *any* lord of Terasia, Acting Governor or no!"

"Your Highness, I understand that—"

"Enough! You'll damned well listen to me. I cannot, and will not, accept the people of Terasia supporting my prolonged stay here. I cannot be a drain on your province's already fragile funds. Do you understand?"

"Yes, Your Highness. Might I—"

"If the next word's 'explain' think carefully if the actual explanation includes any objection, because *that* I won't tolerate."

Wealsman said, "Your Highness, I did take it upon myself to speak to your manservant and, for that, I can but apologise; with hindsight, it probably wasn't the wisest move of my life; however, please put your mind at rest. The money isn't coming from the general taxation pot, sir. It's coming from the money collected from the tribute; that which would be sent to Oedran to your father's coffers."

"Does that make it any better? You are defrauding His Majesty."

"No, sir. His Majesty knows and has agreed with the decisions."

Arkyn sagged into his chair, still furious, but the sting had gone. Why hadn't his father told him? He glanced at Wealsman's concerned face. "I'm sorry."

Wealsman never hesitated. "Your Highness needs not apologise; I do. I should have explained before you found out like this…"

Arkyn got up, abruptly. "Maybe you should, but you didn't. Let's leave it there. I wanted a word on a different matter as well. Have you found out who was responsible for those notes?"

"No, sir, not yet, not absolutely. Have there been any more?"

"No. Not for a couple of weeks or more. I don't know if that will help or not. No-one knows you're investigating anything, do they?"

"No, sir."

"Good. Keep it that way. Thank you, Wealsman. I'll see you at dinner."

Wealsman bowed and left. Once he was well clear of the office, he let out a long breath. He now knew one thing for certain; he never wanted to be on the wrong side of the Prince.

* * *

Arkyn called up Fafnir. Two moments later, he was saying, "Father, why didn't you tell me my stay in Terasia was being financed from the tribute?"

Adeone recognised spent anger in his son's gaze. "Because, quite frankly, I forgot to. It was sorted out weeks ago. How did you find out?"

"I was checking my household accounts."

"I'm impressed by your dedication. I don't think I ever did that when I was on the reviews. Kadeem must have been uncomfortable telling you."

"Erm, well, he didn't exactly tell me. Wealsman had to."

"You were angry?"

Arkyn sighed. "Yes. Was it stupid of me?"

Adeone smiled. “Understandable, rather. We should have told you. I forget, sometimes, just how much you’ve grown in the last few years.”

“I gave Wealsman a hard time.”

“Then, if you feel you should and haven’t already, apologise. I’m sure he won’t bear a grudge. How did the wardship meeting go?”

Arkyn ran a hand through his hair. “Well enough. I dismissed both the steward and governess.”

“Have you talked to Daia about prosecuting the former steward?”

“No. Should I?”

“It might be an idea. It would send out a statement to all stewards of our wards. Think about it. If you want any advice, ask Lord Iris.”

“I will. He’ll be leaving for Oedran on Alunadai.”

“Will you be pleased?” asked Adeone.

“Does it sound too ungrateful if I say ‘yes’? It’s not that he’s been a bad advisor, quite the reverse. It’s just I feel I can’t always be myself. Is that normal?”

“Yes. You learn to ignore the feeling and be yourself. Iris worked with father for too long.”

“He has been a good advisor though. Do you want Irvin to return to Oedran with Lord Iris? I think he’d like time to explore the library here without feeling his grandfather disapproves.”

“Then tell Iris that Irvin is staying with you, if Irvin wishes to. There shouldn’t be a problem. If there is, tell me. Don’t take the whole world on your shoulders just yet.”

“I’ll try not to,” said Arkyn ruefully. “After all, I follow your example.”

“Wait until I see you,” growled Adeone good-humouredly. “At least I can tell you’re feeling better. I’d better continue annoying your Uncle Festus. For saying he’s my Chief Advisor, he can be remarkably laid back about giving advice.”

“Hmm. How many glasses of whiskey have you given him?”

“Enough.”

When the link closed, Arkyn did feel better, but he still felt sick at the way he’d overreacted and knew that the feeling wouldn’t dissipate anytime soon.

* * *

In Oedran, Adeone winked at Landis and called up Dragoris. He obtained a private link with Wealsman, whose worry seeped through the link.

Adeone said, “He’s calmed down.”

“Thank Alcis for that. I should have told him sooner.”

“We both should. He’s young and doesn’t like being sidestepped. It’s perfectly understandable. He’s meant to be managing everything and, because he was ill, we’ve gone blundering in. I hate to think how annoyed he'll be when he realises that we're friends, but I'm still not going to tell him yet. He was saying he felt Lord Iris was preventing him from being himself."

"I don't think anyone's noticed, Sire, least of all Lord Iris."

Adeone laughed. "No, probably not. Keep an eye on him, Percival."

"I will, sir. It'll take more than a dressing down to stop me from doing that. Anyway, I'm still invited to dinner, so it can't be that bad."

Once out of the link, Wealsman ignored the speculative stares from the meeting's attendees. One or two were wondering if it was the herald of change. Was Wealsman's tenure as Acting Governor ending? Would the Prince take over? Wealsman merely finished the meeting with a competence that several found rather annoying.

* * *

On Septadai, Arkyn presided at a banquet, and, the morning after, waved Iris farewell. He spent the afternoon trying to persuade Irvin to move into the Residence, but Irvin pointed out that Silvano would register it as a snub and he hadn't been a poor host. Laughingly, Irvin observed he was closer to the library if he stayed at Silvano's. Arkyn said he'd accept it if Irvin found him something to read as well. By the time the sun set the following day, they'd talked to the librarian – a gentleman who was loath to let any of the books and scrolls out of the building, no matter who was asking for them. Arkyn persuaded him to let him keep them in his rooms at the Residence and should any not meet the librarian's strict standards on their return, then the Prince would have a new copy of the book or scroll taken, or have it repaired. For the librarian's tolerance, Arkyn had a few of the more fragile books repaired anyway.

Chapter 41
REVIEW REPORT

Imperadai, Week 31 – 18th Anapal, 4th Anapcis 1211

Oedran – Carnford Gate

JUST OVER THREE WEEKS after leaving Tera, Lord Iris reached Oedran in the early afternoon. Riding through the city gates, he was truly glad to do so. He wanted to do several things: pay his respects to the late Lord Rale, see his neardaughter and the new Lord Rale and get home for a long hot bath. Protocol dictated he must report to the King first. So, as soon as his secretary had located the report, he rode to the Palace.

At the Outer Office, Richardson greeted him. "Welcome back to Oedran, Lord Iris. His Majesty is just talking to Merchant Chapa. If you wish to wait, I can check if they've finished."

Two minutes later, Merchant Chapa had left and Adeone got to his feet in welcome. "Lord Iris, I *am* glad to see you! How was your trip?"

"Pleasanter than I expected, Your Majesty. It's been a mild winter. I'm sorry to disturb your talks with Merchant Chapa."

"Don't be; I think that he was about to hand me another 'idea', one of the type that normally takes ten men to sort out."

"I'd have thought he'd have run out of those after all these years. The first thing he ever said to me was had I considered that some taxes only hinder trade."

Adeone chuckled. "I can believe that. His numerous ideas do, however, bring prosperity to the empire. Unlike the bandits he's told me are on the roads in Areal, but that's a matter for later. Now, before aught else, I suppose you have a long report for me."

"I certainly have a report for Your Majesty. Shall I send for it?"

Adeone rang for Richardson and, a couple of moments later, the chest Iris had brought with him was carried into the room.

Adeone looked at it and, when the door had closed on the Outer Office, remarked, "I'll have to think of an appropriate way of thanking Prince Arkyn when I see him."

"It's not quite as bad as it seems, Sire. There are some letters for you from the overlords."

Adeone raised an eyebrow. "Petitioning me, no doubt, as to my son's decisions."

"No doubt, sir. There is also a letter from the Acting Governor, I expect outlining his stewardship."

Adeone grinned, reckoning the time was right for Iris to know. "Oh, I expect not. I expect, knowing Percival, it will more likely be full of gossip for my eyes only – a crafty way of it getting here."

Iris had known the King long enough to recognise when a seemingly innocent comment was no such thing; the use of Wealsman's given name was also pause for thought. "Sire?"

"Percival has rarely written to me on official matters since I became King. He tends to depress my day and contact me by messenger instead. He says it's easier, but I expect he simply wishes to see my reaction."

Thinking of everything that he'd ever said about Wealsman, Iris said, "I didn't know Your Majesty is acquainted with the Acting Governor to that degree."

Adeone's lips twitched. "Didn't you? I can't think how that happened. I don't want the friendship known, Iris, which is why I'm leaving the choice of Margrave to your Prince. I want the right man for the province. I don't want to simply appoint my friends to such positions."

"Doesn't His Highness know of the friendship?"

"No. I've never told him. It's complicated, but I have several friends I would rather no-one knew about. To talk to my children about them might well make their existence unintentionally known. I trust your Princes but they are, or at least have been, in the case of Prince Arkyn, children. Children have a habit of talking without realising that what they say might be disadvantageous. Once they're *both* old enough, I'll tell them. Until then, I don't intend to."

Iris remarked, "If I may say so, Prince Arkyn and Lord Wealsman have formed a notable working relationship. Sire, I think I ought to—"

Adeone interrupted without meaning to. "That doesn't surprise me." He noticed Iris' face. "Whatever you've said to Percival is between yourselves, my lord. I will not bother about it unless it was malicious."

Iris relaxed. "Thank you, Sire. My concern was initially at the amount of power that you placed in his hands during the prince's incapacitation. He soon proved to me that he wasn't abusing the privilege."

"Was that all?"

"Not quite, sir. It puzzled me that you permitted his engagement."

Adeone grinned mischievously. "What else was I going to do? He's loved Kristina for many years. He's sent me an invitation to his wedding. There are many reasons for me not to go, but I have been sorely tempted."

"What, if I may enquire, are the reasons, Sire?"

"Many and varied, my lord. This is something I must decide for myself… Though, I think, if news of these bandits is correct, I ought to make a tour of Areal soon."

Iris caught the King's eye. "I didn't see much evidence of banditry, sir, but it would be a dim bandit who would attempt to waylay a Lord of Oedran. I heard that others had a spot of trouble but I put it down to exaggeration. If Merchant Chapa has heard otherwise, he would make sure of his facts before he spoke to Your Majesty."

"Yes, he would. I think I might talk to Governor ReJean and see if there have been any reports in Amphi. I could at least travel there without too many eyebrows being raised. I've not been out of Anapara since, well, since Princess Ella passed away…" He paused briefly. "I miss travelling. I had eleven years of undertaking provincial reviews and then Faran invited me into Lufian and I did need to go and oversee the forts there… Part of me wishes… but that is beside the point. What would you see as the main issues should I travel to Areal?"

"I'd say, sir, that you'll need to appoint a reliable King's Representative in Oedran. The second point I might make is that you'll need a good set of guards with you. How far south were you planning on going?"

"I don't yet know, my lord. I'll no doubt decide there is no way I can manage it, especially looking at the 'report' you have for me."

"It isn't bad, sir. The chest was the most secure means of transportation. I believe His Highness has read this copy and included his comments where necessary, those comments he'd have voiced to Your Majesty rather than making them official."

Adeone nodded. "This might well be interesting. How did you find working with your Prince, Iris?"

Passing the King a scroll box, Iris never hesitated. "It was an experience I'd never have missed, sir. The more I worked with His Highness, the more I wished I could."

"You didn't find his methods incompatible with your own?"

"At first, sir, yes, I did. I found his methods incomprehensible. They do, however, work exceptionally well for him. He had many of the officers and lords showing their true personalities when my methods may not have done so," admitted Iris without subterfuge.

"What was the mood in Terasia regarding the review?"

"I can only speak for the time I was there, sir, but by then, I think, many people had realised that Prince Arkyn was trying to work for them. The alacrity with which he dealt with the fraud in the exchequer startled and pleased many – Rahat and his deputies have been found guilty of fraud. I think some, who realised there were issues, expected His Highness to be less proactive. If you don't mind me saying, sir, the Prince has a fresh-faced look that fools many."

King Adeone beamed. "That he does, Iris. I'm pleased that the people of Terasia accepted him amongst them so readily."

"They've certainly done that, Your Majesty. There was much anxiety for him also, especially regarding the events which greeted him and then with his illness."

"Yes, his illness was unfortunate and I must thank you for taking over what you did."

"It was a pleasure. His Highness' health was of paramount importance, Sire. He appeared to succumb to the fever quickly, but, I believe, having talked to Master Kadeem, it wasn't as rapid as it seemed."

"No, I think perhaps he was suffering at least the day before." Adeone looked at Iris. "I'm sorry that Lord Rale died whilst you were absent, my lord. It can't have been easy."

Iris swallowed. "It wasn't unexpected, Your Majesty, and everyone there was understanding. I should pay my respects to Lady Landis and our new Lord Rale."

Adeone nodded. "He's at Landis House. Now, very quickly – so you can go and take your rest – did the Prince give you any idea whom he'll appoint to the post of Margrave?"

"No, Sire. I advised Lord Kre, but I don't believe he had made a firm decision by the time I left Terasia. I would have thought he'd have told Your Majesty when he had."

"Maybe he will. I shan't ask. I've told His Highness the choice is his as I'm too biased in favour of Wealsman. I've an idea brewing for a wedding gift. Tell me what you think…"

Iris listened with interest. "If you'd asked me before I went south, sir, I'd have advised against it; however, that said, I think the idea holds a lot of merit. It is certainly worth considering."

Adeone smiled. "Good. I'm pleased and I even think it was an honest opinion. I'd like to see his face – but that would be his influence on my sense of humour, so I'll leave the moment for my son. For now, that's all, my lord. I'll read the report and organise a time to see you if I have any questions. It won't be for a couple of days."

Iris pushed himself to his feet. "Thank you, Sire. Before I leave, might I enquire how my son has deported himself in my absence?"

Adeone smiled. "I've no complaints, Iris. Lord Idris has been an effective host at Court and has caused me no disquiet. I've not felt like I've needed to raise anything with him. He's done your name proud."

"That is reassuring, sir. Thank you."

After Iris left, Adeone retrieved Wealsman's letter. He ought to see to business first, but there were times he ignored the knowledge, and receiving a letter from Percival was always one of those times.

An hour later, Adeone opened the review report. There in Arkyn's neat hand was the caption '*The weather in Terasia is atrocious!*' Adeone laughed aloud. Arkyn had threatened to make that the first comment of the report. By the time he reached the end, Arkyn's thoughts and feelings came clearly through his annotations. Adeone could almost hear him saying them. His son had made sure he still was the primary voice in presenting the report. Iris, who hadn't opened it, would have been astonished by the detail and cross-referencing Arkyn had added. So, for that matter, would Wealsman, who had an un-annotated copy. It took Adeone a few hours to read it all. Enough time for Landis to see Iris and to appear and ask how Arkyn had managed.

Adeone let his friend see the annotations.

Landis sighed. "He works too hard for a sixteen-year-old."

"I know, but it's an amusing read. He's given concise and incisive comments. Not to mention blunt."

"Reminds me of another prince who was doing the reviews a decade ago."

Adeone adopted an innocent expression and tone. "I can't imagine to whom you could be referring, Lord Landis."

"No, but I bet Wealsman could."

Adeone had the grace not to try to deny it again. Wealsman always told the truth and could be relied upon to quote verbatim. It was one reason Adeone got on with him. When dealing with so many people, it was pleasant to talk to those who would tell the truth, frustrating at times when the truth wasn't what he wanted to hear, but he recognised its worth anyway.

Adeone re-read the report a couple more times to glean everything he could and read the overlords' letters. Silvano wasn't pleased with the prolonged wait to find the new Margrave, nor with the length of his interview with Arkyn. No complaint would alter the fact it had been long, and privately Adeone was pleased that Arkyn was taking the matter so seriously. He replied to Silvano acknowledging the concerns but adding, diplomatically, that the Prince was in charge of Terasia for the meantime. He used the letter to inform the lord that he couldn't be spared from Tera to attend his daughter's proposed marriage to the Visir in Cearden. Silvano, when he received the reply, took it to mean that he would be the next Margrave.

* * *

A couple of days after Iris reported in Oedran, Adeone requested a link with his son.

Arkyn smiled warmly as it formed. "Sire."

Adeone grumbled, "Don't know what you're so happy about, unless it's giving your poor beleaguered father even more reading to do. Thank you for the chest!"

Arkyn laughed. "I thought you wanted a report, sir."

"Did it have to be such a long one? Couldn't you have told the overlords not to write?"

"I'm sure I could, sir, but I thought you'd be interested in their views – an unbiased examination of my capabilities." Arkyn swallowed. "What did they say?"

Adeone shook his head. "Nothing that need worry you. After all, they're writing to their King about their Prince. It's hardly unbiased. Are you finally relaxing properly?"

"I'm trying to, father. Are you?"

"No, I've got the rest of your report to read!" He laughed. "Don't look like that. I was joking. I finished it a couple of days ago and Iris has just explained his input. Did you really get him to rewrite his reports?"

"Yes, Sire. Shouldn't I have done?" fretted Arkyn.

"That rather depends on your reasons. If you couldn't work with them, you did the right thing. He didn't mind. You've influenced him anyway."

"What makes you say that, father?"

"I've had the law banning weapons in the Administrative Quarter handed to me, signed and sealed by the Etanes. Weeks they've been debating that and wanting clarification, which I've given them. Apparently, Iris went to the debate yesterday, stood up, asked Lord Para what he thought the job of Ealdorman entailed if not seeing that I got a *timely* response to my petitions and promptly called for the vote to be put. Your Uncle Festus told me that after the stunned silence, both he and Fairson seconded the motion and Para found himself outmanoeuvred. He's been trying to delay until your Uncle Scanlon, Anguis and Rathgar have returned from Denshire. Scanlon can't be at the debates, but it would have meant that the law would have had less chance of being passed."

"I'm glad it's been passed but why am I to blame for Iris' actions?" enquired Arkyn, confused.

"Because Iris has always been a fantastic advisor, but he tends to let others lead in the Etanes, especially in controversial debate. I can never, or could never, put a law up for debate through him unless he was Ealdorman. Since he went to Terasia, he's saying what he thinks slightly more. You're to be congratulated. I've been trying to manage that for years."

"There must be more to it than that, Sire."

"Not really, not that I can see. Unless it's because Lord Rale isn't there and Iris is now the oldest Lord of Oedran. Anyway, the result's the same. Weapons are banned in the Administrative Quarter for all but the FitzAlcis, lords, the militia and those ceremonial posts which require them."

"Will people accept it, sir? Doesn't it seem like curtailing freedoms?"

Adeone raised an eyebrow. "Of course it does, and it is, as Aunt Amara is sure to point out. Though, as I explained to your Uncle Festus, most weapons that we banned aren't carried by citizens anyway. The added advantage is that it shows Oedran as a peaceful city and should lead the way for the rest of the empire. Talking of which, how's your reading going?"

Arkyn accepted the change of subject and plunged into debate.

Chapter 42
HISTORY

Alunadai, Week 32 – 22nd Anapal, 8th Anapcis 1211
Arkyn's Chambers

ON ONE COLD, grey day, Arkyn returning to his chambers spotted Karl and Elsa. He stopped for a couple of words, but it turned into a discussion and he invited them back to his rooms. Kadeem greeted him with a highly deferential air he saved for when others were around. Arkyn raised an amused eyebrow, which Kadeem replied to with a neutral inclination of his head. Once in the sitting room with a drink apiece, Arkyn looked at the twins.

"Are you hiding from your teacher again?" (They grinned, caught out.) "Kadeem, go and see Secretary Thomkins. If he wants his children back at their books, I'll not go against him. If he holds no objection to them being here though, apologise to their teacher for me." As the door shut behind Kadeem, Arkyn noted the twin's apprehensive faces. "Let's see what happens, shall we? I expect your father won't mind and it's taken Kadeem's deferential presence elsewhere – two motives, one message. Do you think I'll make a politician?"

"No, sir, you're too honest," replied Elsa.

Arkyn laughed. "I'm glad for that. Now, what have you both been up to?"

"This and that, sir."

"That's the kind of answer I used to give my father when Tain and I had been raiding the kitchens. He never believed we'd been doing anything mundane…"

"I can't believe you'd ever mislead anyone, sir," responded Elsa.

"I'll have to cultivate that. So, what have you actually been up to?"

Karl said quietly, "Trying to find an account of the Cearcall that doesn't send us to sleep."

Elsa grinned. "*Amazingly*, sir, your story got us interested."

Arkyn smiled back at her. "If you're going to be as cheeky as that you might as well call me Arkyn. Formality is for other circumstances. So did you find one?"

"No, so we wondered if… That is if…" Elsa tailed off.

Arkyn nodded. "I can tell you the rest of what I remember, if you really want me to. Again, I can't promise to be a great storyteller or historian."

Karl said, "I'm up for it."

Elsa agreed, so Arkyn continued with his potted history of the Cearcall.

* * *

The Cearcall began to realise how powerful they were. They could store and manipulate large sources of magic and, through helping the kings of the lands, their political influence was widespread. In a world of disparate lands, of countries whose borders were only as good as stability and peace could make them, the Cearcall were an instrument of that peace, of resolutions and redress for infractions – that is they would negotiate terms of peace should skirmishes occur. Their influence meant they had near open access to any palace or place they chose. They had their own laws that governed magic and anyone known to wield it. They created stores of magic in major towns or cities, they even created stores in some buildings. The Palace in Oedran had a couple of globes, though they are now lost.

The Cearcall built comfortable homes for themselves across the lands. Ceardlann, in the Rex Dallin, was one such. A globe hidden deep within its bounds creates and renews the magic of the valley. Its location is unknown and some suspect there is more than one there.

It is lost to the myths and mists of time who first asked if they could manipulate the magic for their own ends. Some speculate that it was the Meithrin, some hazard the Wright. Whether it was a healer or a manipulator is now immaterial. All that is known is they began to see if they could lengthen the span of their lives. They were finding that they'd start something and their successor would continue it. They became selfish.

Then there was born a boy who, by chance, possessed three of the spirits. Some say it was fate, others that it was unfortunate. He could not only manipulate the magic and create illusions, but he could also split his mind. Some historians suggest he cared too much about power. He became known as the Tribility. Though few ever knowingly met him. A mystery in his lifetime, he became a legend in history.

There was an underground movement that wanted the Cearcall to release the stored magic so that others could use it. The Darkal were still trying to find a way to do this when they found the Tribility instead and hid him. Did they fill his head with possibilities? Probably. But the boy's own dreams must have been part of what came next. The Cearcall met in their tower, now protected by an impregnable fortress. They had heard of the existence of the Tribility and were determined to find him and remove the spirits he possessed.

He could feel them searching for him. Travelling to the Low Plains, he climbed Ull's Watchtower – the column of rock left from which Ull had fallen to his death – and looked towards the Cearcall Tower. He could feel them getting closer and closer. He managed to use their searching against them and effectively sent his mind into theirs instead. He saw the truth of what they were doing. Saw them using the magic for their own ends and it frightened him. He managed to block their search and created illusions of himself all over the lands.

The Cearcall, creators and destroyers of kings, weavers of magic and ower, omniscient and omnipotent, spent *twelve years* chasing phantoms.

Twelve years to the day after he had first seen what they were planning, e boy stood once more on Ull's Watchtower. The full moons were bright, or it was a Grey Day. Even across the miles, the boy, now a man, aged venty-four, thought he could see the glow of the Cearcall Tower. He sent is mind out and then hit a barrier. The Cearcall had realised what he had een doing.

He knew they were there. He had followed the news of their travels and ustrations. Had even been drinking in the same tavern as their apprentices ne night. It is said he witnessed them showing off their skills and learned ore than they realised about their aims, their destinations and their art. It s a pleasant tale, though I've never seen evidence it happened.

Did he know from that meeting that the Cearcall would be at the tower? Did they always meet on Grey Days? Did he know of the Wandoril eputation and caravan approaching Cearcallead? We will never now find ut. What made him climb Ull's Watchtower? What made him hunt out nswers that night? We will never know.

When his mind hit the barrier, he didn't stop. He knew that in every rmour there is a chink, a point of weakness in its creation. As our knowledge f magic has waned, we have lost the knowledge of what the chink might ave been. Could it have been a mistake? Could it have been a trap? Could e Cearcall have used the Tribility's arrogance against him? Again, we can nly speculate, for what came next was so cataclysmic it shook the world.

Having found the weakness, the barrier no longer worried him. He ould explore the Cearcall Tower at will, or at least, as he wasn't a seer, e could send his senses out and learn of feelings, of weakness or strength n the stones, in the very air around his senses.

After that night, the Tribility disappeared. No-one knows how he did it, r why. Did he mean to destroy? If he had just been a sensor, could it have appened? Was the fact he was a manipulator and splitter part of the puzzle? For that which hands make whole can be torn asunder. The globes, the magic he Cearcall had hoarded, destroyed them as he released it. With a glare so right it shadowed all lightning, with a boom so loud it shook the mountains, vith a devastation so complete it laid waste all in the vicinity, the Cearcall Tower exploded.

Cearcallead became Denshire: the burnt land. Its rivers swallowed by he earth, it's forests but ashes in the wind, its crops dust.

The Wandoril deputation couldn't get home. Seas were roiling from he explosion. Our sailors even now say there is no way back to Wandarin. Trapped in the lands – never really to be part of them, never to settle down

– the Wandoril became known as the Wanda. They still roam the lands looking for a home.

The star stones were lost. Legends say they have all, at one time or another, been found, though some were hidden again. Without the stones, those apprentices who survived, those who were young or had been left behind to watch over hearth and home, could not form the next Cearcall. There are relics of the Cearcall, just as precious, if not more so. Each of them had an item, one handed down to them by their predecessor. Some were specific to their spirit, some were symbolic, others practical. They are all, though, priceless. Some, which the legends tell us existed, are lost, others, like the Memini's Manuscript here in Terasia, have been carefully conserved but even they couldn't help form a new Cearcall.

Released from the thrall of the Cearcall, the lands revelled. Kings and generals grew confident in their superiority. Fighting erupted. Wars started. Order disintegrated. Civil wars swallowed many lands as power once more became a commodity to kill for. Only Anapara remained peaceful. We began to restore the peace of centuries amidst the trials of war.

* * *

As Arkyn finished, Karl looked up. "Surely someone knows what happened to the Tribility."

Elsa was enthralled. "And what happened to the magic? He had released it."

"History has never discovered what became of him. When he released the magic, he didn't do so in a stable manner," explained Arkyn. "It was transferred into heat and light. It was used up. The largest store of magic ever produced was gone in the rumbling thunder of an instant. That is why there is very little now in the empire."

"But surely more has been produced in the last six hundred years?" mused Elsa.

Arkyn shrugged. "The star stones need to be active to produce a significant amount. They need to belong to someone with a spirit to be so. When they scattered across the lands, they became dormant. As far as anyone knows, they are now inactive. It will take at least six to be touched by the correct spirit to waken any of them. That is what the legends tell us anyway."

"Are there any spirits in the empire now, Arkyn?" enquired Elsa.

"Who knows? They haven't proclaimed themselves if there are. There are some with lesser forms alive, but they were always more abundant. The scryers who were the lesser hue of a seer are relatively numerous. They are the most common though, although artists and wordsmiths are also around."

Karl broke his silence. “Are the lesser hues for the lesser and the spirits for the greater then?”

“No. The concept of the lesser and greater is older than our history. It predates the appearance of Ull – the lesser were originally slaves and the destitute. When the Cearcall became powerful, some were of that section of society and wished to escape the negative connotations such a label provides. Gradually they introduced the word cisan, to represent the lower ranks of society and to give them pride and an identity – the name taken from Cisluna, the lesser-moon; the greater of society started to use the word alunan to describe themselves – from Aluna – and so, as will always happen, concepts changed and a different culture took hold. It became considered a grave insult to describe someone as lesser or greater, and it still is. After the Cearcall fell, the concept of cisan and alunan had wormed its way into everyday life and language. There is now no getting rid of it. The spirits, however, can occur in anyone – for when Ull first brought the stones into the world, there was only one moon, only one protector, only one entity from which we came. All else was a dispute over titles and riches. Since Ull’s creation of Cisluna, and then the adoption of cisan and alunan, things became more complicated. Over the centuries, though, it was clear that the Cearcall was stronger when half were alunan and half cisan. It was better that way.”

“Why?” enquired Elsa.

“Who knows? All the legends say was that it had to be balanced. Maybe it’s something to do with how Ull was pulled onto this world. Maybe it is to do with the fact the Cearcall was formed to stop fighting and create peace. Maybe it is something else. I ought to ask Laioril and see if he knows, but I never seem to get around to it.”

“Who’s he?”

Arkyn smiled. “He’s the Chief of a tribe of the Wanda which camps in the Rex Dallin most years. He tells us the stories when we’re there at the same time. So, if there’s anything wrong with my telling, it’s entirely his fault.”

“I didn’t notice anything wrong, Arkyn,” remarked Karl.

“You’re still awake, so that’s something.”

Elsa grinned. “Yes, but we’re learning of the last six hundred years, when there’s been no magic. It must have been fantastic to be alive when magic was around. Just think, maybe we’d have been able to wield it.”

“What would you like to have been?”

Elsa thought for a couple of moments. “Wasn’t there a spirit whereby you could disappear and reappear wherever you wanted?”

“Yes, a shifter, pretty rare apparently. How about you, Karl?”

“A manipulator. I’d love to be good with my hands. How about you, sir?”

"Magic and kingship apparently don't mix," said Arkyn, "but I suppose I'd have liked to have a hue, rather than a spirit. I'd like to have been a reconciler – one who balances out, one who can bring things to a peaceful resolution. The corresponding spirit was that of a magic balancer: someone who could control the flow of magic. Along with the magic bearer, they assisted the rest of the Cearcall, keeping experiments safe, absorbing magic and giving it where needed. Important skills."

Elsa nodded. "Yes, but surely boring."

"Maybe, but maybe not. They don't have the prestige in the legends of the espiens or healers; they don't have the clear skills of the wrights and memors; they don't have the more fantastical skills of the shifters and splitters, but without the bearers and balancers, magic would destroy instead of help. Whatever else the Cearcall was, they brought peace. They stopped many magic wielders from doing evil. It's said they removed spirits for the good of others. The murderer of King Simeon III of Macia was a rogue healer who used his skill to kill instead of heal. One of Guilbred's *Accounts* tells us what happened—"

Karl suddenly asked, "How have you found out so much?"

"I read. I've several books from your city library here, as well as a book chest I brought from Oedran. The majority of which is about the Cearcallian Era."

Karl chewed his lip. "Could I borrow one, sir? Or could you tell me which one to start with?"

Arkyn smiled. "Certainly you can. Well, you can borrow one of my own. I've promised the librarian I won't let his out of these rooms. Let me just find one…"

Chapter 43
HAPPENINGS

Winter

Tera

DURING WINTER, Arkyn did what he'd promised the Aedile he would and visited the site of the City Assembly. He'd sanctioned the money for rebuilding it and examined with interest the plans. The plot of land was certainly spacious, and the Aedile had found that he could demolish most of the old building, leaving the section he couldn't as a reminder of what had gone before. Irvin, after spending a few days reading up on early Terasian history, told Arkyn he was sure the site was the same as the original Palace of Tera. He'd found an early account and map in one of the books. Arkyn looked at it as well and was suitably convinced. He informed

Wealsman who, noting the lads' enthusiasm for the subject and having heard about the hours spent reading, found a historian in Tera who had no objection to talking to the Prince and young lord. Irvin's excitement was obvious, especially when the historian showed him many texts and maps he'd collected. Arkyn smiled and let his friend pursue his interest in peace; instead, concentrating on the histories relating to the Cearcall kept in the Teran Library. Most correlated with what he'd read in Oedran and at Ceardlann. They even matched with Laioril's stories, though they weren't so entertainingly told.

* * *

Continuing his hunt for the new Margrave, Arkyn spent some evenings entertaining all the overlords, and when he wasn't doing that, he often dined with Irvin and Daia. Kadeem fretted. The Prince managed the evenings without anyone realising how tired he was, but the mornings were characterised by the fact he had to be woken from his slumber. There were also occasions when Kadeem had found him asleep during the afternoon, but he decided the moment wasn't right to broach the subject.

One evening, for politeness' sake, Arkyn invited Lord Melek, as well as Irvin, to dinner. Melek was older than him by some years, but he had been one of Irvin's hosts. It took very little time for Arkyn to understand why Irvin hadn't mentioned Melek. Half an hour after Arkyn's household had cleared the meal, the Prince finally had enough of his condescending and sneering manner. In no uncertain terms, he asked Melek to leave.

It didn't take long for the news to spread that Arkyn had disliked the young lord's company. When he heard, Silvano was irate with his son; Melek shrugged it off. Arkyn would soon be returning north, his influence in the province would cease. His father enquired acidly if he was blind to politics. Arkyn's influence in the province would *never* cease – especially if Lord Wealsman's idea for a gift, on the Prince's leaving the province, was agreed upon.

* * *

Two weeks before the Munlumen, Arkyn made his decision for a new Margrave. He would use the coming of spring to announce his decision and requested that Wealsman had everything ready to hand over smoothly. Wealsman, without the slightest question about who would be taking over, did so – glad that when he married, someone else would be running the province. Arkyn refused to be drawn into any confidence as to whom he'd picked. He hadn't even told his father.

* * *

With the news that the Governor of Areal's wife had died in childbirth,

Adeone decided that a small amount of travelling couldn't do any harm. He would travel to Amphi, capital of Areal, to give the Governor time to grieve with his daughter. His presence would also act as a prevention against the growing threat of banditry in the province, especially if he summoned the Commander of Areal and spent time touring the province.

Chapter 44
TERASIAN ANNOUNCEMENT

Septadai, Week 36 – 28th Bayal, 21st Bayis 1211
Margrave's Residence

ARKYN ARRANGED A BANQUET so he could announce the new Margrave. For some reason, he had wanted to keep the identity to himself until the last minute. It might be unconventional, but as Landis said, traditions could be changed.

Arkyn entered the Margrave's Hall on Munlumen Eve. His quick gaze assessing the spectacle. People were talking in groups dotted around the room, although roughly where they'd need to be for the announcement. The overlords close to the dais, the minor lords and visiting dignitaries one tier back, then the officials, then the merchants and anyone else. Fitz was talking to a couple of latecomers, their hoods still on to protect them from the driving rain. He smiled. His captain was obviously happy with the situation, so he didn't let it trouble him.

Arkyn recognised a lot of the faces; through his enforced stay, he'd become acquainted with many people in Terasia. As his eyes raked over the guests, silence fell and, as he made his way to the central dais steps, the guests parted to let him through. There was a general rearranging of position until Arkyn stood on the dais steps with the overlords flanking him. He glanced along the front row of the minor lords and was pleased to see Wealsman. He had at the end of his working day formally finished being Acting Governor so had reverted to his birth place when precedence was to be considered. Arkyn smiled a half smile. Percival returned it. He was happy enough; from where he was, he could watch Arkyn's face as he made the announcement and see Kristina, who as the hostess was standing to the left of the Prince.

Edward passed the Prince a scroll.

Arkyn started talking in a level and highly official voice, "My lords, ladies and gentlemen, officials of Tera, merchants of Terasia and visiting dignitaries…." He paused theatrically, unrolling the scroll, and turned to Edward. In a stage whisper he said, "Have I missed anyone?"

"I think there's always room for missing *someone*, sir," replied Edward in like manner.

"And guests who don't fall into the above categories. I apologise in advance; I have never been good at making prepared speeches, so I am just going to hand this long..." He carried on unrolling the scroll. "*Very long* scroll..." He reached the end and passed it to Edward, who was by this point trying to keep a straight face. "...to my administrator and improvise. Welcome to the Margrave's Court. As all of you are aware, earlier this year, Lord Portur died at the hands of a traitor. The King informed me I was responsible for appointing the new Margrave and again I cannot but apologise for the delay caused by a trifling case of flu I so inconsiderately managed to pick up. I am happy to say the case is now closed."

The majority of the Terasians in the room were smiling. They had become used to Arkyn's ways, but the visiting officials were amazed at the informal handling of the situation.

Arkyn continued, "I must admit, it was lucky I became ill. It gave me so much more time in which to observe the different candidates – though, I think, *they* were hoping I'd return to Oedran sooner. As many here are aware, the review was fraught with unforeseen problems, the death of the Margrave and the execution of his deputy certainly didn't help matters; I admit my life was made more difficult by these events. It could have been even more so, had it not been for Lord Wealsman, whom *most* will credit with working extremely hard. Some have still caught him with his feet up occasionally though – I cannot imagine what he thought he was doing sleeping at night, there was always more to do."

There were various outbursts of laughter at this and Wealsman merely accepted the praise with a slight inclination of his head. What *was* Arkyn doing? There was a glint in the Prince's eye that certainly spoke of mischief.

"Well, my lords, ladies..." Arkyn sighed. "Let's not go through the list again. Guests, all I can say is I hope Lord Wealsman continues to work as hard, as he has done over the last few months, during his tenure as King's Representative and Governor of Terasia. Lord Percival Wealsman, do you hereby accept the post of Margrave?"

Wealsman gaped, speechless. Visibly swallowing, he eventually said, "How can I refuse, Your Highness?"

"Quite easily; a 'no' normally suffices, my lord." Arkyn was hoping against hope that he wouldn't; he hadn't found anyone else he was happy with to take the post.

In the brief moments that followed, Wealsman and Arkyn shared a glance. The Prince no longer looked mischievous. Wealsman almost thought that there was reassurance in the gaze. He tried to understand what he'd said or done that had made Arkyn pick him. He hadn't been interviewed as the overlords had. He glanced at Kristina and saw her smile; she was enjoying his speechless moment. She gave a slight nod, which he understood to mean she didn't mind if he agreed. Looking along the row of overlords, he noted relief on some faces, astoundment on others and fury on Silvano's. That decided him. If Kristina and Arkyn thought he could do the job, and Silvano wouldn't gain more power, he would take it for the peace within Terasia. Everyone was calmly waiting for his reply.

"I find, I must accept, Your Highness."

"Thank Alcis for that!" came the relieved whisper of a guest.

At the same moment, Edward handed Arkyn a note. He opened it. There, in handwriting that he knew all too well, were the words…

Missed me

PART 4

Chapter 45
MARGRAVE
Evening
Margrave's Hall

ARKYN READ THE NOTE and then reread it. It didn't make any difference. Even without a signature, without punctuation to give him context, it was the first note in Tera that he was pleased to read. It explained the bedraggled guests talking to Fitz.

Beaming, he said, "Thank you, Lord Wealsman; however, before we continue, my lords, ladies and all here present, please greet your King, His Majesty Adeone Altarius FitzAlcis."

Arkyn finished and, turning slightly, bowed to his father who was unfastening the clasp of his cloak, removing his riding hood and handing them to Simkins. Wealsman whipped around and half the people in the hall fell to one knee or curtsied. The other half looked uncertain before following suit.

Laughing, Adeone, in full formal dress, made his way up the dais steps. "I'm sorry, Prince Arkyn, but you have our newly appointed Margrave to thank for my visit."

Rather red, Wealsman replied, "You never actually *accepted* the invitation, Sire."

"I never declined it either. Congratulations on your new post, I am pleased His Highness picked Your Lordship. There is the small matter of you taking the oath, Wealsman. So, as I'm here," he motioned Percival for to kneel.

Arkyn moved off the dais steps. He shot Edward a look that plainly said, '*Did you know he was coming?*' Edward shook his head, grinning. The Prince's pleasure at his father's arrival was evident.

Wealsman moved forward, his gaze never leaving Adeone's face. Had the King known? Why was he really in Tera? Was it for the wedding or for this? Adeone met his eyes and waited as Wealsman knelt. The hall of onlookers fell silent as Wealsman raised his hands palm up, and Adeone placed his on top.

"Do you, Lord Percival Wealsman, hereby swear to govern, in the King's stead, the province of Terasia in accordance with what is right and just for the people of the province?"

"I do so swear, Your Majesty."

"To protect the people from threats and to defend their rights?"

"I do so swear, Sire."

"To send resources when requested by the lawful King or his Advocates?"

"I do so swear, Sire."

"To answer the lawful King's call, in times of peril or peace?"

"I do so swear, Sire."

"To abide by the laws of the empire and the Terasian Settlement?"

"I do so swear, Sire."

"To always give support and honest advice to the lawful King with relation to the oversight of the province?"

Now deadly serious, Wealsman said, "I do so swear, Your Majesty."

There was the merest trace of irony as the King replied, "Oh good, I look forward to that. You may rise, Lord Percival Wealsman, Margrave, Governor of Terasia and Defender of the Southern Marches."

Wealsman rose and, bowing, stood beside the Prince.

"I can't believe you invited him, Percival!" muttered Arkyn by way of greeting.

"To my wedding, sir. He got here a bit early. I'm as confounded as Your Highness."

"Obviously!"

King Adeone turned. "Prince Arkyn, would you like to close proceedings?"

"Thank you, Sire, I'm sure…"

Adeone simply held out his hand. Sighing, Arkyn made his way forward.

"Your Majesty, Excellency, my lords, ladies and gentlemen, officials of Tera, merchants of Terasia and visiting dignitaries… the list just goes on getting longer, doesn't it? Thank you for your patience through what has been another evening that hasn't gone *quite* to plan. I think we're all getting used to them. I hope you will join me in wishing the King welcome and the new Margrave well in his post. All that is left for me is to open the feast. I am sure there was a seating plan that has had to be rewritten but, hopefully, that won't have affected anybody so much that they can't enjoy the banquet which awaits us."

Everybody laughed as Arkyn moved off the dais steps to show he had finished speaking.

As the noise swelled, Adeone said lightly, "I must have a word with your former tutors."

Arkyn watched his father uncertainly, but saw amusement deep within his eyes. "Why's that then, Sire? I was told being able to improvise was good."

Adeone chuckled and ruffled his son's hair.

"Have you ever been introduced to the new Margrave properly, Sire?"

The King said, "Yes, about twelve years ago and I've never been able to escape since. *Have I, Percival*?"

"I can't imagine what you mean, Sire. I'm afraid, Prince Arkyn, I've never let on how well I know the King, but I'm always flattered when he ays it's as well as Lord Landis."

Adeone and Percival shared a glance, dreading the reaction. Arkyn ad been deceived for months. The response bewildered them.

All too aware of the hall full of watchers, Arkyn said, "I should have nown. There were too many chess moves I recognised. Anyway… I uppose I never asked either."

Inwardly, he was cursing. Had he been played for a fool? The hesitancy is father and Percival shared went some way to ameliorate his feelings. 'here was more to their decision than a wish to make him appear a fool. Vhat would Percival have told his father? Would his father have asked? Jo. He'd seen the guilt his father had suffered when he'd made Landis etray confidences the year before. Still, why hadn't they told him?

Adeone laughed again. He glanced at Wealsman. "Who won in the nd, Your Excellency?"

"His Highness, Sire. Might I present Lady Kristina Portur to you again?"

"Of course you may."

As Adeone was introduced to various people, the Margrave's steward rossed to Arkyn, enquiring softly what he was to do about the dais seating.

Arkyn considered briefly. "I'm on the King's right, Lord Wealsman on is left. Everyone else simply moves one place down. Place chairs at the nds of the dais so as not to disturb anything else. His Majesty must have ny chambers, and I shall move elsewhere for my remaining nights here."

"Master Simkins has already mentioned that the King is against that, Your Highness. We have used the rooms Lord Iris was occupying for His Majesty."

"If that is the King's wish, then I cannot override it. Thank you."

The steward left and Adeone caught Arkyn's eye. Walking over to im, Arkyn tried to relax.

"Prince Arkyn, I understand other than impromptu speeches, you have een behaving yourself."

"I'm afraid they are all too kind, Sire. I am more like my brother than eople realise."

Adeone smiled. "A deft way of asking after him. He's well and tearing ound Ceardlann." He looked at the dais where the alterations had been nade. "Such a simple solution. I'm impressed. Come, shall we eat? For 1o-one else can whilst we do not."

Wealsman grinned mischievously. "You could have fun, though, eeing how long they would wait, Sire."

"Percival, your sense of humour doesn't improve with age. Anyway, 'm hungry even if you're too startled at your new position to eat. Did ou really have no idea?"

"No, Your Majesty, especially when His Highness requested that I made sure everything would hand over smoothly."

Arkyn's lips twitched. "Yes, sorry about that, Percival, but I wanted to make sure you could get a honeymoon without worrying."

"Thank you, sir, but we still have no Deputy Governor, as yet, so I'm afraid I'll have to stay here."

Walking by his father, Arkyn said, "Sire, I was going to ask, would it be acceptable if I stayed here for another aluna-month and oversaw the province whilst His Excellency has a honeymoon?"

Adeone glanced sideways at Arkyn, pleased by the newfound confidence that was evident in him.

"I'm sure we can give him that. I planned to go into Gerymor and Denshire whilst I was in the region, but their officials can come here. Your Excellency, you have your honeymoon."

"Sire, I cannot ask… The upheaval—" stuttered Wealsman.

"Oddly enough, I didn't hear you ask in the first place." He chuckled to himself. "Marry Kristina and have a break; trust me, you'll need one before the next few years' work." They reached their seats and the King faced the hall, raising his hand for silence, which fell absolutely.

"Your Highness and Excellency, my lords, ladies and gentlemen, officials of Tera, merchants of Terasia and visiting dignitaries. My apologies for taking up your time with yet another speech. I shall be as brief as possible; for one thing, having had a long ride, I'm as hungry as any of you. This speech is intended to stop any rumour or needless speculation. Twelve years ago, I visited this province to undertake the same duties as your Prince has just fulfilled. Twelve years ago, I became friends with three lords here. Two have since died and I will pay my respects to them over the coming days; however, one is still living. It is on his account I am here. Lord Wealsman – or the Margrave, as we all must now call him – invited me here for his wedding in three days' time. It took me very little effort to decide to come to Tera once again. I'd come with the sole intention of seeing one of my closest friends marry and to revisit a province that I have always regarded warmly. Unfortunately, the best-laid plans of kings often go awry and can be rewritten by princes, it seems. Prince Arkyn *never* told me, or hinted to me, that he had chosen Lord Wealsman as Margrave, and he was, in fact, ignorant of our friendship until a couple of minutes ago. I have nothing but support for the appointment, but Lord Wealsman can hardly have a honeymoon when he's accepted such a position; to leave the province without governance would be unthinkable, and so, as I mentioned, I've changed my plans. I shall govern Terasia directly for the next month and allow His Excellency and Lady Portur their long-awaited honeymoon."

There was a moment of silence before a cheer erupted.

Wealsman rose. "Sire, what can I say but thank you? I am yours to command, *especially* in these circumstances."

Adeone, laughing, nodded and they resumed their seats. Once everyone had started eating Wealsman could absorb everything that had happened. Adeone hadn't known Arkyn's decision. He found that oddly reassuring, as though a weight had been lifted. He hadn't been appointed because he was friends with the King, which meant he still had to work out why he *had* been appointed but he supposed Arkyn had witnessed him doing the job for a couple of seasons and must have considered he'd cope for far longer. Kristina let him brood, but she squeezed his wrist in mute support.

Eventually, Adeone broke the silence. "Percival, are you going to eat or merely upset your cook?"

Wealsman blinked, looked at Adeone blankly for a moment and then at the platter in front of him. He hadn't taken any food from the pies, pasties, roast meats, fruits and desserts laid out in front of them.

"Sorry, Sire. I'm still stunned."

"Well, it's the quietest you've been in my company for years. I'm enjoying the sensation, but if you don't eat, Lady Portur won't forgive us."

The rest of the evening passed off pleasantly with small talk and curiosity. Soon after the end of the feast, Silvano left, but he was the only overlord to make his feelings plain.

At around midnight, Adeone caught his son stifling a yawn. "Arkyn, go to bed if you're tired."

"I'm not really, sir."

His father merely nodded, not believing a word of it. Half an hour later, he saw him stifle another yawn and, peering over his shoulder, caught Kadeem's eye. The manservant walked over.

"His Highness is retiring for the evening, Kadeem."

Giving in with good grace, Arkyn rose. "Goodnight, Sire. I'm glad you're here."

"Night, Arkyn. I must admit, I'm glad to be here."

* * *

After his son had gone, Adeone said, "Is he still tiring easily, Percival?"

"More easily than I think he should be, sir. I think, for all he said the case was closed, it's been taken to a higher court."

"Yes. I was wondering that myself. What does your doctor say?"

"I haven't enquired, Your Majesty. If I needed to know, I would have been told. I'm afraid I left the majority of his care up to Kadeem."

Adeone nodded. "Thank you, Percival. You were, of course, right. I'll talk to Kadeem tomorrow sometime and I'd like to talk to the doctor – ostensibly to thank him."

"Of course. I'll arrange for him to come and see you first thing."

"Should keep me out of everybody's hair for a time… Did you really not tell Arkyn you had invited me?"

Wealsman blushed. "I thought when I sent it that if you accepted it, I would tell him if he were having a bad day. If you declined, it would have been pointless telling him. I was half afraid to mention it because I knew he might not feel as though he could trust me."

"So, you *can* be sensible…"

"That would be a first, Sire."

"Are you meant to disagree with me like this, my friend?" enquired Adeone, tongue in cheek.

"You'd think I were ill if I didn't."

"No, I'd know you were. You're as bad as Festus."

Completely relaxed, Wealsman shrugged. "In my modesty, I doubt that; I don't have as much opportunity."

"My son's just rectified that. I was pleased when he chose you. I've wanted you to be my Representative here for a while. Ideally, I'd have liked Sansky to be your Deputy Governor, but that wasn't to be. I've wanted, on several occasions, to ask Arkyn whom he had in mind, but I also wanted him to make his own decisions. You're a good statesman; I had to hope he'd see that. I didn't send him here for a rest."

"Sire, he certainly hasn't had that. I must commend him. He's been unstinting and unwavering in all his work and decisions. I think even without the attack of flu, he would have worn himself out."

"Yes, that's what worries me, Percival. I'm going to have to have a long talk with him."

"Good luck, sir. He's got a well-defined sense of duty. I can only hope any children I may have turn out to be so praiseworthy."

"If I didn't know you better, Percival, I'd think you were praising for the sake of it. Your children – and you'll have some, I now have no doubt – will appear to be as good as gold, with a mischievous streak that they could only ever have inherited from you. Enjoy the experience, I certainly have."

Wealsman laughed. Several of the guests watched the dais; a few of the older ones wondering how they could ever have believed that the friendship between the two men had waned, or how they could have forgotten it existed in the first place. Both men were obviously happy in each other's company and no-one was muttering about Wealsman's appointment. Some overlords were obviously relieved at not being picked; they and others congratulated Wealsman and welcomed the King in one conversation.

Adeone and Wealsman left the banquet an hour or so after Arkyn, having decided to have a quiet drink away from the interested stares.

Chapter 46
DAGGERS AND LETTERS
Night
Arkyn's Chambers

ARKYN ENTERED his chambers in a conflicted frame of mind. Glad to see his father after so long apart, but questioning if he was truly there for Wealsman's wedding. Had he taken the opportunity the invitation presented to travel to Terasia to correct mistakes made in the review? Were there issues with how he'd handled the Roth situation? Had Iris carried petitions that required the King to travel to Terasia to smooth over his mistakes? Arkyn couldn't remember his father ever travelling across the empire on a whim to attend a wedding before. The last time he'd travelled so far was to Faran's in Lufia, and then there'd been issues with the local forts. Would he really have left Oedran just for a wedding?

Unable to shake off the preoccupation, his eyes lit on the occasional table by his normal chair. Two letters sat there. It was late for despatches, so he crossed and picked them up. He recognised his nearfather's seal – blue wax, a double circle denoting a lord with a simple L at the centre, then a double-storey 'a' in the crook of the letter, above the monogram an O to denote Oedran and below it the letters KD to denote King's Defender. He relaxed before glancing at the second letter, expecting another known seal, but there was no cachet in the wax. Rather distracted, he heard his manservant mention something about sleep.

"I'll be there in a minute, Kadeem. I just want to see what these are."

He broke his nearfather's seal and settled into his chair to read the lengthy letter. Landis apparently had a clearer understanding of how betrayed his nearson might be feeling. He wanted to reassure him that there hadn't been any malicious intent behind them all keeping the secret of Adeone and Wealsman's friendship. Without any condescension, Landis explained how much it had mattered to Adeone that Arkyn made his own mind up, that they had never expected Arkyn would have to work so closely with Wealsman. He explained how worried Adeone had been and how he had almost told Arkyn about the friendship, but by the time Arkyn recovered from his illness, there was a bond formed that revelation would have fractured to the detriment of everyone. They had formed a relationship based on mutual respect and that, for someone in Arkyn's position, should never be undermined. Landis also reassured Arkyn that Wealsman had been so reserved about what was happening that Adeone had, on a couple of occasions, become frustrated. All that aside, Landis wanted Arkyn to know that he was still available if he needed to talk about the situation, fume over the situation, or just find a different situation to talk about.

By the end of the letter, Arkyn's anger cooled. He didn't understand everything, but he did appreciate what Landis had told him and began to believe his father's motives weren't malicious or aimed at making a fool of him. He'd finished re-reading parts of the letter when Kadeem re-entered the sitting room. The pallor suffusing his manservant's face struck him immediately.

"Kadeem, what's—?"

"Sir, would you mind staying in here?"

Realising something had happened, Arkyn shook his head. He broke the uncoloured wax on the second note as Kadeem left the room once again. The content was brief.

Not all surprises are pleasant.

Swearing, Arkyn tossed it into the fire. As if he needed telling that after the last year. He was aware of movement and bustle in his chambers, but was too wrapped up in his thoughts to pay it much heed. Then Fitz told him to remain where he was and he simply nodded, staring into the fire.

"Can I get you anything, sir?" asked Kadeem.

"No, thank you. What's happening?"

"There was a dagger in your bed, sir."

Tired out and numb, Arkyn said nothing.

Kadeem watching him decided others could see to the bedchamber and talk to the guards. "Shall I inform the King, Your Highness?"

Arkyn shook his head. "Tomorrow will do. We shouldn't interrupt the end of the banquet with such news. Not when Wealsman's been made Margrave, it wouldn't be fair to him."

A short while later, there was a peremptory knock on the door and Adeone entered. Languidly, Arkyn rose and bowed. His father jerked his head in dismissal at Kadeem, waiting until the manservant had left before saying,

"Get Arkyn a whiskey, please, Percival, and, thinking about it, us one too."

Arkyn watched his father. "I asked them not to tell you—"

"Fitz was upbraiding the guards. Otherwise, I'm sure they'd have done as asked…"

Wealsman, one ear on the conversation, poured the drinks, sniffed and rang the bell. When the manservant entered, he said, "Get that whiskey checked for poison, Kadeem. I could swear it's been laced with something. See the King's changed as well. Send to my house if needs be."

Kadeem never hesitated. "Very well, Your Excellency."

Once Kadeem had left, Adeone asked, "Certain?"

"Yes, sir. Bitter almond isn't a natural flavouring for whiskey. I am, after all, something of a whiskey drinker."

Adeone smiled. "Yes, as I know, to my cost. Arkyn, are you all right?"

Still numb, Arkyn swallowed. "Shocked, father. I thought I'd done nough to stop the attacks."

Adeone glanced at Wealsman. "Attacks? I know of only one, Arkyn."

Admitting to himself he couldn't hide matters any longer, Arkyn xplained. "I've received odd letters."

"What did they say?" enquired Adeone calmly.

"Nothing specific, just facts... A caltrop could stop a horse, Tain night not grow up—"

"Why in Sicla's Cavern wasn't I informed?" demanded Adeone.

Arkyn met Wealsman's eyes – so he *hadn't* been telling his father things. Adeone saw the glance and followed it. Wealsman knelt.

The King pushed himself to his feet. "Your Excellency has an explanation, presume?"

Touching his father's arm, Arkyn interrupted. "Sire, I ordered Percival ot to tell anyone; I didn't want a fuss."

Wealsman said, "Your Majesty, I *should* have told you."

Adeone regarded him for a long moment. "Would you go against your Prince's wishes?"

Percival saw a glint of amusement. "It rather depends on who else is n the province and asking me questions, sir – you know how I hate dilemmas of that kind."

"Percival Wealsman, you're incorrigible. Get up off your knees before you get rheumatism."

Back on his feet, Wealsman said, "Even so, sir—"

"Percival, I ordered you not to tell anyone," interjected Arkyn. "Father would be more furious if you had told him, I suspect."

Sinking onto a chair, Adeone winked at his son. "Yes, I would have been, but I was wondering how long I could tease Percival for." He sighed. "The odd thing is, I've been receiving notes as well. I'll need to make sure Tain hasn't had any in the morning. When did you get yours?"

"The last, this evening – it's gone into the fire. The others, at various times during my stay. In comparison to the dagger, the poison, it's nothing."

Adeone nodded. "They probably expected you'd go straight for a drink."

"I didn't feel the need for one. Ever since I cut my hand, I haven't wanted o drink when I'm emotional."

"I'd keep that trait private, sir," advised Wealsman. "It saved your life and may again."

Adeone caught his eye and there were no words, just an understanding that, as friends, they were both worried about the same matter. Then Adeone's perception shifted, the air shivered and beside Wealsman stood a ghostly Lord Sansky, watching Adeone and Arkyn with concern written on his features. He placed a hand on Wealsman's shoulder as a friend would in congratulation or support.

Wealsman shivered. "We are alone, aren't we?"

Adeone smiled at Sansky. "For all intents and purposes."

Puzzled, Arkyn enquired, "Why, Percival?"

"Because I feel as though someone else is here. Ridiculous."

Adeone chuckled. "How long have you been Margrave for? You're already paranoid."

Sansky grinning rolled his eyes heavenward in a universal gesture of amused resignation.

Wealsman shook his head. "It must be the events of the evening, Sire."

Adeone glared at him; he didn't want Arkyn reminding of them.

Arkyn saw the exchange. "Father, I'm not bothered. Wealsman's right after all."

There was a knock at the door and Sansky vanished. At a nod from his father, Arkyn granted admittance.

Sergeant Hillbeck entered. "Sire, I've had your rooms searched. Nothing turned up, but that isn't unusual, given our sudden arrival. The commander has had the two guards who were here earlier arrested and is speaking to all the staff who weren't at, or involved with, the banquet, though that isn't promising. Are there any further orders?"

"Not this evening, thank you," replied Adeone. "Pass on my thanks to Fitz and Wynfeld, then carry on with your normal duties, please."

"Sire." The sergeant saluted and left.

"That sergeant is abrupt, Your Majesty," remarked Wealsman.

Arkyn yawned. "Yes, but he's good at his job. He's saved the King's life more than once. I'm sorry, Sire. Will you excuse me if I retire?"

Adeone smiled at his son. "There's no need to apologise, Arkyn." He leaned over and rang the bell. A moment later he said, "His Highness is retiring, Kadeem, and, after you've told me His Highness is in bed, we shall leave you in peace."

"Very well, sir." Kadeem held Arkyn's bedchamber door open. A few minutes later, he reported Arkyn had been asleep as soon as his head hit the pillow.

Adeone seized the opportunity. "Truthfully, how is he?"

"Tired, Your Majesty. He's had a few nightmares which haven't helped, I think. He keeps talking of Prince Tain's energy."

Adeone smiled half fondly. "I bet you don't though. Let His Highness sleep in later." He glanced at a timepiece. "Until at least half past nine. I'll talk with both you and Edward properly tomorrow, but thank you for all you've done over the last few months."

As the King stood, Kadeem smiled. “Thank you, Your Majesty. Your Excellency, the Margrave’s rooms have been prepared for you.”

“Oh, thank you, Kadeem, but, as my fiancée is in the next room, I think it wouldn’t—”

Adeone sighed. “Wealsman, we all know you’ve slept in your office before. It’s too late for you to be crossing the city. If it makes you any happier, I’ll have a guard stationed on your door so I know what you get up to. Though looking at you, all he’ll hear is snoring. Deal?”

“I’m Your Majesty’s to command,” replied Wealsman with a flourish, opening the door.

“That’s a yes then,” grouched Adeone. “Let Hillbeck or Fitz know, please, Kadeem.”

“My pleasure, Sire. Goodnight,” said Kadeem, chuckling only once the door had closed behind them.

* * *

Once in his own small sitting room, Adeone waved Wealsman to a chair, rang for Simkins, obtained drinks not laced with poison and settled down for a talk about the notes.

Feeling as though he was breaking a confidence, Wealsman explained. Adeone sat forward when he started explaining about the nightmares. It was almost what they needed, proof that the notes had had some effect, had caused distress. Once that was certain, then the person who had left them was on very thin ice.

In talking about the nightmares, Wealsman felt strange; he’d talked to Adeone about such things twelve years before when he still suffered from them. He’d not had one since. Was it just that in talking about them he had recognised insubstantial fears? He recalled the dread of being out in the cold, being alone in the world. Had Adeone’s friendship banished that? It wasn’t as though he had been friendless, but maybe there had been empathy rather than sympathy. Studying Adeone, he realised, somewhat sadly, their positions had been reversed: it was Adeone who now had few true friends, and he who had more. He was about to get married when Adeone had become a widower; their lives had never been in tandem, although they had had common themes. Maybe that was what made them such good friends, the understanding and a capacity to listen and remember.

Chapter 47
FOOD FOR THOUGHT

Alunadai, Week 37 – 1st Teral, 1st Teris 1211
Arkyn's Chambers

FOR THE FIRST TIME in a long time, Arkyn was awake before Kadeem entered to rouse him. He stared at the ceiling and beamed. He hadn't dreamed the fact his father was in Tera. Deep down he was relieved by it; he wasn't the highest official in the province. He pushed himself up as Kadeem entered, wishing his manservant a good morning and Kadeem could tell, straightaway, that the Prince was feeling calmer.

"Good morning, Your Highness. I hope you slept well."

"Considering everything, remarkably well, Kadeem. What time is it?"

"Half past nine," replied Kadeem carefully. "His Majesty said to let you rest, sir."

Arkyn sighed. "I was almost pleased to see him." He laughed. "All right, Kadeem, you're off the hook. As it's half an hour later than I thought it was, I'd better get up."

Arkyn left for his bathroom and Kadeem shook his head in a rare show of affection. The Prince would mumble and moan about the interference, but there was no real displeasure behind it this time.

Twelve minutes later, Arkyn entered his sitting room. His father was sitting on the couch reading one of the books that the librarian had sent.

He grinned. "I'm not convinced, sir."

Adeone raised an eyebrow. "What do you mean?"

"The book's upside down."

Adeone chuckled. "I've been speaking with Fitz. You should be quieter walking through your rooms; you might have caught us conspiring."

"It wouldn't be the first time, father."

Adeone pushed himself to his feet and father and son greeted each other as they couldn't the previous evening. The hug lasted for a long moment.

Laughing, Adeone said, "You've grown. I'm sure of it. An inch, I'd put money on it. I wish you'd stop; you're taller than I am."

"I'll try, father, but I'm not certain I'll succeed – Kadeem keeps making sure I eat, you see."

Adeone snorted. "I'll tell him to starve you instead then – that will have to be later though, because I'm hungry. Let's ring for breakfast and then we can see about what we're going to do today. I think Percival is already at his desk, he's besting us; we can't have that."

Arkyn shrugged. "Why not? Let him do all the work; he *is* the Margrave."

Adeone's eyes twinkled. "Tempting, but he is getting married in a couple of days. We shouldn't work him too hard; it wouldn't be fair on Kristina."

"True. Can we save it all for when he returns to his post then? He does like to be busy… Ah, Kadeem, could you serve breakfast please?"

Two minutes later, Adeone and Arkyn were eating and talking quietly. Kadeem, standing by the wall, had to smile. He couldn't help it. Adeone was telling Arkyn about Prince Tain's escapades. Adeone saw him grinning at one point and winked. He didn't mind Kadeem hearing the stories, if only to prepare the manservant for what was waiting at Ceardlann.

They were close to finishing the meal when they heard voices in the antechamber. Arkyn jerked his head at Kadeem.

A few minutes later, the manservant re-entered the sitting room to find both the Prince and King sitting comfortably. Both of them glanced over questioningly.

"Note from Captain Fitz, Sire."

Arkyn said, "I'm impressed he didn't insist on seeing us."

"He tried, sir. Commander Wynfeld took him and Sergeant Hillbeck off to His Highness' office, to await you there."

The King regarded him. "You're an exceptional fellow, Kadeem. Do you know Fitz's story?"

"Some of it, sir, yes."

"Then I'm suitably impressed. Fitz must respect you to listen to you so closely. Maybe you can send and say we won't be long?"

Once Kadeem had gone, Adeone read the note. His face went from thunderous to puzzled.

"Well, *this* I can't believe. We've work to do."

Arkyn pushed himself to his feet. "You can't believe that we've got work to do?"

"No. You'll see. It'll be an interesting introduction to the more unpleasant aspects of kingship."

Arkyn sighed. "I thought I'd had enough of those on this trip."

* * *

They made their sombre way through the Residence. Arkyn leading the way to his office. Adeone saw which one he'd been allocated and grinned.

"I used this one. It's an old friend. Oh look, they're all waiting in a line, isn't it sweet?"

Arkyn laughed. "Your Majesty, should we really—"

"No, but it's never stopped me yet. Morning, gentlemen. You've some explaining to do."

Wynfeld and Hillbeck snapped to attention and saluted. Fitz caught the King's eye and then saluted. There was an unspoken message there. One that said the King had heard only half of the story with the note.

Half an hour later, Wynfeld, Fitz and Hillbeck had left and Adeone had told Arkyn what would happen next. Arkyn blanched.

"Sire, I can't interrogate Lord Irvin. It's ludicrous; he's no more a traitor than Uncle Festus is."

"Do you think I've never had to interrogate your nearfather?" demanded Adeone. "Of course I have. You know I have. Last year, when Gad was watching you and he refused to tell me what was happening. I didn't like doing it any more than you like the prospect of this but, eventually, you must face up to it – people you consider friends can betray you."

Arkyn said, "I know, sir, it's just that I thought that you'd—"

"That I'd take over and protect you from this? No. I know this year has been more troublesome than either of us would wish, but I didn't come down here to undermine your responsibility. I'm here to see Percival marry. If I wasn't here, would you be hesitating?"

"I suppose not, Sire, but then the choices would be very different."

"You could still delegate and have Wynfeld question Irvin," pointed out Adeone. "There is always a choice. You wouldn't be the first member of the family to order others to do the unpleasant tasks. In fact, you'd be following a fine tradition."

Arkyn nodded, feeling sickened. Was he ready to face this hurdle?

Adeone regarded him. Was he pushing his son too far? He watched Arkyn struggle with the decision and kept silent. There'd be much harder fights in his life, fights that no-one could take on for him. So far, his decisions had been extraordinary for his age. His resolve to face up to the harshness of official life had been unswerving.

Adeone's heart overruled his head. "Would you like me to do this?"

Arkyn blushed. "Yes, but I don't think I could let you and still respect myself."

"Then would you prefer it if I went elsewhere? I don't mind going."

Arkyn shook his head. "I'd prefer it if you stayed, Sire."

Adeone smiled. "Then shall we… That is, do you want to summon Lord Irvin? We've got all the known facts."

"This feels wrong, sir."

"Yes, but role reversal can be beneficial and, even as king, you won't always be in command."

Arkyn nodded, rang for Edward and sent for Irvin, his stomach churning.

Half an hour later, Irvin entered the office confidently. Seeing Adeone, he stopped, amazed. Bowing, he was more disconcerted by the Prince saying,

"Disarm His Lordship and leave."

Irvin handed his dagger to the guards who flanked the doors.

As the guards left, Arkyn asked, "Why did you send your apologies last night, Lord Irvin?"

"I didn't, Your Highness," replied Irvin, perplexed.

"You weren't at the banquet in honour of the new Margrave and your apologies were received. I ask again, why did you send them?"

"I received a message through my man that the banquet had been cancelled due to unforeseen circumstances, sir. Feeling tired, I had an early night."

Arkyn rang for Edward. "Have Lord Irvin's manservant escorted here, please, Edward." As his administrator left, Arkyn turned his attention back to Irvin. "Will you swear to me on your family's oath of loyalty and lordship that you did not send any message here last evening, and that you had no knowledge that the banquet was going ahead?"

Adeone inwardly raised his eyebrows. If Irvin were ever found to be foresworn, then his whole family would suffer. Their titles would be removed and Irvin would be tried as a traitor. Arkyn had certainly learnt how to issue an ultimatum for truth.

"Gladly, sir. I swear that I never sent a message here yesterday evening and that I had no knowledge that the banquet had not been cancelled," replied Irvin placidly.

Both Arkyn and the King breathed a sigh of relief.

Adeone said softly, "I hope that is true, for your sake," caught Arkyn's eye and made and small apologetic gesture.

The Prince asked, "Lord Irvin, where is your formal cloak kept and who has access to it?"

"It's in my dressing room, Your Highness. My man and, I suppose, any of my host's household could find it." Curiosity was eating away at Irvin. What had happened that warranted this? It was obviously major, had happened whilst he should have been at the feast and he'd been implicated. He'd never seen his friend so grim before.

"Do you know of any substance that smells of almonds?" enquired Arkyn. "Other than almonds, of course."

"Yes, sir, cyanide has that scent. One of the Kings of Terasia was dispatched by cyanide in whiskey. It's in Lange's *History of the Kings* that the librarian sent. Silly really, because some people can smell it."

Adeone and Arkyn shared a significant glance.

"Did your reading ever tell you how to *get* cyanide?" demanded Arkyn.

"No, sir. I wouldn't want the knowledge." Before he could stop himself, Irvin enquired, "What's happened, Your Highness? Sire?"

The King watched him shrewdly, wondering how his son would react to the question.

Arkyn merely ignored it. "My lord, is the dagger you gave my guard the only such one that you possess?"

Irvin closed his eyes for a moment. Opening them again, he admitted, "Currently, Your Highness. My other dagger has gone missing recently. Pearson, my manservant, can tell you. I had him hunt everywhere for it. All I could assume was that I'd lost it in the city without realising. I was annoyed; it was a cisan-age present from grandfather."

Adeone caught Arkyn's eye and nodded. The Prince pulled open a desk drawer and handed a dagger, hilt first, to the King.

"Would this be your dagger, Lord Irvin?" Adeone placed the weapon on a table and then stood a few steps back.

Irvin walked over and, sensibly not picking it up, studied it. Taking two steps back, he answered the King. "Yes, Sire, that is my dagger."

Arkyn said grimly, "Wait outside, my lord," taking the dagger back from his father.

Irvin bowed and left, none the wiser about anything that had occurred. As soon as he appeared, the secretaries stopped talking.

Edward said pleasantly, "Please take a seat, my lord."

Irvin sat in the only chair there. It just happened guards were flanking it.

Arkyn glanced at the dagger. They all carried them. They were seen as a necessity, as well as a mark of rank. This one was particularly intriguing. Most cisan-age daggers were ornate, or at least bejewelled. If Irvin hadn't highlighted it was a significant gift, Arkyn wouldn't have guessed.

Seeing the puzzlement, Adeone said, "Lord Iris is far more practical than many give him credit for. He knows that it's better to have a tool you can use than it is to make a statement. I think it's where your Uncle Festus gets his view of weapons from."

Arkyn hesitated. "Lord Iris is all about tradition though."

"Yes, including the tradition that it's better to live than die because of stupid mistakes – not that he'd put it like that. He would lay down his life for the empire, for his family and for ours, but he'd rather support all three by living than dying as a gesture."

Arkyn considered that. "Was he… Did he say anything about… well, about the review?"

"A bit. Mostly though, he talked quite a lot about how much respect he'd garnered for you, that you did your family proud in all the finest ways."

"Do you ever get tired of the sycophancy?"

Adeone snorted. "Constantly, but Iris isn't sycophantic. That's why I kept him on as an advisor after your grandfather died. He is careful in what he says, but he's not sycophantic. There's a wealth of difference. He said he found your methods difficult at first, but they work remarkably well for you and, by the time he left, he had grown to respect your work as well as your position."

Arkyn swallowed, blinking hard. "You're really not here because I messed everything up?"

Adeone didn't laugh. He crossed to his son and pulled him into a hug. "Of course I'm not! I'm here to see Wealsman wed and a couple more mischievous reasons, but not one of those is to do with your handling of the review. If you hadn't been here, I might have delegated those reasons, but I wanted to see you."

"I'm glad to see you."

"So I should hope," teased Adeone. "Now, I hate to alter the mood, but what do you make of Irvin's story so far?"

"I trust him. I don't feel like he's lying or hiding anything. Pearson should be able to help with minor details, but I don't think Irvin is foresworn."

"No. He's sensible. Not picking up the dagger proved he's an Iris. I can see his grandfather's teaching in him."

"Yes, so can I," muttered Arkyn.

* * *

Several minutes later, Edward showed Pearson in. Unlike Irvin, he had heard the King had arrived. He hadn't, however, heard anything else.

Arkyn asked, "Who brought the message that the banquet had been cancelled last night, Pearson?"

"A residency courier, Your Highness."

"Would you recognise him again?"

The manservant shook his head. "Probably not, sir. I could give it a go, but I'm not certain."

"Has Lord Irvin lost any property since his arrival in Tera?"

The manservant frowned. "He has misplaced a dagger, Your Highness."

The King enquired, "Misplaced or lost?"

"Is there a difference, Sire?"

Adeone drew a sharp breath. "Just a small one. You can put something down and momentarily forget where you put it. You can, however, find it again. If something is lost, you have little chance of ever locating it."

Without blinking, the manservant said, "Thank you, Sire. I would say then he has lost his dagger – as I and some of our host's household have searched for it in vain."

Arkyn nodded. "Has His Lordship's official cloak gone missing?"

The manservant wondered if the Prince was reading his mind. He said, "I only found out that has been misplaced as I received your summons, sir. I haven't had chance to hunt to see if it is truly lost."

"When did you last see it?"

"Yesterday morning, Your Highness."

"Are you *certain* about that?"

"Yes, sir. I looked it out in anticipation of the banquet."

The King walked over to the cupboard and pulled out an official cloak. "Is this it?"

The manservant hardly hesitated. "Yes, Your Majesty. The hem is fraying. I was going to get a new one made when we were back in Oedran."

The Prince nodded. "Very well. Thank you. You may leave. Ask my administrator to join us, please."

The manservant bowed and left. Edward entered a couple of moments later and turned to Arkyn but the Prince was thinking, so the King said,

"You can remove the guards on Lord Irvin, Edward. We'll want to see Lord Silvano and tell Wynfeld to post a few men at his house. Something odd is happening."

"Sire, I think if we're exonerating Lord Irvin, then he is entitled to an explanation," remarked Arkyn.

The King nodded. "Ask His Lordship to join us, please, Edward."

Half a minute later, Arkyn said, "Lord Irvin, there was a double attack on my life last night and it seems someone wanted to implicate you by using your dagger, cloak and research; however, there were factors that were concerning. The person who entered my chambers still had his hood up, hiding the majority of his face. Your manservant's testimony shows that your involvement is not just unlikely, but improbable as well. Your possessions will be returned to you, although I cannot tell you exactly when yet. In the meantime, for any formal occasions, please feel free to use another cloak; His Majesty and I are not too bothered about it being formal under these circumstances."

Irvin's face was a picture. The mixture of shock, anxiety and relief flickered over it so quickly that Arkyn and Adeone couldn't tell which emotion had been the first. The young lord simply bowed and left, without a word. Once outside the office, he let out a long breath and sank onto the chair he had been occupying. Edward passed him a drink.

Irvin sipped at it. "Thank you. What *exactly* happened last night and why is His Majesty here?"

Edward watched him shrewdly. "There was a dagger in His Highness' bed and poison in his whiskey. His Majesty is here for Lord Wealsman's wedding. His arrival was unheralded."

Irvin sighed. “What happens now?”

“If I might advise you, my lord, I’d go to the library. I wouldn’t return to Lord Silvano’s for a while. I expect there’s going to be some upheaval.”

* * *

Half an hour later, Silvano presented himself, half fuming that there were guards at his house. He handed a scroll to Laus, as Edward – seeing the mood he was in – kept him waiting for a moment as he warned the King and Prince.

When Silvano entered, Adeone said, “Do you have any objections to renewing your fealty, my lord?”

Silvano’s mind raced. What had sparked the request? Were others being asked the same? Were the guards at his house a result of the King’s displeasure at his former connection with Roth? Should he have stayed longer at the banquet? Did he have any right of refusal? One look at Adeone’s implacable face told him he didn’t. Guards were already at his house should he even try to refuse. The guards outside the office were there for a reason. His only solace was that he hadn’t been disarmed.

He kept calm as he replied, “None, Sire. I am my King’s to command.”

The King renewed the oath and then kept Silvano kneeling.

Silvano inwardly cursed. He might not have been disarmed but on his knees, he couldn’t draw a weapon and the King would know that. He fumed at being forced to remain in the obviously subservient position without explanation, but he had emphasised he was the King’s to command and, as the newly sworn fealty ensnared his mind, he had no choice. He’d felt the ties form when he’d originally sworn fealty through Lord Portur on the day of King Adeone’s coronation, but this was something else entirely. He couldn’t put his finger on what, he just knew it was stronger.

“Lord Silvano, in truth, do you trust your household here implicitly?” asked Arkyn

Silvano’s eyebrows flickered momentarily into a frown. He wanted to object to the question, but couldn’t. “In truth, if I had doubts about any of them, sir, I wouldn’t employ them.”

“Can anyone else enter your house and locate items in your guest rooms quickly and easily?”

“I very much doubt it, sir. Why? Has there been a complaint from Lord Irvin?”

Adeone smiled mirthlessly. “There has been more than that, Your Lordship. How many staff do you employ?”

“Here, around twenty, Sire.”

Arkyn asked, “Have any left recently?”

“No, Your Highness, and no-one new has been employed for about four aluna-months.”

Without pausing, Arkyn said, "I'm having every member of your household questioned and all their movements yesterday recorded. As this is a case of treason, there is no right of petition."

Silvano whitened. "Treason, sir?"

"Yes, Silvano, treason and, once again, a double count of treason. You were at the banquet last night; did you not think it odd that Lord Irvin didn't attend?" enquired the Prince acidly.

Silvano again frowned. "Truth be told, Your Highness, I never noticed."

Adeone didn't say anything but his face was eloquent – a host hadn't realised his guest was missing from an important banquet.

Arkyn's feelings mirrored his father's but, instead of commenting, he enquired, "Did you bring any attendants with you last night, my lord?"

"A server and groom, sir."

"You will give their names to my administrator. When you return home, I do not want you questioning anyone or discussing what has happened here, my lord. That's all."

Rather stiffly, Silvano rose. "Your Majesty, might I ask a question?"

"You have just done so," replied Adeone. "You may ask another, however." Was Silvano stupid? Appealing to him when Arkyn had led the interview would get him nowhere.

"Is Lord Irvin under suspicion, sir?"

Adeone regarded him for an uncomfortable moment. "Why?"

Too late Silvano realised it had been the wrong question but doggedly continued, "Because I won't give houseroom to anyone suspected of treason, Your Majesty."

"Lord Irvin isn't under suspicion, but if our findings are correct, you have been doing so for some months, if not years. Be thankful that, unlike my ancestors, I don't hold a master responsible for his servants. You may go."

Chapter 48
REFLECTION

Morning

Arkyn's Office

WHEN THEY WERE ALONE, the King saw strain lines appearing on Arkyn's face. "I somehow doubt that anyone here has told you Silvano and Roth were close friends."

Arkyn tried to relax. "I know they were, sir, but everyone has been *very* careful not to tell me outright. They have dropped hints though. That was one reason I didn't choose him as Margrave."

"That and the fact Percival is good at his job, maybe?"

"It helped, Sire."

They smiled at each other. Father and son looked like father and son: the same style of grin in similar features. The illusion broke as the King became serious again.

"Irvin isn't completely off the hook, you know."

Arkyn sighed. "And now he never will be. I think he realises that, Your Majesty, but the writing on the note wasn't Irvin's."

"What did the note say?" (Arkyn told him.) "Did you receive another surprise, other than my arrival yesterday? Or in the last couple of days?"

"Not really, sir. The significance of that had escaped me."

"It may narrow the field to people here rather than at Silvano's."

"Yes, sir, but someone from Silvano's could have come here ostensibly with a message. If they were pretending to be Irvin, they could have simply walked in. He's had access to my rooms for weeks to read the books the librarian has sent. Then they could have left by the kitchen door later. The dagger and note could be unrelated, even the poison could be."

Adeone considered that. "True, but how would they have known I'd arrived? Other than Fitz – whom I forewarned to get us through the cordon – *no-one* knew I was arriving. Most people in Areal think I'm visiting the ports. Scanlon still thinks I'm closer to Oedran than I am."

Arkyn chuckled. "How have you managed that?"

"I've left Richardson taking documents in and out of an empty office for a couple of days. The Commander of Areal has also been warned not to try to see me. He knows I'm up to something. Oh, and talking of which, I've got to appoint a new Major of Oedran. That, however, is a problem for later. Currently, I think more than one person was working this treason last night, or, as you say, the note and the attack were separate. Other than if it's Silvano's server, he *should* have been in hall all night, until Silvano left, but he could have worked it alone. Do you have any objection to my talking to Kadeem about that? He might have noticed if the man slipped out for a time. Simkins was organising my chambers."

"Of course I don't, father. Shall I get Edward to ask him to join us?"

"In a minute." The King seated himself. Hunched forward, he looked at Arkyn. "Today aside, you work too hard, you do realise that?"

"I do?" asked Arkyn, a frown knitting his eyebrows.

"Yes! How long did it take you to prepare that tome of a report for me?"

Arkyn smiled faintly. "A couple of days for the annotations. I wanted it to be clear."

"It was: crystal. Mind you, it was a bit hard to read, in places, because there was so much detail."

"Oh. I'm sorry, Sire; I'll try to make it clearer next time."

Adeone saw he wasn't joking. He sighed. "Arkyn, my son, it was perfectly all right. I'm just worried you might be making yourself ill. Take it from someone who knows, enjoy freedom whilst you can. Sooner or later, you'll not get a day to yourself."

"We both know if Uncle Scanlon gets his way, it will be sooner though," muttered Arkyn. "I want to be ready," his voice had dropped to an almost inaudible whisper.

Adeone knelt by his son's chair. "You are ready. Apparently, half the officials didn't know which way up was when they left this office. That proves you've mastered the first rule…"

"Which is?"

"Keep 'em on their toes, as Laioril would say. Keep 'em dancing to your tune and tell them to pipe down when they get too loud. Now you need to master the second rule better than I do."

"What is that one?" enquired Arkyn apprehensively.

"Leave enough time at the end of the day to relax and, no matter what anyone tells you, heading up a banquet is *not* relaxing!"

Arkyn snorted. "I've discovered that. I'm worried I'm doing things wrong."

Adeone smiled mischievously. "As Percival would say, you will be king. You can't do it wrong. The only thing I think you might not have mastered is putting your feet up after a day's work."

"I don't know, Sire. I can't sleep standing up."

Adeone laughed. "That, Arkyn, is a very 'Tain' comment. Have you been talking to him over messenger?"

"No, father, he doesn't trust them and so far, has refused to get one. I'd therefore only use Fafnir if it was urgent that I speak to him."

Adeone paused, then changed the subject. "Talking about Ceardlann has reminded me, I want Fitz to retire."

"Why, father? He's been excellent—"

"Not because of any mistake, I just think it's time. I'd like him to have some retirement. Some time when he's not watching our backs. When old Jack passed on, I thought I'd try to get those who've been talking about retirement for a time to do it. Old Quinn said he'd got the easiest job in the empire, guarding the Pillars of Alcis, so why did he need to? Fitz hasn't got the same excuse. I'm going to see if he will. That's all I can do. I won't make him go."

Arkyn nodded. "I'll miss him. He's kept me safe all the way here and whilst we've been here."

"I know. I'll have a word with him. My idea was this: I've brought a commander south with me and stationed him at the fort, telling him to keep quiet on the reason he's here until I've talked to Wynfeld… I want to make Wynfeld the Oedranian Major. The General has agreed; all that I now need to do is ask Wynfeld himself. I say ask but I suppose I mean tell. Then I'm going to see if Fitz will retire. The inn in Dellwood needs a landlord. I know Fitz has talked about running an inn. What sort of retirement it will be, your guess is as good as mine, but I'll offer it to him. If he accepts, I'll retire him before we go home. That way he can travel with us as he should, as a friend. He's earned it!"

Arkyn smiled. "He has, sir. Are you meaning Wynfeld would also travel back with us?"

"That was my plan. What do you think?"

"I can't see a flaw with it, father." He sighed. "Have I said I'm glad you're here?"

"Only a couple of times. I'm sure I can stand hearing it again."

Adeone poured them both a drink before walking over and relaxing into the couch. He put the goblets on the table. Arkyn got the hint and joined his father, who then asked about his reading into Cearcallian history.

"Don't you want to tell Wynfeld and Fitz what we've found out this morning, and what you've planned for them, sir?" enquired Arkyn, confused.

"The first is already sorted, the second can wait." He laughed at his son's expression. "Didn't you wonder why I opened the window a crack? I've had the guard outside of it making notes on their replies, with strict instructions to take himself off to where he can't hear us after I used the words 'in a minute'. I thought Irvin might be easier if he didn't think others were party to the interrogation."

"That, father, is devious."

"That, son, is being a king."

"Why didn't you tell me about Percival?" asked Arkyn uncomfortably.

"Many reasons. Are you feeling betrayed?"

"Yes. Slightly. A bit. It might have helped to know, especially during those first days."

Adeone nodded. "I nearly told you then, but I wanted you to make your own decisions. Percival has been one of my best spies here; I didn't want to undo the work of years."

"You came down to see him marry."

"Yes, I let my wish to see a friend's happiness overrule my common sense. I can't apologise enough for keeping you in the dark, but, had you known, would you have made Percival the Margrave without thought as to the other candidates?"

Arkyn paused. "I suppose it would have made the decision easier, father."

"Had anyone then questioned you as to why you'd promoted a minor lord, could you have given the same reasons you now can? Or would it have been a handful of reasons masking the fact that I wanted him to be the Margrave?"

"I suppose it would have been a mask, but he's still the right man for the job."

"Yes, but this way you've learnt a lot more, and quite frankly so has Lord Iris and so have I… Would you ever have formed the type of friendship you have with Percival if I had told you?"

"I suppose not."

"So I supposed also. Arkyn, can you forgive me? I give you my word that other than enquiring how you were, I never asked Wealsman to betray anything. He wasn't reporting to me from the day you entered Tera. He didn't even tell me of Portur's death; he let you do that."

Arkyn sighed. "I'll forgive you, but I'll have to think of a just reward for Percival."

"I think, by making him Margrave, you've already managed that. He's got years of hard work ahead of him."

They grinned at each other, completely at ease.

Chapter 49
ACQUAINTANCES
Late Morning
Arkyn's Office

WHEN THE INTERRUPTION ARRIVED, it took the form of the newly appointed Margrave. Adeone smiled in welcome and didn't move from the couch. Arkyn, sitting with his back against the arm and his legs drawn up, likewise didn't move. Edward and Percival had both seen him seated thus plenty of times before. When the door closed behind the administrator, the King merely said,

"Get yourself a drink, Percival, and pull up a chair; I'm introducing His Highness to a more relaxed working method."

Wealsman grinned. "It certainly looks like you've both relaxed into it well. Thank you."

When he'd sat himself down, Adeone raised an amused eyebrow.

Wealsman said, "Your Majesty, I've been giving thought as to a Deputy Governor—"

"Surely your *wedding* takes priority, Percival?" despaired Arkyn.

"Not really, sir. Everything is organised, though my tailor might not have appreciated the last-minute alterations to my formal wear. Anyway, as I was saying, the Deputy Governor, I'd like to make a controversial appointment."

Adeone said, "He'll be your deputy, not mine. I never interfered in Portur's appointment of Roth. Appoint whomever you wish. Whom *do* you wish for the post, by the way?"

"I was thinking about the Aedile actually," clarified Wealsman dryly.
Arkyn laughed. "He'll certainly tell you what you need to know about and sometimes what you don't!"

"Yes, Your Highness. He is also the highest-rated official in your report – the un-annotated copy."

Arkyn crooked an eyebrow at his father.

"Can't imagine who told Wealsman about that," remarked Adeone supremely innocently.

"I'll have to take Your Majesty's word for it; however, *father*, please tell me, you *didn't* bring it back with you?"

Adeone went shifty. "I might have done. I thought Percival might like to see what an easy ride he had got, if he were appointed."

"It's an interesting read, Your Highness," remarked Wealsman.

Arkyn muttered, "Next time I'll mark it for the King's eyes only."

The King and Wealsman grinned like two naughty boys caught out.

Adeone crooked an eyebrow. "Seems you let the magic out of the tower, Percival. So, what can I do for you *exactly*? Other than finding a reward for dropping your King well and truly in the mire. If you think Ernst would be best, appoint him."

"Yes, Sire, it's just that the overlords were rather perplexed when I was appointed. The move was unorthodox. If I then appoint a deputy who isn't even a lord… well, sir, I don't want to stir unrest."

Arkyn said, "With the King here, you don't need to worry about unrest."

"Though I do take the point," admitted Adeone. "How about I wait until you are on your honeymoon, then appoint the man over your head? You can pretend to disagree as much as you like."

"Sire, if you were to appoint him, then they couldn't complain," agreed Wealsman. "Especially not as the last deputy to be appointed by the Margrave was a traitorous piece of—"

"Traitor would do. You always did have a florid style when talking about treachery."

"I wonder where I got that from, Your Majesty."

Adeone's lips twitched. "Don't cheek your King, he might not like it."

"I'm sorry, sir," said Percival seriously. "I was wondering whether we could cause some mayhem, for old times' sake."

Without a glance at Arkyn, Adeone remarked, "I'm meant to be responsible now and so are you, *Margrave*."

"I *knew* there was a good reason to refuse the post. Never mind, where we lead, others must follow."

"Yes, but I don't think letting white mice loose in the middle of the Margrave's Hall whilst ladies are dancing would be a good idea – this time."

Arkyn grinned. "I'll try that one."

Adeone looked at him. "You're far too sensible and I'll say, here and now, please *don't* suggest it to your brother!"
Wealsman laughed. "Should I then?"
Adeone held his gaze for a second before saying, "No."
Wealsman sighed. "Right. I'd like to meet Prince Tain at some point. I get the feeling we'd get on well."
"Too well. So that can wait a few years. Do you want me to appoint the Deputy Governor?"
Wealsman thought for a few seconds. "It might be the best idea, sir."
"I'll give it a week. I don't want Arkyn wearing himself out. To tell you the truth, I don't want myself worn out either. Looking at your desk briefly this morning, I think I could well be worn out in three days."
"I'm having Thomkins file most of it away. Did you bring Richardson with you?"
"No. He's confusing orderlies in Areal before returning to Oedran to help Landis. I've brought a junior secretary from my office instead."
"Will Thomkins be needed?" enquired Wealsman.
"Is this the gentleman with the twins who hardly ever see him?"
"Yes, sir." Wealsman wasn't in the least fazed that the King knew about Karl and Elsa. He had gathered in the short time he had seen his friends together that they were close.
Adeone shrugged. "He can show Kenton the ropes, as it were, and then take a well-deserved fortnight off. That should give him a week to point us in the right direction and a week to sort out the mayhem before your return. Where are you spending the honeymoon?"
Percival hesitated. "I've not been home for a while. I thought we'd go there and I can oversee management of my lands directly, for a time. If you don't mind? I've just realised, I need travel leave now."
"There was me thinking that a honeymoon was meant to be so you and Kristina could enjoy yourselves, Percival," observed Arkyn.
With a twinkle in his eye, the Margrave said, "I'm sure there'll be ample opportunity, sir. I will need to sort my lands out though, before I settle into being Margrave and permanently here."
"I think you might find they are already sorted out," revealed Adeone, smiling to himself. "Not that much needed doing."
Wealsman looked shrewdly between his friends, who suddenly seemed a bit too conspiratorial for his liking. "What have you two been up to?"
Arkyn adopted an innocent expression. "Us? Nothing."
Seeing Wealsman didn't believe him, Adeone confessed, "At Arkyn's suggestion, I had the Palace Steward talk to yours. I don't mean the one here. Hopefully, everything should be running smoothly. The Prince

poke to him late yesterday and told him to make sure everything was eady for your arrival. Your travel leave was never in question."

Arkyn added, "You've been working hard as Acting Governor. We ought we could do this for you in return."

"Yes, it wasn't because he wanted peace and quiet at all," teased Adeone.

In a long-suffering voice, the new Margrave began, "Sire, sir—"

Adeone cut across him. "What are friends for? I said you would be etting a honeymoon and so you are. You can, of course, check our work. Ve won't be offended. Just enjoy it."

Wealsman gave in. "Thank you. Though I don't know what I will do vith myself."

"I'm sure you'll find something, Percival. Probably riding around madly. heard you missed the endurance ride again. How is Kristina this morning?"

"Calm, but she has married twice before. I'm the one with nerves."

As Wealsman took a drink, Adeone enquired, "Did I say I'll be giving ne bride away?"

Wealsman sprayed the drink back into his goblet, making a strangled oise and choking slightly. "No, Sire, you seem to have *forgotten* that!"

"How careless of me. After all, she is my ward, in a manner of speaking."

Still choking on his drink, Wealsman croaked, "Does Hale know?"

Adeone chuckled. "He does now. I had to devise a more convincing eason for coming down here than simply the fact I wanted to. Iris came p with this one."

Watching the friends, Arkyn said, "As the Margrave is fond of ointing out, no-one could complain, Sire, you are the King."

Adeone crooked an eyebrow. "Yes, but sometimes it is better to let nem think they can, for a short time at least. Unless, of course, pulling ank for pure amusement is worth it. Talking of which, I suppose I will eed to see Wynfeld."

Getting up, Arkyn rang the bell on his desk. He was interested when aus and not Edward entered, or for that matter Stuart, who had recovered rom his illness. He asked the secretary to inform Wynfeld the King would eed a word when it was convenient. Laus replied that he would.

Adeone looked over. "Well, well, well, still causing trouble?"

Laus knelt, but met Adeone's gaze. "I learned from the best, Sire."

"What are you doing on your knees, Laus?"

"Checking the floor's clean, sir."

"Get up!"

Arkyn glanced between his father and temporary secretary, unsure if e'd mentioned Laus' name before.

Wealsman, on the other hand, was smiling. "Your Majesty remembers aus then?"

"How could I forget him?" remarked Adeone. "The only clerk I've ever had to replace."

"Had to?" muttered Laus.

Adeone eyed him. "Well, I had to find you another job before my father objected to your absurd informality. How have you found working for Percival then?"

"Absolute nightmare, sir. I don't know why I thought I'd get more time off. My nose must be an inch shorter from being against the grindstone so much."

"As you can see, sir, I've not managed to cure the informality," explained Wealsman.

Adeone laughed. "I'd have thought it a miracle if you had, Percival." He took a step towards Laus and extended a hand; the two men gripped each other's elbows.

Adeone said, "I'm glad you're still you, Laus. So very glad. Come back to Oedran."

Laus looked at Wealsman before replying. "Sire, I would, but who would keep His Lordship out of the mischief he gets into at every opportunity? Sorry, I should, of course, have said, His Excellency – which gives him even *more* opportunity for mischief, not that he needed any."

Adeone sighed. "You know you're always welcome there though. I've missed you…"

Laus smiled. "I you, Adeone. It seems an age since—"

"That's because it's twenty-six years since we were boys, Laus. Since my father took note of whom my companions were."

"He had your best interests at heart, sir. We didn't take offence. We knew why he did what he did."

Adeone nodded. "I knew as well but it hurt, it did hurt. I'd just lost my mother…"

"I know, sir. We all felt for you… You have my condolences for all the losses since as well. I've wanted to write so often, but I didn't think it would reach you and it would have jeopardised too much."

"Thank you, truly, thank you. Now, you'd better send for Wynfeld. I do have a job to do."

Laus bowed and left, beaming.

Adeone, shaking his head, looked at Wealsman. "When His Highness told me that he had a temporary secretary, I never dreamt that you'd foisted Laus on him!"

Wealsman shrugged. "You might say, he was the most qualified person I could think of, Sire; and he wanted to meet His Highness again." He turned to Arkyn. "He remembered you from a child, sir."

"I think I've changed," volunteered Arkyn.

Adeone clapped him on the back. "Yes, but Laus used to keep you well entertained. Let me just say, I think it's lucky he's never met your brother."

Wealsman chuckled. "I keep hearing about Prince Tain. I wish I could meet him."

Arkyn grinned, pre-empting the King. "Then you'll have to either wait for him to come here or come and visit Oedran at some point, Percival – obviously when you've got the province back on its feet."

Wealsman said, "Which I really ought to be seeing to now, if you'll excuse me?"

Adeone smiled. "I'll be along at some point either today or tomorrow to receive a briefing."

"I'll look forward to it, Sire. Your Highness."

A few moments later, Adeone watched Arkyn warily. "I'm sorry, there's much I should have told you about my time here, but I didn't want you to be biased."

Arkyn shrugged. "I understand why. Are there any more people to crawl out of the woodwork?"

Adeone smiled. "Only one, but this one is atypical. Laus!" As the secretary entered, he said, "As you're here, you can make yourself useful!"

"I'm always useful, Your Majesty."

"Richardson just died of shock. Can you send for Lady Daia, please?"

"Certainly, sir. Lord Silvano left a scroll with me for your attention as well. Should I bring it in?"

"No. Tuck it away until I want to be depressed."

Laus left whilst Arkyn regarded his father with an odd expression.

Adeone winked. "Trust me, Laus will never change the way he is. There's no point fighting it."

"I wasn't planning to, father. I was just wondering… Is this why you went to such lengths to let Cal live at Ceardlann?"

"Yes. I never want you or Tain to suffer the years of loneliness I did after my mother's death and before I met your Uncle Festus."

Arkyn nodded. "Thank you."

Adeone smiled. "You're my sons, part of me, body and soul. Now, how long does Daia normally take to get here?"

"About quarter of an hour."

* * *

When Daia entered, she'd obviously been waiting for the summons. Her dress was more suited to formal evenings than everyday wear. Her hair was styled rather more neatly than Arkyn was used to seeing. She'd taken thought for her appearance. As she curtsied, she didn't lower her gaze, but watched Adeone's face.

He smiled. "You've grown!"

Daia laughed. "So I have, Sire."

He tutted. "What on Erinna is wrong with 'Uncle Adeone'? You managed it twelve years ago."

"Twelve years ago, I was *six*, sir, and Your Majesty wasn't King."

"A lot *was* different. Come here, my dear."

Daia walked over to him and was oddly pleased when Adeone wrapped her in a hug. She was touched by the emotion in his voice when he said,

"Your father died too young. I am so sorry."

"He should never have picked up a sword again!"

Adeone snorted. "That's unfortunately true. He should have stuck to watching and throwing in hopeless comments. He was better at the comments than the fight."

"I think he proved that once and for all."

Adeone sighed. "Yes, but he was forced to that final fight."

Daia looked at him. "Sir? …Uncle Adeone, what do you mean?"

He motioned to the couch. She sat, her eyes never leaving his face.

"Not 'sir', Daia, please, not through this conversation. My brother is out to murder me. The problem is, we can't prove anything. The point is, he isn't just attacking me and my sons. He's attacking my friends as well. He knew your father and I were close. He even suspected that your father was sending me information—"

"But he was."

"Yes. The problem was he was careless and Scanlon found out. I don't know how, but probably through Roth. Anyway, he spent three years planning an accident. Oh, Scanlon can be devious. Your father never stood a chance. The accident was murder. I'm sorry to tell you all this, but you must know. You and Arkyn have become good friends. You're in the same position your father was. For one thing, you've continued spying for us since your father died. Your father was a brave man, a fantastic friend, and a good statesman. He was just a hopeless swordsman and spy. I'm truly sorry, Daia. His friendship with me got him killed; I'm convinced of it and can never forgive myself for it."

She was silent for a long moment, absorbing the information. "I think he realised he was in danger. From the moment you left, he never treated me as a child without independent thought. He made sure I could think for myself, run a household and our lands. He made sure I was ready for a life without him. I'm certain of it now. I've suspected it for some years, but now I know that that was what he was doing. He knew I had to cope. Uncle Adeone, he *knew* what he was doing. He wouldn't want you to feel guilty and I can forgive you very easily for you weren't to blame."

Adeone caught her eye. "You're not just saying that to salve my conscience, I hope."

"Father, I think Daia's right," commented Arkyn quietly. "After all, I've seen proof she can manage her lands. I'm curious though, Daia... When you're out 'helping the sick', do you mean 'collecting information'?"

Daia chuckled. "That as well. I thought you knew."

"No, this is an example of father wanting me to make my own mind up."

Adeone watched him. "Was it the wrong decision, Arkyn? Honestly?"

Arkyn considered for a moment. "I don't think it was, but next time I'll ask you if there's anyone I should know about. So far there've been three people and I am beginning to wonder who else will appear."

"I suppose that's fair enough, but there's no-one, Arkyn. Now, as Laus kindly informed me earlier, I have a scroll to read from Silvano. Maybe you two should leave me to my work. Daia, you'll dine with us this evening?"

"If you want me to, Uncle Adeone."

"I'll look forward to it."

As Arkyn and Daia left, Adeone yelled once more for Laus. They spent a few minutes reminiscing before Adeone broke the seal on the letter from Silvano.

Chapter 50
MAJOR ISSUES

Afternoon

Arkyn's Office

ADEONE READ THE SCROLL and went from sceptical to cold fury. Silvano's household was suspected of treason and he had the temerity to petition him. He sent for Wynfeld.

"What do you know of Silvano, Commander?"

One look at his King's face told Wynfeld he needed to calm him down. "I know he wouldn't listen to my advice, Your Majesty."

"No, he describes you here as a jumped-up flunkey with ideas far above your natural rank. Sicla's Cavern, I will not tolerate such things! Your worth is never in question. I want you to know that."

"Thank you, Sire. The thought is much appreciated. What else did His Lordship say – if I might ask?"

"Well you might. He has petitioned me to disregard the appointment of Wealsman as Margrave. He states that His Lordship's birth is not compatible with the post, that your Prince is too young to make such a decision, and that he has an improper regard for the traditions of the empire. That his choice is nothing but a vagary of youth and that no upstanding Lord of Terasia can condone such a governor."

Wynfeld's face set. "Then, if I might just say so, Your Majesty, His Lordship is a short-sighted cur with the brains of a worm—"

"For once I'll let you. My description isn't so complimentary. I do not dare put pen to parchment to reply to his letter. Maybe you'd convey my response," suggested Adeone, reflecting that he'd never heard Wynfeld express his feelings so pointedly before. "You will inform His Lordship that at no point did I ever suggest – by look, word or deed – that His Highness' decisions were a matter for a man whose household is under suspicion of treason. You may also tell His Lordship that if he questions the competence of my officials again, I *will* act against him. He is *not* an Advisor to the FitzAlcis. He had better attend to his own affairs before he interferes in mine! What's more, Wynfeld, I shall not accept either a petition or apology from His Lordship in this case. Furthermore, I do not want His Highness or His Excellency to hear of this matter."

"Very good, Your Majesty. Would you like a report on his reaction?"

"If I do, when I've calmed down, I shall request one. The next I shall leave up to your discretion; you may, if you wish to emphasise the message, take a few more men with you. Whatever you decide on that front, I want your competent presence at Silvano's house. Make your presence and authority known. You hold that authority, today, directly from me, without reference to the Major of the Southern Empire, General Paturn or Prince Arkyn."

Wynfeld was astounded; it was virtually unheard of for any king to give that directive verbatim. "Thank you for the trust, Sire."

"After this year, that is never an issue, Wynfeld. Later, when the main business of the day is over, I need to talk to you about several matters, but I'd like Prince Arkyn to be present. Now, I believe you had a message to deliver."

Wynfeld saluted smartly and left. Adeone poured himself a drink, still fuming over the scroll.

* * *

A few hours later, Arkyn was once more talking to his father when Laus announced Wynfeld. The commander entered, saluted, and stood at ease. His uniform was pristine. He'd donned his breastplate over the jupon he'd worn that morning and it gleamed.

Arkyn said, "Thank you, Laus, that's all for today. Get yourselves off."

Wynfeld relaxed. If Laus and the secretaries were leaving then whatever was about to occur couldn't be too devastating or alarming. His Prince smiled at him and there was a note of humour there, as though he knew what Wynfeld was thinking.

Once the door closed, Adeone said, "Nice though it is to see a polished reastplate, Wynfeld, save our eyes and remove it. You're not on parade."

Wynfeld chuckled. "Sorry, Sire. My batman was determined I should ppear in correct uniform when attending on Your Majesty. I gave him ie slip this morning. He ensured I couldn't this evening."

"Simkins corners me in much the same way."

Arkyn nodded glumly. "Kadeem me."

They all laughed.

Watching as Wynfeld undid his weapons belt and laid it on the table. deone enquired, "How have you found Terasia, Wynfeld?"

"Relatively quiet on the rumour front, but, probably because of His lighness' visit rather busy in other ways…" He fumbled momentarily vith the shoulder strap.

"You mean I've kept you working all hours and, for that, I apologise," emarked Arkyn.

"Your Highness, I thank you, but you mistake my meaning. I meant nly that there has been more to do than would be normal—"

Adeone smiled. "So, no doubt, you're anticipating a rest when we epart for Oedran."

Wynfeld shook his head. "I'll be bored, Your Majesty. Idleness is nknown to my nature, especially now."

Arkyn asked, "When wasn't it? You like to be busy, just admit it."

Wynfeld sighed. "I like to be busy, sir."

"Good. I'm pleased about that," admitted Adeone. "Now, I had several easons for coming south. How's your premonition today, Wynfeld? Can ou guess what one was?"

Wynfeld, putting his breastplate down, didn't see the glint in Adeone's ye. "No, sir. I never expected to see Your Majesty here and so have not onsidered the problem."

"Remiss of him, isn't it, Your Highness?" mused Adeone

"Very, sir, and unlike Wynfeld."

"True. Well, he can hardly have heard about something that only a andful of trustworthy men know about. Wynfeld, I have a job for you. Vill you accept it?"

Perplexed and suspicious, Wynfeld said, "Your Majesty, I mean no liscourtesy, but I would like to know what I'm accepting."

Adeone steepled his fingers against his lips, then turned to Arkyn, yes glinting. "He did just say 'What I'm accepting'?"

Arkyn failed to hide his amusement. "Yes, Sire. I distinctly heard him."

"Sirs, what I meant to say—" began Wynfeld, feeling exposed without breastplate and weapons belt.

Adeone made a slight movement of his hand and Wynfeld stopped talking. The King became grave. "I know what you meant, Wynfeld, and I shall stop teasing you. I do have a job for you, and would like you to accept it. Would you at least be happy returning to Oedran with us?"

Wynfeld nodded. "Yes, sir. I'd prefer to oversee the situation in the city myself. I've been thinking about it for a while. Beaver is more than competent, of course, but after the Servants' Stair incident, I'd be happier if there were two heads overseeing intelligence gathering. I think there is more than enough for two officers to do. I'd be happy to take a demotion to captain as well. There aren't any posts for a commander in Oedran and—"

The King raised an admonishing finger. "Let me get a word in, Wynfeld. Alcis, you can talk as much as my younger son at times. Though, I will allow, everything you said is pertinent with the proposition I have in mind. Beaver does need help, that is certain, but another captain will be found. No, Wynfeld, what I have for you does not involve demotion. In fact, just the opposite, I'm promoting you to Major of Oedran, forthwith."

Wynfeld stood rooted to the spot, totally stunned. Eventually, he said, "Sire, my previous words aside, I cannot accept that."

On the sidelines, Arkyn wondered how his father would react to a refusal to obey an order. He'd never been in meetings like this with his father and he was learning with every interaction.

"It is not a matter for discussion," warned Adeone, "but I would like to hear your reasons."

"Because, sir, I'm born cisan, I wouldn't know where to start and there are others more worthy of the promotion. Post me elsewhere, sir. I'm happy as a commander."

"I don't care two hoots of a deaf owl about your birth. I care about your abilities for the job. No-one disputes you have those in abundance."

"Sire, I wouldn't know where to begin—"

"You didn't as a captain either," observed Adeone. "I don't want someone in the post who will accept what has gone before as set in stone. Your remit will cover Anapara and Areal. We need someone we have absolute trust in. Someone who will change that which requires changing."

"Sire, I've had two promotions in three years. I—"

Adeone shook his head gently. "Wynfeld, you've deserved them. You deserve this one as well. What's more, the General *asked* for you, before I told him my preference. Lord Landis couldn't think of anyone better. Advisor Rayburn made no demurral and the retiring Major said he timed his resignation with this in mind. Wynfeld, I hate being autocratic, I hate being despotic, but you will be accepting this promotion. I need someone I can work with, His Highness can work with and whom we can trust."

With various confusions clattering around in his mind, Wynfeld inclined his head. "Very good, Sire. Could I beg of you one favour?"

Adeone nodded. "I suppose you have deserved that."

"I realise that I'm never likely to be a candidate, but, *please*, will you promise not to promote me any further?"

Adeone laughed. "Wynfeld, I shall say that if there is an alternative, I'll examine it closely, but, rest assured, I can't see General Paturn retiring for a couple of years at least. He flatly refuses to consider such a thing. I shall not force him to go."

Wynfeld relaxed. "Thank you, sir."

"I'll just take your oath and the empire can have five Majors for a couple of weeks."

When Wynfeld rose, Arkyn handed him a drink. He took it with a hand that trembled slightly. Arkyn smiled at him reassuringly and he smiled back, still somewhat stunned.

Adeone sat down. "Major Wynfeld, sit yourself down. We've got a lot to talk about and, hopefully, none of it arduous. You'll be pleased to know, I hope, that I warned Maria myself, so your aunt won't be clipping you around the head like the last couple of times."

Wynfeld laughed, wondering how his King had found out. "Thank you, Sire. It did hurt. How is she?"

"Going grey, thanks to Prince Tain's ministrations. She's fine, Wynfeld. You'll have to see her when we're back in Oedran."

"I'll make sure I take the time to when His Highness is next in the city."

"I could give you a Dallin."

"No, sir," said Wynfeld, touched. "I shouldn't be in the valley; it is your retreat and haven and I would feel wrong there. Thank you, though."

Adeone caught his eye. "Thank you for the consideration, but I mean it. If you do feel that you want to go and visit your aunt anytime, let me know. How are the investigations progressing at Silvano's?"

"They're still going, sir. Several people are lying, but I'm uncertain who they're protecting. I'm going to need a couple of days. If possible, I'd like to question them separately and intensely."

"Then you have all the warrants you need. I want to know what occurred. My patience with the traitors in this province is ending."

Arkyn said, "So is mine, sir. Especially as they involved Irvin. At least this can't be laid at Roth's door, or blamed on him."

"I suppose not. How has Erlan Roth behaved himself?" enquired Adeone.

"Wynfeld can say with more authority than I, sir."

"Very well, Sire," reported Wynfeld. "Exceptionally well, in fact. I don't think there'll ever be a problem with his loyalty."

Arkyn glanced at his father. "I think he's loyal, sir. I don't think it's the Roth family we need to be concerned about. I was seriously tempted to make Erlan the Margrave, but did, however, let Lord Iris influence my decision against him."

"I must say I'm pleased," said Adeone, "but only because I wanted Percival in the position. It might be worth remembering your preference for the future. All being well, Percival won't retire for some years, but, at some point, we'll have to pick another Margrave. Now, we're to an early dinner. Major, will you dine with us? Bring your weapons belt. I'll have your breastplate delivered back to the fort."

"I should go and—"

Adeone tolerantly shook his head. "Wynfeld, you'll eat with us first. I think I ought to explain to you a few facts of life: one, food *is* required for continued existence, two, I'm about to introduce you to a *very* useful spy."

Wynfeld laughed. "Then how can I refuse either, sir?"

They left the office still chuckling. Wynfeld, when Adeone told him Daia was the spy, accepted it and told her how to pass information back to him. There wasn't the slightest sign of confusion, which made Arkyn wonder how many other ladies of standing Wynfeld had beguiled into the same service.

Chapter 51
FITZ
Evening
Arkyn's Office

THREE HOURS LATER, Fitz obeyed a summons, wondering what was happening. He'd been left alone for years, to undertake his duties as he wished, but he could feel change in the air. A talk with Wynfeld merely confirmed that the King was making reforms.

He entered the Prince's office and saluted, noticing that both the Prince and the King were there. Both were relaxed, and both regarded him with open, honest eyes from the comfortable seating. He'd always liked the FitzAlcis, from the first days he'd had to deal with them. Prince Lachlan had accepted it when Fitz had adamantly informed him that *no-one* was going to be seeing Altarius. He hadn't pulled rank; all he had done was ask for an honest answer that the King was resting. Fitz had given it and whether it was some mystical skill in the post of justiciar or whether it was simply Lachlan's character he didn't know. All he knew was that Lachlan had known he wasn't lying and was acting in good faith.

He'd seen Adeone grow up, from a bump to a man, had even helped form the man in some ways. He'd taught him to fight, but he knew that Adeone had learnt the tricks of a mental fight from others.

Arkyn, he'd helped to guard. He had seen the young Prince struggle to come to terms with his responsibilities. Behind the scenes, he'd tried to take pressure off the Prince, even telling Lord Wealsman that Arkyn wasn't to be disturbed. He'd recognised Wealsman but hadn't said anything. Wealsman had introduced himself as though they had never met. He'd therefore got the message and, also, realised Wealsman was Adeone's spy. He'd been careful, for Arkyn needed some privacy, but ultimately he'd done his job and guarded the FitzAlcis' interests.

Adeone, looking at the captain, smiled warmly. He liked Fitz's honest openness and no-nonsense attitude. All he'd ever get from Fitz was the truth. It didn't matter if that truth put his life at risk; it didn't matter that it might not be what he wanted to hear. Fitz dealt only in what was.

"Fitz, why the concerned gaze?" asked Arkyn.

"Just suspicious of what's afoot, sir."

Adeone had talked to Arkyn about who would lead the discussion and they'd decided that as Fitz was currently guarding Arkyn, the conversation would fall to the Prince, but that Adeone would help where needed, for neither of them fooled themselves that Fitz would accept retirement easily.

"You could give lessons in premonition. Sit yourself down. Would you like a drink?"

"Thank you, sir. Right up to the point of 'a drink' I was reassured."

"Have one anyway. It's nothing disastrous." Arkyn passed him a tankard of beer.

Fitz eyed him shrewdly. "*Now* I'm *really* worried. What have I done?"

Arkyn seated himself. "Your job? Did you know that old Jack has died?"

"Aye, sir. I'm sorry for it."

"You and me both. He should have had some retirement."

Fitz had the first inkling of what the meeting concerned. "He'd have been bored. *So would I.*"

Adeone held his gaze. "Is that a refusal to retire, Fitz?"

"No, sir; it's simply a statement that, *should* I ever retire, I'd be bored."

Arkyn said, "You've been talking of it for years!"

"Yes, and I do a lot of talking – most of it immaterial to the purpose. Wishful thinking, then I remembers that you can't live your life by dreams."

Arkyn nodded; he understood that sentiment. "Very well, Fitz. Let me just say that we are offering you retirement. We're not ordering it, the King's not insisting on it, but we would like you to consider it. You've a pension waiting, and the King's been thinking—"

"It can be a terminal illness, Sire."

Adeone laughed. "I know, Fitz, but please hear us out. I'd like you to retire, not because of any mistake, not because of anything you've ever done… No, that's wrong, because of *everything* you've ever done. You've become a friend to the FitzAlcis. Support whenever we've needed it. I want to spend some time with you when our respective duties don't have to be considered. I know you've been talking about running an inn; would it interest you to know that the inn in Dellwood currently needs a landlord?"

Fitz cursed inwardly. How long had it taken to make sure that the inn *did* require a landlord? How long had Adeone been planning what to say?

"Sire, what would you say if I said I'd prefer to continue as I am?"

"I'd say that it is your choice and would accept your decision. Frankly, part of me wants you to be at our side, but there is still that part of me that thinks you are owed your own time."

Fitz got up. Adeone was telling him if he wanted retirement it was his, unconditionally, but he could stay, if he wanted to. It was his decision, his and no-one else's. Whatever he decided, Adeone would respect his decision. He glanced at Arkyn; the Prince's features were accepting. He sighed; he was getting too old for the job he held. He'd been feeling it on this trip more than any other. His joints ached and he found he was slower than he had been. Dellwood was a pleasant village. The King often passed by. He wouldn't be isolated, far from it. He thought back to the hours spent talking over a drink with the King. That relationship had started with Arkyn as well, and he liked the easy informality they found.

"Would you come for a drink, Sire?"

Adeone chuckled. "Try to stop me, Fitz. I hope this will enhance our friendship, not end it."

Fitz looked at the King, held his gaze and after a moment gave one purposeful nod. "I can't believe I'm doing it."

Adeone pushed himself to his feet. "Thank you." He walked over to him and held out his hand. "There are no words for what you've done for my family. I want you to know that we'll never forget."

Fitz took the proffered hand. "Sire, I couldn't in all conscience have done anything else. It wouldn't have mattered who you were—"

"Yes, that's what makes you so rare. Now, pass me your sword."

Fitz took a step backwards. "I didn't know you meant straightaway! Who's going to look after His Highness?"

Arkyn said, "Hillbeck is taking over command of your men."

"Sir…" Fitz caught the King's eye, pleading.

Adeone saw something he never thought he'd see in Fitz's eyes, something his son couldn't see: panic. "All right, Fitz, but you're invited to the wedding feast, aren't you?"

Fitz nodded, his eyes still pleading.

"Then I'll say this: when you've dismissed the men for an afternoon ff, you'll be officially retired. You'll be at that celebration as a free man, ot a member of our staff."

Fitz, his heart racing, said, in an official tone, "Very good, sir."

"You will get used to it. I'll even make you a promise…"

Fitz eyed him, not at all reassured.

"I'll let you keep your sword and rank," said Adeone.

"Thank Alcis for that. I don't want to revert to my name, Sire."

Arkyn hesitated, but curiosity got the better of him. "I've always ondered why you're called Fitz. Care to dispel the mystery?"

Fitz sighed. "It's nothing spectacular, sir. I don't think—"

"I'm listening."

Adeone smiled at the guard. "So am I."

Recognising defeat, Fitz sat down. "It's all connected to that first evening, hen King Altarius found out about, about his first family. I was suicidal, I ink. I saw the state he was in; no-one could fail to. He was irate, angrier an I've ever seen anyone before or since. He never gave himself time to ink, ordering the execution of Lord… of his nearfather. After that, no-one ared go to him. I was talking to his guards. We heard a crash. They didn't ove. Suddenly angrier with them than afraid of the King, I went into the ner Office. King Altarius was standing, shaking, looking out the window. le never noticed I was there. I picked up the table he'd knocked over. He ever turned round. I went through to his private rooms. Quinn was nowhere be found. So, I prepared the King's bed, found everything he'd need, icluding a decanter and goblet, and went back to him. He was traumatised. here's no other word for it. He didn't know where he was, who he was ven. I got him to bed, and, as I was leaving, he suddenly asked me my name. told him it didn't matter; my name was immaterial. He asked me why. I aid that if he wanted to order my arrest, I'd rather he didn't know it, and if e wanted to thank me, I was simply a son of Oedran, that there was no need or a name. He said that in that case, as I was a son of Oedran, he'd call me itzOedran. It took a mere minute for it to become Fitz. He needed someone talk to; in that moment, he needed a confidant. I was there, it was pure hance but he talked to me. When he dropped to sleep, I went and stood by is door. Prince Lachlan tried to enter. I told him the King was asleep. He elieved me. He asked me my name and as the King had named me Fitz that vas the name I told him. The following morning, I returned to my regiment. Iy captain gave me the roasting of the year for being absent – and, having een a year for rebellions, that's saying something. I took it; I didn't want to ave to explain, but something that night had made me realise that I couldn't eturn to my former life and so, when my conscription ended, I told my aptain I wasn't leaving. He said I had to and then re-join if I must. It was the only time I ever played on what I'd done. I told my captain to tell King Altarius that Fitz wasn't leaving the army. The captain told me not to be a fool and that he certainly wasn't going to be telling the King anything, even supposing that he could get to see him. Yet he must have mentioned it to someone for the following day I found I was ordered to the General's office. I found your father there, Sire. He said, quite simply, that I didn't have to leave the army, and, in fact, there was a spot in the King's Guard that had my name on it, if I wanted to accept. I couldn't do anything other than accept, he was the King. The following day I reported to him. I'd been given his guard to oversee. I told him I was cisan born and I'd meet too much prejudice as a captain. He laughed and said that, from then on, he'd be guarded by sergeants. There's never been a Captain of the King's Guard since. I accepted promotion in the end but only to help protect him better as I didn't trust any of the layabouts Lord Iris was proposing making the Captain of Intelligence. Technically, I'm the last conscripted soldier from 1169."

Adeone watched him. "You think that story is unspectacular?" He shook his head to dispel incredulity. "Fair enough. So, what is your name?"

The captain laughed. "Fitz, Sire. Any other would be the bane of my life."

Adeone and Arkyn looked at each other.

Arkyn said, "We can live with that, if you can."

* * *

When Scanlon heard Adeone had reached Tera; he was irate. What did his wastrel spies think they were doing to miss such an obvious trick? He could have used the fact the King was virtually alone to his advantage. Seven men travelling together should have been conspicuous – especially when it was obvious that one was of high standing. The idea Adeone might have discarded the obvious for the duration of the ride never even occurred to the Justiciar. He, himself, would never have stooped to a disguise. Moreover, he wanted a serious and painful word with his spies in Terasia, all of whom had assured him there was no evidence that Wealsman had stayed such close friends with Adeone. He couldn't be blind to Adeone's manipulations if he was going to succeed in revealing them to the world. He decided to have a painful word with the advisors who had assured him all was well. Maybe now was the right time to visit Oedran. It didn't take long before he told the newly married Visir that he was leaving for home.

Chapter 52
CARRYING ON

Cisadai, Week 37 – 2nd Teral, 2nd Teris 1211

Kristina's Rooms

THE FOLLOWING DAY, Wealsman – who hadn't had two minutes to himself the day before – walked in on Kristina, waving the maid out. His heart lifted as his betrothed smiled in welcome.

Leaning down, he kissed her. "Our invitation brought more than we bargained for."

"Yes, but then the King did say it was due in part to your influence on his sense of humour, Percival. I think it's called being blown up by your own magic."

Wealsman sighed. "Don't you start finding the situation amusing as well. You know tomorrow I have to promise, not to your father but to the King, that I will care for you better than he could! Plus, I have to do it on bended knee!"

"Don't let it get you down. His Majesty thought it was quite amusing one way or another."

Percival ignored the bad joke; worry eating at him. He sank onto the seat next to her, groaning. "How can I ever care for you better? It would mean I was foresworn."

"No, it won't, for I would never accept the King's care over yours. You should know that by now."

Percival studied her face. "I still wonder though."

"Stop wondering." Before he could say anything else, she kissed him. This time, it was more than a peck. By the time Wealsman released her, he was wondering why he'd visited her. Kristina wrapped her arms around his neck and continued.

After a moment, Percival broke away and pushed himself to his feet. "Kristina, I have to go and brief the King on the running of Terasia. The last time he was here was twelve years ago, and this review has changed quite a lot."

"Then you'd better go… Percival…"

Rather distracted, Wealsman said, "Yes?"

Kristina bit at her lip, turning away. "Never mind, it can wait."

Her unease disquieted him. "What is it?"

"I don't know how to say this, but it looks as though I might be with child. I have missed a course."

Wealsman sank onto a chair. They'd taken a risk, but he'd never thought it would happen. He held out his hands; as she took them, he said, "I can't say I'm disappointed." This time it was he who started the kiss and didn't break away. When he did, he stated, "I must tell Adeone."

Kristina stared at him, horrified. "Tell the King his ward, or whatever I am, is carrying *before* she gets married?"

He nodded. "Unless you want to? He must know as we do. Otherwise, it can be construed as treachery, though not treason."

Kristina paled. "Then you had better."

Leaving her extremely tense, Wealsman went to his office. He found Adeone already there, talking to Thomkins.

The King took one look at his friend's face and dismissed the secretary. "What's happened?"

Extremely nervous and formal, the new Margrave said, "Your Majesty, I've just been speaking to Lady Portur and it seems… Well, Sire, it seems… Oh, Sicla. How can I put this? It seems…"

"Yes, you'd got that far."

"It seems, sir, that, well, that Kristina is carrying a child." His eyes raked Adeone's face and he was reassured to see neither anger nor hostility there.

Instead, Adeone was amused. "I know. I've known since the banquet."

Wealsman sank onto a chair, his head in his hands. "How did you know? She's only just told *me*."

"I watched Ira go through pregnancy three times and Lady Landis six, not to mention Lady Aelia. I can recognise the signs. I'm glad, very glad, and no-one else need know that we knew today."

Wealsman sagged; Adeone hadn't seen him so drained before. He passed him a drink, squeezing his shoulder kindly.

"Regain your strength then go and tell your Kristina I'm not at all bothered. You've loved each other for so long. Marriage is only a formality."

Wealsman said tiredly, "Thank you, Sire."

The King smiled. "I think I heard 'Adeone' there not 'Sire'. When you see her, invite her to an informal dinner with me tonight, if you'd be so kind. After all, you won't be in the Residence and she shouldn't be alone the evening before her marriage."

* * *

When it came, the evening was calm. Wealsman was puzzled to find Arkyn waiting for him at his house. The Prince merely smiled, remarking that he hadn't thought it fair that the Margrave had to spend the eve of his marriage with no company. Wealsman outwardly accepted the explanation.

When they'd dined, they settled comfortably with drinks by their hands and the chess pieces ready.

Without consulting Wealsman, Arkyn said to the server, "That is all for now, thank you."

Wealsman gave an almost imperceptible nod and the man left. It was unusual for a guest to dismiss the servants, and Arkyn wasn't prone to playing on his rank. Once the door had closed, Wealsman quietly enquired whether Arkyn was going to reveal the real reason for his visit.

Arkyn said loud enough to carry beyond the door but not so loud as it would seem unnatural, "Let's see if you can beat me tonight, Percival. You start." Lowering his voice, he added, "If you promise me not to overreact."

"I'll promise you that, sir."

"Earlier today we arrested Lady Portur's maid for spreading rumours that Her Ladyship is with child. She is now writing a statement refuting all such claims. The doctor is examining Her Ladyship, as we speak, and the King is investigating the matter… Percival, just listen to me! You won't get very far. My guards have instructions from the King not to let you leave here tonight, so sit back down. The doctor will find that she is not expecting. By the way, I meant to put my congratulations somewhere into that explanation."

Half frightened, half furious, Wealsman said, "Will find she is *not* —? What has the King done?"

Arkyn eyed him. "Your Excellency promised you wouldn't overreact. What do you suppose His Majesty has done other than show the doctor where his loyalties lie?"

Wealsman took a steadying breath. "I… I'm sorry. I just… Oh, Sicla!"

Kindly Arkyn murmured, "Don't apologise. You are worried for Kristina, that is all. Father would have told you all of this if he could have done; however, as he can't be in two places at once, I am telling you… Are you ready to listen?"

Wealsman nodded – the game of chess forgotten.

"Hale took the rumours to the King earlier today. *After* you had told him Her Ladyship was carrying. His Lordship received the assurance that the King would investigate the *rumours*, which he did. The source of them was easily discovered; the guard who's been stationed in the kitchens pointed her out. Kristina's maid has discovered she's overreached herself. To slander anyone under the King's protection could be construed as treason, as it ultimately slanders the King's judgement. She was given the option of revoking her statement publicly or facing that charge. She decided to go for the former option. It seems she wasn't certain enough of her facts."

Shaking, Wealsman had his head in his hands. "And Kristina?"

"She is having supper privately with the King. The only addition to the itinerary was the fact Artzman was there talking to the King about my health when she arrived. He stayed to check the validity of the rumours. She will have undergone a consultation with him. An interrogation of the household could have been worse for both of you. I will replace some of the Residence guards for lack of discretion, you have my word, but sleeping in your office really wasn't the wisest thing you could have done. Nor was visiting her *after* late evenings with me."

Wealsman's voice shook. "She is afraid of doctors. I can't bear… I'm sorry. This has all come as something of a shock."

"Percival, I'm telling you this because tomorrow there will be the question asking if anyone knows any impediment to marriage. You know that, in Terasia, if a lady is already pregnant, she cannot marry until the child is born. It is *certainly* an impediment to marriage. The King wants to be sure he has a doctor's report from this night to prove she's not carrying. He also wants to make sure you are ready for the response to the question and don't overreact if someone does claim Her Ladyship is pregnant. We've silenced Hale and the maid, but that doesn't mean someone else won't try to disrupt proceedings."

"But the doctor won't be blind and he won't lie, even for the King."

"Father has drawn up a list of questions. If Kristina answers them truthfully, she's fine. She had a case of food poisoning not long ago. That could still be making her sick after large meals, especially as she refused to see a doctor. There could have been delayed shock from Portur's death, meaning her cycle was disturbed—"

"Sir, she cannot deny she hasn't had a course recently."

"She won't have to. The question we came up with was had she bled recently. Yes, it sounds crude but a cut finger can bleed. If Her Ladyship agrees, the King will cut her finger tonight so they can honestly say she started bleeding when in the King's company. As you have pointed out before, Percival, who will doubt the King's word? They will, in their haste to seem loyal, interpret it in the manner they think it should be."

Wealsman suddenly laughed. "*We*, sir?"

Arkyn blushed. "I owe you quite a bit as well – my life for a start."

"I'm not sure that I deserve this though."

"We are, so stop doubting your King and Prince. Kristina will be perfectly well. Come on, it's your move and I need to increase my lead."

Wealsman gazed blankly at the game. Arkyn took one look at him and cleared the chessboard. They talked instead.

Chapter 53
WEDDING

Tretaldai, Week 37 – 3rd Teral, 3rd Teris 1211
Tera – Wealsman's House

THE MORNING OF Lord Wealsman's and Lady Portur's wedding dawned fair and crisp. The city was alive with guests. Having spent the night at Wealsman's, Arkyn rose and dressed formally in readiness. He'd just finished fastening his belt when Wealsman's manservant informed him that Wealsman was sitting staring at the wall and wouldn't move. Arkyn motioned for the man to lead the way.

He entered Wealsman's rooms. "Percival, Kristina can't marry you if you're not there."

"Why is she doing so, anyway?"

Arkyn waved the servants out. "Because she loves you. Any fool sees that. What's more, you can't keep the King waiting. So, on your feet, Your Excellency. That's right. About turn. Good. I'll just tell your man you're about to need his help and, to make sure you get to your wedding, I have orders from the King to go to the alcium with you. That is another reason I invited myself here last night. Now, go and have a shave like a good Margrave."

Wealsman left without a word. Arkyn rang for the manservant, who entered rather impressed to find that Wealsman wasn't there.

Smiling, Arkyn said, "If he starts to dally again, tell him His Majesty is waiting. I'll wait here for him."

A couple of hours before, in the Margrave's Residence, Kristina re-entered her bedchamber after breakfast. A figure was rearranging the hastily left bed covers, tutting whilst she did so. Kristina laughingly greeted the only attendant she had ever felt any affinity for. Her old nurse turned around, hands on hips.

"Hmm. You've aged a bit, my lady. Looking wiser too."

Kristina walked over and hugged her. "What are you doing here? I mean, I'm pleased to see you, but how…?"

The old nurse sniffed. "Seems the King and Prince know what they're doing. Now, come on, we've got to get you ready for your wedding day."

Kristina laughed. "My third wedding day. I'm getting used to them."

"Yes, but we both know this is the only one that has ever counted, don't we, my lady?"

Feeling seven years old again, Kristina left for her bathroom.

Her old nurse wasn't the only person she recognised running around after her that morning; the others, though dear friends, weren't quite in the same league. Amongst them was Daia – who'd be one of her bridesmaids. Two hours later, at half past ten, she was looking radiant in an ivory silk dress embroidered with entwining leaves in bronze and honey threads. She made her way to the entrance hall of the Residence where she found the King, in full formal dress, giving orders to guards in brightly polished armour.

Adeone walked to meet her. "My lady, if Lord Wealsman isn't made speechless, I shall think he is ailing."

Kristina's eyes danced. "I hope he isn't made too speechless, sir."

Adeone winked. "So do I. It would seem a shame after everything else. Are we ready?"

Kristina paled. "I don't know if I am, Sire."

He murmured reassuringly, "Just take a deep breath and let it out slowly. Fix your eyes straight ahead and watch the fun commence."

She chuckled. "Is that what you do at official functions, Your Majesty?"

"Yes. Now, if you don't mind, I'll link my arm through yours. For support for your nerves and then you can hold me up as I try to stop laughing at Percival trying to be sincere as he kneels to me."

* * *

Arriving at the alcium after a brief journey, Adeone alighted from the coach and offered Kristina his hand before re-linking his arm in hers and motioning to the guards to open the alcium doors. The sight that met their eyes was stunning. Fragile blossom scented the air, the blooms hung from balconies and worn by guests. Kristina's breathing deepened as they walked along an aisle formed by guards who saluted as the King passed. They reached the circular open space in the centre below the representation of the stars.

The alcia approached Adeone. "Why have you come?"

"To marry Lady Portur to a man worthy of her love."

The alcia demanded, "Who claims this lady's love?"

Kristina breathed in sharply as Wealsman appeared; she hardly recognised him. His dark-blue tunic was piped with red cord. The open neck revealed a crisp ivory undertunic decorated in threads that matched her dress. Someone had told tales, but his eyes betrayed that he hadn't been shown her dress. His hair was so neat that she wanted to mess it up, just to recognise the man she knew.

"I, Lord Percival Wealsman, Margrave of Terasia, do claim her love."

The alcia waved him forward. "Do any here have knowledge why these two may not marry? Is there any doubt as to their love for each other?"

Adeone was thinking, *'That line is new, Arkyn'*. The marriage wording wasn't entirely set down in law and he had no doubt who had requested the extra line; it had the simple duplicity that his son excelled at.

Adeone, Kristina and Percival faced the guests. For all their fears no-one, confronted with the full splendour of the King in state, was stupid enough to speak up.

The alcia said to Adeone, "There has been no objection, Sire."

The King glanced at Wealsman, who dropped to one knee. Those close by almost thought he was shaking.

"Lord Percival Wealsman, Margrave of Terasia, will you promise that your care for Kristina will surpass my own?" enquired Adeone.

"I give you my promise that I will try my hardest to make it, Your Majesty."

"Will you promise to never let harm befall her if you can prevent it?"

"I will, Sire."

"Promise to never force your wishes on her and give her unstinting love through trouble? Will you give her stability and trust?"

"Your Majesty, I promise that. Here I make my own vow that all I have is hers, my love, my land, my life, my heart, from now to eternity."

"Lady Kristina Portur, do you return and accept the terms here laid down for your marriage?"

"With all my heart, Sire."

King Adeone smiled at her. "Then I cannot object to your union. Lord Wealsman, what are you doing still kneeling? Your wife needs your arm."

Wealsman pushed himself up and Adeone put Kristina's hand in his.

"Lord Percival Wealsman, Lady Kristina Portur, I hereby bestow upon you both my blessing for your marriage and wish you a contented life together." In a whisper he added, "Just remember, Kristina, if you have any trouble with him, I'm your last guardian and outrank him."

She laughed at the look on Wealsman's face. She murmured, "Thank you, Sire. That will come in handy."

Wealsman, trying to keep a straight face, held her gaze. "Lady Kristina Portur, will you here accept my family name and become *my* lady?"

In a voice so resolute that some men quailed, Kristina vouchsafed, "I will, Lord Percival Wealsman."

Percival relaxed. "Then we are bound."

Kristina smiled. "We are bound."

Each spouse slipped a ring on the other's finger.

The alcia stepped forward. "My Lord and Lady Wealsman, may the blessings of your ancestors be with you."

Applause broke out as Kristina and Percival made their way to the waiting coach. Adeone and Arkyn followed them and mounted their horses. They set out after the coach and only then did the alcium gradually empty of the other guests.

Chapter 54
DISARMING FEAST
Afternoon
Margrave's Residence – Entrance Hall

ONCE ALL FOUR OF THEM were in the entrance hall of the Residence, Adeone, with the broadest smile Percival had ever seen on his face, said, "Congratulations to you both. This day has been a long time coming."

Percival grinned. "Thank you, sir. I think it was worth waiting for."

In a mock severe voice, Adeone remarked, "There is no status here today, Percival; in company or out, I am Adeone to you and your wife. I will not have it any other way, my lord."

Percival eyed him. "We might agree to that, *Sire,* if you could also drop the lord and lady!"

Adeone laughed. "Consider it done, Percival. Now, go on with you both. Kristina will need to remove the train of her dress, otherwise she'll be tripping herself up as you dance." Adeone took Kristina's hand and kissed it. "I meant it; I want to know if you ever have a problem with that rascal."

"I'm sure I've got a few tricks up my sleeve, Adeone, but thank you."

Wealsman groaned. "I'm sure you have, Kristina. The King was right, however; you need to remove the train of your dress."

Adeone enquired, "Tell me something, Percival. What is so hard about using my name that your wife can manage to overcome but you can't? Now, the guests are arriving. Go on with you."

They left as Adeone and Arkyn began to welcome the guests for the feast before entering the Margrave's Hall. Arkyn watched his father's face as Adeone saw the dais, with its central chair, and summoned the steward.

When the man arrived, the King queried crisply, "This feast is being held in honour of Lord and Lady Wealsman. I am merely a guest and I will not, by my sudden arrival, remove His Excellency and Lady Wealsman from their place of honour. I will sit as is traditional on the bride's left. They are the centre of attention. His Highness is on the groom's right. See to it, please."

The steward bowed as Adeone strode off. Twelve minutes later, the alterations had been made. Moving through the guests, the King was perplexed to find a scroll in his hand. Who had handed it to him? He caught his manservant's eye. Simkins approached and bowed.

"Give this to Kenton, please. I'll read it later, if he thinks I need to."

"Very good, Sire." Six minutes later he was back saying, "I believe all the guests have arrived, sir."

Adeone nodded; somehow, he had taken over the proceedings from the steward. He wasn't concerned; it kept happening to him and always had. He made his way over to Arkyn.

"Feeling up to taking over for me, for a short time?"

Arkyn agreed; thinking that it was both annoying to be asked, after the last few months' worth of responsibility, and also pleasant that his father thought him capable of managing. He couldn't, however, work out which was the overriding emotion.

* * *

A few minutes later, Adeone extricated himself and left the hall in search of the happy couple. He found them sitting close together in Kristina's rooms. Percival's hair had resumed its usual disordered appearance.

Smiling, Adeone said, "Don't get up. I just thought I'd let you know the hordes are assembled, when you're ready and not before."

Percival looked at Kristina. "How long do you think we could keep Adeone waiting?"

Before any of them had the chance to say anything else, Kenton apologetically entered and bowed after a brief knock.

"Forgive me, Sire, but I think you should read this scroll immediately."

Annoyed, Adeone held out his hand. Kenton's posture alone hinted at something serious. Having also sensed it, Wealsman stood up.

Two minutes later, Adeone cursed, "Alcis be dark, how stupid is he! Death and damnation! I take it you have taken appropriate action, Kenton?"

"I've asked Captain Fitz to talk to His Highness whilst Major Wynfeld organises a posse of men," clarified his secretary.

"Good. Tell Wynfeld I will want to interview Silvano again, so to remove him from the guests as well. Then I want the guard doubled and the dais guests searched. Nobody threatens my closest this much – be they friends or family! In fact, disarm *all* the guests with my apologies – when Silvano starts playing up, tell him to shut up. He's given more than house room to traitors. He gave one life." As Kenton left, Adeone turned to a stunned Wealsman and Kristina. "Kristina, I know Percival will tell you later what this is about, but could you just wait in the next room, please?"

Kristina left. It might be her wedding day, but Adeone was still the King. Wealsman looked at his friend and then, passing him a drink, asked what had happened.

Adeone ran his hand through his hair. "Hale and Melek Silvano have been plotting. They were behind the latest attacks on Prince Arkyn – but not the notes – something to do with a dinner and revenge for Roth's execution, and they planned to kill either you or Kristina, today. Their preference was you. It seems Hale *really* didn't want you to marry Kristina. Aluna, help me keep my temper. I'm close to losing reason."

Percival took his friend by the upper arm. "They'd have had a bloody good fight on their hands, Adeone. I never go anywhere without a dagger. I've taught Kristina a few tricks as well. Plus, the hall would have been full of guards."

Adeone shook his head. "No, it wouldn't have been! I told them not to bother. The only ones there would have been Fitz and Wynfeld as guests; once they had seen to their duties. It is Fitz's last day as a guard as well. As soon as he's dismissed the men and joined the throng, he is a free man."

"I don't think that would have stopped him."

Adeone snorted. "No, it wouldn't but I can live in hope that he'll have a peaceful retirement."

"At least this latest wasn't treason."

Adeone sighed. "Percival, as *Margrave* you are my Representative; it *is* treason to attack your life! I would have thought the events of this last year would have etched that into your brain."

"Adeone, nothing happened. It was caught in time."

"Yes, but will the next be?" fretted Adeone. "Scanlon's behind a lot of this and I can't prove it. No-one will name him, *no-one*, and one of these days he'll kill one of us. What happens then? I can't bear to think of it. If it's me, who will care for Arkyn and Tain? If he gets one of my sons, how will I have the will to fight him? I've lost too much of my family already." Adeone remembered it was Wealsman's wedding day and apologised.

"Don't be a fool, it's fine. Can I point out that you've doubled a guard that wasn't going to be there…?"

Adeone chuckled. "Relaxing well into the informality, aren't you? Wynfeld will sort it out. Ask Kristina to join us before I get maudlin."

Twelve minutes later, Adeone's secretary once more entered and told the King his orders had been carried out. None of the guests had protested, the conspirators had been detained and Wynfeld had declared himself satisfied. Adeone nodded in dismissal and then turned to Wealsman.

"Shall we go and celebrate?"

"As I said before all that, I can keep you waiting… revenge is sweet."

"Dessert won't be if you continue like that. Just think about how much more opportunity I *will have* in the near future. I'm now running Terasia directly. Are you still proposing to keep me waiting, Percival Wealsman?"

"I half think it might be worth it, but the look Kristina is giving me is telling me that she is hungry and I'd better not keep her waiting."

Adeone's lips twitched. "That's the way it should be. You're now married, Percival, as is exemplified by the fact that you're more afraid of your wife than of your King. Come, lead the way."

Percival shook his head. "*No*. We go down together."

Adeone agreed to keep the peace. When they reached the Margrave's Hall, Wealsman spotted the new dais arrangement.

Softly he enquired, "Who…? I gave strict orders the seating was to emain as it was."

"That's a pity. I gave strict orders to change it. It seems my authority till overrides yours, Percival."

Kristina was trying to keep a straight face, as Percival muttered, Knew there was a reason not to be friends with the King. I get made the *Margrave* and my friend *still* outranks me."

"Not today, Percival. That's why the seating has been reorganised. 'oday, I am your wife's former guardian. Now, are you going to lead the vay, or do I have to push you?"

Percival realised the guests were watching the exchange with interest, ven though they couldn't hear what was being said. Adeone also realised hey were the only men still with a weapon. Motioning Hillbeck over, he ook his dagger from his belt and passed it to the sergeant. Wealsman took he hint and did likewise.

As they walked to the centre of the dais, Wealsman commented, Unarmed at last, Adeone?"

The King replied quietly, "No. Though I hope I don't have to retrieve he other from under my mantle."

Adeone and Kristina sat whilst Wealsman made a short speech. The ext was Adeone's and he rose, saying,

"I think I am going to take a leaf out of Prince Arkyn's book and improvise. As those of you who were at the announcement a couple of days ago will now, I have been friends with the new Margrave for many years. As you will also remember, I had no idea that Prince Arkyn was choosing Wealsman as Margrave. I had come to Terasia with the sole intention of seeing him marry – r at least that's what I've told him over the last two days. I did, however, have n ulterior motive. I have a wedding gift for His Excellency, one that has been planned for many weeks." He turned to Wealsman, who was looking extremely ncertain. "Percival, I shall try to be brief. You have been an invaluable support o me over the last few years. His Highness has already honoured your loyalty nd statesmanship, but I must honour our friendship. I thought long and hard bout what I could give you to mark this day. Then I thought of who you are, man who never likes to be bored, who likes to be busy. This being before His Highness handed you Terasia to govern. You've today married a lady you have oved for many years. I know you are both content with your lives; that Kristina vill be happy as your wife, but I still had to find a gift. So, I thought long and hard and finally came up with an idea I could live with, and one I hope you both can." He turned and took a bunch of keys on a long string from Simkins. 'Lord Percival Wealsman, Margrave of Terasia, will you please kneel?"

Watching the King's face, Percival did as requested. Keys generally meant one thing, and Wealsman knew how crafty Adeone had been as his heart and head started arguing their joy and fear simultaneously. His friend could at least have warned him, given him a chance to have a say a chance to object, to— *'That's why he didn't'*, whispered a voice in his head. *'Because he knew you too well.'*

Adeone said, "Now, you've taken more oaths than I can remember though I expect you can."

"Yes, Sire, there was—"

"Percival, that was rhetorical!" Adeone winked at him. "I have here the keys of all the manors formally of Lord Portur's tenure. In thanks and gratitude for twelve years of unstinting friendship, on this your wedding day, I name you as an Overlord of Terasia." He placed the keys around Percival's neck, pinned on a badge of office and didn't dare look at Kristina who had moved and stood with a hand on her husband's shoulder.

Wealsman swallowed. "Sir, our marriage was gift enough, but I thank you; your wedding present has given me even *more* work to do." He raised his hands as though to swear fealty.

Adeone laughed and reached down to help his friend back to his feet "I'll apologise to your lady for that one. Kristina, can you forgive me?"

"Of course I can. It should keep him quiet." She hugged her husband

Adeone clapped, a still stunned, Percival on the back before turning to the hall. "I must just add that this is no precedent for future actions." He sat down and crooked an eyebrow at Wealsman.

The new overlord said, "Thank you, sir. I think I'll just open the feast before Your Majesty has any more ideas…"

Adeone chuckled. "See it as your influence on my sense of humour, Percival."

As Percival sat down, a ripple of laughter and slight clapping spread. It seemed the gift had met with a certain amount of appreciation. That or they liked seeing him lost for words, which – knowing some guests – was a more likely explanation.

"When do you want me to renew my fealty, sir?" he enquired a few moments later.

Adeone crooked his finger so that Wealsman leaned closer. Then crooked it again. Half leaning over Kristina, they heard Adeone whisper,

"Never, my friend."

Kristina chuckled to herself as both men sat up, still silently arguing. Wealsman lost by the expedient of Adeone ignoring him.

Halfway through the feast, Percival enquired, "Just to clarify something, Adeone, where *are* Kristina and I going on our honeymoon?"

"I've warned your new steward that you'll probably be calling on him, but, Percival, everything should be working how you like it. This has been planned for some weeks."

Percival shook his head. "It must have been, but I still can't believe you've done it! What of my own lands?"

Adeone smiled. "I thought your second son, when you have one. Just enjoy it. You deserve it."

Wealsman saw Kristina chuckling to herself. "What's so funny?"

"You are. You question everything. You're an overlord and Margrave of Terasia, stop moaning."

Adeone laughed. "Thank you, Kristina."

Percival mumbled something nobody heard, but Adeone and Arkyn were willing to bet it was something to do with finding a just reward.

The feast continued without incident and, when the guests had gone, Percival and Kristina left for Wealsman's house. Adeone and Arkyn spent a pleasant evening in the Residence simply talking. The traitors could wait until the morning. They had given up with the tolerant approach. Neither exactly minded their lives being threatened, it came with the rank, but Wealsman's and Kristina's were another matter, *especially* on their wedding day.

Chapter 55
TRAITORS

Imperadai, Week 37 – 4th Teral, 4th Teris 1211
Adeone's Chambers

AS ADEONE AWOKE the next morning, the events washed over him in a crescendo of different emotions. He swore. The previous day should have been happy; material concerns, such as the fact people were out to kill each other, should have remained in the shadows. Wanting the first part of his day to be over, he rang for Simkins. The manservant entered and noted the King's mood. He was all but silent until his silence became oppressive and Adeone snapped at him for it.

On reaching the Margrave's office, Adeone found Thomkins and Kenton both waiting. Kenton bowed and smiled; Thomkins merely seemed nervous. Adeone sighed. Why couldn't he be in a foul temper without people becoming scared? He tried to shake himself out of it, but he couldn't. His actions had risked his friend's life. He sent for Wynfeld, hoping that being busy would assuage the feeling of guilt. A few minutes later, Arkyn joined him and there was an unspoken agreement that they'd handle the morning interviews together; they both had a good reason for wanting the truth.

Warned by Kenton, Wynfeld knew of his King's mood, but unlike Thomkins wasn't nervous. He'd often witnessed his King in such moods, and had, on a couple of occasions, caused them. He entered the office and saluted smartly.

Adeone glanced over. "What are they saying?"

Wynfeld knew who he meant: Hale and Melek Silvano. "Absolutely nothing, Sire. We've tried everything that won't leave a physical mark. They simply refuse to talk."

"You are convinced of their guilt?" enquired Arkyn.

"Yes, sir. I've been watching the Silvano household for many months. It's also been noted, on several occasions, that Hale and Melek have never been on speaking terms until shortly after Lord Portur's death."

Adeone nodded. "I'd have been astonished if they were. What of Silvano's conduct? Was he part of the plotting?"

"He's chastened, Sire, and has abided by all strictures in place." Wynfeld was honest. "We've no evidence he was involved. He is merely a lord who thought he was about to be made Margrave: ambitious and proud. We're sure Hale and Melek were working alone. There is one thing I must mention: Lord Silvano has never formally released Lord Melek from being his responsibility."

Adeone was astounded. "Melek is twenty-five. Sicla. That's complicated matters." He sat with his hands steepled against his mouth. "I need to see the Terazi, and I need to speak to Silvano after that. I will also have to talk to Hale and Melek, see if they admit their treason in front of me. If they don't then they will have to stand trial. Whether Silvano joins his son, I will decide after I speak with the Terazi." As Wynfeld left, Adeone cursed. He saw the confusion on Arkyn's face. "Children must be formally released from their parents' responsibility in Terasia. Technically, as Melek hasn't been, Silvano is also a traitor. Melek is still classed as a child in law here."

"That's… unfortunate."

Adeone snorted. "That's an understatement."

* * *

Half an hour later, the Terazi entered the King's office and knelt. Arkyn smiled at him as Adeone looked over.

"Thank you, Your Honour, you may rise. Before we go any further, I must thank you for the support you gave Prince Arkyn at the beginning of the review."

The Terazi was serious as he said, "Your Majesty, I did only as my conscience advised."

"Then maybe you could do so again. Has anyone informed you why I had all guests disarmed yesterday?"

"Yes, sir, a complication I would not have wished on any wedding party, let alone Lord Wealsman's."

In that instant, Adeone was disposed to like the Terazi, even though the man answered to Lord Scanlon. "Quite, Your Honour. Hale and Melek Silvano are currently refusing to answer questions. We also have a complication: Silvano never formally released Melek."

"That is unfortunate, sir. I am sure you're aware that Silvano must, therefore, take some of the blame and responsibility—"

"In my grandfather's day, he would have faced execution, Your Honour. Some might still say that is an appropriate course of action; however, I believe it would do more harm than good. This province will not benefit by being an overlord down, certainly not one whose lands are so vast. What do you advise?"

"Your Majesty, I am no advisor. I can but state the law."

Adeone liked the honesty. "Very well. Tell me the law."

"There are two courses of action, Sire: either Lord Silvano accepts all responsibility for his son's actions and stands trial alongside him, or he disowns his elder son, swears a binding fealty – one higher than truth-binding – pays a heavy fine and gives over the care and education of his remaining children into Your Majesty's hands."

Adeone got up and paced over to the window. "A heavy toll either way."

There was a knock on the door and Wynfeld entered. He saluted and watched his King's eyes; in them, he could see the disquiet that other men might have missed.

Moments later, the Terazi had moved to one side and Silvano was on his knees in front of Adeone.

"What do you know of the treason planned for yesterday, Silvano?" snapped the King.

"On my life and lordship, nothing, Your Majesty," replied Silvano. Pale, sleep deprived and visibly shaking, his voice was obviously under tight control. He knew what was at stake.

"Look at me!" commanded Adeone with such force that Arkyn jumped.

Silvano raised his gaze; he saw the King's implacable face. By the time Adeone had finished explaining his options, there was no option if he wanted his younger son to inherit. He renounced Melek and swore a speech-binding fealty. Adeone had considered a life-binding one, but no-one would ever give credence to Silvano again. Unlike Captain Haster's treachery, this was known by the world. There was also the consideration that, unlike Haster, Silvano's temperament would likely kill him through the binding. Adeone didn't need Scanlon twisting that into a form of murder. With speech-binding, Silvano could never speak against them again. His speech was bound to Adeone's wishes until Adeone or his heirs decided to release him.

When Silvano rose to leave, Adeone added, “You would do well to persuade Melek to talk to me, Silvano. Wynfeld will see you have six minutes with him. You are not to discuss anything else. I hope I’ve made myself plain.”

Once Silvano and Wynfeld had left, Adeone asked the Terazi to stay, then glanced at Arkyn. His son met his gaze, but there wasn’t equanimity in his eyes. Seeing a father disown his son had disquieted him.

Adeone crossed to him. Half-whispering so the Terazi could pretend not to hear, he said, “He’s protected his family, Arkyn – not let them starve. He had no option.”

“Surely, sir, something could have been done.”

“No. There was nothing. They weren’t estranged, they weren’t under separate roofs and they weren’t step-father and son. I’ve still got to take some action, but I can’t now strip him of his lordship or put him on trial and he knows it. These decisions are tough. I won’t lie about that, but we must make them.”

“It still seems harsh for actions not of his making.”

“Arkyn, listen to me carefully. He is responsible for the man his son has become, as I am for you and as father was for myself and Scanlon.”

“Yes, but you and Uncle Scanlon are very different.”

Adeone smiled sadly. “I had my mother’s influence as well, Arkyn. My father wasn’t as bitter with life when I was born and mine and Scanlon’s formative years were very different because of it. I grew on a crest of love, he on the crash of grief. It doesn’t excuse what he is but it does help me to understand. Your grandfather was an autocrat. There’s no other word for it. It worked for him, as you’ll remember.”

“Yes, sir, but I’m just trying to accept what’s happened.”

“I can appreciate that. If it helps, I’m not certain my father would have given Silvano a chance. He’d have had him arrested and charged and I doubt that Silvano would have offered a life-bind fealty test.”

* * *

Six minutes later, Hale entered the King’s office. He neither bowed nor knelt. Adeone eyed him steadily, but to no effect. Arkyn glanced at the senior guard with him and flicked his eyes. Dring swept Hale’s feet out from under him and the lord landed on the floor with a thud. With his hands tied behind him, he was unable to break his fall, and his nose took the impact. Dring reached over and pulled him up into a kneeling position by his hair. Blood was running down Hale’s face. The sergeant had no love of traitors and was determined to make sure they understood their actions nullified any former status. Hale’s neck was taut, his head forced back, whilst Adeone seemed supremely unconcerned.

The King said, "Hale, I'd like to advise you to make this easy. Did you now of Melek's actions on the day of my arrival? Did you plan to kill ord Wealsman yesterday? Or your daughter, come to that."

Hale kept silent and, for all his head was forced back, managed a sneer be proud of.

"I have several accounts that say you did," continued Adeone mildly. Do you wish for a prolonged ordeal? If you do not answer me today, then iere will be one. You will be handed over to my men, and a case will be repared against you for the Terazi to hear. When it comes to treason, I have hand my men almost unrestricted licence. I want the truth of the matter."

Hale stayed silent. Dring looked at the King, who raised an eyebrow. 'aking out his dagger, the sergeant pressed it against the taut flesh, not uite cutting it.

"Hale, do not make this hard on yourself for your children's sake. Did ou plan to kill Lord Wealsman?"

Hale was silent. Adeone jerked his head at the sergeant. Dring hauled ie lord to his feet and pushed him out of the room.

Adeone said to thin air, "Why is he such a bloody fool?"

"Because he hopes to be found not guilty, sir," replied the Terazi. "If he dmits it to you, he dies before the sun rises on a new day. If he goes to ial, he believes there is hope."

Adeone sighed. "I suppose that is true enough. Do you mind conducting ie trial here?"

"No, Sire. I think it might be better than having them taken to Oedran. shall look forward to whatever evidence Major Wynfeld has collated. Ie seems to me to be a remarkable officer."

Adeone said, "Thank you. I wonder if Silvano has talked any sense ito Melek."

'wo minutes later, Melek Silvano's interview went the same way as Iale's had. The only thing that made him react was the news his father had enounced him and left him to his fate. For Melek, that was the greatest etrayal. He had thought he had his father wrapped around his finger, that e'd be there to fight for him and that his influence would prevail.

When Melek had been removed, Adeone enquired, "Do you truly hink you'll ever get a confession, Wynfeld?"

"Not and leave them fit for trial, sir. We can try the psychological ricks, but I'm not hopeful."

The Terazi said, "Major, try every trick for the next week. I'll put their rial in for a fortnight later – should give scars time to heal."

Adeone turned to him. "Your Honour, there is no need for you to make uch a move."

The Terazi inclined his head. "There is every need, Sire. I value Lor Wealsman's friendship and I would that they and others realise tha silence is not an option in cases such as this."

"Then, Wynfeld, you have your orders. Terazi, thank you for all you help and advice. Prince Arkyn, please stay a moment." Once alone wit his son, he said, "What do you think comes next?"

Arkyn shrugged. "Getting Irvin out of Silvano House and then mundan paperwork."

Adeone laughed. "Yes, that about sums it up."

Before an hour was up, Irvin was relocated to Portur House. Both Adeon and Arkyn considered Wealsman wouldn't mind and Irvin certainly didn' when he realised how close it was to the library and the City Assembly, wher he'd been watching the men dig the new foundations and uncover ancien walls. He'd told Arkyn they'd found a small gold bear hidden in one wall. Wa it was proof of the old palace? Bears and power being synonymous in Terasia

When that was sorted, Kenton handed over a scroll from Wealsman Adeone unrolled it, intrigued.

Things can only get better. There's a fresh supply of whiskey in the office and I've left my cook behind so you can sample his puddings once again. If you need peace, my staff will look after you. Thank you.

Adeone tossed the note at Arkyn, who read it and smiled, despairin that Wealsman had thought about their feelings the morning after hi wedding. He poured both himself and his father a whiskey and they sa for six minutes before facing the day's mundane paperwork.

Chapter 56
DEPUTY GOVERNOR

Imperadai, Week 38 – 11th Teral, 11th Teris 1211

Adeone's Office

A WEEK LATER, Thomkins entered the Margrave's office to find the King watching the gardens.

"A confirmed list of Gerymorian and Denshirian ambassadors, Sire."

"Thank you, Thomkins; I can't wait for their arrival. Tell me something… I do not mean to interfere, but when are you going to tel your children that their mother has forsaken them?"

Thomkins for the merest second resented the question, and then remembered that the King was a father with motherless children. He'd begun to like the King, so answered honestly. "I don't know how to, sir. It would almost be better had she died."

Adeone turned to him and Thomkins saw a haunted look in his eyes and cursed himself for a fool. Maybe some pains were never eased by time.

Adeone said, "Maybe it would, but a father's duty is as hard whatever the cause of loss. Do you not think they need to know?"

"Yes, sir, I do, but there are other issues at hand."

"I do not mean to pry, Thomkins."

Thomkins broke in quickly. "I realise that, sir. I just don't know how to tell them that I'm dying and their mother wants nothing more to do with them."

Adeone's heart plummeted. He hadn't seen that coming. He realised he'd had a similar dilemma when explaining to Arkyn that Scanlon wanted to kill them all. Crossing to the decanters, he poured two whiskies, handing one to Thomkins and pointing to a chair.

"Such things are never easy, I speak from experience, but our children have the right to know the truth. They will come to terms with the knowledge, but to deny them it and then to have them left out in the cold is unforgivable, don't you think?"

"Yes, sir, it's just finding the words. I wasn't the youngest man when I married their mother and so I've always thought that she would be there for them when I've died, but now I have to face the knowledge that she won't be. They're full young to face such things."

"I know there are arguments why mine and my sons' situation is different, but the loss of a mother is still the loss of a mother. I and my sons have pulled through."

"Yes, sir, but you weren't deserted."

"I know that," whispered Adeone. "I suppose you have to make your children feel that they haven't been. You've spoken of your passing. If it isn't impertinent to enquire, how long has your doctor given you?"

"A while, sir. I should see them turn cisan-age, at least I hope to. I will have to cease work in two years, at the outside… I don't know how to tell Lord Wealsman."

"Might I suggest directly? He can then find another official secretary, not that you will be easy to replace. I remember Portur saying he was sure you were a wordsmith."

"Lord Portur was a smooth talker, Your Majesty."

"Yes, I had witnessed that side of him." Adeone sighed. "Does your brother know?"

Thomkins shook his head. "I've not had much to do with him since King Altarius took him north. He'd care for Karl and Elsa, I know, but it's getting them north when—"

Adeone put a hand on the secretary's arm. "Thomkins, *when* anything happens, Lord Wealsman will keep an eye on your children; I'll make sure of that. Having worked so hard for so many years, you're entitled to a pension. Don't force yourself to carry on working if you'd rather spend your remaining time with your children. It isn't worth the heartache."

Thomkins looked at the King, reassured by the confidence that had been given away. "I'll give Lord Wealsman my resignation in a couple of aluna-months' time as I wouldn't want anyone to think I disagree with his attaining the post. I don't. I can't think of anyone better and am pleased I've had the pleasure of working for him. I could just have done with a bit more sleep on occasion."

Adeone chuckled. "Yes, I heard he has been working hard. Now, I suppose I'd better deal with this list of ambassadors. Actually, that can wait. Can you send to Prince Arkyn and the Aedile?"

"I'm afraid Ernst's in a meeting, Your Majesty."

"Then get him out of it."

"He's chairing it, Sire," replied Thomkins uncertainly.

Adeone grinned. "Then get him out of it *politely*. After that, you can leave. I'm sure Kenton can cope. I'll see you in a couple of weeks."

Thomkins said, "Very well, sir, and… Thank you."

Adeone nodded. It had been by pure chance that he'd discovered Madam Thomkins had disowned her family – pure chance, and a spy network.

* * *

The courier sent to the Aedile was astounded when he handed Ernst the note.

Instead of getting up at once, Ernst said, "I shall be there presently."

It took him six minutes to conclude the meeting and when he presented himself at the King's office, he was sent straight in. Rising from a bow, he noticed, with equanimity, that Prince Arkyn was also there.

Adeone said, "Sit down, Ernst."

Disconcerted by the request and the fact the King had used his name, Ernst gingerly sat.

"I've been re-reading the review report and Prince Arkyn and I have been considering the only post left to fill. Lord Wealsman's deputy must be honest and reliable. Having given it thought, it seems, from *everything* that's been said, that you would be the best person to take the post."

The Aedile embodied confusion. "Pardon?" He recollected himself. "What does His Excellency say, Majesty?"

Adeone regarded him quietly. "The Margrave has accepted the idea."

"Then, as Lord Wealsman has no objection, I would be stupid to refuse. I'm not sure I'll be any good, but I'll give it a go."

Arkyn shrugged. "We think you'll cope – if you can work your way through other people's prejudice."

Adeone smiled. "I'll take your oath and then explain a few things to you." Once the oath was taken, Adeone continued, "It may interest you to know that Lord Wealsman suggested you and Prince Arkyn said he couldn't think of anyone better. The reason *I* appointed you was to keep the traditionalists happy, or not in open rebellion, at least. Whatever Lord Wealsman feels he *has* to say when he *discovers* you've been appointed, put your mind at rest. He wanted you."

Still in shock, Ernst nodded. How had he gained such status? Where did he start with the job? Who could he ask for help?

Arkyn empathised with the confusion on Ernst's face. "The former Deputy Governor's clerk will give you a quick run through of what's needed, Ernst. I say quick, but it probably won't be."

Adeone added, "We'll be sending things along to you over the next couple of weeks. If you have any questions, don't hesitate to ask to see Prince Arkyn or myself. There are various ambassadors due from Gerymor and Denshire over the next fortnight, just to add to the headaches."

The Deputy Governor pulled a resigned face. "I'm sure I'll cope, Sire."

Adeone smiled. "I hope so. Thank you, Your Excellency. That, for now, is all. Yes, you do, as you have no title, get the honorific as well."

Somewhat confused, Ernst left. Adeone chuckled to himself. Once the man got over the shock, he'd make a good Deputy Governor. Over the next fortnight, he proved it. When Adeone and Arkyn were busy talking to the ambassadors, he competently managed anything urgent. During a few hectic days, Adeone left the running of Terasia almost exclusively to him.

Chapter 57
RETURN

Imperadai, Week 40 – 25th Teral, 4th Souis 1211
Adeone's Office

LEAVING HIS FATHER'S OFFICE three weeks after the wedding, Arkyn saw Wealsman walking towards him. Smiling at each other, Arkyn held the door to the office open and, passing the papers he was carrying to Kenton, entered with Percival.

"Sire, the renegade returns."

Adeone looked up. Settling back and laying down his pen, he said, "What happened to your honeymoon, Percival?"

"I'm not here to take up the reins, you'll be sorry to hear; it's more than my life's worth. Kristina and I were talking; you were right, I didn't have much to do on the estates. She suggested we returned to Tera because I had this strange idea that I might like to spend some time in your company before you leave. That is, if you can both stand it?"

Adeone laughed. "*If* we can stand it? You mean we have the option?"

"Yes, *Your Majesty.*"

"Good. Then I'll choose to put up with your company, though I'll not speak for my son."

Arkyn grinned. "I'll cope. I'll watch you beat him at chess, father. How is Lady Wealsman, Percival?"

"Well enough. I don't think she's stopped smiling yet."

Adeone sighed. "The verdict is being returned on her father today."

Percival sat down. "She knows he is guilty, sir, and, other than the duty of feeling sad that he will die, she isn't upset. They have never got on. I think, truth be told, she will be relieved."

"I had a feeling that might be the case, but I find it is better not to try to predict a reaction to bad news. Tell me something, is her brother made in the same mould as his father?"

Wealsman regarded Adeone shrewdly. "No, Sire. He tries to please his father for an easy ride. He's not bad. Younger than Kristina. She was the eldest and therefore got the most hassle. Would you like to meet him?"

Adeone thought for a time. "Yes, but I'd rather that no-one knew we have met. Percival, maybe…"

"I can arrange a dinner and you can drop by unexpectedly, Sire."

"Yes, but people would know we had met," remarked Adeone patiently.

Arkyn passed them both a drink. "True, father, but it certainly wouldn't appear planned. He is in Tera at the moment."

Adeone raised an eyebrow. "I know."

Wealsman was momentarily disconcerted. "He thought you didn't."

Adeone smiled. "I know exactly which lords are in Tera and I am getting daily updates as to who they're talking to. I do in Oedran as well. When are you proposing this meal?"

"When would you find it easy to get away, sir?"

"Sometime next month: when you're in post; however, I should be able to get away before seven tonight, if friends didn't come and interrupt me."

"I know when I'm not wanted… I'll see you tonight then, Sire?" suggested Wealsman innocently.

"Depend upon it. That is, if Her Ladyship can cope with an unannounced visit from the King."

Straight-faced, Wealsman said, "I think she's getting used to them."

Adeone laughed. "Too true. Now go on, get out of here. Some of us have *your* work to do."

Wealsman bowed and left, grinning. Arkyn followed, picking up his documents and enquiring of Percival how he'd found his new lands. As Percival replied, he respectfully took the papers off Arkyn, carrying them to the Prince's office and staying there for some time continuing the conversation, during the course of which he managed to elicit the ıformation that Arkyn had had another note, which he hadn't mentioned › Adeone. The Prince passed it over.

Support only supports those who are toppling

Seeing Arkyn had taken it to heart, Wealsman persuaded the Prince ıat it was nonsense. Privately furious, Percival decided he would confirm ho had been leaving them and requested permission to talk to others.

Finally admitting that Wealsman needed help to say who had been ɛsponsible with any conviction, Arkyn agreed.

* * *

'wo hours later, Adeone was informed Hale and Melek Silvano had been ɔnvicted of treason. He finished working for the evening before *suddenly* eciding that, as Wealsman was in Tera, he'd visit him.

Adeone entered the drawing room where Percival, Kristina and her rother were ensconced; all three rose. The Wealsmans smiled in welcome, ut Kristina's brother paled and knelt. Adeone looked at Wealsman, who ıid lightly,

"Sire, might I present my wed-brother, Thaddeus Hale?"

"I'm pleased to meet you, Thaddeus. You may rise. Lady Wealsman, I'm ɔrry for the news you received today. I came to see if I can do anything."

Kristina remarked sadly, "It would hardly be appropriate, sir. Though, ıank you."

At an invitation from Wealsman, Adeone sat down. A servant offered im a drink and then, at a word from Wealsman, left them all alone. Adeone ɛt the goblet down on a table very deliberately. He faced Thaddeus.

"Before tonight is out, I will take your fealty. No, Percival, wait. I ıould have taken more heed to the fact that Hale didn't want you two to ıarry. I should have persuaded him instead of ordering his co-operation; ıerefore, I am proposing to implement the same fine on the Hale Lordship s I have on the Silvano one. A twelve per cent fine on your net income ɔr twelve years. Will you accept that, Thaddeus?"

Thaddeus didn't know what to say. He looked at Wealsman, who was ʌatching the King's implacable face. He glanced at Kristina, who odded. Swallowing, he agreed.

"Good. Kneel once more, please." Adeone took his honour-binding ath and then sat back down. He said to Percival, "I'm sorry. I told you ou'd get dragged into work. The other thing I came about was the half of ıe Roth lands now in my guardianship. Could you oversee them for a me? Maybe some of the income could be put to good use, to offset family xpenses, maybe; after all, yours will grow soon."

Wealsman understood the underlying message to help Thaddeus out, f necessary. "I think I could manage that, sir. Thank you."

Adeone turned to Lady Wealsman. "I promise that is all the work I shall be conducting in your house this evening."

Kristina smiled. "It is not an issue, Your Majesty. Might I invite you to stay for dinner?"

Adeone accepted the invitation. "Thank you. That would be kind. Especially if we can drop the formality. How are you finding being married to Sicla's apprentice?"

"Oh, I'm coping nicely. Have I thanked you yet for sorting out our new lands? It seems Percival is free for a time."

"Good, I'm pleased. Though both Arkyn and I thought he'd probably find something else to do…"

Gradually, the talk of the evening became increasingly informal. Thaddeus was perplexed to hear the mischievous side of the King's personality. Then Wealsman joined in and by the end of it, he was seriously wondering whether he was in the company of the King and Margrave or two boys. Kristina smiled at him, knowing what he was thinking. Any dinner at which their father had presided was strictly formal. Suddenly, he smiled back. Adeone caught the grin and winked. By the time he left for the Residence having refused a bed, they were all joking and laughing.

* * *

Adeone found Arkyn entertaining a newly arrived ambassador from Gerymor. He entered his son's rooms to find him having a pleasant time talking to another of his old 'friends'. Made even more pleasant because the official had absolutely no scruples about telling the Prince anything the King had got up to during a review. Adeone, sitting down and accepting a drink from Kadeem, eyed the official before saying,

"I see you've not changed much at all then: still the same old tattler."

The man beamed. "I've got to keep my hand in. How is Your Majesty?"

"Well – until I heard you'd arrived in my absence. I was hoping to get the chance to tell you to keep my secrets."

"I'm sorry, sir. I thought Prince Arkyn might need some entertainment in your absence. Your Highness, I take it all back, your father, the King, was the model of propriety."

Adeone merely smiled fixedly. "Now, now, I wouldn't perjure yourself. Lying in front of your King *isn't* a wise move."

"Very well, sir. Your Highness, your father, the King, was a model of propriety during his *working* day."

Arkyn merely inclined his head noncommittally.

Adeone took a sip of his drink. "There's no mischief here."

Ogilvie didn't take the hint. "Your Majesty's unannounced visit was a serious whim then?"

Adeone stilled. Ogilvie knew he'd taken things a step too far without the King having to say anything directly on the matter.

"It was hardly unexpected. I had received an invitation from Lord Wealsman. We'll talk about the Gerymorian mines tomorrow morning. I hope you have a relaxing night."

Ogilvie merely rose, and, bowing low, left.

Rather intrigued by his father's reaction, Arkyn said, "Lord Ogilvie told some interesting stories, Sire."

"Yes, I expect he did. He has the habit however of exaggerating facts. I was a lot more serious than he and Wealsman make out."

Arkyn smiled. "I know, father. I take all their stories with a pinch of salt. How well do you know him?"

"An aluna-month-long acquaintance, during the review. Since then, we've corresponded on official matters, wrapped up in unofficial chatter, but that is all. I know him well enough for him to take slight liberties, but not for that many. He is nowhere near Wealsman's standard. I'll never drop the formality around Ogilvie."

That told Arkyn everything. "He hadn't been here long enough for me to hear anything I think you would wish I hadn't, father."

Adeone raised an amused eyebrow. "How long did you suffer his company for?"

"About an hour. I mostly asked about Gerymor. It kept him off other matters. How was Percival?"

"Well enough. I've taken an honour-binding fealty from Kristina's brother and imposed a fine on the Hale Lordship, the same that I imposed on Silvano's. So, he is now Lord Hale. I know the court verdict stripped him of everything, but given all that's happened here, and the fact I've only fined Silvano, it seemed fairer and better all round. Can you get Edward to draw up the relevant paperwork for the Terazi, please? The witnesses were Percival and Kristina."

"Certainly, Sire…" He changed the subject deftly. "I had a letter from Tain earlier. He's well; still mischievous at any rate."

"I expect I'll find a tome waiting for me then. I've been looking at our trip home. Hopefully, we'll be in Oedran in plenty of time before the Munewid. I'd like to involve you in the Petitionals. They're two days of complete mayhem, but I think you should be there this time."

"I'll look forward to it, father."

"You won't by the time you've accepted the hundredth petition with a smile wrapped on a serious persona. I'll get Tain in Oedran as well. You two can have some time together before you have to do the Anaparian Review. Then I suppose I'll have to see about getting a judge to teach him. I'd rather it's one of Uncle Lachlan's old guard than one that Scanlon has appointed though. I just know Scanlon will stick his nose into the matter. He left Denshire shortly after my arrival here, an interesting coincidence—" (Arkyn suddenly yawned.) "I'll leave you to sleep."

"Sleep seems very elusive at the moment."

Adeone rang the bell, concerned. "The sooner you go to bed, the sooner you'll sleep."

Arkyn pushed himself to his feet. "I eventually get off to sleep all right. It just doesn't seem to refresh me at the moment."

Adeone also rising said, "I could always get you some official reports to read… they send me off into a deep sleep. A cold bath normally wakes me up, but then all I want to do is snuggle back into my nice, warm bed. Simkins never lets me though."

Arkyn was smiling and yawning. Kadeem, entering, took one look at him before pointedly opening the bedchamber door. Adeone left, concerned that over a season on from when Arkyn fell ill, his son was still drained. He'd certainly talk to Doctor Chapa when they returned to Oedran.

Chapter 58
CONTROVERSY

Alunadai, Week 41 – 1st Geryal, 8th Souis 1211
Adeone's Office

FOUR DAYS LATER, Adeone looked up from his desk as Kenton asked if he had time to see Wealsman, Roth, Kre and the new Deputy Governor. Rather intrigued, Adeone agreed to.

"A deputation? I hope whatever I've managed to get wrong can be put right."

All but Wealsman became worried. He said, "Your Majesty, if there's anything you've got wrong, I don't think anyone would dare tell you—"

"You would. So, gentleman, what can I do for you all?"

"Could we talk in private, sir?" enquired Wealsman.

Adeone considered him for a moment before saying, "Thank you, Kenton. I'm sure I'm physically safe enough with Their Excellencies and Lordships. Mentally… others shall judge that when Wealsman's gone." The door shut behind the secretary and Adeone became serious. "Please take a seat, gentlemen, and explain why you're here."

When seated, Wealsman explained, "Sire, we'd like your advice and guidance on a matter of importance to us all. Your Majesty and His Highness are leaving for Oedran soon. I've had organised the traditional banquet—"

"You're meant to be on your honeymoon!"

The Deputy Governor remarked dryly, "He kindly delegated the task to me, Majesty."

Adeone laughed. "All right, one to him. Go on, Wealsman."

Now with a glint in his eye, Percival continued, "As you know, sir, it's traditional to give the *reviewer* a gift." The emphasis was slight and for Adeone's ears only. "We wondered—"

"You're right, it is my son who should receive that gift."

Roth, Kre and the Deputy Governor relaxed.

Wealsman nodded. "So I thought you'd say, sir. Thank you. We've been trying to think of a fitting gift for His Highness for a while. He's done much for the province with the review."

"Yes, more than mine did. I know it, even if no-one will say it to me."

Wealsman caught his eye and grinned. "Give me chance, Sire. I was just getting to that bit."

Everyone laughed and then realised what he'd said.

Adeone rolled his eyes. "Now you're causing the disquiet, Wealsman. Get on with it and leave impudence for another day."

"Sir. As I was saying, His Highness' work has been notable, there isn't only that though. The overlords, myself, the city officials—"

Adeone said lightly, "Strange, I thought I'd made you an overlord."

Ernst, realising Adeone was in a light-hearted mood, joked, "He's in love, Sire. It does make some men forgetful."

On the sidelines, Lord Roth chuckled softly. Lord Kre looked scandalised; he'd never had much to do with the FitzAlcis and this audience wasn't going how he'd imagined it would, or should.

Adeone enquired, "Do you think there's a remedy for it?"

"Hard work, Majesty. *Very* hard work."

Wealsman muttered, "Thank you, Ernst. I'll remember that."

Adeone laughed. "No, you won't, Wealsman. We've just determined you're in love and are forgetful, if that's ever possible with you. Carry on with whatever plans you have all come up with – that is, if you can remember them."

Wealsman purposefully sounded like he was trying hard to restrain himself. "Very good, Your Majesty." He relaxed. "We feel that the events of His Highness' stay mean that something extra is required this time. We need to be seen to make reparation in some measure."

Adeone frowned. "Your Excellency, reparation is a word rarely heard and only in grievous situations."

Wealsman caught his eye. "If it had just been Roth's treachery, I would never have used it, but there has been much occurring. Not all of Terasia's making, I'll allow, but His Highness could have jumped to conclusions. His illness came on after he arrived here. He might have been poisoned, but he accepted it as an ailment. He didn't order an interrogation of all his and the Residence's staff; he could well have done so—"

Adeone knew what Percival was skirting around. "All right, Percival, I take the point."

Wealsman sighed. "That's fortunate, sir. You'll see why. I mean no disrespect."

Adeone caught his eye and there was silent humour there. Watching them, Kre realised Adeone hadn't over-exaggerated the friendship. If anything, he had understated it. Lord Roth was also wondering if that was the case. He speculated on why Wealsman had insisted on them accompanying him. Their new Margrave might have been happier explaining this in private.

Wealsman was speaking. "...We thought, after all that he's been through here, we owe him something more than the traditional fine ceramic. He's interested in the Cearcallian Era. He's read much that is in our library. The librarian has been impressed by the speed he's returned the scrolls. Anyway, we thought we'd like to make the Prince a present of a book."

The hairs on Adeone's neck stood on end. "A sensible idea, even for you, Percival, but why do I think you're about to suggest something extremely controversial?"

"Maybe because I am. We realised there is only one book that this province could give His Highness that is of the right significance – for any other he could have copied. We'd like to give His Highness the Memini's Manuscript, Your Majesty."

Adeone jumped to his feet, running his hand through his hair. He walked a few paces from his chair before turning and saying, "You do realise what this would mean?" All the men were on their feet. He tried to calm down. "That book has caused rebellions and assassinations. It caused the Age of Tyranny, or at least was a catalyst. It should have been handed to my ancestors, as tribute, twenty-five years after the province joined the empire but the lords wouldn't... the grievances, the murder of a king to keep it here and now you'll tamely hand it to my son?"

"I wouldn't say 'tamely', sir," clarified Wealsman. "We know its history. We know its worth. King Arlis permitted us to retain the book on the understanding that when we found a man of the FitzAlcis worthy of it, we should hand it to him. We feel that man is the Prince, sir... Sir?"

Adeone ignored him. "Roth, Kre, is this the feeling of *all the* overlords?"

Roth and Kre glanced at each other, they'd expected some sign of happiness, not distress, but Erlan answered honestly,

"All but Lord Silvano, Sire, and he agreed with the gift in the end."

"What were his objections before?"

"The Prince's age, sir." It was Lord Kre who had spoken.

Adeone turned to him, seeking reassurance. “He agreed in the end, ·ithout coercion?”

“Yes, Your Majesty. He knows that he has lost his influence; he is a roken man, sir. His objections ended with his son’s treachery. I believe e realised he must do something and agreeing to this might help, but never olve his situation.”

Erlan said, “Sire, my nearfather was reluctant but, I believe, it was iore in memory for my father than for himself. I truly believe that.”

“How is he, Roth?” asked Adeone.

“As Lord Kre says, broken, sir. He’s hardly seen a soul for weeks. He eeds time to adjust.”

Adeone nodded. “Keep an eye on him, my lord. You’re both in a imilar situation.”

That unsettled Kre. He’d have expected Adeone to appear more hard-earted, even in a relatively private meeting. He began to have an honest espect for the man rather than the king.

“*Has* the City Assembly *agreed*?” enquired Adeone.

Ernst nodded. “Yes, sir. We all feel the time is right and, without causing ffence, I hope the fact we aren’t presenting it to a king should help dispel ny curse on it.”

Adeone tilted his head. “I shall accept the point without offence.” He ank onto his chair. “If you are all determined, and I see you are, then I an’t advise my son to refuse the honour, but I hope you can understand ·hy I am hesitant.”

“Your Majesty, we do understand,” Wealsman said reassuringly, “and , for one, would like to thank you for that hesitancy. It has reinforced, in ıy mind, that we are doing the right thing.”

“That’s the kind of twisted logic that I expect from you, Percival.”

Wealsman caught the King’s eye and smiled wryly, “That’s me, sir, wisted,” but he saw the initial reaction draining from his friend. “Also, or once, that’s all I needed to see Your Majesty about.”

Relieved, Adeone nodded. “Thank you, gentleman. Please continue to eep this matter private. Wealsman, as you seem to have decided to ignore ıy instructions regarding your honeymoon, I’d like a word.”

The other three left. Wealsman poured Adeone a drink. He put it down nd squeezed the King’s shoulder. “Thank you for agreeing. I couldn’t hink of anything else when I’d thought of this.”

Adeone said, “Do you know how much blood has been spilt for ossession of that book?”

Wealsman took a deep breath. “After reading what it would allow me o, I have a fair idea.”

“Ah. So you are a memor then. I’ve wondered for a while.”

"Yes, and I'd rather that book never betrayed the fact. I thought it could be safe at Ceardlann. No-one can fight for it there. Put it with the Skifta's Sword and—"

"Percival, I don't *know* if you're doing the right thing."

"If I'm not, I'll be the infamous one in our history books. I just don't know whether to warn Arkyn."

Adeone groaned. "Neither do I. I'd say let his reaction be honest. Percival, I think I should explain something to you…"

Wealsman's apprehension was soon eclipsed by Adeone's revelation that he was a medium and had, on the night of his arrival, seen Sansky standing by Wealsman's shoulder. Later, when Kristina noticed his thoughtful mood, all he'd say was that it was interesting to find that friends could still astound him.

* * *

Meanwhile, Adeone had sent for Wynfeld and informed him of what had been agreed. After the shock had worn off, Wynfeld became his normal practical self and asked what his King wanted doing about transporting the manuscript back to Oedran.

Once they'd discussed the details, Adeone said, "Your Prince requested the name of a sergeant to promote to captain, I believe, Wynfeld. One to act as liaison with the fort here for the Margrave's protection."

"Yes, sir. We all think Dring would be best."

"Then see I get his commission to sign as soon as possible. After what Wealsman's proposed, he might well find a few disgruntled Terasians around. Not everyone will be happy that he's giving us their greatest treasure. I'd rather no accident befell him quite yet. By the way, I understand from the Exarch that Jones wants to move on."

Wynfeld nodded. "Yes, sir. I thought Paras – to guard the Domini."

Adeone eyed the Major. "I'm sure the fact that your Prince is undertaking the next review in that city has nothing to do with the decision."

Wynfeld grinned. "Of course not, sir. Whilst we're talking of the movement of men, sir—"

After a brief knock, Arkyn entered the office. Wynfeld rose and saluted.

Adeone raised an eyebrow. "Whatever that document is, it can wait. Wynfeld's about to ask for something, I can tell by the look in his eye."

Arkyn chuckled. "So can I, Sire. What is it, Major?"

"Nothing disastrous, sir," replied Wynfeld, "but maybe momentous. I think I've got a sensor at the fort here. Corporal Butterworth thinks that he may be a medium, but there's more to him than that. He spotted the kitchen lad that first day; he helped discover that Melek Silvano was responsible for the dagger—"

Adeone interrupted, "What else has he 'discovered', Wynfeld? I don't mean the small things; I mean about people here."

Wynfeld paused; his King's tone had been harsh. "Your Majesty, I don't know if I should—"

Glancing at his father's set face, Arkyn snapped, "Major, the King just asked you a direct question – *answer it!*"

Wynfeld said, "Apparently, Ull's Legacy affects Lady Daia, Lord Irvin and Lord Wealsman, Sire. Lord Wealsman is probably a spirit holder; the others have hues. He says that there are a couple more people here, but he can't pinpoint who."

"When did he say that, Major?"

"The last three nights ago, sir. He was guarding the gates here – as for his conclusions before that, a few weeks ago."

Adeone got up and paced over to the window, his back to the room. "Confine him to the fort until we've left. I don't care what excuse you use, but you'll not tell him that is my order. Do you understand?"

Wynfeld was puzzled. "Sir? For what reason? He could be useful; I was going to ask to take him north with us."

"No! Send him elsewhere, promote him to sergeant. I don't want him anywhere near Oedran. I want your assurance that you'll do it."

Confused and perplexed, Wynfeld said, "You have it, Sire, but might I have some explanation?"

Arkyn watched his father's back. "You have your orders, Major, and if you question His Majesty again, I'll have you court-martialled."

Wynfeld took the hint and, saluting, left, for once annoyed that his King wouldn't explain his reasons.

Arkyn said, "He's gone, Sire."

"I'm sorry for that, Arkyn, but don't trust in magic to rule. Now, I've got to get on. Leave whatever it is on my desk."

Disconcerted by the abrupt dismissal, Arkyn left. Adeone collapsed into his chair. Who was the second unknown? He was the first. Would he ever know, or wasn't there enough time to find out? Was his son the second? Did he have a hue or spirit? Either way, he probably owed him and Wynfeld an apology.

Chapter 59
FINAL NIGHT

Septadai, Week 41 – 7th Geryal, 14th Souis 1211
Margrave's Residence

SEPTADAI DAWNED with the hints of a clear day. Wealsman had been back at his post for a couple of days and, much as they'd happily stay for longer, Adeone and Arkyn would be setting out for Oedran the following day to leave enough time for contingencies. Breakfasting together, Adeone talked Arkyn through the obligations to the province they were leaving and the protocol surrounding the leaving feast, including not refusing the gift offered.

Overseeing the final preparations for their journey, Arkyn could almost taste the tension building. Something was going to happen that night, and he didn't know what. After events in Tera, he wanted to be safely in Oedran, or, more preferably, at Ceardlann. Wishing the evening was over, he dressed with extra care. With his father in the city, he didn't like the idea of being found wanting.

Adeone wouldn't have noticed. What Wealsman planned would be one of the most momentous events of the century so far, probably the most momentous gift given to a reviewer in well over a century, if not in centuries. One of the last known treasures of the Cearcall, still at large in the lands, would join the others ensconced at Ceardlann, behind heavy protection.

The King and Prince entered the Margrave's Hall; their gaze taking in the decorations, tables, dais and a newly placed pedestal at the feet of the dais steps and central to the hall, covered by a rich cloth of black and gold. Percival and Ernst had done their province proud. The magnificence of the hall manifested itself, more so than it had at any other time during the Prince's visit. Percival walked over to greet them and Adeone made a joke. Arkyn relaxed. How could he have been nervous? Percival was still the same. His father's presence was supportive and the hall welcoming.

They made their way to the dais. Adeone seated himself without a word at the centre of the long table. Arkyn on his right followed suit. All the overlords then sat, leaving only Wealsman on his feet at the King's left hand. Gradually the guests fell silent, ears open for Percival's speech. Whether they knew what was coming or not, they all realised that the occasion would be momentous.

Wealsman's nerves didn't show. He recalled all the other banquets from the visit, all the other moments and speeches. Could he do this event the justice it deserved? Rarely did anyone get the chance to know they were about to make history.

In a mellow voice, one which suited the atmosphere and the coming event, he said, "Your Majesty, Highness, my lords, ladies and dignitaries, welcome, once more, to this hall and Court. A feast awaits, but I must ask for your tolerance in allowing me to speak first. Your Majesty, further to an earlier conversation, my speech is still directed to our Prince. Your Highness, all in Tera and Terasia, will be sorry to see you depart on the morrow. Your strength and good humour through all the tribulations of your visit has been an example and inspiration to us all. None here could ever have predicted a worse beginning to your visit, none can condone it. Your resolve in facing that event was worthy of your ancestors and has provided much anticipation for the years ahead. I hope that you do not mind me saying this, but your illness was a matter of distress for many Terasians. Nothing could have been hoped for more at the time than a swift and full recovery. You returned to your duties with an unfailing enthusiasm, and a will to see those duties through to the conclusion you wished for. I can speak with some authority when I say that your efforts for Terasia were relentless. The added duty of finding a new governor for this province is a job that many men would have baulked at, but Your Highness dealt with it practically; I, for one, can't complain about your choice. Actually, having seen my desk, I might just have to retract that."

The laugh he wanted resounded.

Arkyn watched him with anticipation, hating being spoken about. "Careful, Your Excellency, I might change my mind."

Wealsman bowed slightly. "It is your prerogative, sir. As I was saying, though, your decisions have only benefited this province, although events might have made you take a different course. The review was a masterpiece, one that will be remembered in Terasia for many years. I think I can speak for the province when I say that we feel only gratitude. The tradition that the provincial reviewer receives a gift from the province he has visited is as old as the empire. Terasia's gift is normally the domain of the Margrave. As this province has been without a governor for some months, all the overlords and City Assembly officials have had a say in our gift. All have agreed to it. A break with tradition this might have been but one I hope all can understand. Terasia has been part of the empire for centuries. For those centuries, our greatest treasure has remained here, against all odds; its worth, as tribute, is great – its worth as a gift even greater and it says what we wish to say to you, sir, better than anyone here can express it. In thanks for all your endeavours on our part, in thanks for your statesmanship and good humour through all you have suffered, we in Terasia would like to make *you* a gift of the Memini's Manuscript."

He gave a curt nod and a covering was removed from a pedestal at the foot of the dais. The manuscript with its new inlaid box stood there for all to see. The box alone was worth a lord's ransom, the manuscript a province's.

Arkyn stared, blinked, coughed, and took a drink of water. He couldn't think, couldn't speak. For a few seconds, he found it hard even to focus.

Percival smiled. "Your Highness, I think we can all see you are speechless, but let me put your mind at rest; you didn't mishear. From this day forth, the Memini's Manuscript is your property. His Majesty has forgone all claim to it."

Still dumbfounded, Arkyn glanced at his father.

Adeone verified Wealsman's words. "It is a gift freely given by Terasia."

Arkyn swallowed. Distressed, he found his voice. "I cannot be the man of legend this would suggest. I thank you for the compliments, Your Excellency, but I cannot..."

He looked at Adeone, whose features clearly said it was Arkyn's decision, but his eyes held the merest trace of a warning.

Arkyn took a breath. Aware of what the day meant, he rose from his seat, shaking. "Your Excellency, as you have said, I was speechless. Part of me still is. I cannot find the words to express what I feel about the honour you have done me. I have enjoyed my time here, truly – all events aside – I have found Terasia to be welcoming. It has been a pleasure to work with you and for this province. I have no wish to rebuff your thanks. I have only respect for this province; therefore, although I might think the ceramic more appropriate, I shall accept your gift with many thanks, many, many thanks. I hope I can prove worthy of it over the coming years."

As Arkyn re-seated himself, his stomach churning, every person in the hall, guests and servants, started clapping.

When the noise quietened, the Margrave replied, "Your Highness, your acceptance of the Memini's Manuscript honours our province as much as we wish to honour you. Not in tribute, but in respect, this gift is given."

With that, he seated himself and motioned to the servers.

Adeone considered his son with a mixture of concern and pride. Ignoring the assembly, he got up. As everyone else rose, Adeone took his son firmly by the shoulders, looked into his eyes, and pulled him into a hug. When his head was by his son's ear, he whispered, "Your mother would have been exceptionally proud of you."

Arkyn turned his head so that his face was hidden from the room. Father and son broke apart and nodded at each other.

Wealsman realised Adeone had been right not to warn Arkyn. Everything the Prince was showing was genuine: the shock, the emotion, the complete incredulity – not even a consummate actor could have recreated it. It was the truth, and it was what they needed to see.

Adeone and Arkyn had sat back down – Arkyn still in shock. Kadeem epped forward and passed the Prince a goblet of warmed wine. Arkyn hook his head.

"No, thank you, Kadeem. I want to feel this. I'll drink water for now."

Kadeem bowed and left again, smiling. The whole of the dais had eard, or were told, what the Prince's words had been. Unconsciously, rkyn had just increased his standing.

* * *

y the time the feast was over and the dancing had begun, Arkyn needed breath of air. Excusing himself adroitly, he got up and walked from the all. Adeone caught Wynfeld's eye and made a small gesture meaning e Major followed his Prince.

Arkyn entered the Residence courtyard and the first still night of spring. hen the last vestiges of winter breeze blowing from the mountains rippled round him and he shivered, wrapping his arms around himself for armth. Wynfeld who'd stood by the door watching the shadows and his rince took his official cloak and draped it around Arkyn's shoulders.

Without looking at him, Arkyn said, "Thank you, Wynfeld. Why did ey do it?"

"Because they think you're the right man for the honour, sir."

"I'm nothing special. I'm sixteen! I've been standing here trying to athom it out. Can I ever truly absorb the fact that they gave me such a gift?"

Wynfeld smiled. "At the risk of sounding like Kadeem, sir, in time it ill become clear. Everything happens for a reason."

Arkyn laughed. "You do sound like Kadeem. All we need now is the ne about the fact that the reason might be clouded, but in time, those louds will part."

"Or it'll start raining."

"You're incorrigible, Major. Was it *their* choice?"

"Yes, sir, but there was a deputation to His Majesty to inform him eforehand."

"I'd guessed as much. Why didn't he warn me?"

Wynfeld felt uneasy. He didn't like predicting his King's reasons. "I on't know, sir. I might suggest it was because reactions to such moments hould be honest and unstudied. It can reveal much of one's character."

Arkyn sighed. "I hate to imagine what everyone just learnt of mine. I uppose I'd better get back to the hall. I must talk to Lord Wealsman and ake my leave of the overlords and Deputy Governor."

* * *

t the door, Arkyn shook his head at the Master of Ceremonies to stop he gentleman announcing him. Instead, he padded over to the pedestal t the base of the dais. He gently ran his hand over the book. The aged leather barely seemed to hold together and yet there was no weakness about the volume. In the light of the candles now surrounding the book embossed lettering stood out clearly.

FOR ALL IS TRUTH BETWEEN THESE PAGES,
HANDED DOWN THROUGH THE AGES,
ALL THE VAGARIES OF OUR PAST,
LONG MAY THESE OUR STORIES LAST.

He fancied it tingled beneath his touch, but it was most likely dormant excitement. Irvin was close by, talking with Daia, and they caught the Prince's eye, smiling discreetly. Irvin especially would sell his soul to open the book; it must contain some of the greatest stories ever untold.

An arm went about his shoulders. His father stood beside him. It was a few moments before the appreciative silence was broken.

Adeone said, "Come, we have duties to perform."

Arkyn sighed. "I could look at this all night."

"Yes, I know, but we do have a ride ahead of us tomorrow. There'll be time enough in the years to come." He murmured, "You'll have to put it in its new box and seal it. Might I suggest you do it now?"

Arkyn nodded. If the book wasn't on display, he wouldn't be so distracted. The King called for wax and Arkyn was aware not only of the silent magnificence of the hall but also of the interested watchers and the genuine feeling of expectation. He found he was shaking too much; suddenly he was as nervous as he had been when he'd heard the conclusion of Wealsman's speech. He swallowed and tried to master the nerves. He couldn't.

He turned to Wealsman. "Your Excellency, for the honour of Terasia will you not lift this precious gift to its new resting place?"

Adeone smiled, a neat solution. Wealsman stepped forward. As he lifted the book, it seemed to warm to his touch. He laid it carefully, reverently in its new casing saying, "For Terasia, a gift freely given."

Arkyn, hands still shaking, pulled the lacings of the box shut and then applying his seal to the ends, said, "In thanks and in gratitude, a promise to keep this gift safe, for *all* our descendants yet to be born – for this gift is their history as much as ours. Terasians, one and all, I thank you."

With that, the wax cooled, and Arkyn ran his hand over the box. He stood back a pace and nodded to Thomas and Alan. They put the case on a stretcher-like board covered in black and gold velvet and passed out of the hall. Arkyn sighed with relief and turned to Wealsman. Two moments later the hall was, once more, full of dancing couples. Wealsman, though, had one more surprise.

Very quietly he said, "Sire, Your Highness, I've a confession to make…"

Adeone and Arkyn exchanged a glance, turned back to Percival and each raised an eyebrow.

Wealsman grinned. "The Manuscript was Terasia's gift to His Highness, but I *am* the Margrave and I have traditions to fulfil, especially as I owe you both so much. In each of your rooms should be a gift from myself and Kristina. I hope you're not too upset with me to accept them."

Adeone laughed. "I bet mine's a cask of whiskey."

Wealsman said, nonplussed, "There might be that there, yes, Sire. Plus, several fine, very thin, glass goblets from Denshire, so much better for examining the colour—"

"Do you have any respect for the ceramic tradition of your country?"

"Certainly, sir, as His Highness will discover."

"As father guessed, so shall I try," mused Arkyn. "It will be specific and personal and with an irony to my visit. This visit has been a maze of sidesteps and a game of chance and tactics; therefore, I suspect my gift is a chess set – either made of ceramic, or the board at least made of that. How close am I, Percival?"

Wealsman muttered, "Remind me never to play cards with either of you. How did you *both* guess? I sense a trick."

Arkyn chuckled and looked at his father.

"Did I forget to mention that the head of my spies is currently stationed in Terasia?" asked Adeone innocently.

"Not exactly, sir. You forgot to mention he was watching my every move," muttered Wealsman, surveying the hall.

Arkyn laughed. "He wasn't, so don't worry, Percival. We hadn't a clue, but let's say as you know us so we know you."

Wealsman smiled. "I can live with that, Your Highness."

Adeone nodded. "That's lucky because it's the best offer that you'll get. Come on, our duties await."

"You could be deaf, sir."

"Percival Wealsman, you'll not catch me that way twice! Especially not as we're meant to be responsible."

Arkyn struggled to keep a straight face. "Am I meant to be sensible then, Sire?"

Adeone sighed. "No, but I hoped you wouldn't follow my example."

Laughing, the three of them made their way along the dais. Silvano knelt when Adeone reached him. Seeing the pallor of the overlord's face, Adeone raised him by his elbow and murmured a few reassuring words. Silvano's face cleared. All the reprisals for his son's treachery had been taken and there would be no more. They reached Lord Roth and he too knelt. Adeone raised him also and made the same promise. Erlan's face, though it hadn't been so haunted, became less preoccupied.

Arkyn said to him, "Thank you for your hard work, my lord."
Lord Roth smiled. "Your Highness, I could do no other."
"I hope to see you again one day – maybe in Oedran?"
"It would be a pleasure, sir."
By the time they left the hall together and walked companionably back through the Residence Adeone and Arkyn were exhausted.

* * *

At the top of the stairs, instead of each going their own way, the Prince invited his father for a drink. Realising his son needed time to unwind, Adeone accepted.

After talking about the events of the feast, Arkyn admitted, "If there's one thing I regret, father, it's not finding out who left those notes. They've been puzzling me for months. I found one earlier that said, *'All events are corrupted by history'*."

Adeone regarded him. "Wealsman's given me a report of his thoughts. I'm pretty certain I know who left both sets."

Arkyn frowned. "Why didn't he give me the report?"

"I thought you'd been troubled enough by them already. I'll give you the report to read, if you want it, but I'd rather wait until we're in Oedran. We can deal with both sets at the same time, and I want to see if Landis' conclusions are the same as Wealsman's and Wynfeld's. The last one I got said that *'Loyalty is but a servant to respect and respect must be earned before peace will reign. Respect can't be bought'*. Not bad, I thought, certainly getting more philosophical, aren't they?"

"That's one way of putting it, sir. I'd have thought you'd have wanted the men arrested."

Adeone shrugged. "I do, but I also want to be sure. The notes aren't outwardly threatening, more factual, but they are still malicious. I cannot in this case order execution, as any judge would tell you, but I want to take advice; I'm thinking of inviting James Tancred to dinner. He'll tell me truly what I can do."

"Couldn't we deal with it through our household rules?"

"Yes, we could," admitted Adeone. "Have you discounted the guards?"

"All right then, through military law – they're still our staff."

"Yes, they are. If I might make a suggestion, you should think about what reprisals you could take under our household rules and military ones. You need to decide how these letters have affected you."

Having almost been poisoned twice, ordered executions, and seen men die in front of him, the notes hadn't been the worst of Arkyn's experiences and, much as they had affected him, no-one had died. "I suppose they haven't. They were a nuisance more than a problem."

Adeone eyed him. "Tell me, when did you first have a nightmare?"

"How did—?"

"Kadeem and Wealsman are worried. Kadeem had to answer my questions and Wealsman knows what suffering from nightmares can be like. He used to be paralysed by them."

Arkyn bit back anger. Kadeem couldn't refuse to answer questions and Wealsman obviously empathised more than he'd suspected. "I had them when I was younger."

Adeone held his gaze. "All children suffer at one time or another. You hadn't had one for years before this trip. I could put it down to extra duties, but I'm not convinced it was. *When* was your first nightmare?"

Arkyn sighed, defeated. He could twist and turn, but his father would get the answer out of him; if he'd been talking with Percival, he already knew. "The first evening I was taking notice of the world after my illness. Wealsman was there."

Adeone took his son by his shoulders. "Arkyn, look at me, look me in the eye and tell me you don't believe that the note found that night was responsible for that nightmare."

Arkyn swallowed and held his father's gaze. Suddenly he couldn't lie. "It was responsible for it, wasn't it?"

"Yes, which means the note has caused you distress, lasting distress. That is against everything—"

"Yet if it wasn't the fact that I'm FitzAlcis, it wouldn't matter—"

"The point is, that you *are* FitzAlcis. The empire has expectations of us, Arkyn. If we don't act, then we lay ourselves open to greater hurts, greater wrongs. Even in the empire's laws are writs against such letters as we have received. Not all crime is physical." Adeone laughed at Arkyn's puzzlement. "Thank your stars that your brother will be the one who has to work out those intricacies. Now, I'd suggest you ask for your household book at some point soon and have a read of it."

"Father, just tell me one thing. Is it Kadeem or Edward?"

"Not if our information is correct." (Arkyn sagged with relief.) "There's never any guarantee that they won't turn traitor at some point. Remember, never get too close to them."

"I know that, sir, I just… After everything they've done for me this year, I was dreading the possibility it was one of them."

Adeone nodded. "Put your mind at rest. We'll deal with it in Oedran. Until then, you've got to work out how to come to terms with the fact you own the Memini's Manuscript. I'll leave you to rest."

"By considering it as history's. I'm only its guardian."

"I really ought to do something about Kadeem's influence on you."

Chapter 60
TAKING LEAVE

Alunadai, Week 42 - 8th Geryal, 15th Souis 1211
Margrave's Residence

AS ADEONE AND ARKYN took what sleep they could, the members of their household, who hadn't been acting as servers at the feast the night before, finished packing their personal effects. Some of the heavier luggage had already been sent on its way, but there was still an impressive array of carts, more than on Arkyn's trip down, for now there was not only the Prince and his household but the King, Lord Irvin and Major Wynfeld – all with associated luggage and attendants. Wynfeld, viewing the melee, groaned. The idea of getting it all the length of the empire was a feat he wished others could have undertaken. He'd move a regiment without a second thought, for the men were disciplined and knew where they all had to be and what they all had to be doing, but civilians were another matter. Fitz walked up behind him and clapped him on the shoulder,

"Don't worry, Major, it'll be a military exercise soon enough."

Wynfeld laughed. "You'll give me a bad name, Fitz."

"No, merely a sensible one. Approach it like a military exercise. It's the only way, *trust me.* I've moved the FitzAlcis more times than I care to think about. Their staff will be organised; Simkins and Kadeem have seen to that."

Wynfeld nodded. "I can imagine they have. I've borrowed a secure chest for the Memini's Manuscript."

"Good. We don't want that going missing. What did the King work out for it?"

Wynfeld lowered his voice. "There are a few pieces of furniture that Wealsman's said he'll send on by sea. The manuscript is going with them; if there *are* bandits in Areal, it should be safer."

"Makes you wonder why we don't go by ship as well."

Still talking quietly, Wynfeld said, "I expect it's because our Prince should meet as many of the Arealian lords as possible – as well as anyone else en route. We've a couple of hours yet, breakfast?"

"The army doesn't march on an empty stomach. Well, not recently."

* * *

Arkyn awoke when Kadeem called him from sleep. He looked for the last time at the ceiling over his bed.

"For all I wish to be home, I'll be almost sorry to leave here."

Drawing the curtains, Kadeem smiled. "We've been here a while, sir. 's understandable. Even the dampest of places can worm their way into person's heart."

"True. I won't miss the damp. Are we ready to leave?"

"I believe so, sir. I saw Major Wynfeld and Fitz getting their breakfast short while ago; therefore, I surmise, they're happy with arrangements. ord Wealsman is also making sure we're in the right places at the right mes. His Excellency and Lady Wealsman have invited Your Highness nd His Majesty to breakfast with them."

"I shouldn't keep them waiting then. That many honorifics in one entence normally means I'm in trouble if I do."

short time later, Arkyn entered Wealsman's dining room and smiled at is father and the Margrave. Daia was also there, talking softly with ristina. He seated himself by his father and had the strange sensation the pic of conversation had been changed to the subject of their trip north. Nevertheless, he happily immersed himself in the issue until Wealsman's ervants served their breakfast. As they finished, Simkins informed them hat Irvin had arrived with his luggage. Adeone and Arkyn made their ersonal farewells before they left Wealsman's rooms. There would be no ue privacy once they were in the Residence courtyard.

The entrance hall was full of clerks and Residence staff, each and every ne of them bowed as Adeone and Arkyn walked through their midst aying their farewells to those they recognised. Outside, Irvin was talking Karl and Elsa. Arkyn glanced over and, excusing himself to his father, vent to say goodbye to the twins. He saw Karl put a miniature golden bear nto his belt pouch with a grin at Irvin. The twins beamed when Arkyn eached them.

"Take care of yourselves, twins. I'll miss our talks."

Karl nodded, but, as always, Elsa was the spokesperson.

"We'll miss them too, sir." She then held out a small ceramic pendant vith a bear's paw print stamped on it. "For you, sir, for luck. We won't eed it travelling to Gerymor anymore."

Arkyn, who'd heard from his father that the twins would be staying in 'erasia, was touched. "Thank you. I'll wear it always."

"That's the idea, sir."

He laughed and gave them both a hug. "Well, we're for Oedran. Keep miling, twins. Come on, Irvin, the King's waiting."

Having unobtrusively watched the scene, Adeone could tell that rkyn had missed his brother and was glad he'd found friendship with he twins. When the Prince reached him, he said, "All ready?"

"Yes, Sire, it seems like it. Thank you, Kadeem."

He swung his cloak around his shoulders and then put the pendant Elsa had given him over his head, tucking it safely beneath his tunic. Adeone wondered if Arkyn was truly unaware of what such honest actions told everyone around them. Arkyn, on the other hand, thought the twins deserved to see he meant what he said. He had been as touched by their offering as he had been dumbfounded by the Memini's Manuscript.

Adeone turned to Wealsman and held out his hand. "Your Excellency you can get to work without interference now."

Wealsman took the offered hand and, kneeling, kissed the signet ring "My king, I would rather have your interference than your absence."

Adeone applied the merest pressure to get Percival back to his feet. "I'l remind you of that one day, my friend."

Wealsman merely inclined his head. "I'm sure the day can't be soon enough, Sire." Thinking that Adeone would soon throttle him, he turned to Arkyn. "Your Highness, words can't express what we feel at your leaving."

"You mean there aren't enough synonyms for 'glad', Your Excellency?"

Adeone laughed.

Wealsman couldn't keep a straight face. "Or rather for its rhyme of sad, sir. I hope your ancestors watch over your journey and return you safely to Oedran."

Arkyn knew that he shouldn't but he couldn't help but lighten the tone. "We'll be out of your way there, Your Excellency." He sobered "Thank you, Wealsman, for all you've done. This visit would have been very different, not to mention more difficult, without your support."

Wealsman merely bowed. He had a couple of words with Irvin, who'd been saying goodbye to Daia, and then turned to Major Wynfeld. "Keep them safe."

"I'll do my best. I've left Dring in charge of Your Excellency's guards."

In the voice of one who wants an explanation for something he should have seen coming, Wealsman said, "My guards?"

Adeone and Arkyn were suddenly having an intense discussion Arkyn finally caught his eye and winked. Wealsman sighed.

"My guards. Right. Thank you, Major. I'm sure Sergeant Dring and I shall get on well."

Wynfeld chuckled. "Captain Dring, Your Excellency – our King promoted him."

Wealsman shook his head as though to rid it of the unbelievable. He watched as Adeone and Arkyn swung themselves into the saddle followed by all their entourage. He was by the King's horse and Adeone gripped his shoulder tightly.

"Look after yourself, Percival."

"You too, Adeone. Ride safely."

He took a step back as Adeone urged his horse forward. Arkyn glanced round when they reached the gate; he saw Percival with his arm around Kristina watching them leave and Daia talking to the Thomkins twins.

Chapter 61
A CLEAR ROAD?
Evening
Terasia

THAT EVENING, they overnighted at a small fort: Edgewood; whose captain was all too aware of the status of his guests. Even if it hadn't been the King and elder Prince, there was Major Wynfeld, enough of a visitation on his own. Adeone noticed the relative ease with which he and his son were greeted as opposed to the anticipation with which Wynfeld was. Was it a good thing or not? It probably was. Junior officers should obey the senior ones. He would give those senior officers their orders.

That night Adeone, Arkyn and Wynfeld looked over their route for the following days. They'd pass from Terasia into southern Areal, characterised by gentle slopes and weather perfect for growing grapes. There was nothing to cause concern there. No hiding places for trouble to congregate. They were all wary. Scanlon knew where they were. If the three of them met trouble on the road, it could hand him the empire.

* * *

Nine days later, they overnighted at Myddlenor Fort, at the border of the Arealian Tribute and Laird Skaner's lands. Here, the landscape was more troublesome with dense thickets, a few gorges and fast flowing tributaries of the River Arden. Looking over the maps with Arkyn and Wynfeld, Adeone was impressed at the speed with which Wynfeld located spots for trouble. Several scouting parties were despatched and Adeone postponed their journey for another day. The parties returned far from empty handed.

Adeone crooked an eyebrow at Captain Sanders. "How many?"

"Five alive, three dead, Sire. We think there's more in the region. I've patrols on the road. We found this lot napping at their camp. Along with quite a lot of gold, all neatly stored in bamboo casings—"

"Show me," interrupted Arkyn. Once he had some in his hand, he said, "This is Terasian tax, Sire."

Adeone nodded. "Sanders, see it sent to Terasia forthwith for the attention of the Margrave. As to these bandits, give them over to the law when we're away." After Sanders saluted and left, Adeone asked, mischievously, "Do I ask the bandits how they obtained Terasian tax?"

Arkyn said, "Is there any doubt, Sire? Someone, close to home, gave it to them. Or, at any rate, made sure they received it."

"Yes, I thought so too. I wonder if he'll save them?"

"Probably not. They've failed him. He'll see they hang for it, if only so the next group try a bit harder."

Adeone sighed. "Most likely. At least we can set out again at first light. We should, therefore, get an early night. Wynfeld, stay a moment. I want a word."

Watching his elder son leave, Adeone pursed his lips. Arkyn was certainly giving a good impression of a normal sixteen-year-old, but it was clearly an act. He'd see Chapa when they reached Oedran. The journey north wasn't the right time to state his concerns.

He looked at Wynfeld. "Get Sanders." Once the captain was in front of him again, Adeone said, "I've been having reports handed to me all year about bandits in Areal, Sanders. Why did it take our arrival for you to send men out?"

Sanders blinked hard. "I… We had searched before, sir, but without success."

"Yet today you found men napping in their camp. That was strangely fortunate, wasn't it? Remarkably well timed. Major Wynfeld will be talking to you about why this isn't acceptable. I should not have to delay our journey for you to search the countryside. Do I make myself plain?"

"Yes, Your Majesty. I shall resign."

"No, you won't. That won't fix the issue. If I hear any other reports of bandits in this region of Areal, I will reconsider your position. You can leave." Once he'd gone, Adeone frowned. "Major, see this situation isn't repeated as we ride north, please. That's all for today."

Wynfeld saluted, left and went to despatch riders north. Every fort was tasked with making the capture of bandits and felons their priority.

* * *

Scanlon heard about the failed attempt later that evening. His reaction wasn't placid. His plans had been set back years through lack of funds, and it was unlikely Adeone and Arkyn would meet the accidents he'd planned on the road. Being so distressed, he made sure others felt it.

His closest private advisor, careful of his own skin, followed orders. He was left with the dilemma of how to placate a man who had just proved himself capable of killing another with his bare hands. The fact the dead man had been condemned anyway was an issue Bantling didn't think was relevant to his current predicament.

Once the initial rage had dissipated, Scanlon began to rebuild his plans. It was important that when he finally attained his goal, it should appear an unfortunate accident. Adeone was being remarkably obliging by not announcing their feud. There was a strange traditional honour that intrigued Scanlon, for Adeone had no respect for tradition. The Terasian Review showed Arkyn was made in the same mould. All the better. He had the support of several men on the understanding he would restore traditions beneficial to men of rank.

Chapter 62
REACHING OEDRAN

Imperadai, Week 45 – 4th Lufial, 18th Geryis 1211
Anapara

ADEONE AND ARKYN SET OFF on the final leg of their journey, glad that, since Myddlenor, their expedition north had been uneventful. No fort on their route had wanted to be found negligent, so every person was stopped and asked their business on the road. Some complained, Adeone didn't. The Lords of Areal, who hosted or rode with them for a day, were also remarkably correct, although, on a couple of occasions, Adeone told Arkyn that they weren't to be trusted. Arkyn accepted the advice, knowing that his father would have evidence to support the supposition.

As the silver pine waymarker for the Rex Dallin came into view, Adeone and Arkyn decided that they'd much prefer the quicker route. Everyone else would take the slower road, but they would go via Ceardlann. The only people with permission for the valley were Fitz, Hillbeck, Edward, Kadeem and Simkins. They'd leave Major Wynfeld and Lord Irvin jointly in charge of everything else, with strict instructions to reach Oedran by the following day.

Wynfeld hesitated. "Sire, you have no guards."

Adeone smiled. "We have Fitz and Hillbeck and the resident guards will meet us near the gate." He saw Wynfeld's face. "Fine, send four with us to the gate. They'll just have to catch you up later."

Satisfied, Wynfeld carried on towards Carnford and ultimately Oedran.

Once in the Rex Dallin, Fitz asked innocently, "Shall I ride to the lodge and get the guards, sir?"

"Don't you dare," replied Adeone, to general chuckles. "It's good to be home."

"You've fifteen miles yet."

Arkyn smirked. "*We've* fifteen miles, Fitz. You're not getting out of it."

Feeling remarkably relaxed and carefree, they rode through the Rex Dallin at a quick pace, greeting anyone they met. It was the middle of the evening and they were within three miles of Ceardlann when Adeone looked at Arkyn and saw his exhaustion. He decided he wanted to talk to Landis and Chapa. He turned to his son.

"I'm going to ride on tonight. Bring Tain and Elantha with you tomorrow. I'd like to see them, but I get the feeling I should be in Oedran."

Arkyn nodded. "Right, father. I hope everything is well."

Taking Hillbeck and Simkins, Adeone started down a different path towards the Pillars of Alcis and the road to Oedran. Arkyn looked at Fitz.

"*Now* you get the guards to meet him at the Pillars."

Fitz chuckled, called his messenger, and contacted the resident captain. When he broke the link, he said, "I'm not sure your father will appreciate it."

"Better safe than sorry. Come on."

* * *

On reaching Ceardlann, Arkyn made his way to the sitting room he, Tain and Cal used. He curled up in the window seat. Two minutes later, like a thunderbolt with an overdeveloped sense of direction, Tain entered.

"Arkyn, you're back!"

"Obviously. How are you?"

"Bored. How was Tera?"

"Interesting. Lots of meetings though. Why are you bored?"

"Cal's been in Oedran for a month and Elantha's all right, but she's a girl. Father said there've been attempts to kill you."

"They didn't succeed, so you won't have to be king."

"Uncle Scanlon says that I don't have to be a justiciar either if I don't want to be."

Arkyn stared at his brother in consternation. "But surely you want to be?"

"I don't know. It all seems so boring. Why would I need to be? Uncle is doing the job."

"It's your inheritance, Tain. It's your duty. Like becoming king is mine. We don't have much choice in the matter." Needing time to think, he said, "Why's Cal in Oedran?"

"Don't know. His father sent for him about a fortnight ago. Can I come to Oedran with you tomorrow?"

Before Arkyn could answer, Kadeem entered with a loaded tray.

"Thank you, Kadeem. I see you've been farsighted enough to bring two plates and beakers."

"I thought it would probably be best. Saves Prince Tain borrowing yours. Your room is ready, sir, when you are."

"Thank you. Have you let Maria know that His Highness and Lady Elantha are travelling with us to Oedran in the morning?"

Kadeem grinned at Tain's whoop of joy as he confirmed he had.

* * *

luttering about the guards, Adeone reached the Palace. He entered the uter Office, where his administrator rose and bowed, smiling.

"Is Lord Landis keeping you working, Richardson?"

"Yes, Sire. *Apparently,* there's no rest for the wicked."

"Then, as you're one of the good around here, *I* won't keep you longer is evening. Get yourself off for the day."

Richardson sighed. "Thank you, Sire. I'd be glad to."

Adeone merely walked into the Inner Office. Landis looked up and, eeing him, grinned widely before rising, bowing and moving out from ehind the temporary desk.

Adeone closed the door. "You might as well sit down, Festus. I'm not oing to stop you working, as you seem so keen. I've never heard ichardson admit to being glad to finish for the day before."

Signing the last document, Landis said, "He'd hardly admit as much you, Sire, would he?"

Adeone groaned, "Don't. You sound like Percival. Why *are* you verworking Richardson?"

"It is unintentional, Sire. I've had to arrest Jacobs."

Adeone held his gaze. After the hard ride from Amphi, the last thing e wanted to do was to deal with business.

Landis saw that. "It will wait, Sire."

"Will it? How long has Richardson been without help?"

"Two weeks, sir. I didn't want him to be but he insisted he'd be fine."

Adeone tossed his cloak onto a table, exasperated. "This is Richardson, andis! *Of course* he *said* he'd be fine! He might even have believed it. he point is, he normally has two secretaries and he's just managed with one. Kenton won't be back until tomorrow. Edward's at Ceardlann. Contact im. Give him my apologies, but ask him to get here for eight tomorrow orning. I'm not having Richardson without help."

Landis did as requested. When he broke the link, Adeone was gazing lankly out of the window.

"Edward's riding on tonight, sir."

Adeone shook his head. "He's too damned conscientious by half. Why id you arrest Jacobs?"

"Those letters, sir. There's no doubt he was the one leaving them. I've ad Beaver questioning him, but he won't say a word about why, and it oesn't solve the fact that Prince Arkyn was also receiving them."

"It does ..." Adeone explained what had been concluded in Tera. "I've ot even told Arkyn who was responsible yet."

Landis nodded. "It makes sense. If Jacobs—"

"Have you finished everything for the day?" asked Adeone.

In a childish voice, Festus said, "Yes, sir. Can I come out and play?"

Adeone laughed. "I suppose so. Come and have a drink. I've told Richardson he can leave for the night."

"Then I have little option. I'm glad to see you."

"I'm glad to be back. What's more, I'm glad Arkyn is home."

As they made their way through the King's bedchamber to his private sitting room, Landis asked how Arkyn was.

"Looking too tired for my liking. That reminds me…" Adeone rang the bell and a couple of moments later, his manservant appeared. He carried on, "Simkins, can you discreetly tell Doctor Chapa I would like a word tomorrow, please?"

Simkins smiled. "I will do my best, Your Majesty." Without being asked he passed them a drink apiece and left the decanter within reach.

Once he'd gone, Landis said, "Is Arkyn still unwell?"

"Something isn't right with your nearson. He's tiring easily. The doctor in Tera insisted it was probably another sickness. A few of Arkyn's retinue did come down with one, but I'm not convinced. All he needed to say next was it's because Arkyn is growing to make me distrust him entirely."

Landis said satirically, "They are their stock in trade answers, Sire."

Adeone nodded. "They certainly are. Festus."

"Oh, whilst I remember. I had a request – well, more of a suggestion – from Judge Tancred. He didn't want to disturb your travels, but he was thinking that the next justiciar normally starts their training proper when they are about twelve… As Tain turns twelve on the Munewid he wondered if he'd like to attend a mock trial he's setting up as an end-of-year exercise for some of the Law School students. I said that you didn't want His Highness in Oedran if you weren't, given the situation… Anyway, now you're here would there be any problem with His Highness attending?"

Adeone said, "I can't see one. I'd prefer it if nobody knew Tain was there, but that might be a bit difficult."

"I could always take him along slightly later and we could sit at the back. Tancred won't highlight the fact he's present."

"That's true. All right, arrange it. I was going to send Tain back to the Rex Dallin the day after tomorrow, but he can stay here longer. He can spend some time with your brood as well."

"He'll probably like that. I think he's bored without Cal around."

Adeone stilled. "Why isn't young Cal there?"

"I thought you knew, his father sent for him about a fortnight ago." Seeing Adeone's lips press together, he changed the subject. "How was the trip back?"

"Peaceful. Only that one planned ambush. Scanlon is slipping. Has he visited Oedran in my absence?"

"Once. I listened, then ignored. He soon went away. Though there was an incident when someone was waiting for me with a dagger. You'd have thought they'd have been more inventive; after all, I never go anywhere without a sword. Then again, they couldn't hide a sword but they managed to get the dagger past the yeomen. All right, before you say it, I hauled in the Chief Yeoman. There hasn't been another incident since."

"Good. Not good that they attacked you, just good you survived and good there's not been another attack."

"I'm pleased you qualified that. I'd feel unappreciated otherwise."

Adeone snorted softly. "Having seen my desk, I might have more reason to not appreciate you."

"This is where I escape by pointing out you're looking tired. Riding from Amphi to here in a day, even by the Rex Dallin, is good going. I'll leave you to rest."

"What you mean, Festus, is that you've not only worn my administrator out but yourself as well!"

"Sometimes I wish I wasn't quite so transparent. I did, however, mean it when I inferred I'd leave you to get the beauty sleep you need."

"Some need it more than others… Goodnight, Festus."

Festus laughed. "Night, Adeone."

Chapter 63

TONGUE LASHING

Pentadai, Week 45 – 5th Lufial, 19th Geryis 1211

Inner Office

THE FOLLOWING MORNING, Landis talked Adeone through everything that had occurred in his absence. Doctor Chapa appeared around eleven and Adeone explained that he was worried about Arkyn. Halfway through the conversation, Richardson announced the Princes and Lady Elantha. Adeone quickly asked Chapa to wait in his sitting room as Tain hurtled across the room to his father and Arkyn grinned at the scene. Tain, as normal, seemed to have a hundred and one questions whilst Elantha stood quietly by. Adeone answered them all patiently, before saying,

"There's something that we've got to see to, your brother included."

Tain chewed at his lip. "I can't stay here?"

"Not this time. Maybe another. Run and tell Maria that you'll both be dining with me later. Go and visit Landis House. I'm sure you've plenty to plot about with your nearcousins."

Tain grinned, gave a brief bow and left. Elantha hesitated, crossed to Adeone, and gave him another hug.

"I'm glad you're home, Uncle Adeone."

"Me too, little flower. Are you going to visit your cousins?"

She glanced at Landis.

Her wed-uncle chuckled. "The girls will be pleased to see you as will Finian. I'm sure the twins will be too busy plotting with Tain to disturb you."

She nodded. "I'd like to see them," she left with a grin at Arkyn.

Adeone watched the door close behind her before turning to Landis. "Get Jacobs here from whatever cell you've put him in. We'll wait for Wynfeld, but I'd be happier if we got it sorted as soon as possible after that." When Landis had left, Adeone said, "Stuart and Jacobs left those notes."

"Stuart? Why would he…?" started Arkyn, flummoxed.

"Because Jacobs believed Edward's post should have been his and Stuart was his protégé, for all he still held the same post in the end, he wanted to discredit Edward, thereby leaving the post for Jacobs to assume. He miscalculated though. Edward found one of the notes and handed it to Wynfeld, who did some investigations. Neither ever told you because they didn't think you needed to be distressed. When you told me that Wealsman knew I later asked him if he'd mentioned it to Wynfeld, he said that he hadn't but that Wynfeld had asked him a couple of odd questions. I asked Wynfeld what he was investigating. I had a meeting with both him and Wealsman and the conclusions both reached were the same. Landis told me last night that he'd arrested Jacobs. Even without the evidence that Wynfeld and Wealsman had collated, he'd come to the same conclusion."

Arkyn balled his fists. "I'd never have thought Stuart would have been foolish enough to do this, especially when the assumed offence wasn't against him."

Adeone watched his son's face sink whilst considering the revelation. Was he blaming himself for not seeing the bitterness? Adeone was tempted to ask, but even asking would put the thought in Arkyn's head if it wasn't there already and he didn't want to do that. Arkyn had to work out how to handle these situations for himself. Eventually, seeing a change in the depth of his son's contemplation, he enquired,

"Did you read your household rules?"

"Yes, Sire; is there any other option?" asked Arkyn softly.

"No. Other than handing them over to the law and I would rather not do that. I don't know if your uncle has had a hand in this but, if he has, giving them over to his justice will not be advantageous. It would highlight that all is not well with our staff. If the people working for us are known not to respect us, then it undermines our authority."

Arkyn nodded. "I understand that, sir, but if we order a whipping and dismissal, they're likely to harbour a grudge, resentment that might well be used against us."

"That is always a risk, but they knew of the discipline when they took their posts, to think themselves immune is foolish. It is a standard discipline for most households of men of standing."

"Yet why must we lay the first stroke?" fretted Arkyn.

Adeone understood what was bothering his son. "It has several reasons for existing. It shows that we will take action, it shows that we have been informed of the transgression and it also allows us to rid ourselves of our distress without taking it out on any others around us. It isn't pleasant. Our lives are not as easy as many would suppose."

Arkyn sagged in his chair. "I know that, sir. I just… I don't know if I can."

Adeone sat by him. "I could take this off your shoulders but—"

"I've taken up other responsibilities already. I'll do it, sir."

A knock at the door interrupted their solitude. Adeone granted admittance and Richardson entered to tell Adeone that both Landis and Wynfeld were waiting. Adeone glanced at Arkyn, who shrugged, so the King nodded to Richardson. Once the Major had been announced and they were alone, Adeone said,

"Wynfeld, you've made good time!"

Wynfeld smiled as he relaxed from his salute. "A dawn march is good for everyone, once in a way, sir."

Adeone glanced at him, amused. "So, you did turn it into a military exercise. Good. Always work in the way best for you. Now, have you got Stuart outside?"

* * *

Three minutes later, Jacobs and Stuart were in the Inner Office. Adeone asked them to explain their actions. They denied that they'd ever done anything. Arkyn looked Stuart in the eye and quoted one of the letters. A flicker gave him away and he knew it. He started to blame Jacobs, saying that his mentor had forced him.

"Shut up, Stuart. Such feeble excuses aren't worth the effort taken to spout them," snapped Arkyn. "You were the whole length of the empire away; do you suppose we are so naïve as to forget that?"

Stuart blanched and fell silent. Jacobs, however, started a tirade. The Prince was a child, a kind child. He didn't know how to handle situations without someone holding his hand.

Arkyn listened for several moments before interrupting. "Jacobs, excuses and diatribes are not relevant. You might have other plans, but we don't care."

Jacobs was momentarily speechless. It didn't last.

Adeone got up. "Major, have Stuart taken outside."

The two guards holding Arkyn's secretary removed him from the Inner Office. Adeone regarded Jacobs, who was still muttering. In the intense gaze of the King, he fell silent.

Adeone said, "You've never been this bitter before. Who's got to you?"

Jacobs glowered. "Got to me? Why does anyone have to have 'got to me'? Not all life is a conspiracy. Not that you'd ever realise that. It's easier to assume that someone else is manipulating people than accepting that we don't like you—"

Wynfeld clicked his fingers and the guards twisted Jacobs' arms painfully up his back.

Adeone watched, apparently dispassionately, before saying, "Because, Jacobs, if you'd had a tendency to treachery, it would have manifested itself long before this year. You've worked for my father as well as me. I could order your tongue loosened but, for all those years of good service, I would rather not resort to such crudity."

Still angry, Jacobs blanched. Unless he started talking, Adeone would keep his word. Moreover, with Landis and Wynfeld present, his answers would also have to satisfy them. They were more than capable of asking painful questions and had the authority to do so, with no reference to the King – Landis would order those questions under his remit as a Defender of the King's Life, Wynfeld under his remit as Chief of Intelligence.

Adeone watched the realisation dawn on the secretary's face and the defiance fade.

When Jacobs spoke, it was obviously the truth but the passion was still there. He told what they'd worked out. That he believed he should have been Arkyn's administrator. That he thought rights due to, and owing to, tradition, had been ignored without any attempt at acknowledging that they existed. He'd been muttering about it one evening with a friend. A couple of days later, he had overheard another man grumbling about something else. He couldn't remember what. The discontent fed upon itself, and was inflamed every so often by this other man. Adeone asked for a name, but Jacobs didn't know it. He told what he could remember: as it turned out, not much. There was one distinguishing feature though, a scar which ran from the corner of his left eye straight down to the corner of his mouth. Wynfeld heard the description and shot a significant glance at the King. Adeone racked his brains; somewhere, sometime, in a report, or face to face, he knew that man. Jacobs finished by saying that if he'd stopped to think, or had had time to cool down, he'd probably have accepted what had happened but, instead, he'd found he couldn't dispel the feeling that he'd been sidestepped, passed over and made worthless by a younger man, and an orphan at that. He finished speaking and Adeone, still the epitome of gravity, ordered,

"Take him out."

The guards did so. Adeone's gaze fell straight on Arkyn. His son was clearly unhappy. Adeone motioned Wynfeld and Landis to the other end

: the room. He never saw Wynfeld shake his head at Landis when he ent to pour his nearson a drink.

Adeone murmured, “What is it?”

“Such passion for tradition. He had a good job; Stuart had a good job…”

Adeone held his son’s gaze. “Have you learnt nothing about loyalty, rkyn? It matters not to whom the loyalty is given, it is always powerful ıd dangerous. It changes men and women until they are blind to right ıd wrong. That is why we must be careful how we behave. For people ill follow our example.”

Arkyn fought against the rebuke. “Sire, I—”

“No, Arkyn, I know you realise it, but do you know it in your heart? o you know what men are capable of for reasons which seem slight?”

Arkyn sagged. “I’m learning, father.”

Adeone grasped his shoulder again. “I know that, son. I ask too much f you at times.”

After a short pause, Arkyn asked, “Yet if we are never to question hat has gone before, how can we progress?”

“That is why we must question; we just need to remember that not veryone will agree. Now, what would you suggest for reprisal? The law ates their fingers would be broken if they were found guilty.”

Arkyn lost colour. “We can’t do that to them.”

“I must admit, I feel the same way. All that is, therefore, left to us is use our household rules. I’m sorry that that is also unpleasant.”

Arkyn took a deep breath. “It’ll have to happen. Father, what of fterwards? They could end up being dangerous. They know so much of ow our offices work, who is important to us, everything.”

Adeone watched him shrewdly. “Wynfeld, do you need a couple of lerks? Confined to barracks and under your constant eye? I’m thinking or all the mundane tasks.”

Wynfeld caught the King’s line of thought. “I think that could be rranged, sir. They’ll have slight freedoms. If they’re kept on the FitzAlcis aff, you can determine their arrangements, and they would still be bound y their oaths.”

Landis overheard the proposal. “A sensible course of action, Sire. I ras worried if they were to be dismissed completely.”

Arkyn sagged onto a chair. “I just wish the whipping could be forgone.”

Adeone pursed his lips. “This time it can’t but maybe you could look ver our household rules and see if they could be updated? However, let’s et this over with.”

ix minutes later, Stuart left with a bloody streak across his back. Jacobs ft without blood drawn, but he knew that would change. In the Inner

Office, Arkyn's distress was palpable. Adeone dismissed Landis and Wynfeld. Once the door had closed on them, Arkyn dropped to his knees, shaking, gasping for air. Adeone got him a drink but left it on his desk. He then dropped down beside his son, hugging him close.

"It was never going to be easy."

"I'm sorry, father, I should be harder than this."

Adeone shook his head. "No. Be glad you feel like this. I am for you. If you'd been carefree, I'd have been more worried. Your uncle uses this punishment for all misdemeanours he can. What's more, he finishes the job himself and has no mercy – every stroke is harder than the one before. I'm *glad* you feel what you do right now. *Never* forget how sick you feel, how utterly disgusted you are. This probably won't be the only time you have to do this, or witness it, but please never *enjoy* it."

"I think I'll promise you that. I feel sick."

"Just take a drink – if only to get your breathing back under control. One last thing, Arkyn, and we can put this year behind us. Talk to Chapa – for my sake, if not for yours. He's waiting in my sitting room."

Arkyn took in his father's concerned face and agreed – support and reassurance worked both ways.

Chapter 64
SUSPICIONS AND SURPRISES

Late Morning
King's Sitting Room

DOCTOR CHAPA SMILED at Arkyn as he entered the King's sitting room. His shrewd eyes assessed the Prince carefully. Arkyn was looking a little tired but not so much as to concern Chapa after a so long travelling.

"I know that look, doc," said Arkyn amused.

Chapa purposefully rearranged his features into an innocent smile.

"Still not convinced, doc."

"I do my best, Your Highness. Might I ask how you are?"

"His Majesty is worried."

"His Majesty is always worried about his family. It's why I'm employed. How was the trip, sir?"

As Chapa listened, he did an examination. Arkyn's pulse was fine, his whole being though radiated fatigue and Chapa was concerned. It had been months since Arkyn had been ill. He should have been far better by now.

Arkyn saw the thoughtful look. "I'm just drained after everything that's happened today..." He explained about the anonymous letters and their consequences.

"Unpleasant, sir. Are you worrying about it all?"

"Maybe a bit. If I could have done anything… The normal self-blame, I suppose. I should have noticed Stuart wasn't content."

"I doubt he'd have let you notice, sir. Traitors bent on destruction don't generally give themselves away easily. Those who do are impetuous or uncaring of their skin. Stuart wanted revenge, not your downfall."

"I'd say that makes him more dangerous, doc. At least I have guards to deal with the impetuous assassins. Roth nearly poisoned me because he wasn't impetuous."

Chapa squeezed Arkyn's wrist. "I'm very glad he didn't succeed, cousin, though I wish I'd been with you in Terasia."

"Father and Uncle Festus probably needed your ministrations. They generally get into more trouble than I do."

Chapa chuckled. "You might have a point, sir, but I could obviously never agree."

"Obviously," said Arkyn with quiet mischief. "What's your prognosis?"

"Put your feet up and don't let the mayhem bother you for a couple of days and it should help. To that end, I'll just pay Kadeem a visit."

"Be kind, doc. He's done well this last year."

* * *

After speaking with Kadeem, Chapa thoughtfully walked to the King's Corridor and then decided he needed to talk over his suspicions with Adeone. He entered the Audience Chamber considering how to approach the matter and into the Outer Office where he crooked an eye at Richardson.

"Twelve minutes."

Chapa nodded and passed over his bag, knocked at the Inner Office door and entered when requested.

Adeone looked over. "Come in, doc. How is he?"

"Resting, sir." Chapa hesitated. "I don't quite know how to say this, Your Majesty, but I don't think it was flu."

Adeone crooked an eyebrow. "Come and sit down first."

"No, Sire. I'd rather not."

"Is he dying?" asked Adeone, the colour draining from his face.

"We're all doing that, sir, but no, not imminently."

Adeone let out a long breath. "Sit down, cousin, and tell me."

Chapa sighed. "Sometimes, young Adeone, you're far too understanding. I have only a gut feeling—"

"You'll not have guts in a minute."

"I think the illness was induced, sir. Something that caused the symptoms, the presentation of the ailment. As it affected His Highness adversely, it was poison; however, I have no proof. My supposition is based on the fact no-one else was ill. Flu is usually contagious. None of the people nursing Prince Arkyn fell ill."

"Thomas, Stuart and the clerks—"

"Had colds much later and weren't nursing His Highness. With flu, I'd have expected someone to present symptoms, probably Kadeem given the amount of time he was with His Highness. He says they were all fine."

"It's not certain though?"

"No, your Majesty, it's not certain. As I said, it's my gut feeling knowing that flu tends to infect others. Given how well protected His Highness is, how limited his contacts are, he doesn't push his way through crowds, for example, I would have expected illness within his household and staff at the same time, or illness within the Margrave's Residence."

Adeone pursed his lips. "All right. I understand what you're saying, but *how* could my son have been poisoned?"

"Any number of ways, sir."

"Is that how helpful you're going to be?"

Chapa chuckled. "Food or drink is the preferred method, sir. My guess is before they reached the Margrave's Residence."

"Why?"

"From recollection, when Roth almost poisoned him more fatally, Wynfeld and Fitz had a guard stationed in the kitchens and another who accompanied the Prince's meals to his rooms. So, my guess is that the drugging took place before they arrived. Some poisons work slowly. His Highness was fit before going to Terasia. That could have saved his life."

Adeone swallowed. "Could it have been Stuart?"

"Unlikely. *Highly* unlikely: a clerk generally wouldn't be involved in His Highness' victuals."

"So, there's another traitor in his household."

"It's possible, sir, but I have no proof for any of this. I don't want to destroy anyone—"

"And I don't want my son poisoned!"

"No, cousin, neither do I," said Chapa quietly.

Adeone swore. "Sorry. Do you think it's Kadeem?"

"No."

"That's definite."

Chapa snorted. "Adeone, you know as well as I do that the Kadeems are contented with their lot. Kadeem has known the Prince for years and cared for him with a dedication that few would manage. He's not a threat. If anything, he's an asset because traitors must get through him."

Adeone nodded. "I can't trust him indiscriminately though. I need to see Wynfeld and get more checks done on the Prince's household, don't I?"

"It would probably be a good idea, sir."

"I thought it was only Cousin Henry who gave me work."

Chapa chuckled. "He gave me lessons, sir."

"Well, he gave me some too. Go and talk with Kadeem and alert him to the possibility. I don't want Arkyn told, but if Kadeem can limit those household members with access, I'd be grateful."

"I'll tell him, sir. Now—"

"I'm fine, thank you," interrupted Adeone, recognising the tone.

"Can't blame a man for trying."

Adeone chuckled. "Get you gone, cousin, and ask Richardson to send for Wynfeld."

* * *

When the Major entered, Adeone didn't miss the quick sweep around the office his eyes took.

"Your Prince is finally resting." He waved to a chair. "I need you to do some discreet enquiries into his household. Chapa isn't convinced the illness was natural."

Wynfeld swore. "We checked everything, sir."

"Yes, but I think we need our minds putting at rest. The doc thinks it could have been slow poison administered before he reached the Residence. I'm not convinced. He could equally have picked something up at the village hostelry, but it is odd no-one else was ill."

Wynfeld nodded. "I'll see what we can discover, sir."

"Thank you. Now, we're back in Oedran. Any qualms?"

Wynfeld smiled, sitting down. "What about, Sire? Being Major of Oedran or seeing my aunt?"

Adeone snorted. "Either really, but I can only imagine that Prince Tain's nurse is proud of her nephew. Go and see her before you report for duty at the barracks. I'll grant you half a day's unofficial leave."

"Thank you, sir. It's much appreciated."

"Yes, well, you'll need it. Not to worry you, but you're now in charge of the Barracks of Oedran, Anaparian and Arealian Legions and after General Paturn, you're the highest officer of my army and I want to make changes. You're still the commanding officer of intelligence regiment. How much you delegate to Captain Beaver is up to you. I'd like you to be directly in charge of the half-regiment used for training. Other than that, I think it's time to get a post for a commander at the barracks. It should take pressure off the General as well. I'm not usually in favour of more layers of command, but in this case, I'll make an exception. Find a commander, Major. Then there are two things I need you to attend to as soon as possible. One is to talk with Captain Edmonds and discreetly revise the training schedules given current threats. The second is to examine your old regiment. Beaver failed to get Jacobs talking about the notes, and Lord Landis' life was attacked when we were in Terasia—"

"His Lordship was *attacked*?"

"Yes, with a dagger," said Adeone. "He wasn't injured this time, but I'd hardly say it was an ideal situation and I'm not exactly happy about it. I'm sure your very presence will inspire honesty. I want a report in a week's time telling me that *you* know what went wrong and that it won't be happening again. I also want you to appoint another captain to help alongside Beaver. He is far too overworked. I believe that's where the problems start."

"Leave it with me, Sire."

"One last thing, Major, I should have told you in Terasia, but old Jack left you everything he owned. Richardson has the information."

Wynfeld's face said everything; Jack had been the closest thing that he'd had to a father figure growing up in Lord Macaria's household. He'd left that household to join the army late in 1193 and had been saddened to hear the old groom had died but had never dreamed Jack had regarded him in the light of a son. He couldn't find anything to say, but Adeone smiled, needing no response.

As Wynfeld left, Adeone wondered what the reaction to his presence would be at the barracks. He had a reputation for getting things done. As Major of Oedran, he had more weight and authority behind his orders. He was the senior Major of the empire, and the empire only had four Majors in total. It wasn't bad for someone who had merely been a sergeant three years previously.

* * *

An hour later, Landis reappeared in the Inner Office to let Adeone know that Jacobs' and Stuart's punishment had concluded. Both men had endured it stoically and neither had been surprised to find they were still under oath and being sent to work at the barracks. Jacobs especially realised it was intended as a prison.

"How's Arkyn?"

Adeone explained Chapa's conclusions. Landis pursed his lips, but that was all the comment he made. Inwardly, he resolved to pay Wynfeld a visit and make sure that the investigation was thorough.

Adeone saw it. "Wynfeld is now Major of Oedran, Landis. He knows his responsibilities."

Landis chuckled. "Sorry. Can I see His Highness?"

"Of course. He's in my sitting room."

Landis entered the sitting room and then crept out again. Once back in the Inner Office, he said, "Fast off, covered with a blanket. He looks so young in sleep still."

Adeone smiled sadly. “He’s grown more than I ever expected this year. He’s faced trials I never did during the reviews and he’s met them head on. Let’s get lunch and then you can depress me with everything else that’s happened since I’ve been gone.”

They were sharing stories when a flustered Richardson entered.

“Landis House is on fire.”

“Tain?” exclaimed Adeone.

CHARACTERS

FAMILIES

FITZALCIS	King Altarius Apolinar	King of the Oedranian Empire 1168-1204
	King Adeone Altarius	King of the Oedranian Empire 1204-present
	Queen Ira	King Adeone's wife
	Prince Arkyn Adeone	King Adeone's elder son
	Prince Tain Lachlan	King Adeone's younger son
	Princess Eliza Elania (Ella)	King Adeone's daughter
	Prince Lachlan	King Altarius' brother
	Lady Amara	King Altarius' sister
	Lord Scanlon	Justiciar of the Empire
	Lady Aelia (nee Rale)	Lord Scanlon's wife
	Lady Elantha	Lord Scanlon's daughter
LANDIS	Lord Festus Landis	Lord of Oedran, Defender of the King's Life, Chief Advisor, nearfather to Adeone's children
	Lady Cornelia Landis (nee Rale)	Long-suffering, hardworking Lady of Oedran
	Lord Julius, Lady Julia	Eldest children, twins
	Marcelea, Antonia, Lucius, Ira	Younger children
IRIS	Lord Ignatius Iris	Lord of Oedran, Deputy Chief Advisor to the King
	Lord Idris Iris	Lord Iris' son
	Lord Irvin Iris	Lord Iris' grandson
RALE	Lord Fingal Rale	Lord of Oedran
	Lord Finn Rale	*Lord Rale's son – deceased*
	Lady Malinda Atgas	*Finn's wife – remarried*
	Finian Rale	Lord Rale's grandson

KING'S RETINUE

Richardson	King's Administrator
Simkins	King's manservant
Doctor Chapa	King's Physician and cousin
Jacobs, Kenton	King's Secretaries
Sergeant Hillbeck	Sergeant of the King's Guard

ARKYN'S RETINUE

Fitz	Officer of the FitzAlcis, captain of Arkyn's guards
Kadeem	Arkyn's manservant
Edward	Arkyn's administrator
Thomas	Kadeem's deputy
Alan	Footman
Stuart	Edward's deputy
Halien	A guard

SCANLON'S RETINUE

Bantling	Advisor

CEARDLANN

Calumiel Galdwin	Arkyn and Tain's friend
Comptroller	Gentleman in charge of Ceardlann
Maria	FitzAlcis Nurse

TERASIAN CHARACTERS

OFFICIALS	Lord Portur	Margrave – Governor of Terasia, Overlord of Terasia
	Lord Roth	Deputy Governor, Overlord of Terasia
	Terazi	Chief Judge of Terasia
	Percival Wealsman	An official of Terasia
	Rahat	The Statisman – in charge of the exchequer
	Ernst	The Aedile – in charge of public works
	Doctor Artzman	The Margrave's doctor
	Thomkins	Margrave's secretary
	Laus	Wealsman's secretary
COURT	Lord Silvano	Overlord of Terasia
	Lord Simble	Overlord of Terasia
	Lord Erlan Roth	Lord Roth's son
	Lord Melek	Silvano's son
	Lord Hale	Minor lord of Terasia
	Lady Kristina Hale	A lady dancing
	Lady Daia Sansky	A King's ward

OTHER

OEDRAN	Merchant Chapa	King Adeone's cousin
	Jack	Chief groom at the Palace of Oedran
	Captain Pixney	Captain of the Palace Guard (Oedran)
	Aldhouse	Chief Yeoman of Oedran, head of law enforcement
ARMY	General Paturn	Head of the King's Army
	Commander Wynfeld	Commander of the King's Army (Terasia)
	Captain Beaver	Captain of Intelligence
	Sergeant Dring	Sergeant in Terasia
	Captain Sanders	Captain of Myddlenor Fort

DELVINGS

Lexicon

OF THE MOONS

ALUNA	The larger of the two Erinnan moons
ALUNA-MONTH	Four weeks
ALUNAN	The higher section of society
ALUNAN-AGE	Twenty years old. Alunan become adults in law
CISLUNA	The smaller of the two Erinnan moons
CISLUNA-MONTH	Three weeks
CISAN	The lower section of society
CISAN-AGE	Fifteen years old. Cisan become adults in law

FOR THE ANCESTORS

ALCIA	A guardian of the ancestor's memory
ALCIUM	A place to remember the ancestors, for blessing new life, for contemplation and for funerals.
MOONSHI	Chief Alcia in Oedran

ON RELATIONSHIPS

NEAR*	Named when a child is born, *nearparents* act as mentors for a child and would act as guardians should the child be left orphaned. Nearparents' children are *nearcousins,* unless the child lives in the same house, then they're *nearsiblings*
WED*	This prefix denotes relatives married into the family, rather like the suffix *in-law*
KINAKIN	Related by marriage but beyond the immediate family. So a child's wed-family would be kinakin to the child's parents.

IN OEDRAN

KING'S ADVOCATES	A group consisting of the King's Defenders, heir and Representatives in the empire
TRINICULUM	A formal dining room at the Palace
ETANES	The law making body, made up of the Lords of Oedran and twelve cisan members
EALDORMAN	The person keeping order in the Etanes debates
YEOMEN	Law enforcers

HONORIFICS

SIRE, MAJESTY	The King
GRACE	The Queen
HIGHNESS	Princes
ELEGANCE	Princesses
EXCELLENCY	King's Representatives
MY LORD	Lords
MY LADY	Nobel Ladies

FEALTIES

FEALTY	A declaration of loyalty from one person to another: a declaration to take up the fight for the liege by the vassal
TRUTH- BINDING	In addition to fealty, the vassal swears to speak to the truth to the liege when required.
SPEECH- BINDING	In addition to truth-binding, the vassal swears never to reveal anything confidential, never to say anything to annoy the liege, to speak only for them not against them.
HONOUR-BINDING	In addition to truth-binding, the vassal swears only to work for the honour of the liege, not against them.
LIFE-BINDING	Melding all aspects of truth, speech and honour bindings, the vassal ties their life force to the wishes of the liege. If they annoy their liege, they feel pain. If they commit treason, the vassal will die immediately.
VALLEY-BINDING	Specific to the Rex Dallin, this binding is said to be life-binding but may stop short of death.
OTHER BINDINGS	There are oaths which fall short of the recognised fealties, that are sworn when taking on specific duties or when an employer requires it.

ON MONEY

DARL	Gold coins
TALENCE	Silver coins, twenty to a darl
CRESCENTS	Bronze coins, twelve to a talence

The Cearcall and Ull's Legacy

t the beginning of the reckoning of years, the Majistar Ull brought agic to Erinna. Twelve star sapphires controlled the creation of the agic. Ull gifted the star stones to twelve individuals, each with a magical irit. For six hundred years they, and their successors, controlled magic ı Erinna, formed laws around it and maintained peace. In the year 600, ey died, blown to the winds when magic, wielded by the Tribility who eld three spirits, destroyed the Cearcall Tower in Denshire. Since 600 agic has been weaker, almost dormant. Some stones were lost, their cation hidden by history, along with some items related to the members the Cearcall.

Title	Spirit	Stone Colour	Item
Amser	Timer	Turquoise	Amser's Watch
Beran	Bearer	Black	Beran's Pendant
Espier	Espien	Yellow	Espier's Glass
Jeci	Illusionist	Blue	Jeci's Ring
Meithrin	Healer	Pink	Meithrin's Vial
Memini	Memor	Grey	Memini's Manuscript
Rheol	Balancer	White	Rheol's Needle
Sennachie	Seer	Green	Sennachie's Bowl
Sentire	Sensor	Red	Sentire's Knife
Skifta	Shifter	Purple	Skifta's Sword
Sundrian	Splitter	Orange	Sundrian's Whistle
Wright	Manipulator	Brown	Wright's Box

ach magical spirit manifests differently from healing hurts to splitting e mind, from creating illusions to manipulating objects.

Iore than one person at any one time can hold a spirit, but only one spirit ielder can possess the star stone and unlock its full power.

ach spirit has a collection of *hues*, lesser forms of the spirit, which may anifest in anyone.

eople who wield magic are said to be affected by Ull's Legacy.

Provincial Information

Province	Capital City	Lord of Oedran
ANAPARA	OEDRAN	PARA
AREAL	AMPHI	RALE
BAYAN	GARTH	RATHGAR
DENSHIRE	CEARDEN	CEARIS
GERYMOR	RY	RYSON
LOW PLAINS	EYLLYN	IRIS
LUFIAN	LUFIA	LUX
MACIAN ISLES	MACIA	MACARIA
PALE LANDS	MEITH	LANDIS
SERPENT ISLE	ANGUIN	ANGUIS
TERASIA	TERA	TERAN
TRADERE	BYFA	FAIRSON

Province	King's Representative	Chief Judge
ANAPARA	DOMINI OF PARAS	CHIEF JUDGE (PARAS)
AREAL	GOVERNOR	KENNER
BAYAN	EXARCH	ESCHERVIN
DENSHIRE	VISIR	HAKIM
GERYMOR	DEY	BORSHOLDER
LOW PLAINS	TUCHLIN	DOMESMAN
LUFIAN	SAGAMORE	DEEMSTER
MACIAN ISLES	FENCIBLE	DOMARE
PALE LANDS	JARL	LAGHMAN
SERPENT ISLE	PASHA	TUOMARI
TERASIA	MARGRAVE	TERAZI
TRADERE	SATRAP	ARCHON

Province	Symbol	Colour
ANAPARA	THREE CROSSED ARROWS	PURPLE
AREAL	A KEY	SILVER
BAYAN	A BIRD IN FLIGHT	ORANGE
DENSHIRE	A TWELVE-POINT MYSTIC ROSE	BROWN
GERYMOR	A SET OF SCALES	WHITE
LOW PLAINS	AN EYE	GREEN
LUFIAN	A FLOWER AND SNOWFLAKE	BLUE
MACIAN ISLES	A TRISKELE OF THREE SPIRALS	RED
PALE LANDS	A VIAL	PINK
SERPENT ISLE	A CURLED SNAKE	YELLOW
TERASIA	A BEAR'S PAW PRINT	BLACK
TRADERE	AN HOURGLASS	TURQUOISE

Notes on Time

WEEKDAYS	ALUNADAI	FESTIVALS	MUNEWID	FIRST DAY OF SUMMER FIRST DAY OF THE YEAR
	CISADAI			
	TRETALDAI		MUNPYRAM	FIRST DAY OF AUTUMN
	IMPERADAI		MUNDIMRI	FIRST DAY OF WINTER
	PENTADAI		MUNLUMEN	FIRST DAY OF SPRING
	HEXADAI		*These festivals are known as Alcis Days and are marked by both moons being full*	
	SEPTADAI			

ON TIME		
1 MINUTE	=	60 SECONDS
1 HOUR	=	72 MINUTES (12 X 6 MINUTES)
1 DAY	=	24 HOURS
1 WEEK	=	7 DAYS
COURT CYCLE	=	12 DAYS
1 FORTNIGHT	=	2 WEEKS

Season	*Aluna-month*	*Week*	*Cisluna-month*	*Season*	*Aluna-month*	*Week*	*Cisluna-month*
SUMMER	CEARAL	1	CEARCIS	WINTER	RALAL	25	RALIS
		2				26	
		3				27	
		4	MIDDIS			28	NORIS
	TRADAL	5			ANAPAL	29	
		6				30	
		7	TRADIS			31	ANAPCIS
		8				32	
	LOWAL	9			BAYAL	33	
		10	LOWIS			34	BAYIS
		11				35	
		12				36	
AUTUMN	MACIAL	13	MACIS	SPRING	TERAL	37	TERIS
		14				38	
		15				39	
		16	EASIS			40	SOUIS
	MEITHAL	17			GERYAL	41	
		18				42	
		19	MEITHIS			43	GERYIS
		20				44	
	SERAL	21			LUFIAL	45	
		22	SERIS			46	LUFIS
		23				47	
		24				48	

POSTSCRIPT

To you, my reader…

Thank you.

I hope you enjoyed *Tera*, the second book in the *Treason and Truth* series.

Please consider leaving an honest review of this book wherever you el most comfortable. Reviews really help readers find their next book and help authors find their next reader.

Acknowledgements

uthors rarely get to publication without help and support. They sit and rite in snatched hours or minutes. Sometimes stories flow unceasingly om their fingers, clamouring to be heard amongst the din of everyday fe. When the last scratch of the pen and click of the keyboard is done, en comes the editing, the interior design, the cover…

My journey has not been solo. From my friends and family who have ad, re-read and given me honest feedback to you, the reader that got is far, I say thank you.

This book is dedicated to Hugh, who has supported me throughout my fe, and whose love of history and knowledge has infused into how I rite and the world I have built.

Explore Erinna

Please visit https://erinna.co.uk for more about the Erinnan Legacy or sign up to The Court Newsletter for freebies and news.

Milton Keynes UK
Ingram Content Group UK Ltd.
UKHW010112180724
445629UK00004B/43